PRAISE FOR MATTHEW FITZSIMMONS

PRAISE FOR *POISONFEATHER*

An Amazon Best Book of the Month: Mystery, Thriller & Suspense category

"FitzSimmons's complicated hero leaps off the page with intensity and good intentions, while a byzantine plot hums along, ensnaring characters into a tightening web of greed, betrayal, and violent death."
—*Publishers Weekly*

"[FitzSimmons] has knocked it out of the park, as they say. The characters' layers are being peeled back further and further, allowing readers to really root for the good guys! FitzSimmons has put together a great plot that doesn't let you rest for even a minute."
—*Suspense Magazine*

PRAISE FOR *THE SHORT DROP*

". . . FitzSimmons has come up with a doozy of a sociopath."
—*Washington Post*

"This live-wire debut begins with a promising lead in the long-ago disappearance of the vice president's daughter, then doubles down with tangled conspiracies, duplicitous politicians, and a disgraced hacker hankering for redemption . . . Hang on and enjoy the ride."
—*People*

COLD
HARBOR

ALSO BY
MATTHEW FITZSIMMONS

The Short Drop
Poisonfeather

COLD HARBOR

THE **GIBSON VAUGHN** SERIES

MATTHEW FITZSIMMONS

THOMAS & MERCER

Text copyright © 2017 Planetarium Station, Inc.

Published by Thomas & Mercer, Seattle

www.apub.com

Amazon, the Amazon logo, and Thomas & Mercer are trademarks of Amazon.com, Inc., or its affiliates.

ISBN-13: 9781503943353 (hardcover)
ISBN-10: 1503943356 (hardcover)
ISBN-13: 9781503943346 (paperback)
ISBN-10: 1503943348 (paperback)

Cover design by Rex Bonomelli

Printed in the United States of America

First edition

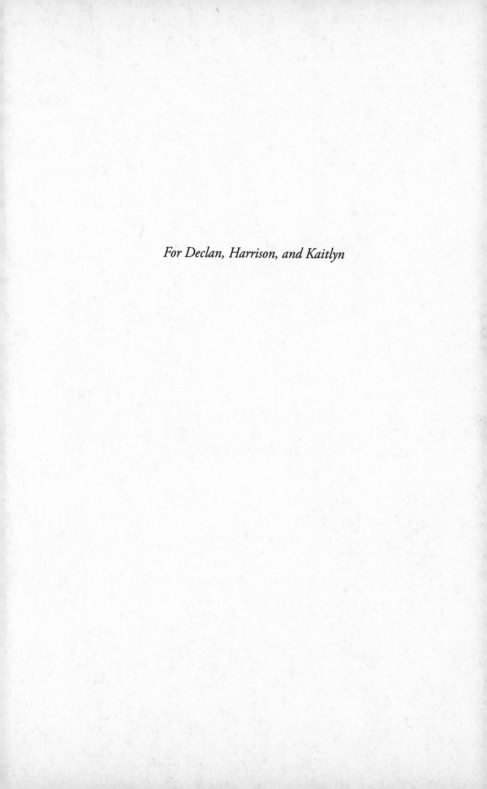

For Declan, Harrison, and Kaitlyn

CHAPTER ONE

The door would never open.

The prisoner accepted that now.

How old was he? He couldn't be sure. Another mooring post that had drifted out of sight in this windowless cell. One thing less anchoring him to the world beyond these walls. This cell where the lights were never off and time had overrun its banks and flooded his minutes, hours, and days so that he could no longer tell where one moment ended and the next began.

Meals arrived in his sleep. Always while he slept. Sometimes he would pretend. Simply to see a human hand would be a comfort. To know there was someone on the far side of the door. He hadn't heard a sound from outside since they'd put him here. Not even when he pressed his ear to the door and strained against the silence. Not a voice. Not a cough or a prayer, a footstep or any proof of life. So he would mimic sleep like a child on Christmas morning, hoping to catch a glimpse of someone, anyone. But they always knew. How did they know when he lay so still?

Were they inside him?

The meals never varied. No breakfast or lunch or dinner. Laid out on the floor—no tray, plates, or utensils. He ate with his fingers, the same tasteless bars, processed beyond recognition, for every meal. He couldn't say he ate three times a day, because what was a day? When the food came, he ate. When it was gone, he didn't. Never hungry until the food came, and then ravenous, as if it had been a lifetime since his last meal.

No mirror—he longed to see his own face. To confirm he was still himself. Maybe they had changed that too while he slept. Were these his arms? His legs and feet? His stomach? His chest? They looked familiar but maybe only because they were all he ever saw. Was he *he*? If he could only see his face, he felt reasonably certain that he would know the answer. He knew the question itself was madness, but it ate at him until sleep claimed him. Blessed sleep.

This was hell, and the door would never open.

The prisoner accepted that now.

If he died, would anyone come? Would the door open at last, or was this also to be his tomb? No, the door would never open. He accepted that now.

In despair, he had run at the wall, slamming his forehead against the unforgiving cinder block. He woke on the floor in a halo of blood. His meal waited in the usual place.

The blood had long since flaked away, leaving a rust-hued outline. He found it pretty and adopted gnawing his arms until he broke the skin. Dripping blood on the floor carefully to see what shapes he could make from it. Cave paintings of himself.

When they'd put him here, he had yelled defiantly. Sworn that they would pay. That he would never break no matter what they did.

He was broken now, and they had done nothing.

His cold fluorescent sun reflected off the white walls of the cell, seeped between his fingers, through his eyes, and cast shadows on his mind.

He longed for a moment of darkness.

Afraid of what the dark might bring.

At first, he could sleep only with an arm draped over his eyes, but now nothing prevented his sleep. Sleep was all he had, and he embraced it. Waking became a hateful thing.

To survive, he retreated further and further into memory. Reliving the finest moments of his life over and over. His wedding. Kissing Nicole at the altar. Their first night together in their home. The birth of their daughter, Eleanor. Adding new chapters, rewriting the past. Unmaking his mistakes. He and Nicole were still married. Still living on Mulberry Court in their sturdy, two-story Cape Cod. He could hear Ellie playing upstairs, but she never came down, and he never went up.

Eventually he began to talk to his memories and to the people in them. Living inside them. They made good company and would sit silently while he ate, listening to him ramble on. On one level, he knew they weren't real; on another, they were all he had. Did not wanting to be alone mark you insane?

Then came the time when the memories spoke back. They took the guise of Suzanne Lombard—his Bear. She was a little girl again, before tragedy struck, as he needed her to be. She told him about the secret passage. That she could take him away. As long as his body stayed behind, the guards would never know that he had escaped. This he knew to be a dangerous precedent, but he didn't hesitate. He preferred madness to the lonely white walls.

The first night, Bear took him by the hand and led him away. She led him out through the secret passage to her family home in Pamsrest. They found a comfortable chair, and he read to her as he had when he was a boy. Nestled against his shoulder, Bear turned the pages for him.

She told him that Ellie was doing well, growing up. Healthy and happy. He asked if he could see her, but Bear shook her head and told him it wasn't possible. The prisoner wanted to argue but knew it was for the best.

Bear squeezed his hand. "You have to survive," she said. "For her."

"The door will never open," he said.

"She's all that matters now."

Bear turned the page. When she became sleepy, he folded a corner to mark their place. She took him back to his cell but promised to return soon.

The next night, the prisoner followed his father to the old diner in Charlottesville. Their Sunday-morning ritual. They sat at their regular table and ordered from a waitress who looked delighted to see them. It was the week before his father died, yet somehow his father knew everything that had happened in the years since his own funeral. When their breakfast came, his father told him why he was there.

"The man who put you here."

"Damon Washburn." The prisoner whispered the name like a prayer in an abandoned church.

"He has to pay."

The prisoner agreed but explained that the door would never open, that he'd accepted it now.

His father winked his trademark wink. "Our time will come."

The prisoner didn't believe that, but planning revenge helped to pass the intervals when sleep would not come. So together they began to strategize. Eventually it was all they ever talked about. His father had an incredibly cunning mind, and the cruelty of his plan shocked the prisoner.

His father saw it on his son's face. "I'm done with people pushing our family around and getting away with it. Do you understand me?"

The prisoner looked away, ashen-faced and ashamed, but his father wasn't finished.

"This is all because you let her live. After what she did to me, to Bear. You let her live."

Calista Dauplaise.

The prisoner, knowing better than to speak her name aloud, said only, "I'm sorry."

"Never again."

"Yes, sir." The son followed the father back to the cell. He tried to apologize again, afraid that his father might abandon him in this place. His father only smiled and hugged him.

"I won't die again. Because of you."

It was true. The following week, when the son came home, he didn't discover his father hanging from a rope in the basement. Instead, beer in hand, his father was turning thick steaks on the grill in the backyard.

"Your mom will be down in a minute," his father said. "Why don't you set the table for three."

His mother, who had passed away when he was three, would be down in a minute. And even though she never did come down to join them, it was a comfort knowing she was close by.

Through the secret passage, the world existed only as the prisoner needed. It was a seductive power—to experience his life as he wished it had been—and he used it to escape his cell at every opportunity. Why shouldn't he? If he could, he would gladly die to end this solitary existence. To escape this hell. He would do anything his keepers asked. If only they would ask. But they never would. The door would never open. He accepted that now.

And then, after a thousand years or perhaps only a single day, something unforeseeable happened.

The door opened.

CHAPTER TWO

The aircraft banked to the left and continued its descent. Beneath the hood, Gibson Vaughn's ears popped. A small detail, but one that made him believe that all this might actually be real. Could you hallucinate a change in cabin pressure? He hoped not.

During his imprisonment, he had imagined his release innumerable times—it was the cruelest trick that his mind played on him—and now he feared that this was but another of his elaborate fantasies. It concerned him that he couldn't easily differentiate one from the other. Frustrating that, even though he knew intellectually that he'd lost his mind, he still couldn't bring it to heel. He leaned forward in his seat to take the tension off the shackles that bound his wrists and ankles. His hands tingled as sensation rushed back into fingers. It felt so real. It had to be real, didn't it?

Supposing for a moment that it was, he still had no idea how long they'd been in the air. His captors had dosed him with something to calm him, and by the time it had worn off, they'd already been airborne. It had been a blessing, protecting his mind from too much, too soon. After so long in solitary confinement, the world beyond his cell door had been traumatic—an overload of brutal sensation. It had overclocked his senses, overwhelming him, and at first he had fought the guards like a lunatic. Simple human contact had felt like fire on his skin; human voices had been a dentist's drill grinding into a brittle molar. Ironic, since it had been all he'd craved. It had taken three men to wrestle him to the ground and sedate him.

Strong hands on his shoulders pressed him back in his seat, checked his restraints, tightened his seat belt. The vibration of the aircraft's hydraulics hummed as the landing gear extended. That felt real too. Fear and excitement swept through him at the prospect of landing. He didn't know where, or even why, but it was something new, and that was enough.

Duke Vaughn snorted from the window seat. "You really believe that? This is a trick, son. They flew you in a circle. You're going right back into the same cell. To break you."

"I'm already broken," Gibson whispered from under the hood.

The aircraft touched down on the runway. Gibson was thrown forward as the plane decelerated in a roar. When it lurched to a halt, hands lifted Gibson from his seat and marched him down the aisle. He shuffled forward in abbreviated, manacled steps. A knife of cold wind cut through his clothes. He dug in his heels, whining like a beaten dog, and struggled back from the open door, certain that they meant to throw him from the aircraft. A hand clamped around the back of his neck; an unsympathetic voice told him to calm down. Gibson remembered the plane had landed. How had he forgotten that already?

The hand at his neck guided him down the airstairs. He stumbled on the last step but righted himself before he sprawled across the tarmac. A short distance from the aircraft, the voice ordered him to kneel, shoved him roughly to his knees when he was slow to comply. In the wind, he heard a click. He braced for the bullet that would put an end to his life. Instead, the shackles came off. The voice told him to lie facedown and lace his fingers behind his head.

The runway was a block of ice, so cold it hurt his bones. But it was a wonderful pain, the pain of being alive. Outside. Unbound. A miracle.

The door had opened. The wind blew right through his lightweight clothes, and he laughed crazily at the sensation. The engines of the plane powered up and began to recede into the distance.

"Hello?" he called out.

No reply.

He called out again, then once more. Gibson struggled to his feet and yanked the hood free. The daylight, reflecting off snow that had been shoveled to the edge of the runway, burned his retinas. He shielded them with his hands, squinting as his eyes adjusted to the glare. He looked about wildly to confront his jailers but saw none. At the far end of the runway, an aircraft climbed the morning sky. The sky. Dear God, the sky. Vertigo swept over him as his mind tried to make sense of it. A kaleidoscope exploded before his eyes. Heart galloping. He dropped back to his knees and cowered at the overwhelming grandeur of a gray winter's morning, certain that this must be dying.

His nausea passed, his vision cleared, and he dared uncover his eyes. A hundred yards away stood a corrugated hangar and, beyond that, a simple office. There had to be two feet of old snow on the ground, salt brown. The airfield looked vaguely familiar, but his mind pulled in a thousand different directions, and he couldn't place it. At his feet sat his old duffel, the one he'd had with him when the CIA had taken him. Shivering, he knelt, unzipped it, and pawed through his dirty clothes. They were all lightweight spring clothes that he'd taken to West Virginia a lifetime ago. Little use in winter, but he put on his windbreaker for all the good it would do.

Bear's baseball cap was missing, and he panicked until he remembered that he'd left it with Gavin Swonger. He wished he had it now; he thought it might tell him definitively if any of this was real. Could this be real? Had he gone through the secret passage without knowing it? He dug through the duffel again but found only a plastic bag. Inside were his wallet, his keys, and his phone. The phone had long since lost any charge. He put it in his pocket, if only to feel normal.

Across the runway, another hooded man clambered to his feet. The man had also been lying facedown on the runway, but his gray suit had been the perfect camouflage. Gibson watched the man pull off the hood and look around in confusion. Even under the shoulder-length hair and matted beard, Charles Merrick was unmistakable. The last person Gibson expected, but, seeing him, Gibson knew it couldn't have been anyone else. The same man who had condemned him to that damned cell.

The two men, standing on the lonely runway, their wild hair dancing in the wind, must have been a strange sight. Loose snow tumbled across the runway as they stared each other down like defanged gunslingers. In the early days of his imprisonment, Gibson had dreamed of what he'd do if he ever saw him again. But as time had passed, he'd felt less and less about Charles Merrick. His father had argued that the man was an animal and had done what animals do when cornered. It would be foolish to expect anything different; the blame belonged elsewhere. With those who should have known better. With the CIA and the man who called himself Damon Washburn.

"You!" Merrick's voice echoed off the trees that ringed the airfield.

Trees . . . Gibson realized where he had been delivered. It had been spring the last time he'd seen this place, so he hadn't recognized it now. He was back in West Virginia—Dule Tree Airfield. The CIA had dumped the pair at the very place where they'd taken them, God only knew how long ago. Six months? A year and a half? Longer? What had happened to warrant their release? His mind didn't feel capable of solving that particular riddle. More than that, he didn't care. He was free and could think of a lot of places he'd rather be than standing on a runway with Charles Merrick, contemplating the implications of his release.

Actually, there was only one place he wanted to be. One person he wanted to see. Ellie. How old was his daughter now? How many birthdays had he missed? The question snapped him from his inertia. Without a word, he slung his duffel bag over a shoulder and turned his back on Charles Merrick. He had no use for the man. At the edge of the runway, he scrabbled over the snowbank and set off across the field for the airfield's office and perhaps a phone. The snow was knee-high, and it took exaggerated steps to break through the icy shell. Badly out of shape, he labored across the field with his heart and breath hammering in his ears. Duke walked behind in the path Gibson had cut through the snow. His father began to sing:

> "Sire, the night is darker now,
> And the wind blows stronger,
> Fails my heart, I know not how;
> I can go no—"

"Shut up, Dad."

Every so often Duke would get to singing. If Gibson didn't nip it in the bud, it could go on awhile, and he was in no mood for Christmas carols. He needed to get gone from this place. Away from Charles Merrick. It didn't occur to him that Charles Merrick might feel differently.

Merrick tackled him from behind and sent him sprawling. The two men struggled in the snow, Merrick keening, "You . . . you . . . you . . ." As if he had much more to say but didn't know where to begin. The rage in his voice said enough. Gibson wriggled free of Merrick's grasp and tried to stand up in the deep snow. Merrick crawled after him and pulled him back down just as he got his feet under him. The two men wrestled again—a feeble, slapstick version of a fight. After so long in captivity, both men tired quickly. They gave up and lay there in the snow, panting and holding on to each other like castaways.

Bear stood nearby with a copy of *The Fellowship of the Ring* under one arm, head cocked to the side, watching Gibson. So thin that she didn't break through the snow but stood atop it like an angel. Her gossamer sundress fluttered in the wind, and her feet were bare; Gibson worried that she'd catch her death. She balanced the book on her head and put her arms out as if on a tightrope.

"It's time to go home," she said. "Ellie is waiting."

Gibson nodded happily, tears in his eyes. "I didn't know if I'd see you again."

"You're silly," Bear answered.

"You're going to wish you hadn't," Merrick said, not seeing Bear and assuming Gibson meant him.

"Are you coming?" Bear asked.

Gibson pushed Merrick off. Merrick rolled onto his back and lay there wheezing. Gibson stood and brushed off the snow. He looked around for Bear, but she was nowhere in sight. She'd gone on ahead. Good. He hoped she found someplace warm. He fetched his bag, keeping a wary eye on Merrick in case he caught a second wind.

"You did this," Merrick moaned.

Gibson didn't have the energy or inclination to argue the point. Merrick didn't matter to him. All that mattered was getting home to his daughter. He left Merrick in the snow and trudged toward the airfield's office. He tried the door—locked. No hours posted at the door. Gibson peered through the window but didn't see a clock in the gloom. Based on the sun, it couldn't be much after dawn. It was far too cold to wait around to see if anyone showed up to work. If this was a Sunday, he could be waiting a long time. His eyes fell on an office phone; he could call his ex-wife and let her know he was on his way. But that would mean breaking in. Jeopardizing his newfound freedom by committing such a pedestrian crime seemed foolish. He had a far bigger crime in mind. The one he and his father had planned together.

He cast one last look toward Charles Merrick, who lay motionless in the snow. Maybe he'd had a heart attack. Gibson hoped not. He wanted the disgraced ex-billionaire to live a long, penniless life. That would be the best revenge of all.

With that cheery thought to warm him, Gibson started down the airfield's dirt road for home.

CHAPTER THREE

At the bottom of the hill, Gibson paused beside the "Dule Tree Airfield" sign to consider his options. Looking up and down the road, he couldn't see any signs of human life. If his memory served, and he didn't know that it did, the airfield was pretty damned isolated. So which way to go? Left or right? Right led back to the town of Niobe. It would take more than a day on foot. No one would pick him up looking like a deranged mountain man. Besides, Niobe held a lot of bad memories, and he didn't know that he'd be welcomed there.

Left it was. It felt better to be moving toward home and his daughter, forward not backward, and perhaps he'd get lucky and stumble upon a town.

The conditions made for slow going—snow had been plowed high onto the shoulders, where it had melted and refrozen into sharp white teeth. That meant walking along the edge of the icy road in sneakers. After a tractor trailer sent him sprawling onto the snowbank for safety, he crossed the road and walked against traffic so at least he'd get a good look at the vehicle that killed him. The wind strengthened as he walked, funneled through the gully between the woods to either side of the road. Gibson leaned into the wind, eyes watering. After a quarter mile he couldn't feel his face. He stopped, shivering uncontrollably, and put on every shirt in his duffel bag. With a Marine Corps T-shirt, he fashioned a crude keffiyeh to cover his neck, mouth, and nose. He zipped the windbreaker up tight, tucked his hands up into the sleeves, and set off again. He looked ridiculous, but it would slow the creep of hypothermia.

Around the bend, he caught up with Bear, who stood under a tree reading her book. Her dress fluttered in the wind.

"Aren't you freezing?" he asked.

"I'm fine," she assured him. "Walk with me?"

They walked side by side. Neither spoke, but her company helped keep him going even as he felt himself weakening. An aching hunger and thirst constricted his throat. Maybe if he lay down in the snow, he'd wake up back in his cell? There'd be food waiting for him; he'd never wanted one of those bars more in his life. Funny the things you found yourself missing.

"Don't even think about it," Bear said, reading his mind.

"I'm tired."

"You slept on the plane."

"That's not what I mean."

"Ellie's all you've talked about. You can't quit now."

At the mention of his daughter's name, Gibson felt ashamed. For all the pleasure it had brought to plot revenge on Damon Washburn, it had been Ellie who had kept him alive. Seeing her again was the only hope that captivity hadn't stolen, yet he already wanted to take the easy way out. He lowered his head and shuffled forward until he became hypnotized by the progress of his feet. He couldn't feel them anymore, so it reassured him to see them hard at work.

When he looked up again, he saw modest houses set back from the road. He should ask for help, but the idea of knocking on any of the doors terrified him. It would mean talking, and not to someone like Bear or his father who understood what he'd been through. The people inside these houses would see only a madman in a windbreaker.

13

Or mistake him for an escaped convict, which he supposed wasn't too far from the truth. There had been a time when persuading people had been second nature to him, but now he couldn't remember how. What would he say to them? How would he even begin?

Duke Vaughn leaned against an old Ford pickup truck with a "For Sale" sign in the window. His dead father beckoned to him, and Gibson went up the driveway. Bear had vanished again. She and his father avoided crossing paths, he'd noticed. They didn't seem to get along so well these days.

"I can't do this," he told his father, eying the home's front door.

"You know how many doors I've knocked on in my career? Asking perfect strangers to vote for my candidate?"

Gibson shook his head. "Looking like this?"

Duke conceded the point. "I'm not saying you don't have certain liabilities. You used to like a challenge."

"It's not a challenge. It's an impossibility."

"Most people would say Damon Washburn is impossible. But we're going to do that too. But first, you have to knock on this door."

"What do I say?"

"How much cash do you have?" Duke asked.

Gibson didn't know. He leafed through his wallet and counted ten crisp twenties. He didn't remember having them when he'd been captured. A gift from the CIA? Mighty generous of them to give him severance pay for time served. Not that two hundred dollars would take him very far. He still had his credit cards, but they would have been frozen for nonpayment a long time ago. He looked at the clean-cut kid on his driver's license with a feeling close to nostalgia. It was valid until his birthday in 2021. He wondered if it had expired.

Gibson caught his reflection in the window of the truck. Unwinding the T-shirt from around his head, he considered the man staring back at him, foreign and familiar in equal measures. The face of a vagrant, feral and adrift. But at least he finally had an answer to the question that had tormented him. He was still him. Such as it was. But it wasn't a face you opened your front door to. He looked unfit for human company. The hollow sockets of his eyes were the red of septic bandages. His beard unfolded like a tangled thicket to his chest, and his long, matted hair fell to his shoulders. Gibson attempted to comb some discipline into it, but his hair felt like barbed wire on his blue-black fingers.

"Doubt a couple hundred bucks is enough to get you this sweet baby." Duke winked and patted the pickup. "But who knows, maybe they're in the mood to negotiate. Just give 'em that old Vaughn charm."

"Oh, I'm sure that'll work wonders."

"That's the spirit." Lately, his dad acknowledged sarcasm only when it suited him.

Gibson went up the walk to the front door, debating whether he'd make a worse impression with a T-shirt wrapped around his head or in full Sasquatch mode. In the end, he left off the T-shirt, opened the glass storm door, and rang the bell. A boy no older than eight threw open the inner door. A wall of heat greeted Gibson, making his face tingle. The boy wore a tank top and shorts and looked up at Gibson from under a Cincinnati Bengals helmet.

"You don't look so good."

From the mouths of babes.

Gibson opened his mouth, but nothing came out. He pointed at the pickup. The door closed, and Gibson heard the boy hollering for someone.

"You're going to have to do better than pointing at things, Tarzan," Duke said.

"I'm working on it."

A woman in her fifties, clutching a bathrobe at the neck, came to the door, makeup half done. She opened the door an economical crack, gave him a once-over, and asked his business. Gibson stood there in mute panic, mind a blank. Despite the cold, sweat rolled down the back of his neck. The woman's eyes narrowed, and she started to close the door when her eyes fell on the T-shirt in his hand.

"You a Marine?" she asked.

He nodded.

"Use your words," Duke said.

"Sing me the hymn," she said.

"Ma'am?"

"You heard me. And don't be giving me no Halls of Montezuma neither, just skip on down to the third verse."

He knew it. Every Marine did. They could have left him in that cell until his brains were scrambled eggs, until he couldn't remember his own name, and he'd still know every word to the hymn. But the idea of saying so much petrified him. He opened his mouth and shut it again.

"I ain't got all day," she said.

"You can do it," Duke encouraged.

Gibson cleared his throat and rasped out, "Here's health to you and to our Corps. Which we are proud to serve; In many a strife we've fought for life. And never lost our nerve. If the—"

"All right, that'll do." Her expression softened. "What do you need, son?"

"Home," he managed.

She nodded as if she knew exactly where he meant. "I let you inside . . . you going to do something stupid? Cause me to shoot you?"

He shook his head.

"Then take your shoes off and come warm up."

"You did it," Duke said, exulting. "This is the first step, son. I'm proud of you."

He didn't share his father's enthusiasm and felt like a kid who'd won a trophy simply for showing up.

She led him down a hall to the kitchen, where he sat at a small table, luxuriating in the warmth of the house. She brought him a glass of water and a banana. He gulped the water and devoured the banana; the smell of the peel made him want to cry, the first real food he'd seen in who knew how long. She took the glass and refilled it for him. The boy danced into the kitchen, football helmet swaying loosely on his head. He spiked an imaginary football and dashed out again.

"I need that boy back in school already." The woman chuckled. "He's going a little stir-crazy."

Gibson nodded—a topic he knew intimately. He'd been that kind of kid himself at that age. Ellie had inherited it from him. Her idea of sitting still was running in circles.

"Ma'am, what's the date?"

Her eyes narrowed. "Well . . . you must have tied one on tight. Don't know the date. It's December 26."

He'd wanted to know the year but feared that would be a bridge too far. He'd missed Christmas with Ellie by one day. One last fuck-you from the CIA. Well, Ellie and he could still celebrate. It wasn't too late for that. What child wouldn't leap at a second Christmas morning?

"My name is Cheryl."

Gibson hesitated. "John," he said. He didn't know why he'd needed to lie to her.

"So where is home, John?"

"Virginia. Near DC. I have enough money for a bus ticket if I can get to Morgantown."

She refilled his water while she thought that over. "Can't be driving you to Morgantown. I'm on shift at eleven."

"I understand. I appreciate your—"

"But maybe I could drop you at the truck stop up on the I-79. You could hitch from there."

Gibson nodded gratefully. She left him alone in the kitchen and went to finish getting ready for work. He got up to refill his water glass, stood over the sink and drank it down, and then filled it for a fourth time. The clock on the microwave read "9:42." It was 9:42 a.m. on December 26. Such mundane information, but it felt like an important gateway between the netherworld he'd been in and this place. Tempting to call it the real world, but he held off, at least for now. He still harbored doubts.

On the far wall hung a framed photograph of a young woman at attention in her dress blues. He raised his glass to her.

Semper Fi.

CHAPTER FOUR

Cheryl dropped him at the truck stop and refused the money he tried to give her for gas. He thanked her and shook her hand when she offered it. Her hand was strong, skin worn and calloused. His first human contact. It reawakened a sense of belonging to the land of the living. A profound difference for a man whose cell had been his whole world.

Inside the door of the mini-mart stood a rack of newspapers. Gibson picked up a copy of the Charleston *Gazette-Mail* and saw the year. Eighteen months. They'd kept him in that cell for eighteen months. He would have believed had it been eighteen years. However long it had been, it felt like a lifetime. How would he begin to explain it to Nicole? He'd missed two of Ellie's birthdays. His daughter was nine. He was thirty-one. That his confinement could have lasted much, much longer offered scant comfort now.

"How do you think Damon Washburn celebrated his birthday?" Duke asked, leaning against the counter. "Bet he threw himself one hell of a party."

The thought of it burned.

Gibson bought the newspaper and a tall bottle of water. He had the woman at the counter run his credit card, but as he suspected, it came back declined. Connected to the mini-mart was a simple restaurant;

he seated himself and put twenty dollars on the table so the waitress would see that he could pay. The menu was a single laminated page, but it overwhelmed Gibson. Accustomed to eating the same food for every meal, he didn't know how to choose for himself. How did something so simple become a life-or-death decision? When the waitress came around, nose wrinkled in distaste, he pointed blindly at the menu and held it up for her to see.

She took the menu and brought him a double cheeseburger. He ate it too fast and gave himself a stomachache. But like a dog that didn't know when it was full, he ordered a second. Waiting, he read the newspaper front to back, and, even though it contained mostly local stories, it represented one more delicate strand tethering him to the world. Over the newspaper, he studied the truckers at the surrounding tables, looking for a kind face. Either none of them had kind faces or else he'd forgotten what one looked like.

It was Bear's turn to play cheerleader. "You can do it. It's Christmas. People feel generous at Christmas."

Gibson didn't know about all that, but took a deep breath and stood up.

"Excuse me," he began. All heads swiveled to see who was disturbing their morning. He forged ahead. "I'm looking for a ride to Morgantown to catch a bus home. I've got a little money, not a lot, but I can put some toward gas. I'm a former Marine, a little down on his luck. If you could help, I'd be grateful. Thank you and merry Christmas." He sat back down and stared at the newspaper, flushed with embarrassment. So that was what begging felt like; he didn't think he'd ever look at a homeless person the same way again.

Bear smiled at him supportively, but no one leapt at the opportunity to offer him a ride. After a moment's hesitation, the room returned to its meals and conversations, agreeing to erase the interruption from its collective memory and get on with its morning. Gibson finished his second burger and ordered coffee, thinking of alternate ways to

Morgantown. In the end, he opted for the individual approach. He'd greet each new truck as it arrived and appeal to the driver. Make it personal. So much human interaction sounded painful, but he would do it if it got him home to Ellie.

Resolved, Gibson paid the check and headed out. A man stopped him on his way to the door and said he'd drop him in Morgantown. "That's my rig," he said, pointing to a semi at the far side of the lot. "Leaving in twenty."

"See?" said Bear. "It's Christmas."

Seventy miles an hour saw them pull into Morgantown in a little over sixty minutes. The trucker, who never offered his name, dropped Gibson off in front of Mountaineer Station. Gibson offered him forty dollars, the trucker took twenty, and the two men shook hands without ever having spoken more than necessary. Gibson had been grateful for the silence. His brief taste of freedom had exhausted him—every inter-action, every decision. Some part of him longed for the inviolate routine of his cell. The irony could not be any more plain—he'd dreamed of escaping constantly, but now, a few hours after his release, all he wished was to be back where he felt safe. Is this what institutionalization did to the mind?

He looked up at the bus station. Only eighteen months behind schedule. He'd been on his way to Morgantown when Lea's desperate text had brought him back to Niobe. How different his life might be if only he'd ignored her. He would never have met Damon Washburn. Never crossed paths with Charles Merrick.

It had been some detour.

His good luck held—the next bus departed in ten minutes. That gave him only enough time to buy a ticket, use the restroom, and find a seat toward the back of the bus. For a time, he watched the traffic on the highway, but soon enough the bus rocked him to sleep. He woke with a cry, certain he'd find himself back in the confines of his cell, disoriented when he didn't. A passenger across the aisle stared suspiciously his way. Gibson sat up and rubbed the sleep out of his eyes. He judged they must be in Maryland by the way the snow had thinned as they moved out of the mountains. So close now. Bear wandered back and sat beside him. They played the alphabet game out the window until he caught the passenger staring at him again.

It was past seven when Gibson got into the serpentine cab line outside Union Station. A mix of holiday travelers and business commuters returning from Philadelphia and New York on this crisp December night—Gibson didn't belong among them. Above his head, great wreaths hung between the arches of the station. He kept his head down and shuffled forward in line. The attendants who orchestrated the cab line hustled to keep things moving, but it was still twenty minutes before he reached the front. Duke waited in line with him.

"What are you going back there for?" Duke asked. "You really think they want to see you?"

"It's my family."

"It's an ex-wife and a girl who barely knows her deadbeat father who's been in a CIA black-site prison for eighteen months. Son, that's not a family, that's a guest appearance on *Maury Povich*." Duke paused to let that sink in. "So . . . what? What do you think is going to happen? You'll roll up to their door looking like Chewbacca's prom date, and they'll welcome you in with open arms? Are you even thinking this through?"

Gibson looked at his father imploringly. "I have nowhere else to go."

"That's not a good enough reason to go someplace."

"What would you have me do?"

"What you promised me." Duke's face was inches from Gibson's. "You want Nicole to respect you again? Then prove to her you're a man who deserves respect. Damon Washburn has to pay. If you go to her now, looking like this? Nothing good will come of it. I promise you."

An attendant pointed Gibson toward a waiting cab. The driver protested that he'd been saddled with a bum and wouldn't unlock the door until Gibson showed him his money. Mollified, the driver punched Gibson's destination into his GPS and drove up Massachusetts.

The idea of reuniting with his daughter thrilled him, but his father had given voice to all his rawest fears. What if he had been gone too long? What if Ellie didn't remember him? Maybe he should wait, get himself cleaned up so he didn't frighten her. Twice he leaned forward to ask the cabbie to take him to a motel and stopped himself. He didn't have money for such a luxury; more than that, he needed to see Ellie to remind him why he still wanted to be alive.

"It'll be all right," Bear said. "Nicole will understand. She knows how much you love Ellie."

"What if I frighten her?"

"You won't. You're her daddy."

"But what if I do?"

"She'll get over it," Bear reassured him.

The thought of Ellie shrinking away from him was too horrible to imagine. Gibson caught the cabbie's narrowed eyes in the rearview mirror.

"What are you doing?" the cabbie demanded.

"Sorry," Gibson said. "Just thinking out loud."

"Don't."

"He's mean," Bear said.

Gibson gave her a pleading look to keep quiet. He didn't want to get thrown out of the cab. He was almost home.

"Well, he is," Bear said, getting in the last word. But after that, she held her peace.

They left the beltway and wound their way up into the residential neighborhood where Nicole and Ellie lived. Where he had lived once. Gibson sat forward, resting his forearms on his thighs, and tried to slow his racing heart. The cab pulled over to the curb. Gibson took a deep breath and looked out the window.

It was the wrong house.

The cabbie had brought him to the wrong house.

The cabbie repeated the address he'd been given—53 Mulberry Court—and showed Gibson on his GPS. Gibson didn't understand. Could he have forgotten the address of the house that Nicole and he had bought together? The house where Ellie had been born and grown up. The house he'd fought to keep when he couldn't find a job. Was he *that* crazy? He tried to think of the right address, but his head was so murky. Gibson tried the handles, but his doors were locked. The driver repeated the fare, and Gibson thrust all the money he had left at the cabbie, who counted it carefully before consenting to unlock the door.

Gibson stumbled out of the cab and spun slowly in a circle. He recognized everything. The houses across the street. The neighbors. The tree with the gashed trunk where a teen driver had jumped the curb and plowed into it. Everything was the same. Except the house. Where was the house?

He really had lost his mind. Or worse, maybe he hadn't ever left his cell. This was nothing but another of his excursions through the secret passage. He couldn't countenance how real it all felt, but there was no other explanation for this cruel trick of his mind. All he wanted now was for Bear to lead him back to his cell. He called her name, but she didn't answer. Maybe she was playing hide-and-seek the way she sometimes did. He ran down the street calling her name and looking behind parked cars.

At the corner, he gave up and slapped himself hard across the face. Trying to wake himself up. Unwilling to remain trapped in this fun-house mirror of his memory, he pinched the skin on the back of his wrist until it bruised. *Please take me away from this hell,* he begged the evening sky.

"Bear. Please come back. Help me," he whimpered, hoping she wasn't too far away to hear him. "Please."

Nothing. He looked up at the street signs that named this the intersection of Macomb Lane and Mulberry Court. He went back up the street, reading the numbers off the houses: 47, 49, 51 . . . He recognized all these houses. Everything was as he remembered it, but when he stopped outside 53 Mulberry Court, it was still the wrong house. Twice the size of the house he remembered. The wrong color. The wrong style. His head throbbed. Maybe this was the right house. Maybe they were inside waiting for him, and he'd only remembered the house wrong. That had to be it.

A silver car pulled into the driveway. A man in a suit got out. He looked Gibson up and down, not appearing overly impressed. He started toward the front door but reconsidered and crossed the yard and met Gibson at the gate.

"Can I help you?" the man asked.

"Do you live here?"

"Who are you?"

"Is this 53 Mulberry Court?"

"Yes, it is. Can I help you?" the man asked a second time.

The front door opened. A woman looked out with a baby cradled against her hip. Two small boys pressed forward to see what the fuss was about.

"Tom, what's going on?"

"It's okay, honey, just keep the kids in the house."

"How is this your house?" Gibson said. "What happened to the old house?"

The man stiffened. "Who are you?"

"I used to live here. What happened to the old house?"

The man turned back to his wife. "Shut the door. Call the police."

"What's going on?" she asked, voice rising.

"Get the gun from upstairs. Don't open the door."

The wife paled but didn't move, frozen between doing what she'd been asked and going to her husband's defense.

"What happened to the house that was here?" Gibson asked again.

"It burned down," the man said.

Gibson fumbled with the gate's latch, trying to get in. This was some kind of a trick. "What are you talking about?"

"The house burned down," the man said again and put both hands on the gate to hold it shut.

Gibson felt an emergency-room dread, the kind that comes from trying to guess what kind of news a doctor brings based upon her body language. "What do you mean, it burned down?"

"Stop. Please just stop. You're scaring my kids."

Gibson looked up at the boys' faces, saw their fear. He let go of the fence and stepped back, hands up. "I'm sorry. Can you just tell me what happened? Was anyone hurt?"

"I don't know. We only moved in a few months ago."

"Who did you buy from?"

"Through a broker. Look, there's obviously nothing here for you. My wife is on the phone with the police. You should just leave."

Gibson took one last look at the imposter that stood where his dream home had once been. He backed away from the gate and lurched away down the street. At a storm drain, he knelt and vomited. He squeezed his eyes shut and willed himself back into his cell, but when he opened them, he was still on Mulberry Court. He prayed for it not to be real. But what if it was? And what if they'd been home? Oh God, what if they'd been home? Numb and lost and with nowhere to go,

Gibson walked in an aimless, straight line, hoping to find the passage back into his cell.

"I warned you not to go back there," Duke said.

"You knew?"

"I didn't think you could handle it. I'm trying to protect you from yourself."

"Take me back. Please," Gibson said. "I can't be here anymore."

A police cruiser passed him and stopped at the curb twenty feet up the block. A uniformed officer, barrel-chested in his body armor, stepped out. The owners of 53 Mulberry Court hadn't been bluffing.

"Evening, sir. Can I have a word with you?" The officer's voice was light and friendly.

Gibson didn't break stride. He was all talked out for one day. The cop could shoot him for all Gibson cared, but he wasn't stopping for anyone. He had to get back to his cell. The passage had to be nearby.

"Sir. I just need a few minutes. Can you stop for me, please?"

When Gibson still didn't, the officer stepped onto the sidewalk blocking his way. A second cruiser turned the corner and approached from the other direction. An old, atrophied part of Gibson's brain warned him that this could only go badly for him. He didn't listen and changed directions to evade the officer, who moved sideways to stay in front of him. The cop raised a hand, palm out.

"Sir. Stop walking, okay. Right there." The man had asked nicely twice, but now his voice hardened.

Ahead, Gibson saw a break in the fence beside the sidewalk. The secret passage to the place where his old house hadn't burned down and Nicole and Ellie were safe and happy. Gibson dropped his duffel bag, took a quick step to his left, and tried to stiff-arm his way past the officer. A little head start so he could make a break for it. If he reached the passage, they wouldn't be able to follow. But putting a hand on the officer took the situation from tense to downright unfriendly.

The officer took hold of Gibson's wrist and, turning, drove his forearm into Gibson's triceps just above the elbow. The leverage on the joint forced Gibson to the ground. Gibson kicked out at the man, desperate to get free. His foot connected with the officer's knee. The cop grunted and let go for a moment. The second cruiser screeched to a halt and bounced up onto the curb, blocking the way. Another officer leapt out. Gibson scrabbled down the sidewalk on all fours until the first officer Tased him. A knee drove into his back, and the officers wrestled handcuffs onto him, then flopped him on his back.

Duke winked down at his son. "You pick the damnedest times to stand on principle."

CHAPTER FIVE

Gibson spent the night at the police station. He'd managed twelve uninterrupted hours of freedom before finding his way back into a cell. Apparently, he had struck an officer, but Gibson remembered little of the encounter. He recalled something about a police cruiser and a struggle but only flashes after that. He attributed the gaps in his memory to the Taser burn on his back. The wound was bruised and raw, and he passed a fitful night, dreams of fire and pain chasing him from sleep anytime he closed his eyes. Ellie screamed for him from her bedroom window.

"Is this real?" he asked his father, who loomed over him each time he woke.

"Does it matter?"

"What kind of an answer is that? Just tell me that Ellie is all right."

"Why would I bother? It's not like you listen to anything else I say."

In the morning, a taciturn officer moved Gibson to an interview room and left him handcuffed to a table. Gibson asked the officer about Ellie and Nicole, but, as with the night before, he received no answer. For his family's sake, he had desperately wanted this all to be another of his elaborate delusions, but deep down he knew it was real.

Hours passed before anyone came to talk to him. He stewed at the injustice of it, layer upon layer of anger stacking up like dry cordwood waiting for a spark. He felt on the verge of a child's tantrum until Bear asked him to read to her. She, too, felt devastated about the fire, and he could see that he was being selfish. They read quietly until she calmed down. Eventually, the door opened. Gibson paused midsentence and handed the book back to Bear. A plainclothes detective carrying a file sat across from him. The man had smug, confident eyes and combed his short blond hair forward in a Caesar that he smoothed compulsively with the flat of one hand. He introduced himself as Jim Bachmann.

"How are you this morning?" the detective asked as though meeting Gibson for a round of golf.

"Don't lose your cool," Bear said, getting up to leave the room.

It was good advice that Gibson wasn't sure he could follow. He wanted to pummel Detective Jim Bachmann, smear blood in the man's eyes, and ruin his perfect little haircut.

"Don't tell him anything," Duke said. "He's probably CIA like Washburn."

Gibson thought Duke was being paranoid.

"No one will tell me about the fire," Gibson said.

Duke let out an exasperated sigh.

"We'll get to that," the detective said.

For the next thirty minutes, the detective advised him of his rights while implying that it would be a mistake to invoke any of them. "You want a lawyer, we'll stop right here, but after that I can't do anything for you." It was a hell of a performance—lawyers and the courts were the enemy, and only good old Jim Bachmann could straighten this mess out. Gibson marveled at what kind of fool would fall for it until he realized that he hadn't asked for a lawyer yet.

"Can you please just tell me if anyone was hurt?"

Detective Bachmann sidestepped the question, unmoved by Gibson's plea. "You answer my questions, then we'll see about yours."

"My daughter . . . is she okay?" Gibson said.

"We can discuss all that after you answer my questions."

Gibson studied Jim Bachmann. He'd always had a talent for reading people and tried to pick up the detective's intent from his body language. His mind couldn't bring the man into focus, and the detective's face remained a cubist jumble of angular planes. Gibson slumped back in frustration. "Why was I stopped?"

"Officers responded to reports of someone matching your description causing a disturbance at 53 Mulberry Court."

"There was no disturbance. We just talked."

Bachmann made a note. Gibson realized he'd admitted to being there.

"We only talked. I swear."

Bachmann smiled agreeably. "The homeowner told a different story."

"So they Tased me in the back?"

The detective looked sideways at Gibson. "You failed to comply with the officer's verbal instructions. Then you assaulted that officer. That's why you were Tased."

"I don't remember doing that."

"Don't worry. That's what body cams are for. That's one-to-five, by the way." Jim Bachmann opened his file. "So . . . 53 Mulberry Court. That was your ex-wife's address, right?"

Gibson nodded, immediately uneasy at the mention of Nicole.

Duke looked over the detective's shoulder at the file. "Son of a bitch is setting you up for something."

"So what prompted the unexpected visit?"

"I thought I was under arrest for assault. And if you have it all on body cam, what do you even need to question me for?"

"Don't worry about the assault. The officer is a friend. If you help us with our investigation, then I'm sure he could be convinced to let it drop."

"What do you actually want?"

"Can you account for your whereabouts the day your ex-wife's house burned down?"

The question caught Gibson by surprise, but he understood now why he was here and why the family had freaked out. Nicole's house hadn't burned down; it had *been* burned down. And he was a suspect, probably the only suspect. Disgruntled, unemployed ex-husbands automatically went straight to the top of the list. The assault charge was nothing but a pretext to question him about the fire. It made him angry all over again.

Bachmann repeated his questions.

"Don't answer that," Duke advised.

Gibson glared at his father. He didn't need to be told that paranoid tales of CIA kidnappings and black-site prisons would go over badly. The detective followed Gibson's eyes to the empty wall where Duke had been and jotted down another note. Gibson doubted it was flattering.

"Mr. Vaughn, I can't clear you if you won't answer my questions."

"You already cleared me."

"Have I now?" Bachmann said with a practiced, condescending smile.

"Well, you have nothing on me, so if you haven't, you're either stupid or a liar."

"Don't kid yourself. I got you six ways and Sunday." Bachmann didn't look amused now.

"Bullshit. I know you don't because I had nothing to do with it. This little dog and pony show is just to see if I'll incriminate myself."

"Gibson . . ." Bear pleaded. "Don't."

She wasn't wrong. Antagonizing the detective wasn't helping anything, but Gibson was tired of humoring this jackal. "Was. Anyone. Hurt?"

"Spare me, all right?" said Bachmann. "If you cared so much about your kid, you wouldn't have burned down her home."

The eighteen months he'd spent wondering if he'd ever be released had been hell, but it was nothing compared to the last twelve hours not knowing if Ellie were alive or dead. He didn't know that he wanted the answer, but not knowing was the most dreadful purgatory he could imagine. Bachmann's sneer was the proverbial last straw. Gibson snapped.

"Was anyone hurt?" he screamed, toggling from calm to rage in the blink of an eye. "Is my daughter safe, you fuck?"

Spittle flew across the table. Gibson's chair hit the back wall as he surged at Bachmann, stopped only by the handcuffs. Bachmann jerked backward, caught off guard by Gibson's Jekyll and Hyde. A pair of uniformed officers burst through the door, ready to crack heads, but Bachmann got between them and Gibson and ushered them back out into the hall. Gibson raged against his handcuffs, unable to subdue the stream of threats and expletives pouring out of him or the tears that coursed down his face. Bachmann shut the door and put his back against it. He waited for Gibson's storm to blow itself out.

Gibson slumped to the floor, arms twisted over his head by the handcuffs still attached to the table. It should have hurt, but he felt nothing at all.

"Are you about done?" Bachmann asked.

"Please . . ."

Bachmann looked down at Gibson and took pity on him. "No one was home, Mr. Vaughn. Your daughter and ex-wife are alive and well."

Gibson absorbed the news. Something hard and jagged loosened in his chest, and he took a newborn's first breath. The sense of relief was primal, and he prayed thankfully to the god of little children. Too adrenaline scarred and exhausted to move, Gibson needed the detective's help to sit up in the chair again.

"Thank you," Gibson said.

"Do that again, and I'll put you back in the cage for a week."

"Where's Ellie?"

"That's not pertinent to this—"

"Where are they?"

"They're not anxious to see you. You have to understand that much. Your ex-wife took out a restraining order against you, so I wouldn't tell you even if I knew."

The words "restraining order" reverberated in Gibson's ears. He caught Duke's eye, who only shook his head and looked away. The detective carried on talking at him, but his words were fuzzy and indistinct.

"Now I've answered all the questions I'm going to, so how about you return the favor? Where were you the day the house burned down? Where have you been?"

"Away," Gibson said. "On my own."

"Don't get cute with me. I'm all out of good graces for the day."

"I don't know where I was."

"You don't know where you've been for the last eighteen months?"

When Gibson stuck to his story, the detective started from the beginning and asked all his questions a second time. Then a third. After that, Gibson stopped paying attention. Someone had burned down Nicole's house, and he hadn't been there to stop it. Something else Damon Washburn would answer for. From the corner of his eye, he saw Duke nod in agreement.

"How can you not know where you were?" Bachmann asked for the hundredth time.

Finally, Gibson slipped up and told the truth. "I don't know. I was locked up."

Bachmann sat forward.

"Gibson," Duke said. "Careful."

"You were in prison? Where?"

"I told you I don't know," Gibson said.

"You don't know where you were in prison?"

"Ask the CIA."

The detective wore the expression of someone who'd started a conversation at a party with a normal-looking person but found himself trapped arguing whether Jimmy Hoffa had Kennedy killed. Duke wore the same expression but for different reasons.

Bachmann said, "You were in a CIA prison?"

"Yeah, that's right."

Without a word, Bachmann rose and left the room. He was gone long enough for Duke to lecture Gibson on the virtues of silence. Bachmann returned in the company of the uniformed officers. Some kind of decision had been reached.

"If we have follow-up questions, do you have a number where we can reach you?"

"I don't have a phone."

"Mr. Vaughn, do you have a home? Somewhere you live?"

Gibson shook his head.

"Is there someone we can call? Who could pick you up?"

Gibson thought about that a good, long while even though the list was good and short. There was his aunt in Charlottesville, but that was a good two hours away, and the idea of mixing her up in any more of his legal troubles did not hold a lot of appeal. She'd been through enough on account of him. Everyone else he knew was dead, missing, or wanted nothing to do with him. Finally, he gave them Toby Kalpar's name. He didn't like the idea of getting Toby involved either, but there simply wasn't anyone else.

CHAPTER SIX

With his slight frame and contemplative, scholarly air, Toby Kalpar looked as out of place in a police station waiting room as he did behind the counter of the Nighthawk Diner. After his divorce, Gibson had moved into a one-bedroom apartment within walking distance of the Nighthawk. The apartment was dreary and depressing, and cooking wasn't among the skills he'd picked up in the Marines. The diner had become a home away from home. He'd spent countless hours at a booth in the back, job hunting. Somewhere along the way, he and Toby had become good friends. The older man had offered Gibson much-needed perspective and advice, for which Gibson had been grateful, even if he hadn't always been able to follow it.

He fought the urge to slip out the door. All these strangers judging him were just that—strangers. It would be something else entirely from Toby. Before he could escape, Toby caught sight of Gibson. If he had a reaction to Gibson's shabby appearance, he masked it well. Toby pushed his glasses high up on his nose, put his arms around Gibson, and hugged him fiercely. Gibson wept bitterly at the warmth of Toby's embrace, who, misunderstanding the reason for the tears, held him all the tighter. Bear, who had a soft spot in her heart for Toby, stood nearby smiling.

"I didn't know who else to call," Gibson said out in the parking lot. It was dusk, and a light, freezing rain had begun to fall.

"I'm glad you did." As was Toby's way, he didn't ask the questions that must have been on his mind, content to let the truth unfold in its own time.

Gibson meant to ditch Toby now that he'd been released, but he had questions that needed answering first.

"Where are they?"

"Let's talk about it in the car," Toby said.

"Just tell me."

Toby held open the car door and waited patiently. "I'll tell you everything on the way home."

Gibson eyed the car warily. It felt like a trap. What was home? *Where the hell was that?* But Toby refused to say anything more, so Gibson got into the car with his duffel bag across his lap in case he needed to get away quickly. Toby started the car and adjusted the heat. The windows had iced over, and light filtered through, ghostly and pale. Ghazal played quietly over the stereo. Toby and Sana Kalpar had emigrated from Pakistan more than twenty years ago, and in many ways had embraced the customs and culture of their adopted country. But Toby's father had been a ghazal poet and singer of some renown, and it was still the music Toby preferred when he felt homesick in the winter months.

In the car, Toby told the same story the detective had. Nicole's house had burned to the foundations. Fortunately, no one had been at home. Clear indications of an accelerant. No witnesses.

"The police think I did it," Gibson said.

"You weren't here to defend yourself. It looked . . . well, it looked bad."

"Where's Ellie?"

"I don't know."

Gibson became angry. "Don't tell me that. Why wouldn't Nicole tell you?"

Toby sighed. "Because she knew that I would tell you if you ever came back."

That, and all it implied, hit home. Gibson sat back and looked out through the small patch of defrosted window. Nicole had disappeared with Ellie. Taken out a restraining order against him and run. She believed him capable of doing this thing. It had come to that.

Gibson got out of the car, certain that he would be sick. Toby followed him, urging him to get back in.

"I can't," Gibson said. "Appreciate you springing me, but I'm not your problem."

"You are not a problem. Please, get back in the car."

"And go where? What will I do?"

"You will need time to figure that out," Toby allowed.

"He's right," Bear said. "You need time to find Ellie."

"I don't know how," Gibson said to both of them. Before the cell, he would have counted planning and decision-making among his skills, but now he saw no way back. Nicole and Ellie were gone, and he was out of time. If he had a gun, he didn't know that he wouldn't put it in his mouth. He couldn't think of a single reason not to—all his reasons had gone into hiding.

"Ellie," Bear answered. "That's always the reason."

"Just leave me," he pleaded with Toby.

For the first time since Gibson had known him, Toby became visibly angry. "Get in the car, stubborn ass. I will not tell you again." Toby was famously gentlemanly in his language, and even that much profanity sounded awkward from his lips. "You'll be a martyr on your own time. But I am not going home to Sana to tell her that I saw you and left you in a parking lot in the rain. No, you will not dishonor me this way."

"Toby—"

"Get in the car! Or I will . . . I will kick your backside." Toby snatched Gibson's duffel bag and made a show of putting it in the trunk, slamming it shut. Then he got back in the car and sat there waiting, both hands on the steering wheel, until Gibson slipped back into the passenger seat.

Toby said, "I apologize for my language."

Toby and Sana Kalpar lived in a town house in Arlington. Together they owned the Nighthawk Diner, and one or both was always there. Sana wouldn't be home until late, so Toby parked on the street, leaving the garage for his wife. Gibson stood in the entry hall while Toby turned on lights in the living room. It was a warm, lived-in home. Gibson had always harbored an ignoble jealousy for Toby's tight-knit family, but he found it doubly painful now. Pictures in frames dotted every surface, and on the walls hung a gallery's worth of art. The work of Toby's only child, Maissa—a gifted artist who had attended Corcoran School of the Arts & Design. Last Gibson knew, she'd moved to San Francisco but was having trouble finding steady work. Toby doted on his daughter, and it had pained him to see her struggle.

"Maissa has a job," Toby said with his typical clairvoyance.

"That's so great. Doing what?"

"Graphic designer for an advertising agency."

"Does she like it?"

"No." Toby smiled. "But one step at a time."

Two cats, one gray, one black, wound between Toby's ankles and disappeared down the hall toward the kitchen. Toby apologized and followed after his hungry pets, telling Gibson to make himself at home. Gibson couldn't decide how to do that, and when Toby came back from the kitchen, he still hadn't moved.

"Well, you didn't run out into the street, so I suppose that's progress," Toby said, but his joke couldn't hide his unease. "So, my friend, I have a question."

Gibson tensed. Toby had held off asking Gibson any questions, but here they came. He had no idea how he would explain the last eighteen months.

"Are you aware of how dreadful you smell?"

Not the question Gibson had expected. "I thought that was you."

"A retort." Toby looked relieved, as if Gibson's feeble joke assured him that he hadn't let a crazy person into his home. "I knew it was still you."

Gibson wasn't so sure, but it felt good to be recognized all the same.

Toby said, "In all seriousness, my friend, you are rank."

He led Gibson upstairs and showed him into Maissa's bedroom. She visited only once a year, but her parents kept the room just as she'd left it. For the most part, it was a grown woman's room but with vestiges of her adolescent affections. In one corner, a watercolor rested on an easel as if Maissa had set down her brush for a moment and would be back any second.

If Gibson lived to be one hundred, the shower would go down as the best of his life. It took three applications of Maissa's coconut-scented shampoo before his shoulder-length hair began to feel clean, four for the beard. He lathered in conditioner, leaned against the tiles, and let the water beat down. In a trance, he stayed there until the water ran cold.

He toweled off and watched the stranger in the mirror brush the tangles out of his hair and beard. It was slow going; patches had matted together in haphazard dreadlocks. He badly needed a shave, but it would take a barber—or a grounds crew—to make headway in this thicket. In the meantime, he borrowed one of Maissa's hair ties and put his hair back in a ponytail. If his former commanding officer could see him now, there would be hell to pay. He'd be right at home in Saskatchewan . . . or Brooklyn. Where he didn't feel at home was in his own skin.

"This is a good move," Duke said. "We need a base of operations."

"Can you just *not* right now?"

Duke pointed an admonishing finger at Gibson. "Toby Kalpar is on a need-to-know basis only, and he doesn't."

The smell of bacon frying roused Gibson from his thoughts. His last meal had been the truck-stop burgers in West Virginia, and the thought of Toby's cooking caused his stomach to turn giddy backflips. Toby cooked at the diner only in dire emergencies, but the man knew his way around a kitchen. Gibson pulled on his jeans, his least dirty shirt, and followed the scent downstairs to its source.

"Just in time. I was about to call the Coast Guard," Toby said, sniffing the air. "You smell like a piña colada."

"Take it up with Maissa."

Toby plated a pair of omelets and drizzled them with sriracha. He set them at a kitchen table already weighted down by a platter of bacon, sausage, and potatoes; toast; cantaloupe; and a pitcher of orange juice, fresh squeezed or Gibson would eat his musty T-shirt. Gibson and Toby shared a love of breakfast and saw the time of day as no impediment.

The two men tucked in to Toby's impromptu feast. It beat a truck-stop burger all to hell; the man could straight-up cook. Gibson was halfway through his omelet before it occurred to him to say so. Toby reached across the table and gripped Gibson's shoulder for a moment, said nothing. Gibson felt human for the first time in as long as he remembered and put his hand over Toby's. Then he saw Duke lurking by the door, watching, and the feeling was gone.

"Do you think it was me?" Gibson asked when the food had gone to meet its maker.

"The man I knew could not have done it." Toby rose to clear the plates, considering the question further. "Are you?" he asked. "The man I knew?"

A fair question. It was Gibson's turn to pause before answering. "I don't know. I don't know who I am, but I didn't do that. That much I can tell you."

Toby nodded and shrugged his shoulders. "That is good enough for me. Now get up and help me with the dishes."

When the kitchen was squared away, the two men moved to the living room for coffee. Toby did much of the talking, telling stories from the diner and catching Gibson up on his family. Gibson could feel his friend trying to draw him out.

"Why don't you ask me?" Gibson asked.

"You'll tell me when you're ready."

"Don't know I ever will be."

Toby nodded over his coffee. "A risk I am willing to take."

"I'll leave in the morning."

"And do what?"

———

Gibson got into bed, still brooding about Toby's question. He already knew Duke's answer and that Bear had another. He'd made promises to each of them and could feel their impatience, waiting to see whom he would disappoint. He feared the answer would be both. An unfamiliar instinct to lie down and die had coiled around his heart. He'd experienced his share of hardship: the death of his father, his arrest and trial, the end of his marriage. He'd always picked himself up and soldiered on, always found a fight to rally him: his father's memory, his freedom, his daughter.

This felt different.

The people he wanted to fight for didn't want him. He could track down his ex-wife and daughter, but if Nicole feared him enough to disappear with Ellie, then what good would it do? If he had lost Ellie, then he feared that his incarceration had stripped him of more than just his sanity.

"That's why Washburn has to pay," Duke growled.

"That's why you have to find Ellie," Bear whispered.

Accustomed as he was to a bare mattress, the sheets hung around him like a straitjacket. He kicked them off, twisting this way and that, unable to get comfortable. He switched off the bedside lamp. The sudden darkness, viscous and bitter, rose up, enveloping him like a black ocean. It filled his lungs, choking him. Gibson flailed wildly. Knocked the lamp off the table. He sprawled out of bed after it, clawing at the floor until his hand closed on the lamp. He turned it on and clutched it to him, shaking and hyperventilating. In time, he got up and switched on every light in the room, each one restoring a part of his calm. He went and splashed water on his face. When he came back to the bedroom, his father was sitting on the bed. Duke did not look pleased.

"Look what they've done to you."

Gibson looked away.

"You really can't think of anything worth fighting for?" Duke asked. "You're really going to lie down for them? That's what he wants, you know."

"Who?"

"The man who put you in that cell. Does he get a pass? What about our plans? Or was that just all talk?"

"I have to find Ellie. Anyway, he's CIA."

"And you're a decorated Marine who helped get bin Laden. Will you just be a footnote in his career? A name he can't quite remember after you crawl off to die. That sit well with you?"

43

"No," Gibson admitted.

"Then make him remember you."

When Duke had gone, Gibson lay on the floor beside the bed. It felt more comfortable to him than a mattress. Bear came and flopped down on the bed. She peered over the side at him.

"Ellie needs you."

"You don't know that," Gibson said.

"I do. She does. You can't let anything stop you. You have to find her. You found me. Remember?"

"Bear, I found you too late."

Bear smiled down at him. "Then hurry."

CHAPTER SEVEN

Gibson woke to an empty house. Not even seven a.m., but Toby and Sana had long since left for the diner. Gibson had once asked Sana how she could work those hours. She told him it wasn't work if you loved it. He'd known exactly what she'd meant.

His body made a tired plea for more sleep, but Gibson ignored it and popped right up from the floor. He could rest after he found Ellie.

He took another shower for the simple pleasure of hot water. He dressed in the same clothes as the night before. Laundry wasn't at the top of his list this morning. Clean clothes right out of the dryer would be luxurious, but he needed to earn it.

He felt surprisingly normal; maybe a shower and a good meal with a friend had been all it took to reset. He hadn't seen Duke or Bear yet this morning, and he took that as an encouraging sign that he was putting his ordeal behind him. Full of optimism, he went downstairs, where he found Duke reading the newspaper. So maybe he wasn't ready for a clean bill of health quite yet. Over the newspaper, his father watched Gibson plug in his laptop.

"I'm not going after Washburn," Gibson said.

"So I've heard."

"Do you understand why?"

"Hey, it's your life, kid."

Gibson hadn't expected his father to give up so easily.

"It's a little humbling actually," Duke said.

Here it came. "What is?"

"I was chief of staff for a US senator. I could talk a socialist into lowering taxes on the wealthy and an evangelical into voting against school prayer. Now I can't even out-argue a child. I must be slipping in my old age."

"You wouldn't do the same if it was me?" Gibson asked.

"Like I said, it's your life. I'm just a dead man who the world still thinks was a suicidal loser. What do I know?"

Gibson decided not to bite. He'd been subjected to this guilt trip for the last eighteen months. Instead, he pointed to the newspaper spread out on the table. "Mind if I . . ."

"Oh, by all means, don't let me get in your way." Duke took his newspaper into another room.

To Gibson's relief, his laptop booted right up despite eighteen months on a shelf. He hacked a neighbor's Wi-Fi and logged into his e-mail, looking for anything from Nicole. He found plenty, but it all predated the fire. Before the fire, a steady stream of correspondence flowed between them. Then nothing. Total radio silence. It was too depressing to contemplate, so out of morbid curiosity, he Googled himself.

In his absence, theories about Gibson's involvement with the death of Vice President Benjamin Lombard had proliferated. AmericanJudas. com—a popular conspiracy website that had been the first to post evidence placing Gibson in Atlanta—continued to lead the charge. It painted Gibson, a disaffected former Marine, as a high-tech Lee Harvey Oswald who'd had an irrational obsession with Benjamin Lombard for more than a decade. But to hear American Judas tell it, Gibson was only a hapless pawn—the triggerman—in a tangled conspiracy to alter a presidential election.

It was so wildly off the mark that Gibson could only shake his head. The truth was both much simpler and far worse. There was no mention of Niobe, West Virginia, or Charles Merrick, but the arson and subsequent disappearance of Nicole and Ellie Vaughn had been exhaustively detailed. Further proof that something nefarious had happened in Atlanta.

A raft of sightings in the last year placed Gibson everywhere from Las Vegas playing high-stakes Pai Gow to eating Oreos on a ferry from Victoria, British Columbia. Great, he thought, they'd turned him into Bigfoot. God, he hoped Ellie didn't see this garbage until she was old enough to understand it. Gibson closed the browser tab; it was time to get to work.

Computers had been a sanctuary for Gibson ever since he'd been a boy. They'd always made sense to him on an intuitive level, and hacking had originally been an abstract intellectual exercise—breaking into networks merely a puzzle to solve. Disappearing into work that he could control while his life descended into chaos had kept him sane. He imagined it was like that for anyone who was good at something.

It had a similar effect on him now, and, as he ran diagnostics and updated the machine's drivers and operating system, something of the old Gibson Vaughn returned. His vision began to clear around the edges, and the asbestos haze clouding his thoughts slowly dissipated. He drove himself faster and faster, enjoying feeling sharp and reveling in the simple pleasure of work. Duke and Bear must have also recognized it because they made themselves scarce.

Thirty years ago, people could disappear into America and reinvent themselves. Now it took meticulous planning and a commitment never to reach out to your old life. For most, the lure of the Internet proved too great to resist—the urge to Google yourself, or search Facebook for the people you'd left behind. The simple truth was there was no such thing as starting a new life. The best you could manage was a convincing rebranding. A fresh coat of paint, but that was all. You might change your name. You might even change your face. But you couldn't change the person underneath, and the person underneath would still have the same needs and wants, the same habits and tastes, the same strengths and weaknesses.

Once Gibson admitted that he could find no trace of Nicole or Ellie Vaughn, he fell back to what he knew about his ex-wife. Nicole Vaughn was an avid reader, and still would be no matter what name she had adopted. Over the past decade, Nicole had reviewed well over a thousand novels on Goodreads, a website for book lovers. She served as a reader for a host of novelists and received advance copies of new books. Her network of followers read her reviews and trusted her recommendations. Although he couldn't find her original Goodreads profile, Gibson would bet good money that she'd only changed her user information rather than delete it entirely. The Nicole he knew would have had a very hard time leaving that investment behind.

Playing a hunch, he searched prolific book reviewers on the site looking for anything that sounded familiar. A profile belonging to a "Gwen Hodges" stuck out to him—similar genres and now with nearly two thousand reviews. She had been productive in his absence. But the reviews themselves were the kicker. Nicole had a distinctive writing style, and when they were married, she would read her reviews aloud to him before publishing them. He could hear her voice in Gwen Hodges's writing now. He kept reading until he felt certain.

Next, Gibson searched the website of Manhattan public relations firms, which conveniently posted photographs of their agents. He settled on a young associate named Anne DeWitt. Anne had a kind, open face. His next step was to spoof an e-mail address that appeared to originate from her firm. Then "Anne" wrote an e-mail detailing her attempts to reach Nicole. Anne had a terrific thriller by a promising debut author and wanted to send Nicole an advance reader copy to review. Gibson wrote three drafts, tweaking the tone and wording, before e-mailing it to Nicole's mother.

Phishing a sixty-year-old made Gibson feel more than a little dirty. Nicole's parents were not very tech savvy and had joined the twenty-first century only under duress. He could think of dozens of ways to hack them, but a phishing attack felt the least invasive. He didn't want to intrude upon her mother's life more than necessary. They'd never warmed to Gibson, and somehow this tactic proved all the things that they'd always thought about him. Duke strolled past the kitchen and complimented his son for his chivalry.

"You're so noble. It's a goddamn inspiration in these dark times."

Gibson had nothing to say to that. He felt guilty hacking Nicole, and he struggled to differentiate himself from a stalker. From any of the estranged ex-husbands on the news who forced their way back into lives better off without them. Bear had argued that this was different. That Nicole had run because of a misunderstanding—she thought Gibson had burned down the house. Once she knew that it was all a mistake, things would go back to normal. Bear sounded so compelling, and God knew, Gibson wanted to be convinced. He missed Ellie terribly.

His laptop announced an incoming e-mail. Nicole's mother had taken the bait. To her credit, Elizabeth Anne didn't cough up her daughter's address to a stranger on the Internet. At least not without exchanging a few e-mails first.

They traded messages all afternoon. Nicole's mother peppered "Anne" with questions. Gibson kept it light and upbeat, stalling at least thirty minutes between messages. Couldn't come across as too eager, and when he felt it starting to drag out, he sent a brief reply and then ignored her next message entirely. Anne DeWitt was a busy woman and had better things to do than beg an amateur reviewer to read a book. Two hours passed. Gibson held his breath until an apologetic note arrived along with a PO box outside Seattle.

Bear did a happy dance around the kitchen.

The PO box was a smart move—one more firewall between Nicole and the outside world. But not from Gibson. A five-minute phone call to the store manager in Seattle netted the PO box owner's name—Gwen Hodges. Humans were always the weakest link in any security. He hung up the phone and got back to work. An hour later when Toby got home, Gibson was staring at Gwen Hodge's house on Google Street View, contemplating his next step.

Finding Nicole, he was beginning to realize, had been the easy part. Approaching her would be a whole other mess, and he didn't really know where to begin. He wouldn't be able to pretext his way past her as he had the store manager. It would require the truth, and the truth depended on how you arranged the facts.

"You're still here," Toby said, managing to sound both sardonic and delighted in the same breath.

"I'll leave in the morning."

"Enough with that. Please."

Toby chatted at Gibson for a few minutes, still doing an admirable job pretending that the long-haired ghoul in his kitchen was, in any way, normal. One of Toby's kitchen staff had a pregnant wife. A false alarm had forced Toby to sub for him midshift. It had not left him in the best mood. Toby excused himself to take care of his chores. He returned a few minutes later.

"I have laundry to do," Toby said and held up Gibson's duffel bag. "Mind if I disinfect whatever is in this?"

"Only if the incinerator is full."

"Agreed," Toby said and left him alone in the kitchen to contemplate Nicole.

This morning, Gibson had experienced a moment of self-righteous anger. He'd imagined meeting Nicole face-to-face. She'd stolen his daughter from him, and he hadn't done anything wrong. But a day of cyberstalking his ex-wife had cost him the high road, and now he wasn't sure what to do. Armed with her address, he could book a ticket to Seattle and confront her at home. But try as he might, he couldn't find a way to say it that didn't sound like an ambush. What was he hoping to achieve? Other than scare a woman afraid enough to take out a restraining order and confirm all her suspicions about him.

E-mail, he decided, was a safer option. He could take his time and formulate his thoughts. It gave him the best chance to convince her that he hadn't burned down her home. It was certainly better than showing up unannounced on her doorstep. The only problem was, he needed an e-mail address for her. Try as he might, he couldn't find one. She'd no doubt known that would be how he'd look for her.

That's when Gibson remembered the old emergency e-mail account that they'd set up when he'd been on active duty. An anonymous account that had no connection to either of them, and from which neither had ever sent an e-mail. In the event of an emergency, either one of them could send an e-mail back to the account itself, creating a closed-message loop. If she hadn't deactivated it as well, he could try reaching out to her that way. He logged into the account to begin drafting his message to her. In the inbox was a single, unread e-mail dated six weeks after the fire; the subject line read: "Gibson." He took his hands off the keyboard, as if afraid they'd accidentally open the Pandora's box. At the kitchen sink, he threw water on his face—it had worked the night before but now succeeded only in making him wet—then went back to the kitchen table and read Nicole's message:

Ellie is safe. I hope that you are too. Although the fact that you still haven't made contact makes me imagine the worst. I pray it's not true, but I can't imagine what could have kept you away.

The police have confirmed the fire was arson. I didn't want to believe it, but there's no question. They've labeled you a person of interest in the investigation. It's important to me that you know that I don't believe you had anything to do with it. I've told the police over and over that they have the wrong idea about you and that their portrait of you doesn't resemble the real you, but they won't listen to me.

I won't believe you started the fire, but I do think the fire is because of you. I think whatever you got yourself mixed up in the last two years tracked you back to your daughter and burned her home to the ground. So while I don't blame you for what happened, I'll never forgive you either. No one put a gun to your head. You chose this path for your own selfish reasons, and you're too smart a man not to have known there would be repercussions.

Gibson, I don't think you're a bad man, but you're bad for your daughter. I don't know if you're alive or dead, but I am taking her where the people who want to hurt you can't hurt her. If anything of the man I married remains intact, you'll understand that and help me protect her by staying away. I imagine you'll find us if you try; I'm begging you not to try.

For Ellie's sake, you have to let her go. Give Ellie
a chance at a safe, normal childhood. Trust me to
take care of her, and stay away. Please.

Gibson stood up and backed away from the computer. Unable to be still, he paced through the house, desperate for a counterargument that would neutralize hers. At a loss for what to feel, think, or do. Afraid, on a bedrock level, that Nicole's e-mail was the most honest and true thing he'd ever read. He could find no fault in Nicole's belief that the fire connected back to him.

Bear looked up mournfully at him. "You have to respond."

"And say what? She's right."

"She can't do this," she said. "Ellie needs you."

Gibson wasn't so sure Bear didn't have it backward. His reasons for going to Seattle were all selfish ones. Ellie would make him feel sane again. Ellie would love him. Ellie would save him. It wasn't the responsibility of a nine-year-old to take care of her father. And what did he really offer his daughter in return?

He stopped at a framed photograph of Toby and Sana with their daughter. Gibson took it off the wall, either for a closer look or to smash it to pieces. If he had matches, he would burn their picture-perfect home to the ground. Then he heard Toby moving around upstairs, and his breath hitched. With both hands, he rehung the photo, chastened for even thinking that about his friend.

But an old, familiar anger had flared back to life. A coal cradled in the ash of a dead fire. The same anger that he'd turned on Senator Benjamin Lombard after his father's death and that had fueled his pursuit of Charles Merrick's stolen fortune. The anger that had sustained him during his eighteen months in solitary confinement. Toby and Sana didn't deserve to be on the receiving end, but Gibson knew who did. The CIA agent who had ordered him taken into custody at Dule Tree Airfield.

Damon Washburn.

In his heart, Gibson knew that if the CIA agent hadn't imprisoned him, without due process, he would have been here to stop the arsonist, or at least to draw the threat toward himself instead of Nicole and Ellie.

Damon Washburn would answer for that.

Somewhere, Damon Washburn was living his life, having scraped Gibson off the heel of his shoe. That would change now. Gibson wanted Damon Washburn to think about him as much as he thought about Damon Washburn.

Toby appeared in the kitchen. He held a watch. It looked expensive. Toby looked at Gibson quizzically and held it out to him.

"It was among your dirty clothes. Does it belong to you?"

Gibson took the watch and looked at it. He'd found it in the hallway of the fifth floor of the Wolstenholme Hotel in Niobe. It had been a chaotic, bloody scene, and he'd put it in his pocket without much thought. It must still have been there when Damon Washburn seized him at the airfield. Gibson looked at it now. It looked expensive, but Gibson was no judge of such things. He remembered there'd been an engraved inscription on the back. Turning it over in his hand, he read, "Merrick Capital 1996–2006." Duke's revenge on Damon Washburn came with a price tag, and the watch would fetch good money from a collector. Problem solved. Gibson smiled to himself. There was a perverse symmetry to Charles Merrick bankrolling his plans for Damon Washburn.

"Can I borrow a car tomorrow?" Gibson asked Toby.

"Going somewhere?"

"I think I need a trim," he said.

"Well, maybe just a little off the top anyway," Toby deadpanned. "I think that can be arranged."

Gibson thanked him, and Toby went back to his housework.

Duke stepped into view. "Are you finally ready to do what needs doing?"

Gibson said, "Why didn't you warn me about Nicole?"

"Kid, all I've done is warn you. You had to see for yourself."

"You're a son of a bitch."

"One of us has to be," Duke said.

"You really think it will change things?"

"You'll be a whole new man."

"All right," Gibson said, capitulating.

"Say his name."

"Damon Washburn."

"That's right," said Duke. "Now make him remember you."

CHAPTER EIGHT

Gibson passed another night on the floor, lights on. In the morning, he found a laundry basket of clean clothes outside his bedroom door. An old winter coat and sweater hung from the doorknob. Toby had left him a note along with car keys and a hundred dollars. The note advised him to bundle up and listed the address of a barbershop. At the bottom, the note read, "Come and give Sana a hug when you look presentable. She sends her love."

As he weighed his options for the future, Toby and Sana made a compelling argument for rejoining the human race. Just as Damon Washburn made the case for scrubbing his hands of the whole miserable experiment. Unfortunately, as much as he admired the Kalpars, he wasn't like them. And of the two paths, only Damon Washburn gave Gibson a sense of purpose.

Gibson would thank Washburn for that when he saw him.

He turned over Toby's note and wrote a list of errands. Everything he'd need to begin his hunt. Step one: even if he no longer felt at home in the world, he would need to pass for someone who did. He wouldn't get very far looking like he'd escaped from an asylum.

The sleeves of Toby's sweater and coat were too long, but Gibson wore them gratefully. He scooped up the money and car keys and packed his duffel bag. He wouldn't spend another night under their roof. Toby and Sana saw him as a reclamation project, but he had no intention of being reclaimed. Damon Washburn would pay, and Gibson, in turn, would pay the price to see that he did.

Bear cleared her throat. "What about Ellie? You promised to take care of her."

"I am."

"You're giving up. Coward! What kind of father does this?"

"A bad one."

"You promised. How can you do this?" Arms crossed, Bear waited for an answer and stomped her foot when he started getting ready to leave instead. "I hate you."

"Yeah," Gibson said. "I hate me too."

Gibson had been driving since he was thirteen, and sitting behind the wheel of Toby's car, he felt thirteen again. He circled the block a couple of times until he started to get the hang of it.

The Arlington barbershop was both resiliently old-school and multicultural. Three of the six chairs were staffed by Greek men in their sixties, the fourth by a Filipina woman, the fifth by a young African man with an indomitable smile, and the last by a stout Brazilian woman who sang as she worked. Five of the six chairs were occupied, and several customers waited for their regular barber. Customers and barbers alike paused at the sight of Gibson, who stood awkwardly in the doorway, fighting his urge to flee.

One of the Greek barbers, lounging in his chair reading the *Post's* sports section, whistled appreciatively at the apparition in the shop's doorway.

"God has sent us a wise man," the barber said. "What tidings do you bring us from the east?"

The shop roared with laughter.

"And what has he done with his two friends?" another asked, picking up the joke.

"Where's the frankincense?" bantered a third.

When the barber saw Gibson hadn't joined in, he hopped up and beckoned to his chair. "Come in out of the cold, my friend. Come. Sit."

The shop sprang back to life after Gibson took a seat. The barber swept the cape around Gibson and studied him in the mirror. He tried and failed to run a comb through the rat's nest of Gibson's hair.

"You offer a unique challenge, my friend. What are your intentions?"

"High and tight," Gibson replied.

The barber didn't understand, so Gibson held up his thumb and forefinger, half an inch apart. "That long." He narrowed his fingers until they almost touched. "The sides."

"And the beard?"

"Gone."

The barber nodded his head in agreement. "A fresh start. You are a wise man after all."

The barber went to work with electric clippers, hair falling away in long sheaves like winter wheat to the scythe as a face that Gibson recognized slowly reemerged. When the beard was no more than stubble, the barber reclined the chair and lathered his face with warm foam and shaved him with a straight razor. The barber held up a mirror so Gibson could judge his handiwork.

"An improvement," said the barber. "Very handsome."

Gibson studied his gaunt features in the mirror. He'd lost a lot of weight but looked almost civilized. Almost. The running scar that laced his neck from ear to ear lent him a frightening aspect. It would make him too memorable, and he would need to let his beard grow back. But it was nice to be clean-shaven for a moment. He traced the old wound with his fingers—a permanent reminder of how close he'd come to dying in the basement of his childhood home, and of the man who'd tried to hang him there. The man had told him that it would take a long time to die when hanged from that height. The short drop, he'd called it. Perhaps, Gibson thought, he was still dying in that basement and everything since had just been a fantasy.

He couldn't be that lucky.

"Stop thinking like that," Duke said.

"Get out of my head."

"You're not the only one he hung in that basement, you know. But I don't have a scar. No one came to save me."

"I was only a kid."

"Always an excuse."

"That's not fair," Gibson said.

He realized that the barbershop had fallen silent and that all eyes were on him. Watching the crazy man talking to thin air. He apologized meekly and tried to pay for his haircut.

"Keep it," the barber said. "Merry Christmas."

Bear was waiting in the car—a little dark cloud of judgment. She and his father were taking turns beating up on him today.

"Bear. Not now. Please."

She didn't move or blink.

"What?" Gibson asked. "What do you want from me?"

"You're going to regret this."

"I'm not safe to be around Ellie."

"And you think getting even with Damon Washburn will help that?"

Gibson tried to convince her, but it came out all wrong. Bear continued to press her case all the way over to the bank, even after he had parked. His head ached, and he needed to go in and see if he had any money left in his account, but he didn't trust himself around people with Bear hectoring him this way. Gibson was sick of listening to her. His mind was made up. It might not be a perfect plan, but it was the plan he needed. He snapped at Bear to give it a rest, and when he glanced over again, she was gone.

In the bank, Gibson left fifty dollars in his account and withdrew the balance: $810. His credit cards had both been frozen due to non-payment; he couldn't afford to pay them off and wouldn't be able to sign up for new ones without a job and a home address. The bank would have issued him a new debit card, but given his shopping list, it would be better not to leave an electronic footprint. So, all of his worldly possessions came down to these: $860, the contents of his duffel bag, and Charles Merrick's gold watch. His old landlord would have long since evicted him from his apartment and sent his things to the dump. Financially, no great loss; the apartment had been only the approximation of a home, and he hadn't owned anything of monetary value. But he was sorry to lose his personal effects, especially the photographs of Ellie.

Gibson made a series of stops after the bank. A navy surplus store for a winter-clothes starter kit and boots. A computer-repair shop for a used laptop. A house with a room for rent on Craigslist that would have been perfect except it had no separate entrance. Gibson couldn't have anyone keeping tabs on his comings and goings. So until he found something that fit his needs, he took a room at a rundown motel. At a convenience store, he bought two flip phones to replace his smart-phone, which couldn't be reactivated without a credit card. While the manager rang up his purchase, Gibson stared at the tired rotisserie hot dogs making their lazy circuit. It was time, he realized, to give Sana that hug.

The holidays were in full swing at the Nighthawk. Toby took his festivity very seriously. Every square inch of the diner had been deco-rated. The Vince Guaraldi Trio played over the stereo, and Gibson felt the warm crush of voices as he pushed through the door. He grinned despite himself. Sana came out from behind the counter and wrapped her arms around him. When they broke away, Sana cupped a hand to his cheek and frowned at him.

"I will not forgive you for shaving before I saw you."

"Your husband thought it best."

Sana harrumphed. "He is so delicate, I swear."

She thrust a menu in his hand and promised to visit when things quieted down. Gibson took his favored booth in the back and ran his hands over the familiar table. The very spot where George Abe had once recruited him to join Jenn Charles and Dan Hendricks in the search for Bear. In a way, it had all started right here. As much as anything can ever be the start of anything. Gibson recognized in himself the basic human need to arrange the events of his life into digestible stories. Stories needed beginnings; this was his. One of them anyway.

Accepting George Abe's offer had been the first in a series of choices that had led him to his present circumstances. The strange part was that, despite all that he had endured, he was hard-pressed to say which decision he would undo, given the chance. Individually, each had seemed necessary and right. It was only when he took a step back and looked at the big picture of his life that he saw where they had led him. Led them all.

George Abe had been missing since Atlanta.

Jenn had gone after him. Alone. No one had heard from her since.

Of the original team, only Dan Hendricks had so far eluded the curse. He lived an isolated existence in California, keeping a low and extremely paranoid profile. He'd skirmished with the same contract killer who had tried to hang Gibson. It had rattled Hendricks, who believed with fatalistic certainty that eventually the killer would return to finish what he'd started. Maybe he hadn't eluded the curse after all.

Before his disappearance, Gibson had talked to Hendricks every couple of weeks. Checked in to trade notes and see if he had heard from Jenn. Gibson remembered clearly the morning that he had said good-bye to her at the motel outside Atlanta. They'd been through one hell of an ordeal to solve Suzanne Lombard's disappearance, and it had frayed their uneasy alliance. By the end, they had all needed to go their separate ways, but that was one decision that he would have made differently if he'd known it was the last time he'd see Jenn.

When the waiter came, Gibson asked for a black-and-white milkshake and ordered his father's favorite breakfast. Milkshakes and eggs—picturing Jenn's horrified reaction to the combination made him smile. Maybe he should reach out to Hendricks. It had been eighteen months. There had to be news, one way or the other. But if it were bad news, Gibson didn't know if he could hear it. He'd already heard all that he could stand. Instead, he stared out the window until Toby put his food on the table.

"It's not such a bad face," Toby said with a smile. "But on second thought, I prefer the beard."

"Thank you." Gibson held up the car keys and the hundred dollars.

"Why do you have your bag with you?" Toby wanted to know.

"I still had a little money in my checking account, so I rented a room," Gibson lied.

"Good. That's a good step. I'm impressed. What will you do next?"

"Well, I thought I'd eat and do a little job hunting." It was the truth. If he wanted any chance of getting away with what he had in store for Damon Washburn, he would need to construct a convincing narrative of a man attempting to rebuild his life. A permanent address was his first priority, but a job would be an important next step.

"Then I will leave you to it," Toby said.

"What?" Gibson asked. Toby had a funny look on his face.

"It's hard to believe you are the same man I collected from the police two days ago. It shows character, my friend. You are going to be all right."

Toby squeezed his shoulder and left the table before Gibson could reply. He ate slowly while the diner filled with the evening rush. Once, a bustling diner had provided comforting, peaceful background noise, but now all the sound and movement felt oppressive. He couldn't keep up with all the stimuli, and his vision distorted at the edges like a television channel with bad reception. Something out of another era, which is how he felt. He mopped up the eggs with his toast and looked around, hoping to catch sight of Bear or Duke.

He hadn't seen either one since the bank. All afternoon, he'd counted that as a sign that maybe he could function without them. But he'd depended on them to survive that cell, and he missed them now. It also worried him that knowing Bear and Duke weren't real did nothing to diminish his affection for them. Then again, no one understood what he'd been through the way they did.

He looked around for them again.

This was not healthy. He knew that rationally. They were a crutch of his mind. Missing figments of your imagination was insane. They weren't his friends because they weren't real. He repeated it over and over to himself without conviction. Something inside him felt irreparably broken, and he didn't see how to do what needed doing while entertaining the ghosts of his past.

"Don't be so melodramatic, son," Duke admonished him. "Glad to see you still clean your plate."

Right on cue.

Gibson pushed his plate away and ignored his father.

"Very mature," Duke said.

"I'm not talking to you in here. People will think I'm crazy."

"You *are* crazy," Duke pointed out.

"Am I?"

"You are now. In there, you were sane. Out here . . . not so much."

"So stop talking to me."

Duke shrugged and winked at the elderly couple staring in their direction. "Thing is, sport, I'm not talking to you. Reflect upon that."

Gibson took out the refurbished laptop that he'd paid cash for at a storefront repair shop in Arlington; the machine didn't have a lot of pop under the hood, but it would get him where he needed to go. The purchase had put a serious dent in his bankroll, especially given that he already owned a laptop. But Gibson didn't see any other way. It had occurred to him that his original laptop had also been in the custody of the CIA for the last eighteen months. God only knew what kind of malware had been installed. He could tear it apart like Gene Hackman and still never trust it again. There could be malware embedded all the way down in the motherboard and chipset. He'd drive himself crazy—crazier—looking. He'd wipe it and sell it as soon as possible.

"Easy there, cowboy," Duke said. "That old computer could still come in handy."

Gibson looked at his dad questioningly.

"If they're watching," said Duke, "then why don't you show 'em what they want to see?"

Why hadn't he thought of that?

"You did," Duke said with a wink.

Assuming the Agency was keeping tabs on him, he could use the old laptop on free Wi-Fi at coffee shops and public libraries to establish a pattern of behavior for his watchers to take in: job and apartment hunting, shopping for a used car, contacting his credit-card companies to set up a payment plan. Anyone watching would see a reformed, upstanding citizen trying to rebuild his life. Then he would switch to his burner laptop and hunt Damon Washburn.

"Now you're thinking," Duke said.

Toby reappeared to clear the table and ask a favor. The wife of his dishwasher had finally gone into labor for real, leaving Toby short-handed. Gibson packed up and followed Toby into the back, where he was put to work. He washed dishes for four hours, and when Toby pulled him off the line, Gibson had himself a part-time job.

All in all, not bad for his first full day back in the real world.

CHAPTER NINE

On New Year's Eve, Gibson worked the morning rush at the diner before taking the metro into DC. He changed trains at Gallery Place and rode the Red Line uptown. At Van Ness–UDC, he exited and climbed the long, broken escalator up to Connecticut Avenue. A wave of vertigo hit him as he emerged into the open air. He put his hands on his knees and squeezed his eyes closed to keep from panicking. Bear counted slowly backward from twenty, which helped settle him down. He stood upright and took a deep breath. She smiled at him, and, when he felt steady, they walked up the hill to the Chinese embassy to see the Fisherman.

Finding Damon Washburn had proven complex.

An intensive two-day search had confirmed what Gibson had suspected eighteen months ago—Damon Washburn didn't exist. Whomever Gibson had rescued on the fifth floor of the Wolstenholme Hotel in Niobe, West Virginia, his name wasn't Damon Washburn. Gibson wished he'd stopped to get some answers from Charles Merrick in the snow. He'd briefly considered tracking Merrick down again, but he didn't relish the thought of their meeting again. Nor did he care to imagine what it would take to compel Merrick's cooperation or how much he would enjoy compelling it. Still, it was a better option than launching a penetration attack on the CIA's employment records. He might be crazy, but not even he thought that a good idea.

"There might be another option," Duke had pointed out.

Hence today's trip to the Chinese embassy.

Damon Washburn hadn't been the only spook in Niobe. Gibson had also crossed paths with a Chinese operative who'd wanted Charles Merrick for his own reasons. In retrospect, perhaps Gibson should have suspected that he was with the Ministry of State Security. But the man in the fisherman's vest had offered information that Gibson had badly needed, and Gibson hadn't asked why. He still didn't know the Fisherman's name but bet that if the Fisherman knew Charles Merrick, then he also knew Damon Washburn.

"Why are you here?" Gibson asked Bear.

He knew she didn't think much of Duke's plan. She thought he should devote himself to finding a way back to Ellie. In her opinion, his vendetta against the man calling himself Damon Washburn would only make things worse. But when Gibson had challenged her to describe what worse might look like, she couldn't come up with an answer. Since then, she'd held her peace on the subject, still clearly disapproving but not abandoning him. Gibson didn't understand why.

"Because you're going to need me," she said.

"I can do this without you."

"I know," Bear agreed sadly. "That's when you'll need me."

The limestone walls of the Chinese embassy rose into sight. The old embassy had been located in a pair of dilapidated apartment buildings at the top of Kalorama near the Taft Bridge. A look unbefitting of the new China. In 2006, a new embassy had been commissioned, modern and sleek. Designed by renowned architect I. M. Pei, it reflected China's twenty-first-century ambitions. Bear refused to go inside but said she would wait for him by the curb.

The front doors opened into a grand entrance hall large enough to feel deserted despite the heavy traffic. Security was intense, but a scrupulous job had been done concealing the dozens of cameras blanketing the entrance. Gibson walked to the center of the hall and stood there. He waited patiently, chin up so that the cameras could get a good, clean look. He made no hostile moves, knowing that simply standing in an embassy with no apparent business would draw attention. It took security only a minute or so to approach him.

"Do you have business at the embassy?" a guard asked.

"No," Gibson replied, keeping his eyes up toward the cameras.

"Then I must ask you to leave."

"Poisonfeather."

The guard looked at him blankly. The man had no idea what that meant, but it wasn't intended for him anyway. Gibson said it again to make sure he heard.

"Tell him I want to make a deal."

"Please leave, sir, or we will call the authorities."

"Tell him I will be back tomorrow. And the day after that. And the day after that."

To the guards' credit, they didn't lay a hand on Gibson and ushered him courteously off embassy grounds. Bear stood across the street, waiting for him. She still wasn't dressed for the weather but didn't look bothered by the cold wind that whipped her dress around her knees.

"How did that go?" she asked.

"I guess we'll see."

They walked back down the hill and turned south on Connecticut Avenue past a series of stately apartment buildings. They entered a small commercial district. On the left, he saw a service station and a small strip mall that seem out of place in such tony surroundings. To his right, Gibson looked up at the marquee to see what was playing at the grand

Uptown Theater—the last of the old DC movie houses. His father had taken him there to see the twentieth-anniversary rerelease of *Star Wars*. They'd sat in the first row of the balcony with their feet up. It had been awesome.

Across the street were restaurants, bars, and a few stray shops. Gibson went down the stairs into a cramped basement pool hall with a retro fifties vibe. The Christmas decorations were still up, and the bartenders hurried around setting up for an influx of New Year's revelers. Gibson found a seat at the bar, ordered a beer, and waited.

After a few hours, the bar began to fill up, and a waiting list grew for one of the six pool tables. The bar stocked board games, and Bear pestered him to play Settlers of Catan, but Gibson knew he'd get himself thrown out playing games by himself. She groaned and spun on her stool, kicking her legs aimlessly until someone took her seat. After that, Gibson kept himself company. An hour before midnight, he paid his tab and made the long train ride back to Virginia. He rang in the New Year on an empty platform at Metro Center.

"Happy New Year, son."

"You too, Dad."

"Ought to be a better one."

"That's a pretty low bar," Gibson said, trying to make himself comfortable on one of the concrete benches.

"Exactly," Duke said, once again immune to sarcasm. He walked to the edge of the platform and sang an old Pogues song in a clear, rising voice.

Gibson pulled his coat tight around him, rested his chin on his chest, and listened to the ghost sing.

It was only nine p.m. on the West Coast. Maybe Nicole was getting ready to go out for the evening. Ellie might still be awake, sitting on the edge of the bed, helping her mother pick an outfit. Maybe Nicole had a date. He hoped she did, even as the thought made his heart ache.

He still hadn't replied to her e-mail and was no closer to knowing what to say.

"Happy new year, Nicole," he said to himself.

Good to his word, Gibson returned to the embassy each day to stand in the lobby until escorted outside. Then he retreated to the pool hall to nurse his beers. On the fourth day, embassy security met Gibson at the door and barred his entrance. He repeated his message to them and then stood on the sidewalk outside the embassy under their watchful gaze. The temperature had dropped all week, dipping into the twenties at night, and by the time Gibson sat down at the bar, he was cold straight down to the bone. He ordered an Irish coffee and it tasted so good that he ordered a second. Then he settled in to wait, passing the time trying to come up with a plan B.

A little after nine o'clock, a group of Chinese came down the steps—three men and two women, all in their twenties. The men wore suits and the women, dresses: one red and one green. Overdressed amid the T-shirts and jeans of the regular clientele. They took a tray of balls from the bartender and racked them on a table in the back corner. Two of the men began rolling cues back and forth across the table, looking for the least warped one. The third man and the two women returned to the bar and ordered a round of drinks. They leaned against the bar beside Gibson and talked animatedly in Mandarin while the bartender made their drinks. The man told the women a joke, or what Gibson assumed to be a joke based on their laughter. Gibson glanced at the group, hoping to make eye contact, to see some spark of recognition, but they took their drinks back to their pool table, paying him no mind.

Gibson exhaled in disappointment, asked for his tab, and went to use the restroom. When he returned, one of the Chinese women was sitting in his seat and, in an embarrassed, almost childlike voice, was asking the bartender for a new drink. She crinkled her nose to convey that it was too strong. While the bartender remade her drink, Gibson stood to the side and counted out bills to pay his tab, then lifted his glass to finish the dregs of his beer. He waited until she stood to reclaim his coat from the back of the stool. He zipped it up and went up the stairs and into the night.

He rode the long escalator to the bottom of the Cleveland Park metro. Down on the platform, he walked away from the few passengers waiting on a northbound train to Shady Grove and sat on one of the concrete benches. The digital sign said the next train was twenty minutes away. Gibson crossed his legs at the ankles and thrust his hand into his jacket pockets, trying to get comfortable. His fingers closed around a scrap of paper that hadn't been there before. He glanced up and down the platform before unfolding it. In small type, it listed an address in Columbia Heights. Beneath that, it instructed him to take the metro to Woodley Park and walk from there. Gibson grinned to himself as he tore the paper into shreds; he'd gotten someone's attention after all.

"I can't believe that worked," Duke said. "We're on a roll now."

Gibson rode the metro one stop, disembarked, and walked east along Calvert Street toward Adams Morgan. No doubt he was being followed, but he didn't have much skill at spotting tails. Gavin Swonger had proved that on more than one occasion, and if that dopey hillbilly could follow him undetected, Gibson didn't like his chances of spotting trained agents of the Ministry of State Security. Anyway, what did it matter? If they wanted to confirm that he was alone, then he was fine with that.

On Columbia Road, two Chinese men came out of nowhere and muscled him into an alley. One of them pinned him against a wall while the second patted him down. They took his phone and wallet and swept an electronic baton over him, looking for a wire. They discussed him in Mandarin and, satisfied, shoved him back out onto the street before disappearing up the alley.

"Not even waiting for you to get to the meet," Duke said. "It's a good sign."

"How is it a good sign? I just got mugged."

"Well, it wasn't one of those muggings where they shoot you."

Gibson shook his head at his father. "One time, I'd like the good news to be better than I didn't get shot."

Duke shrugged. "Maybe start small and work up to it."

The address led Gibson to a row house on Thirteenth Street. A real estate agent's "For Sale" sign stuck out of the small dirt patch that qualified as a front yard in this neighborhood. The house was pitch-black, but Gibson went up the stairs and tried the front door. Unlocked. He went into the foyer. The old hardwood floors creaked under his feet. He wasn't sneaking up on anyone, so he called out a greeting. No response. He walked through the unfurnished house.

He found the Fisherman sitting patiently at a folding card table in the kitchen. Gibson's phone and wallet were on the table. At the back door, a bodyguard trained his gun on Gibson. Another bodyguard materialized behind Gibson and searched him a second time. When he finished, the bodyguard spoke in Mandarin to the Fisherman.

The Fisherman gave his men curt instructions and offered Gibson a seat at the card table. Gibson sat. The two men regarded each other, not long-lost friends by any stretch but each curious about the other. The fisherman looked fitter, jawline sharper. His fishing vest had given way to a tailored suit.

"My men do not speak English," the Fisherman said to Gibson. "Do not worry about them."

Thoughtful, but Gibson didn't worry about them for their English fluency, rather the guns in their hands and the cold, expectant way they watched him—like a pair of herons watching a meal swim around their feet.

"Is that a new scar?" the fisherman asked, gesturing to his throat. "You had a beard last I saw you."

"There's no such thing as a new scar."

"Profound. Fresh wounds, old scars . . . is that the idea?"

"Something like that."

"It was foolish. Coming to the embassy."

"Sorry to inconvenience you," Gibson said.

"Not for me. For you. Did you not consider that my embassy is under constant surveillance by your government?"

Gibson hadn't and knew that he should have. It underlined how occluded and sloppy his thinking had become. Not that he would have acted differently, but it worried him that it hadn't even crossed his mind. He would need to be more careful.

"Are you so anxious to be sent back?" the Fisherman asked. "Do you miss it?"

"Sometimes." It slipped out, his honesty surprising them both. "Do you know where I was?"

The Fisherman shook his head. "Not specifically, no."

"I never told you how good your English was."

"Or I yours," the Fisherman said. "What is it you want?"

"I want the man who sent me to that hellhole. I want his name, where he lives. I want him."

"Well, after your performance this week, he may want you too."

"I don't want to wait that long," Gibson said.

"Describe him to me."

"Tall. Thin but muscular. African American. He'd taken a hell of a beating so I can't really say much about his face. He called himself Damon Washburn, but that's not his real name."

"No, it is not."

"So you know who he is?"

"I do. What do you intend to do when you have him?"

"Help him understand what he did to me."

"And so what . . . ?" The Fisherman sat back and crossed his arms. "What makes you think I will furnish you with that information?"

Gibson took a breath, keenly aware of the line he was preparing to cross but even more aware that he no longer cared. "Because I know the identity of Poisonfeather."

The Fisherman's eyes narrowed, but Gibson couldn't tell why. One more example of his diluted instincts. Poisonfeather was a prized American intelligence asset inside the Chinese politburo. The Fisherman had risked everything to pry the name of the mole from Charles Merrick in Niobe. Gibson had stopped him then. He figured it ought to be worth Damon Washburn's real name to the Fisherman now.

"Merrick told you?" the Fisherman asked.

Yelled it at him was closer to the truth. Gibson had spent eighteen months in a cell for hearing it.

"That's right," Gibson said.

"You want this man so badly that you are ready to betray your country?"

"Just returning the favor."

The Fisherman ran a thumbnail back and forth beneath his bottom lip. "And all you want in exchange is the real name of this 'Damon Washburn'?"

"So we have a deal?" Gibson asked.

"I'm afraid that we do not."

"Why? You were willing to kill for it back in Niobe."

"I was, yes. Circumstances, however, have changed."

"How have they changed?" Gibson heard his voice rising but couldn't control it.

"Poisonfeather is dead. He was executed for crimes against the People. Why do you think you were released?"

Gibson slumped back in his chair. He'd been so overwhelmed since his release that he'd never stopped to ask to stop the most basic of questions: Why had he and Merrick been freed in the first place? The answer was obvious. Because they no longer represented a threat to the United States. The Fisherman had neutralized Poisonfeather.

"How?" Gibson asked. "Merrick didn't get a chance to tell you."

"True. It would have been simpler had Merrick told me, but with the data points I acquired in Niobe, I was able to reconstruct and track the traitor through Merrick's financial dealings. It simply took more time."

"That must have been quite a feather in your cap."

"Clever," the Fisherman said.

Gibson hadn't intended to be clever, and it took him a moment to discover his unintended pun. He played it off with a tight smile.

The Fisherman said, "In actuality, it was a feather in my superior's cap."

"You gave him the credit?" Gibson asked.

"That is how it works in my country. But when he was elevated, I was elevated along with him. Had I hoarded the credit, then I would have made an enemy instead of an ally."

"Congratulations."

"You know, in a way, you owe me your freedom."

"Well, thank you for that," Gibson said. "So if you already have Poisonfeather, why are you here?"

"Because as much as we enjoy your charming visits to the embassy, I need them to stop."

The Fisherman shifted to Mandarin and spoke to his men, who listened attentively. One bowed his head sharply and went out the back door. After a moment, Gibson heard a car start. The second bodyguard raised his gun. Gibson tensed, imagining the real estate agent's reaction to discovering his body in the morning. The Fisherman stood and gave Gibson a hard look.

"So, our business concluded, I will not be seeing you at the embassy again."

"No, you won't."

"Good. I'm glad we understand each other."

The Fisherman shifted to Mandarin, and the bodyguard holstered his gun. The bodyguard helped the Fisherman on with his coat and held the back door open for him. The Fisherman paused, half in, half out of the door, and looked back at Gibson. "Damon Ogden," he said, pronouncing the name carefully. "You had it half right. The man you want is named Damon Ogden."

Gibson looked at him, dumbfounded. "Why?"

"I'm curious to see what happens."

"Thank you."

"I hope you find what you need." The Fisherman pulled the collar of his coat tight. "Because they will bury you for this."

CHAPTER TEN

Gibson liked working the industrial dishwasher. Over its roar, he couldn't hear anyone and was grateful for the peace it granted him. Anyone but Duke Vaughn, whose voice he heard perfectly. They had paid their first visit to Damon Ogden's neighborhood that morning, and Duke hadn't stopped scheming since.

When Sana put a hand on his shoulder, Gibson jumped a mile. Sana apologized profusely. Gibson apologized profusely. They both apologized once more for good measure, and then Sana pointed to the front of the restaurant: a police officer was here to see him. Gibson stifled his first instinct, which was to flee out the back. He didn't like the visit coming so soon on the heels of his reconnaissance of Ogden's neighborhood.

"Be cool," Duke said. "You haven't done anything illegal yet."

"Besides meeting with the Chinese? Maybe they know what we've planned."

"Boy, you really think they'd send one measly Virginia cop if they knew that? SWAT would be dancing on your back."

His father had a point. This was something else. Gibson peeled off his heavy rubber gloves, dried his face on his apron, and went out front.

Detective Bachmann, perched on one of the counter stools, pointed to the stool beside him. Gibson sat and studied his hands.

"Nice haircut," Bachmann said. "Like a whole new man."

"Thanks."

"Are you?"

"What do you want?" Gibson was in no mood to banter. Duke stood off to the side and tried to get his attention. Gibson ignored him as best he could; he was getting better at blocking out Duke and Bear when he was around people.

"Just checking up on you. You seemed disoriented the last time we spoke. Wanted to see how you're settling in. You have a job. That's a good start."

"Living the dream."

That didn't satisfy Bachmann, so Gibson gave him a family-friendly version of his recent activities: the basement room he'd rented and his landlady, Gloria Nakamura, a widow and a curmudgeon with a dim view of the government, who was more than happy to take the rent in cash so long as Gibson paid in advance and didn't bring women home. Bachmann asked for Gibson's new address while somehow making it seem a friendly gesture. Gibson thought it a good trick and gave the address to the detective, who jotted it down in his notebook.

Gibson fed him a line of bullshit about updating his résumé and straightening out his finances. He left out the reconnaissance he'd been doing of the abandoned power plant that met his needs exactly. Instead, he told Bachmann about buying a 2002 Yukon on Craigslist. That he'd taken it for a test drive and that it ran well for a vehicle with 180,000 miles on the odometer. But he left out that he'd paid for it from money raised by the sale of Charles Merrick's watch to a collector. He left out all the other interesting items that the Charles Merrick Gold Watch Fund had bankrolled. And he definitely left out tomorrow's trip to

Longman Farm to buy the hard-to-acquire items on Duke Vaughn's shopping list.

He didn't tell the detective how badly he wanted a gun. How it had caught him by surprise because he intended to take Ogden alive, so why did he need a gun? He'd never felt any particular fondness for firearms. The Marines had taught him their care and use—five weeks of training before they'd entrusted him with live ammunition—which had instilled in him a healthy respect for their capabilities. But that was all. To him, firearms had always been tools and nothing more. He'd never felt an attachment to them before. Not the way he did now. This craving to feel the weight of a loaded gun in his hands.

Ordinarily, acquiring a gun couldn't have been easier. There were hundreds of ranges and gun shops in Virginia, but all would require a background check. If he were on a watch list, it would raise all kinds of red flags at Langley. Flags that he could ill afford, given his plans for Damon Ogden. His best bet was the secondary market: a gun show where sellers weren't required to conduct background checks so long as they had no reasonable expectation that the buyer intended to commit a crime. Unfortunately, the next regional gun show wasn't for another month, and Gibson had no intention of waiting that long. He asked himself who he knew who would have black-market contacts. One name leapt to mind. And that name owed him . . . At least that was how Gibson saw things.

"Have you looked for your ex-wife?" Bachmann asked.

"Found her." Gibson saw no reason to lie about that.

Bachmann looked disappointed. "You remember that restraining order?"

"Does this look like Seattle to you?" Gibson asked.

"Still, you think that's wise?"

"You know, I had a father, but I remember going to his funeral. So for the life of me, I can't figure out who the fuck you are."

"Good one," Duke said with a grin.

Bachmann shrugged. "You go anywhere near her, and you'll find out pretty fast who I am."

Gibson stood, his interest in this interview waning.

"Walk me out," Bachmann said, finishing the last of his coffee.

"Walk yourself out."

"Hey." Bachmann took hold of Gibson's arm. "That assaulting-an-officer charge can come back anytime. So be a good boy and walk me out."

Bachmann held his gaze until Gibson relented and followed the detective out into the cold. Bachmann unlocked his car and sat in the driver's seat to start the engine while Gibson stood and shivered.

"Given any more thought to your statement?"

"You mean, did I suddenly remember burning down my daughter's house?"

"Did you?"

"Nicole told you I didn't."

Bachmann shrugged in a familiar gesture of *seen this, done that.* "Yeah, a woman defending her loser ex-husband. A first in the annals of police work."

"I can't help you, detective."

Bachmann tried a different tactic. "Well, let's say for a second you didn't do it. Any ideas who would want to settle a score with you?"

"Me?"

"Don't even start with that. We both know your history, Vaughn. If it wasn't you, it was someone sending you a message. Your family was just the envelope."

Unfortunately, Gibson did have ideas. Too many. But he wasn't about to share his suspicions with a Virginia detective. That would only raise more questions that Gibson couldn't afford to answer. Besides, figuring out who'd burned down the house wasn't his priority. The fire was only a symptom. Ogden was the disease.

"You do, don't you?" Bachmann said.

"No, not off the top of my head. But I'll sleep on it."

"You do that," Bachmann said amicably, shutting his door. Through the glass, he winked at Gibson and mouthed the words "I'll be seeing you."

Gibson stood in the parking lot and watched until the car was out of sight. A red Acura pulled into the just-vacated spot. Two couples got out, men from the front, women from the back, even though one of the women was a good three inches taller than either of the men and could have used the legroom. The foursome laughed together about some joke from the car and gave him a wide berth as they bundled into the diner. Gibson felt a visceral, contact hate for them and stood in the cold, wondering why. They'd done nothing to warrant his rage. It wasn't until he passed them on the way back to the kitchen that he recognized it for what it was: jealousy. He resented their laughter, their happiness, their easy camaraderie. Gibson wished he shared such a bond with someone who was not a ghost.

His thoughts went to Jenn Charles. Missing for two years now. Neither he nor Dan Hendricks had seen or heard from Jenn since Atlanta. Before the eighteen months in a cell, Gibson had hunted for Jenn and George Abe but found not a trace of either. Now when he thought of them, it was in the past tense. He realized that while he'd been locked away he'd quietly declared them dead. He hoped he was wrong. He missed Jenn and on some level knew that she was one of the few people who could help him. Ironic, given that she didn't particularly like him. But she understood him. Toby liked him but didn't remotely understand him.

On impulse, he took out one of his new phones and dialed the last number he knew for Dan Hendricks.

Surprisingly, Hendricks picked up on the second ring. "Who's this?"

"It's Gibson."

There was a sizeable pause. "Is Tupac or Elvis with you?"

"Not recently."

"Damn. Looks like I lost the dead pool. Where've you been?"

"It's a long story. How are things? What have I missed?"

"The Cubs won the World Series," Hendricks said.

"You are kidding me." Gibson wasn't a Cubs fan, but he loved baseball, and it reminded him how out of touch he was with the world.

"You really didn't know that?"

"I didn't."

"Cubs took it in seven."

"Well, that's just fucking fantastic."

"Chicago seemed to think so."

"Have you heard from Jenn or George?" Gibson asked, working up the courage to raise the question that he'd called about.

Another pause. "No. Nothing."

Gibson felt himself sag, physically and emotionally. "What do you think that means?" He knew exactly what it meant but needed to hear it said in plain English. Hendricks had picked up one hell of a bedside manner during his twenty-year stint as a cop in Los Angeles. Gibson could count on him to pull no punches.

"It means it's been over two years. Either they're dead or they wish they were."

Gibson let that sink in. It was a harsh assessment, but he could find no fault in it. Two years was a long time. Too long. He could add another name to the list of people that he'd failed.

"You still there?" Hendricks asked.

Without Jenn to connect them, Hendricks and he didn't have much to say to each other. Gibson had never been Hendricks's favorite person.

"I gotta go," Gibson said.

That seemed to surprise Hendricks, who traditionally was the one in a hurry to get off the line. "You all right? This a good number for you?"

"Probably not for long," Gibson said. His plans for Damon Ogden would involve swapping cell phones regularly.

"Keep in touch. Maybe we'll get lucky."

"Well, it is a new year."

Hendricks chuckled at that. "Auld lang—"

Gibson hung up and went back inside. He had a lot of dirty dishes to clean.

CHAPTER ELEVEN

Gibson had been to Longman Farm once before.

Nineteen months ago. Starting him down a long path that had led to his detention by the CIA. It had been the height of spring. The countryside had sparkled with new life.

Not like today.

Today the barren trees reached up like dying nerves into the low-hanging sky. This was another beginning, and Gibson couldn't help but read stark metaphor into the landscape.

"Kid, you're starting to get on my nerves with all your moping around," Duke said.

"Mind your own business, then."

"Isn't there a ball game on?"

"It's January," Gibson said.

"That means pitchers and catchers report next month. Getting close."

Gibson flipped on the radio, looking for anything to distract his father. He found an oldies station with Jackson Browne singing about life on the road. Duke sang along, and for once, Gibson didn't mind so much.

Gibson didn't see the sign that marked the break in the trees that led back to Longman Farm. He realized his mistake a mile down the road and swung out onto the shoulder to turn around. He'd missed it the other time he'd been here, and a prickling déjà vu raised hairs on his neck. Another bad omen.

Duke snorted and shook his head.

Back at the turnoff, Gibson thought that the old sign might have seen a coat of yellow paint since he'd been here last. They bumped up the uneven gravel road to the gate that announced Longman Farm officially. The rusted gate had been fixed, and the long, curving drive up to the big house had been repaved. Everywhere he looked, Gibson saw mended fences and other indications of upkeep. Last time the farm had been practically falling down around itself, but no longer.

Gavin Swonger waited on the front porch like an upright nail. The last eighteen months might have been good to Longman Farm, but time hadn't worked any magic on Swonger's beard. It was the same mangy patchwork of scruff and acne. Still, there was something different about him that Gibson couldn't quite put his finger on. Something in Swonger's face had changed, his features heavier, eyes purposeful and silent. Or perhaps it was his heavy work pants, the boots, or the thick sleeveless fleece over a flannel shirt. All Swonger had ever wanted to be was a farmer. He looked the part now.

Apart from the black pistol in his hand.

Bachmann had asked if he had any idea who had burned down Nicole's house. Swonger hadn't been one of the names Gibson considered. They'd had their differences in West Virginia, but Gibson thought they'd parted on good terms. Almost friends. Then again, perhaps that had been the money talking.

Gibson stopped the Yukon but left it in gear. Just in case he'd been wrong about Swonger. But when Swonger ducked his head to see who was behind the wheel, Gibson realized that he hadn't carried the gun out onto the porch specifically for him. He'd simply seen an unfamiliar vehicle come up the drive and reached for a weapon. A strange way to greet company. Maybe life hadn't been so good at Longman Farm after all.

Gibson killed the engine and eased out of the driver's seat, hands in plain sight. He'd parked so he could keep the Yukon between himself and the porch.

"Hey, Swonger." Gibson pointed to the pistol. "That for me?"

"Gibson?" Swonger asked, half greeting, half disbelief.

"More or less."

Swonger nodded but didn't come rushing down from the porch to embrace him. Movement around the side of the house caught Gibson's eye. A man he didn't recognize had eased into a crouch and sighted a rifle on him. Not exactly a hero's welcome.

"Where you been at?" Swonger asked.

"Away."

"Away? This ain't the time for no games." Swonger's thumb flicked off the safety—maybe the gun was for him after all.

Gibson realized what was different about Swonger. When they had first met, Gibson had dismissed him as one more yard-boy ex-con who talked a whole lot tougher than he'd ever hope to be. It had taken time to recognize the intelligence behind Swonger's surly, antagonistic posturing. Longer still to respect Swonger as a man, despite his bluster. All that had burned off now. There was a calm, a lean simplicity to the ex–car thief that hadn't been there before.

"It's hard to explain," Gibson said.

"And you so good with words. Why you here? Let's start with that. This about your house?"

The question caught Gibson by surprise. Maybe it had been naïve of him not to connect Swonger to the fire. This was going to take an ugly turn if Swonger were mixed up in it.

"Why?" Gibson asked. "You have something to do with it?"

"That what you think?"

"Not until just now."

Swonger looked away, thinking. "Let's take a drive."

"Where?"

"Ain't far. We'll take your car." Swonger finally came down from the porch but gestured with a hand for Gibson to put his hands up. "Cole's got to search you."

"Cousin Cole?" Gibson asked.

"Yeah," Swonger said. "He got released six months ago."

"Nice to see a man turn over a new leaf," Gibson said as the man with the rifle frisked him.

"He's clean," Cole said, standing back up.

"All right," Swonger said. "Let's take that drive."

Swonger got in the passenger side and rested the gun on his thigh. Cole got in the back beside Duke, who stared daggers at the back of Swonger's head.

"Go for his gun," Duke said between gritted teeth. "He was in on it. He's taking you somewhere to bury your body. Do him before he does you."

"We don't know that," Gibson said sharply to the rearview mirror. He didn't like this side of his father. Duke had changed since Gibson had decided to go after Ogden. Hardened. It bothered Gibson but not as much as the knowledge of what he might do if Swonger had been involved with the fire.

"Don't know what?" Swonger asked, glancing at Cole in the backseat, who shrugged in confusion.

"What?" Gibson said dumbly, realizing his mistake.

Swonger gave him a puzzled look. "You all right, dog?"

"Yeah, I'm fine. Where are we going?"

Swonger directed him around the big house and deeper onto the farm. Cattle stood glumly in a frozen field and watched the SUV disappear around a bend and down a sloping hill. Swonger glanced back and forth from the road to Gibson. As if Gibson might vanish if Swonger didn't keep a proper eye on him.

"Here," Swonger said, pointing to a gap in a tall hedgerow.

Gibson pulled in and stopped before the blackened ruins of a house. Fire had gutted it, collapsing the roof except for a portion in the back corner, which stood defiantly against the elements. The surviving brick walls left some semblance of a floor plan, and the fireplace rose like the charred spine of an animal sacrificed to a primitive god.

"Welcome to Casa Swonger."

While Longman Farm belonged to Hammond Birk's family, Gavin Swonger's father had been the longtime farm manager. Swonger had grown up here. His family had lived on the property and done the lion's share of the day-to-day work.

"What happened?" Gibson asked, staring out at the house.

"Consequence happened." Swonger wouldn't say more.

Mesmerized, Gibson got out and walked up the brick stairs and into the house. Swonger yelled that it wasn't safe, but Gibson didn't care. Some part of him needed to stand in the ruined house. He clambered up and over the debris from the collapsed upper floor. Running his fingers across the charred end of a cracked wooden beam that had been seared to a charcoal tip, his hand came away black. He held it to his nose to smell the cold smoke. A stuffed, one-eyed rabbit caught his eye. It was moldy and sodden; Gibson tried to brush the dirt away but succeeded only in knocking loose the rabbit's remaining eye. He searched the rubble for the eye, and when he couldn't find it, tossed the toy away. What good was a blind rabbit?

Had anything of Ellie's survived on Mulberry Court? He imagined that Nicole must have walked the wreckage of their home, scavenging odds and ends from her life while making plans to disappear. For the first time, he felt grateful that she had run, grateful for his ex-wife's resourcefulness.

Swonger joined Gibson in the ash and surveyed the scene. The gun had disappeared from his hand.

"We made some mess, huh?" Swonger said.

"That we did."

Swonger swore under his breath as if this were his first time seeing the fire-ravaged house.

"Who?" Gibson asked.

"Who you think?"

"Deja Noble."

Deja Noble ran a crew out of Virginia Beach. Because Swonger knew her brother from prison, he and Gibson had turned to Deja in desperation in West Virginia. She'd helped them, but her involvement had come at a price. Gibson hadn't considered her for the arson, but now the symmetry of it made perfect sense.

"Consequence in the flesh," Swonger said. "Hit us the same day as your ex-wife's house."

"Anybody home?"

Swonger shook his head.

"You didn't go to the police?"

"And tell them what?"

Gibson was familiar with that particular quandary.

"You know I carried Deja out of the hotel during the fire? Saved her life."

"Good thinking," Swonger said.

"Guess it didn't make us even."

"Not as such, no. Thinks we set her up and sent her and her men into that hotel to die."

"Which we did."

"Which we did," Swonger agreed.

"So she burned down our houses."

"For starters," Swonger said.

"What about the money? She didn't take it, did she?"

Gibson had cleaned out the last of Charles Merrick's brokerage account and transferred it to the Birks and Swongers. Almost a million and a half dollars. Some of that money had been meant to take care of Judge Birk. It had been about the only good thing to come out of that disaster, and it would hurt to know it had been for nothing.

"No, she don't know nothing about that," Swonger said. "Is that why you're here? The money?"

"Not as long as you took care of the judge like we agreed."

"Judge doing fine. In a home near Richmond. He's all the way gone now. Waste of damn money, you ask me, but he has people taking care of him like you wanted. Got the address you want it."

Gibson nodded, sorry but not surprised to hear the judge's dementia had worsened. When he had time, he'd stop in and pay his respects.

"Where you been, Gibson?" Swonger asked. "And don't give me no 'away.'"

Gibson told Swonger a sanitized version of the last eighteen months, leaving out the part where he'd been driven crazy in solitary confinement. Remarkably, Swonger seemed wholly unsurprised at the mention of the CIA's involvement, as if the government's abetting Charles Merrick's crimes confirmed deep-seated paranoias. Only the end of the story seemed to bother him.

"Motherfuckers just dumped you on the airfield like you was trash? That's cold, dog. Real cold."

"Kind of why I'm here," Gibson said and held out his shopping list. "I need your help."

Swonger looked it over. "Let's go back to the house and cut it up."

CHAPTER TWELVE

The clapboard farmhouse was a beautiful home. Gibson could feel its history in the creak of the floorboards and the way Swonger had to put his shoulder into the front door to open it. Time had done its work, and the old house had eased comfortably into its foundations. The floors rose and fell in rolling swells, and none of the doors or windows sat squarely in their frames. When the wind picked up, the house expanded like a lung and a cold draft whistled through the hallways. Gibson zipped up his jacket, unable to decide if he'd been warmer inside or out.

In the kitchen, Swonger poured him a cup of burnt coffee from a pot that had been sitting far too long. It was hot, though, and Gibson drank it without complaint. Swonger threw fresh logs on the kitchen fire that had burned down to glowing embers. When the wood caught, they sat at a banquette built under the kitchen windows. Gibson looked out on a small, frozen pond beside the house while Swonger read over his shopping list. Swonger's brow furrowed as he tried to guess what it added up to.

"What the hell is all this?" Swonger asked.

"Don't you still have contacts in Richmond? Is it a problem?"

"That ain't even the question, dog. Why you need a Yukon? You drove up in one. And what you need so many protein bars for? You feeding an army?"

"No," Gibson said. "Just one guy."

"That's like a year's supply."

"Two," Gibson corrected.

Swonger stared at Gibson, started to ask a question, then stopped, perhaps realizing that he didn't want to know the answer. He went back to the list instead.

"How clean does this gun got to be?"

"Spotless," Gibson said.

"Ketamine? You planning on tranking a horse?"

"Can you get it?"

"This a farm, 'course I can get it."

"I take it back," Duke said. "I like this guy."

"Okay, then," Gibson said. "So will you help me?"

Two men in work clothes barged in the kitchen door, stomping feet and talking loudly. They saw Swonger and stopped in their tracks.

"Sorry, Mr. Swonger," they said in unison.

"I need the kitchen, fellas. Can you give my dad a hand out on three?"

The men said they would and backed out of the kitchen, repeating their apologies. Swonger met Gibson's eyes.

"Mr. Swonger?" Gibson said.

"You know how it is," Swonger said shyly.

Gibson smiled. "It has a nice ring to it. Looks like you're really handling things here. I think it's great."

Swonger glowed at the praise, but another thought intruded, and he grew somber. "I ain't told you everything."

"Is it Lea? Did she make it?"

Lea Regan aka Chelsea Merrick aka Charles Merrick's daughter had been a friend and ally in Niobe, West Virginia. She'd had her own reasons for hating her father, but because Charles Merrick was her blood, Gibson had never entirely let his guard down with her. Still, they'd worked side by side, and Gibson knew her to be good people. She'd taken a bullet to the chest during the chaos inside the Wolstenholme Hotel. Swonger had pulled her out before fire engulfed the hotel, and the last Gibson knew, she'd been on the way to a hospital. But beyond that, he knew nothing.

"Yeah, man," Swonger said. "She pulled through."

"Good," Gibson said with relief. "You in touch with her? I should let her know her father is out."

Swonger shook his head. "Ain't seen her, dog. She lit out soon as she got out of the hospital."

There was sadness in Swonger's voice that Gibson couldn't decipher. He knew Swonger had been in love with Lea, although he wasn't sure if Swonger knew it. Either way, Swonger had been too starstruck to act on his feelings. Probably for the best. Lea Regan and Gavin Swonger were from different worlds. Wherever she was, Gibson hoped she was safe and happy. He would track her down and give her the news when he had time. He owed her that much.

"So if it's not that, what haven't you told me?"

"I work for Deja Noble now," Swonger said. "I do, but I don't. Tell the truth, whole farm is hers. It's not, but it is, if you understand me."

"I don't."

Swonger told him about Deja's gunpoint ultimatum after the fire. How she'd become a silent partner in Longman Farm, paid off enough of the farm's debt to keep it solvent. That the Swongers would be allowed to remain on the property and manage the farm. That "allowed" really meant "forced." In exchange, the farm would become Deja's personal depot as her crew moved merchandise in and out of the state.

"Did the Birks go for it?"

"Not exactly, but Christopher's share of the money went a long way to convincing him not to force the issue. Not like he was pining away to be no farmer."

"You all right?"

"Course I am. Got everything I ever wanted, didn't I?" Swonger said with a weary chuckle. "So you know, I'll have to let Deja know you was here. Nothing personal, but sometimes her people are watching, sometimes they ain't. Can't risk not telling her. Hope you understand."

Gibson nodded that he did. "Don't jam yourself up on my account. Is she liable to come looking for me?"

"Dog, I'm out of the Deja Noble prediction game. But, yeah, I wouldn't bet against it. She still has some issues to work out with you. She's sore about Truck." Truck Noble was Deja's warship of a brother. He'd used Gibson as a piñata until a bar owner in Niobe had broken a baseball bat over Truck's head. Gibson had claimed responsibility for the whole thing to protect the bar owner from the Nobles.

"What about him?" Gibson asked.

"He's not all there anymore."

"What part of him?"

"The brain part," Swonger said. "Big man don't talk much no more. Deja didn't appreciate you breaking her brother like that."

"Guess that's fair."

"Still want my help?"

Gibson nodded that he did.

Swonger said, "Okay, but I need one thing from you."

"Name it."

"Don't go messing with Deja Noble. I know you, you have that damned honorable streak. Think you always have to balance the ledgers. Far as I'm concerned, the ledgers are balanced as a mother. It ain't ideal, but I got equilibrium. Things are working out right now. Guess I'm asking, can you leave Deja be, knowing what I told you?"

It was a good question. "And if I can't?"

"Then I can't help you. I'm sorry. Lot of her people died in that hotel, Gibson. But weren't nobody home when she burned down our houses. Think on that. She showed us a piece of mercy. Just a little piece. But you go riling her up, she'll pile the bodies up. Yours and mine. Can't risk that collateral."

"And if she comes messing with me?" Gibson asked.

Swonger shrugged. "Pistols at dawn, dog."

Gibson indicated he could live with that. As with Charles Merrick, Gibson couldn't sustain any anger toward Deja or what she'd done. She didn't owe him any loyalty. It had been an eye for an eye, and while hard, it also felt fair. Gibson hadn't been there to speak for himself, so she'd taken it out on Nicole instead. And that was why Damon Ogden still had to answer for himself. The way Gibson saw it, Ogden had owed him loyalty—not to mention his life—but shown him none. *That* ledger he would balance.

Satisfied, Swonger fetched a spiral-bound notebook, and the two men spent the next few hours hashing out the details. Swonger made meticulous notes in an illegible scrawl, asking questions but never prying into Gibson's business. His questions were sharp and raised points that hadn't occurred to Gibson. Gibson marveled at how much Swonger had grown up in only eighteen months. Ultimately, they split the list into two deliveries. Gibson wasn't working on a traditional clock, but the sooner the better—he didn't know how long he could hold his ghosts at bay.

"When you need the first delivery?" Swonger asked.

"Soon as possible."

"Give me a few days."

"Good enough," Gibson said and gave him the number of one of his burner phones. He pulled out a roll of bills wrapped in a thick rubber band. The proceeds from selling Merrick's watch. "How much?"

Swonger sat back, stung. "Not taking your money, dog."

"This is business, Swonger."

"No, it ain't, even. Put it away. You paid all you're going to pay. You hear?"

"Thank you."

The two men shook hands over the table, and Swonger smiled now that it was settled. "Ain't nothing. Just tell me what it was all for someday."

Gibson wasn't sure there'd ever be a someday, but he promised that he would. Satisfied, Swonger walked him to the front door. From the top of the staircase that led to the second floor, a woman's voice called his name. Gibson looked up to see Lea. She smiled down at him, but he was too astonished to smile back. Still, he felt an unexpected rush of happiness to see her.

Two thoughts occurred to him as he glanced at Swonger. First, there had been a time when Gibson had known Swonger's mind thirty seconds before Swonger did. It scared him how easily he'd swallowed Swonger's lie. Swallowed it without a moment's hesitation. The madness that had ground him down in that cell had also eroded his ability to read people. If people had once been open books to him, then he was all but illiterate now. Second, he had no way to know if Swonger would hold up his end of their arrangement. He didn't like having to take it on faith, but what other choice did he have?

As Lea started down the stairs, Swonger let out a cry and bounded up to meet her. She put her arm around his shoulder, and together they came down one stair at a time. She looked pale and terribly thin. Swonger chided her for being out of bed, but Lea shushed him. At the bottom of the stairs, she threw her arms around Gibson. Gibson hugged her back while Swonger fetched a quilt from another room. Swonger put it around her shoulders and eased her into an armchair. Swonger said he'd be right back and went to make Lea a pot of tea. Gibson pulled up a seat close to her.

"What happened?"

"I got shot," she said with a wan smile.

"Eighteen months ago."

"Not like the movies, is it?"

"No, it isn't."

"Bullet went in here." She pointed to a spot above her right breast and then traced the bullet's path. "Clipped my clavicle here, and then bounced south like a pinball. Collapsed a lung. Nicked my intestine. Four surgeries so far. They had to go back in three times to get all the bone fragments. Then the secondary infections. That was not my favorite part. One little bullet. A .22. Can you believe that?"

"Is he taking good care of you?"

Lea's face brightened. "Mama Swonger? He's pretty much kept me going. Same thing with the farm. I don't even recognize that boy some days."

"And you? Are you all right?"

Lea shrugged. "You ever wish you could talk sense to who you used to be?"

"Yeah, like either of us would have listened."

Lea laughed at that until it turned into a coughing fit. Swonger hurried back from the kitchen with her tea and rubbed her back until it passed.

She thanked Swonger and looked at Gibson apologetically. "So enough of my tale of woe, what the hell happened to you?"

Seeing Lea in her weakened state, Gibson hesitated to put more stress on her, but she had a right to know what had happened to her mother and that her father was free again. He took a deep breath and told her. When Gibson came to how he found her mother, Lea looked away and wiped tears from her eyes. She took Swonger's hand and held it tightly. Swonger didn't take his eyes off her.

They'd all experienced the tragedy in Niobe but from different perspectives. Now, they spent the afternoon trading their war stories, filling in details for each other. Duke waited impatiently in the doorway, but Gibson needed this.

"Do you know where my father is now?" Lea asked.

"Only where I'd like him to be."

"We were so stupid. We should have gotten out of West Virginia while we had the chance," Lea said.

"Not sure we ever had one," Swonger said.

The plain truth of that quieted them. They'd all been too arrogant, too righteous, to play it safe. Looking around the room, Gibson saw the price they'd paid for it. They all did. Lea looked suddenly tired and made a joke about a full day's work. Gibson began to feel he'd overstayed his welcome. He made his good-byes. Lea kissed him on the cheek, and Swonger saw him out. At the car, the two men embraced, and Swonger clapped Gibson on the back before stepping back.

In a low voice, Gibson asked, "So are you two—"

Swonger shook his head vehemently. "Naw, it ain't even like that. I just look after her, is all. She keeps the books for the farm. Has like a calculator in her head."

"You should tell her. Life is short."

Swonger looked back at the farmhouse. "Woman like that, dog. You think she don't know?"

CHAPTER THIRTEEN

After the last trailer, the lights in the theater dimmed. Gibson gripped the armrests and tried to quell his rising panic. His foot started tapping, but he couldn't stop it. He stared up at the screen, willing the movie to begin before he lost his nerve.

Since his visit to Longman Farm, he'd been catching a movie at an Arlington multiplex in the afternoons after his shift. If nothing else, it gave him an opportunity to practice controlling his fear of the dark. It embarrassed him. He knew he had other, more serious psychological issues, but panicking every time the lights went out felt foolish. A child's fear. Not that knowing it was irrational did anything to lessen its power over him. Through clenched teeth, he focused on slowing his breathing and holding his foot still. When the projector finally flared to life, his body uncoiled like it had been yanked free of an open power line. He went limp in his seat, exhaled hard, and took a long drink from his huge soda to wet his parched throat.

Not bad, he thought.

Actually, he felt pretty good in general. Since he'd begun prepping in earnest for Damon Ogden, things had improved steadily. Each day a little better. His head had calmed. He rarely saw Duke or Bear. Now that he had a project, he didn't need them as much. Being outdoors barely affected him anymore. Even interacting with people was getting easier, and it no longer hurt to be touched. Duke had promised that if Gibson followed through with their plan, things would get better. So far, so good. His revenge gave him a sense of purpose that drove him. Its planning, organization, and execution felt important in a way that washing dishes for twelve dollars an hour never could.

He'd been keeping late hours, so once the movie started, Gibson made himself comfortable and took a nap. He wasn't there for the movie anyway. It was all part of the plan, and he needed to establish an alibi. Not that he thought anyone was watching. Not now anyway. But afterward, he'd need a verifiable routine. So he made a point of buying something from the concessions line and chatting amicably with the bored staff behind the counter. To make certain they remembered him, he'd twice let his large soda slip out of his hand at the counter. No one ever forgot a serial klutz.

After the movie, Gibson drove to the outskirts of Damon Ogden's neighborhood. Ogden lived alone in a house in Vienna, Virginia, just beyond the sprawl of Tysons Corner. A quiet neighborhood dominated by young families. A place where people felt safe, let their guards down. In the Yukon, Gibson changed into the same distinctive running gear and took his nightly jog past Ogden's house. It gave him the opportunity to scout the neighborhood and plan for contingencies.

The weatherman called it a polar vortex. Gibson called it camouflage. At night, the thermometer had been dipping into the teens, driving all but the hardiest off the streets. The handful of brave souls that he did meet, Gibson greeted with a friendly wave. No one questioned the neoprene hood that covered everything but his eyes. He wanted to be remembered but not recognized. The best way not to seem out of the ordinary was not to be. When the time came, Gibson would be just a hard-core neighbor out for a run. Plus, he really needed the exercise. It felt good to be able to run more than a block without puking into the bushes.

His last stop each night was the abandoned power plant. It had been a godsend. Duke had suggested it when they'd first started planning, but they'd had to wait until Gibson's release to make sure it still stood.

Duke had been chief of staff to Senator Benjamin Lombard when the plant had closed. It had remained a political hot potato in Northern Virginia for more than twenty years. The original proposal had called for the plant to be demolished to make way for new development, which in real-estate-hungry Northern Virginia would ordinarily have been a no-brainer. However, no one had calculated the expense of removing the asbestos, lead paint, mercury, and other hazardous materials. Standard demolition would have had serious environmental implications for the surrounding residential neighborhoods, which meant time and money. One development company after another backed away from the project. So there the old plant remained, undisturbed in all its dilapidated glory. Neighbors paid it no mind, and it had become an all-but-invisible eyesore.

It may have been perfect, but he still had a lot to do if he wanted to make his deadline. He worked until after two a.m., as he did every night. It was grueling, but Gibson enjoyed the work. For the first few days, his back had ached like he'd been through a workout, which he supposed he had. Combined with his running, he felt like he was relearning how to use his body. It was a satisfying feeling. Then, exhausted, he stumbled home to his basement room and slept on the floor until it was time to go to work at the diner.

The next night, after a particularly awful movie involving a white family, demonic possession, and a haunted house, Gibson found a small trailer hitched to the back of his Yukon. The first delivery, right on schedule. Swonger had held up his end. Not wanting to leave his cargo unattended, Gibson skipped his evening run and drove straight to the plant.

A high chain-link fence overgrown with vines encircled the property, but the gate was wide open. Anything of value had long since been removed. A security service drove the property twice a week looking for indications that local kids were partying there. Security never went inside the plant, though, and as long as Gibson kept a low profile and covered his tracks, they never would.

He drove around to the back of the plant and backed the Yukon up to a basement entrance to unload the trailer. He checked the packing tape that he'd put over the basement door's seams. It was undisturbed; no one had been there. The door's lock had broken long before, and it had been padlocked shut with a length of chain. Gibson had removed the padlock with bolt cutters and replaced it with a similar model.

Inside, he flipped on the lights. One of his first tasks had been to replace most of the lightbulbs, this after he'd discovered to his delight that the caretakers still paid the plant's utilities. He went down a flight of stairs and along a narrow, dank service corridor. Ducking under a corroded pipe, he made a left and then a right, moving deeper into the abandoned building. It had taken a whole night's work to clear all the debris, but it had been worth it. He couldn't imagine a more private location for a hundred miles. And what he had in mind for Damon Ogden depended on privacy.

His improvised workbench was just as he'd left it. He took a key from a hook and unlocked the bathroom door. It needed reinforcing. One of a long list of modifications to make to the eight-by-ten bathroom. Swonger's delivery would see to that. But first things first; he went back topside and spent the rest of the night unloading and organizing his new equipment. He had a lot of work left to do if he wanted to be ready by Friday night.

———

Friday's movie featured a misunderstood teenager drafted into a fight against a dystopian oligarch. The key to winning, as best as Gibson could follow, was embracing her individuality. He liked this one more than most of the movies he'd seen recently, although he didn't know what it said about him that he related so strongly to a teenage freedom fighter. Exhausted after a long week, he could have used a nap, but no way he was sleeping. Tonight was the night.

When the world was saved and the credits rolled, Gibson went out to the lobby and bought a ticket for another movie he'd already seen. At the concession counter, he ordered a large soda and made a big show of holding it carefully in both hands. They all shared a good laugh about his clumsiness. Gibson asked them the time and wished them a good weekend. Back in the theater, he found a seat in the back and let the lights dim before slipping out the side exit.

His Yukon was gone. In its place sat a blue 2001 Yukon with Virginia plates. Once again, Gavin Swonger had come through. Gibson thought about considering the proposition that this might be the rule more than the exception.

The driver's door was unlocked, and Gibson found the key under the mat. He took an inventory of the trunk. He counted everything that he'd requested along with the suitcase he'd left in his Yukon for Swonger to transfer between vehicles. Inside the suitcase was an empty backpack that Gibson filled with items from tonight's delivery. Then he got on the road.

Rush hour was typical for a Friday night, but once he got on the Dulles Toll Road, things eased up. He parked at one of the hotels surrounding the airport, chosen for its lack of security cameras. He tucked the Yukon away in an inconvenient back corner, wheels far enough into the adjacent spot to discourage anyone who cared about their paint job. He rolled the suitcase—the kind businesspeople crammed into the overhead bins on flights—over to the hotel and caught a cab to a second hotel, this one in Tysons Corner. In the lobby bathroom, he changed into his cold-weather running gear. He took the .45 Lawman from its clear plastic bag and loaded it. It felt so good in his hand that he only grudgingly put it back in the backpack. He left the suitcase in a dumpster behind the hotel and caught a second cab that dropped him five blocks from Damon Ogden's home. He paid cash and shouldered his backpack as the cab disappeared up the block.

It was going to be another cold one.

Kidnapping an officer of the Central Intelligence Agency was a terrible, foolhardy idea. It could only end badly. But the fact that it was a terrible idea gave Gibson certain advantages. No one had ever kidnapped a CIA officer on American soil. That meant he had the element of surprise on his side. Sometimes foolhardy gave you an edge.

It also helped that security for the intelligence community was reactive rather than proactive. Roughly five million Americans held security clearances, so it simply wasn't feasible to watch everyone. The first line of defense was the individuals themselves. If Damon Ogden spotted trouble—for example, if a foreign national made an approach or if Ogden lost his ID—it was his responsibility to report it. Once the CIA knew of a problem, it would react quickly, but until then, it idled at the starting line.

So, hypothetically, if one of their officers went missing, the CIA wouldn't have any idea initially. It wouldn't be until Ogden was reported missing or failed to show up at Langley that the CIA would be alerted. Even then, the CIA would allow a short grace period—Gibson guessed no more than a few hours—before it initiated a search. Step one would be to call everyone on the missing officer's emergency contact form. If friends and family couldn't help to locate Damon Ogden, the next step would be to send a supervisor to Ogden's home. Within four or five hours, the FBI and the local police would have been alerted. Within twelve hours, the full muscle of the American intelligence community would be mobilized to find their missing man.

Once that happened, it wouldn't take long for someone at Langley to throw the name Gibson Vaughn into the pot along with any other enemies Damon Ogden may have made. After that, they would begin sifting through Gibson's life for any indication that he'd abducted Damon Ogden. Gibson would either need to be off the grid by then, in which case the CIA would draw a bull's-eye on his back that would never be erased, or else right where they expected him to be, squeaky clean, above reproach, just trying to make ends meet at the diner.

Gibson had opted for the latter. For one thing, he didn't have the resources to go on the run. Better to hide in plain sight and give them no reason to suspect him. Let them sniff around; if his plan worked, then he'd be nowhere near Ogden when the CIA let the dogs off the leash. But to do that he'd need a head start. Friday night gave him his best shot. Monday was Martin Luther King Day. If he took Ogden on Friday evening, then alarms at the CIA wouldn't start going off until late Tuesday morning when Ogden failed to report for work. That would give him eighty-four hours to cover his tracks while simultaneously creating a much larger window of time for which investigators would need to account.

The wild card would be if the Agency tried to reach Ogden over the weekend, or if he had personal plans. From what Gibson had been able to ascertain, Ogden's social circle was small, only a handful of college friends. However, he dated a woman, a single mother of two, in Reston. Ogden saw her two or three times a week and almost always on the weekend. Gibson would need to create a convincing excuse to keep her from panicking early. He had an idea how he'd handle it, but it would have to happen on the fly after he'd taken Ogden. It was risky, reckless even, but then, no plan was perfect.

Gibson pulled on his face shield and began an easy jog toward Ogden's house.

CHAPTER FOURTEEN

As night fell, so did the temperature. The wind had a bite to it, driving the wise indoors. It picked up as Gibson turned onto Damon Ogden's street. Two cars sped by on their way home after a long week, and a woman dragged a shivering dachshund up the sidewalk, but otherwise he saw no one, and no one saw him. Jogging past Ogden's house, he found nothing out of the ordinary. He ran a few blocks before circling back. There was no hurry. Ogden was a creature of habit and wouldn't be home before six thirty at the earliest.

One of the quirks of modern home-security systems was that many didn't consider the garage part of the house. It meant that the countdown to enter the disarm code didn't begin until the door from the garage into the house opened. That would be fine except that the signals from most commercial garage door openers weren't encrypted and were remarkably simple to spoof with the right equipment. Unfortunately for Damon Ogden, both his garage door and his alarm system fell into those categories.

A week earlier, Gibson had come out with a simple device he'd cobbled together from a child's electronic toy. It cycled garage-door codes and found Ogden's in less than two minutes. Gibson had then programmed that code into the generic, replacement garage-door opener in the pocket of his running jacket. With the push of a button, he triggered Ogden's garage door now, strolled casually up to the house, and ducked inside.

Gibson shut the garage door and looked around. Despite the single-car garage being packed to the rafters, it didn't offer many places to hide. Gibson added "neat freak" to Ogden's list of crimes against humanity. The boxes, meticulously labeled and stacked along one wall, offered no cover. His best bet was the small blind in the corner created by a kayak and two bicycles hanging vertically from a rack.

Gibson squatted on an overturned metal bucket to wait. When the motion-activated light clicked off, he was ready with a flashlight but let out a small involuntary cry anyway. To pass the time, he rummaged through his backpack, flashlight between his teeth, and rearranged his gear. He pulled on a pair of double-layer latex gloves and a surgical hairnet.

That took all of three minutes.

Then he sat in the dark of the garage and waited. With all his experience, he would have thought that he'd be an old hand at loneliness. But he hadn't had a real conversation since the farm, and the lack of human interaction ate at him. Objectively, he knew it was good that Bear and Duke didn't come around as often. It meant he was improving. But they'd been his only companionship for eighteen soul-crushing months. Even if they were only figments of his psychosis, they were his friends. And he missed them.

Gibson flicked off the flashlight and counted slowly to ten. When he turned it back on, he could feel himself shaking. He let a few minutes pass and tried again, this time to eleven. When his heart stopped pounding, he told himself, he would go to twelve.

The motor for the garage door cranked to life. The sudden noise startled Gibson, who dropped his flashlight. It rolled toward the middle of the garage, beam playing crazily over the walls. Gibson watched all his planning come unraveled with a strange, detached fascination. Then miraculously, the flashlight made a U-turn of its own accord and rolled back to Gibson. He scooped it up gratefully and pressed back against the wall as headlights spilled across the garage. The car eased into its spot, and the engine cut off.

Gibson held his breath.

The driver's side door opened, but Ogden took a moment to balance his briefcase, coffee cup, phone, and keys. Gibson studied him in the dome light. He'd expected a rush of emotion when he saw Damon Ogden again, but in truth he felt only confusion. The man in the car didn't look anything like the man he remembered. Obviously they'd met under less than ideal circumstances—Ogden had been on the wrong end of a beating that night, and the Wolstenholme Hotel had been a war zone. But even so, Gibson would have sworn that he'd know Ogden anywhere. How couldn't he? It was the last human face he had seen for eighteen months. The last voice he'd thought he would ever hear. Their lives were bound together inexorably because of that night in West Virginia. So how could Gibson not know him? How could this man be a stranger to him?

Gibson realized that he had a more pressing concern—his hiding place blocked Ogden's view from the car, but there would be a brief window, between the car and the house door, when he would be in Ogden's field of vision. If Ogden looked this way, he'd have no chance of subduing him quietly, if at all. It would be an all-out brawl, and not one Gibson could be sure of winning, even if he'd been anywhere close to fighting shape. Anyway, that wasn't the plan.

He drew his gun and thumbed the safety off.

The plan hinged on Ogden not knowing the identity of his abductor. It also required that Ogden go into the house and disable the alarm. Gibson needed access to the house, and the security company's log had to show Ogden arriving home as usual. Because when investigators looked at the record of Ogden's cell phone, it would show the phone connecting to a tower in his neighborhood. If Ogden never made it inside the house, then investigators would pinpoint exactly when and where Ogden had disappeared. That would hand them the crime scene, which would shift the odds against Gibson considerably.

Ogden pushed the car door closed with his hip. Gibson crouched lower, his pulse like a freight train in his ears. One step. Then another. Gibson held his breath—one more step and they'd be staring soulfully into each other's eyes. Gibson pressed the button on his garage remote. The garage door began to close, seemingly on its own. Ogden froze, looking around for an explanation—the button by the door into the house, the car itself, then accusingly up at the garage door motor on the ceiling. Gibson used the distraction to break cover, the rumble of the garage door covering any noise he made. He dropped prone alongside the car as the garage door shuddered to a close. In the silence that followed, he watched Ogden's feet under the car turn in a slow, confused circle. Gibson willed him away.

Go on. Go on. You know how glitchy those motors can be.

Ogden and his feet finally took the hint. Gibson breathed a sigh of relief as Ogden opened the house door. The shrill, staccato bleat of the alarm cried out until Ogden punched in the code to deactivate it. Gibson rose to a crouch, counted to thirty, and slipped into the house after him.

Although he'd never been inside Ogden's home, Gibson knew that the garage connected to a combination laundry room and pantry. He knew because all the houses in Ogden's development were based on a few standard models. Two like Ogden's were currently on the market, and the floor plans were posted helpfully on the real estate agent's website for prospective buyers to admire. Or prospective home invaders to memorize.

After the cold of the garage, the warmth of the house prickled his skin. The lights in the pantry were off. Through the swinging door that led to the kitchen, Gibson heard Ogden open the refrigerator. The last thing Gibson wanted was to get drawn into a game of cat and mouse on Ogden's home turf. Better to take him in the pantry and end it quickly. But to do that, he needed to lure Ogden back in this direction. Gibson looked at the garage-door opener still in his hand. Did he dare go to that well one more time? He stepped into the corner behind the kitchen door and pressed the button.

In the kitchen, Ogden swore as the rumble of the garage door opening echoed through the house. Wondering aloud who to call for a faulty garage-door motor, he pushed through the door, which swung back and forth angrily. In the strobing kitchen light, Gibson watched Ogden open the back door and stare accusingly at his disloyal garage. Gibson took two steps and pressed a stun gun to Ogden's neck. The man's back arched painfully as his muscles locked up and he cried out before crumpling to the ground.

For a moment, Gibson stood over Ogden, waiting for a sense of victory. Something. He'd imagined this moment so many times in his cell. But instead of triumph, when he looked down at Ogden prostrate at his feet, doubt elbowed its way to the fore. Gibson pushed it away, mistaking it for simple fear. *Finish the job,* he chided himself—*finish what you set out to do.* Why should he expect to feel anything? He hadn't accomplished anything yet.

It occurred to him that the garage door was still open. Stupid. He ducked down, planted a knee on Ogden's back, and watched the street until the garage door finished closing. Beneath him, Ogden was shaking free. A syringe of ketamine put a stop to that. Gibson knelt on Ogden until the powerful anesthetic took effect. It should knock Ogden out for hours, but Gibson secured his wrists and ankles with zip ties, a hood over his head. No sense taking the chance that he'd gotten the dose wrong.

Gibson searched Ogden, emptying the man's pockets and removing a watch and a ring. It all went into a ziplock bag except for the cell phone and car keys, which he left on the kitchen counter. The ziplock went upstairs with him to the master bedroom. Gibson found a suitcase in a closet and packed enough clothes for a week. Toiletries. The gun from the bedside table. The passport and cash that he found in a bureau drawer. Ogden's college diploma came out of its frame and was tucked into the suitcase. Gibson perused the framed pictures on a credenza, picking one of Ogden's parents. Like the rest of the house, Ogden's bedroom was a pristine affair, and Gibson left it that way.

Suitcase packed, he carried it down to the kitchen and took a tour of the house. He went room to room, making sure that he hadn't overlooked anything. If Gibson had expected to come away with a sense of Ogden's personality, then he'd visited the wrong house. He couldn't get over the utter banality of Ogden's home. The generic, Pottery Barn veneer, everything tasteful while having no taste of which to speak. He'd wanted something more from someone with the power to disappear a man from the face of the earth.

The last door he tried opened into an office. Gibson sat at the desk and tapped the spacebar to wake the computer. He'd brought equipment to hack the log-in, but the computer didn't have one. No doubt Ogden knew better than most that log-ins were a sham.

Gibson used one of Ogden's credit cards to book train tickets to Fort Lauderdale, New York City, and Chicago. Bus tickets to a half dozen other cities. Hotel reservations. Last, Gibson slid a CD into Ogden's computer and initiated a complete wipe of the hard drive. It would take hours, and Gibson would be long gone before it finished, but it would give investigators one more misleading question to puzzle over.

Ogden and his suitcase went in the trunk of his own car. Gibson sat on the bumper to catch his breath. Moving Ogden reminded him how much strength he'd lost in the last eighteen months. Either that or Ogden weighed considerably more than the 190 listed on his driver's license. Gibson checked the time—right on schedule. He borrowed Ogden's thumb to unlock his cell phone and scrolled through Ogden's calendar.

On Saturday evening, Ogden was taking his girlfriend and her boys to a Capitals game at the Verizon Center in DC. Sunday, he was watching the NFL playoffs with "the boys." Other than that, his weekend looked open. Next, Gibson went through Ogden's texts from the last twelve hours, looking for any last-minute plans that might not have made it to the calendar.

Nothing. So far so good.

He read the threads between the girlfriend and the group texts to his friends, getting a feel for how Ogden wrote to each. He was more formal and reserved with the girlfriend, casual and jocular with the guys. Gibson wrote an apologetic text to the girlfriend on Ogden's behalf. Something had come up at work, he'd been called back in, and it looked like it could be a working weekend. Cell phones weren't allowed inside Langley so Gibson wrote that Ogden might be incommunicado if this situation went badly. Ogden was sorry and would make it up to the girlfriend. Gibson relayed the same message to "the boys" but in far coarser terms.

The girlfriend replied to his message, and Gibson spent fifteen minutes going back and forth with her. She wasn't happy. Clearly, this wasn't the first time that Ogden's responsibilities had interfered with their plans. Gibson played the part of the repentant boyfriend stuck between a rock and a hard place.

I have to go in. It's my job.

I know. I'm just disappointed about tomorrow. The kids

were looking forward to it.
So was I. Tell them I'm sorry.

There was a pause. In text, Ogden was reserved and never wrote "I love you" first. Gibson made a point of breaking that rule now:

I love you.
Love you too. Are you ok?
Frustrated. Missing you. Wish it could be another way.

Hopefully the CIA would read something sinister into that text later. But in the short term, Ogden's uncharacteristic display of emotion had the desired effect.

Oh baby it will be alright. Call me when you can.
I'll try. Gotta go.

Gibson didn't reply after that, leaving room for Ogden's colleagues to invent subtext that suited their narrative. Then he placed a call to the main line at the Chinese embassy. He got an automated message, but that didn't matter. He left the line open for two minutes before hanging up. That ought to give them something to talk about at Langley.

Satisfied, Gibson connected Ogden's phone to an external battery. Enough to power the phone for two weeks, not that it would need that long. Next he put the phone and battery in a padded envelope stamped and addressed to Ogden's parents in San Diego. It went out on the front steps. Until it was picked up on Saturday, cell records would show the phone connected to his "home" cell towers. Then its cross-country journey would provide investigators with one more wild goose to chase down.

Gibson backed slowly out of the garage and out onto the deserted street. He shifted the car into drive and waited for the garage door to close for the last time before accelerating away into the night. It was a straight shot south to Dulles. At the hotel, Gibson backed in beside the Yukon and transferred Damon Ogden and his suitcase from one trunk to the other.

He reviewed all the false trails that he'd left for investigators to chase down: train tickets, bus tickets, plane tickets, phone traveling cross-country to San Diego, calls to the Chinese embassy, and Ogden's car parked at a hotel near an international airport. The first rule of disappearing was to make it difficult for anyone to follow you. Creating a sea of misinformation was textbook procedure, and with any luck that would be exactly how the CIA would interpret what Gibson had left for them. He wanted them to think their man was on the run, possibly going over to the Chinese. He wanted them scouring the four corners of the globe far, far from abandoned power plants in Northern Virginia.

Gibson dragged Ogden down the long service corridor into the deep recesses of the power plant. Gradually, the howling wind faded from earshot until the only sound was of Ogden's heels scraping the concrete floor.

In the cell, Gibson laid Ogden gently on his back. Once he unbound his wrists and ankles, Ogden looked almost peaceful. Undressing Ogden, he methodically folded each piece of clothing and stored it in a garbage bag. Getting an unconscious man into a jumpsuit proved to be a nightmare. It was like dressing the world's most uncooperative five-year-old. When she wasn't in the mood, Ellie'd had a way of going limp that increased her body mass. Ogden was worse.

Don't think about Ellie now.

When he finally finished, Gibson sat on the end of the cot and took a last look at his handiwork. He'd been over every square inch of this room a dozen times, but with Ogden lying there, it had stopped being an abstract exercise and become all too real. Over the past week, he'd stripped the windowless, eight-by-ten bathroom down to the floor. The tile, the mirror, the toilet paper dispenser—anything that might be fashioned into a tool or a weapon had been removed. The feet of the cot were bolted into the floor. All that remained of the original bathroom were the toilet and sink.

In one corner, crates of protein bars were stacked to the ceiling. Gibson couldn't stop by three times a day to feed him, but if Ogden rationed himself, he should have no problem making them last. Not that Gibson envied him the constant diarrhea and stomach pain as his body adjusted to its new, one-dimensional diet. It would be unpleasant, but Ogden would survive. Or he wouldn't. That was up to Ogden now. But he had everything that Gibson had been given.

Looking at Ogden on the floor, Gibson remembered waking up in his cell for the first time. The anger. The despair. The hopelessness. Eighteen months. A forced—and now likely permanent—separation from Ellie, the most important person in Gibson's world. That was what Ogden owed him. Gibson wouldn't hurt him, wouldn't kill him. But he'd promised his father that Damon Ogden would know how it felt. In eighteen months, Gibson would let him go. But Ogden wouldn't know that. He wouldn't know how long he'd been there or how long he had left. Wouldn't know if he'd ever be free. This was fair. Just. Eye for an eye. Who knew, Ogden might even make a friend or two while he was here.

Gibson left Ogden lying on the floor of the cell and went out into the hall. He took one last look at the prisoner. He'd check in on him in a few months when the heat was off, but until then, Damon Ogden would be alone with nothing but his conscience for companionship. Gibson swung the door closed, expecting a rush of euphoria. He'd done what he'd set out to do. What he'd promised his father in the cell. When that didn't come, he waited to feel anything at all. Nothing. He felt nothing. He turned the locks and slid the dead bolts into place. It would take a tank to knock this door down.

Now Damon Ogden would finally pay.

Still nothing.

He stepped back. It had been a long day, and he was exhausted. He needed sleep—in the morning he would feel like a new man. Duke had promised him that he would. He wished Duke were here to reassure him. Discouraged, he stowed his gear in a cubbyhole and went out down the service corridor, scattering debris to cover the drag marks. He didn't expect anyone to come this way, but if they did he didn't want to leave a trail of bread crumbs to Ogden's door.

It was a cloudless night. At the top of the stairs, the sky flexed and then crumpled like a beer can in God's fist. It pressed down on Gibson, vertigo spinning him, driving him to his knees. As bad as it had ever been. Static filled his eyes, and he couldn't breathe. Bear knelt beside him.

"One," she said.

He closed his eyes.

"Two."

He took a halting breath.

"Three . . ."

At ten, Gibson climbed tentatively to his feet.

"I wasn't sure I'd see you again," he said.

"You're still being silly."

"Why are you here? I thought you didn't want anything to do with this."

"Because you need my help. I told you that."

"But why would you help me at all? I don't understand."

"Because you came for me. I'm returning the favor."

"I was too late, Bear. I'm always too late."

"No," she said. "No, you weren't. Look at me. Gibson, look at me. My daughter is safe because of you. Catherine is safe. You gave her a chance. You did that."

"Stop it."

"You've helped so many people. Why don't you see that?"

"You're not going to talk me out of this," Gibson said. "He has to pay. He has to understand what he did."

"You will regret this for the rest of your life. You already regret it."

"You would say that."

"I'm not saying it, stupid. You are." Bear began to cry.

He felt terrible, but his mind was made up. The irony of that sentiment was, unfortunately, lost on him. "I'm sorry, Bear. He has to pay."

Gibson got back in the SUV. He started the engine and waited for Bear to get in. She stood in the wash of the headlights, unmoving. He left her there and drove home in silence, trying not to think about her dire warnings. The static in his eyes made it hard to drive, and Gibson needed both hands on the wheel. For the first time in weeks, he couldn't sleep unless every light was on.

CHAPTER FIFTEEN

The next morning, Gibson woke to an awful headache. He'd spent a largely sleepless night tortured by Bear's warning at the power plant. Afraid that she might be right. That this had all been a terrible mistake. And where was his dad? This had been Duke's idea in the first place. Why wasn't he here to explain why Gibson didn't feel fixed? That had been the whole point, hadn't it? But it was as if the ghost of his father knew that he'd written a bad check and wanted to avoid paying up. Gibson felt hollowed out. All he wanted was to turn off his alarm and sleep forever. He lay there listlessly with a pillow over his face.

Why *didn't* he feel better?

Because he wasn't finished. Ogden might be safely stashed away, but Gibson still had much to do. The rest of the weekend was dedicated to being seen. To establishing an alibi and passing convincingly for someone who hadn't kidnapped a CIA officer and imprisoned him in an abandoned power plant. Gibson couldn't very well do that from his bedroom floor. He would feel better once the weekend was behind him.

That had to be it.

He dragged himself from the floor and into the shower. At the diner, he worked a double shift. Operating on only a few hours of sleep, he still had to sell himself as energetic and well rested. He mainlined caffeine all day and feigned a cheerful, upbeat demeanor. After his shift, punchy and exhausted, his body begging for sleep, Gibson forced himself to hang around and eat dinner with Toby. Priority one was minimizing the amount of uncorroborated time he spent between now and when Damon Ogden officially went missing on Tuesday morning.

Maissa was coming home for a weeklong visit in February, and Toby was in high spirits. He talked animatedly throughout dinner while Gibson nodded in the appropriate places. He appreciated the opportunity to listen without needing to contribute much to the conversation. When the plates had been cleared away, Toby remembered something. He left the table and returned with a cardboard box. He put it on the table between them.

"What is it?" Gibson asked.

"It's yours."

Gibson lifted the lid. Inside he saw framed photographs. A bust of James Madison that had belonged to his father. His passport. His discharge papers from the Marines. A tattered social security card and other personal effects. His wedding ring. A bundle of letters in blue envelopes. From a stack of photographs, he picked out one of Nicole holding a sleeping Ellie at the hospital.

At the bottom of the box, he found a framed photograph that his father had kept on his desk. In it, Gibson sat in an armchair, Bear cozy in his lap. She'd been seven, Gibson eleven, brother and sister in all but name. She'd harassed him for a year to read her a book, and when she finally wore him down, she'd been ready with *The Lord of the Rings*. It had taken them two years to finish, but Grace Lombard, Bear's mother, had snuck a photograph that first night. It had come out so perfectly that most assumed it had been staged. To Gibson, the photograph represented an idealized version of his childhood. He hadn't noticed before, but when he saw Bear now, she was the girl from this picture. She even wore the same dress.

He felt a sweeping gratitude to have all these memories back but didn't understand how. Gibson looked up at Toby questioningly.

"I might have bribed your landlord to let me go through your apartment before he sent everything to the dump," Toby said.

"Thank you so much."

"I'm just sorry it's taken until now. I wanted it to be a surprise, but we've been so busy, and I kept forgetting."

"No, it's amazing. I thought I'd lost all of this."

Toby picked out a photograph of Ellie on her first day of kindergarten. "You have a beautiful daughter, Gibson. I'm proud of how hard you've worked to get back on track. How is the job search coming?"

Feeling guilty, Gibson updated Toby about his nonexistent job search. Toby asked question after question, and Gibson's lies became more and more convoluted. It surprised him how hard it was to keep it up. Thankfully, Toby's work soon interrupted.

Around eleven, Gibson dragged himself home. He unpacked the box and set the pictures out on the floor close to where he slept. When he came back from turning on all the lights, Bear was sitting on the floor, looking at Ellie. He braced for another lecture, but Bear didn't say anything. That was almost worse, but Gibson was too tired to argue about it tonight. He stretched out on the floor and fell asleep looking at his daughter.

His alarm woke him at 5:45 a.m. The last thing Gibson wanted to do was to go for a run at this hour, but he got up and got dressed anyway. Then he lurked at his front door, peering out through the curtain until he saw his landlady begin her morning pilgrimage to fetch the Sunday paper. He met the seventy-five-year-old widow on the sidewalk. Normally, Mrs. Nakamura didn't have much to say to him, but this morning she launched into an excited soliloquy about how the Packers were going to trounce the Cowboys. Her green-and-gold Packers jersey flapped excitedly around her knees, and it seemed a little early to be this fired up, but there was no stopping her. She invited him upstairs to watch the playoffs that afternoon. Gibson said he had to drive down to Richmond but promised to stop by if he got back in time.

———————

At first glance, Hammond Birk's retirement home looked like a college campus. The white stone façades lent the main building a magisterial, academic pedigree, and Gibson imagined it would be a beautiful spot in the springtime. He parked the Yukon in a side parking lot and tucked the keys above the visor. He signed in at the front desk and had his picture taken. A nurse issued him a visitor's pass and escorted him to Jefferson Hall, the pretentiously named south wing.

As they walked, the nurse explained that Judge Birk slept most of the time now. His dementia had entered stage six, which made completing even simple tasks now a challenge. Speaking had become increasingly difficult over the last twelve months. The last time they'd seen each other, the judge had emerged from his haze long enough for a conversation. There would be no such reunion today.

Sure enough, they found Hammond Birk sleeping peacefully. The brochure from the lobby described it as a suite, but the judge's room felt like a hybrid between an economy hotel and a hospital. The air freshener couldn't mask the smell of antiseptic any more than the handmade throw could disguise the hospital bed. Still, it was a vast improvement on the broken-down trailer where Gibson had found Birk eighteen months ago. Gone were the matted beard and filthy clothes. The judge looked clean, comfortable, and well cared for.

Dementia had stolen the judge's mind while still on the bench, and Charles Merrick had stolen his retirement. Gibson had stolen a piece of it back for him. It wasn't much, but it comforted Gibson knowing the judge would see out his days with some dignity, despite the enormous cost. Here, at last, he could point to something decent that he had done.

Gibson sat in an armchair beside the bed and opened two of the RC Colas that he'd brought—the judge's favorite—placed one on the nightstand even though the judge wouldn't drink it, and clinked the glass necks together. He sat watching the judge sleep.

"Did I ever write you about the accident?" Gibson asked the judge. Gibson and the judge had traded letters for years, but Gibson couldn't remember if he'd ever mentioned it. He hadn't thought of the accident in almost ten years, but it had been on his mind the last few days. "I had a forty-eight-hour leave, but a hurricane had made landfall in North Carolina and was dumping rain up and down the seaboard. Authorities were telling people to stay off the roads, but I hadn't seen Nicole in months, and there was no way in hell I was spending it on base. So I borrow a buddy's car—a little Corolla—and I haul ass home. Funny thing was, because of the warnings, the roads were deserted, so I made great time. I remember being in the outside lane, going too fast. Stupid, but I just want to get home and see my girl." Gibson paused, picturing the moment. "Coming around this slight bend, the car hydroplaned. Started spinning. I took my hands off the steering wheel because I didn't want to be holding anything when this piece-of-crap Corolla slammed into the trees at eighty miles an hour. It was like being on one of those Tilt-A-Whirl rides at the fair. Three perfect revolutions across the highway. Everything slowed down the way it does. I remember this moment when I knew I was going to die and there wasn't a damn thing I could do about it. It was weirdly peaceful."

The judge slumbered, oblivious. In a way, Gibson envied him.

"Anyway, I've been thinking about it a lot recently. How lucky I got. One second, I'm spinning, the next I'm sitting on the side of the highway facing the wrong way. They'd lined the side of the highway with these big rocks that had stopped the car like a ship running aground. I was fine. Airbags didn't even deploy. Bottom of my buddy's car was chewed all to hell, though."

Gibson opened another bottle of RC and sat in silence, thinking. He felt like he was in that car again, spinning out of control.

"Sometimes I think you should have sent me to prison like the senator wanted. Better for everyone."

The judge had offered Gibson the Marine Corps instead of prison. It had been the greatest kindness anyone had ever done him, and it felt dishonest and self-pitying to wish it away. He might not be wanted in his daughter's life, but going to prison would also have meant that Ellie would not have been born. Wishing he'd gone to prison was selfish, pure and simple, and absolutely typical. Like the fact that visiting the judge was just one more piece of his alibi, should anyone come asking for it.

The room was warm, and Gibson dozed off in the armchair. He woke late in the afternoon, groggy and stiff. He yawned and sat up to stretch. Across the bed, Deja Noble sat lazily shelling pistachios. He recoiled at the sight of her, unsure if she was real or another figment. Either way, he felt the calm return that had abandoned him when he'd locked Damon Ogden into his cell. She looked up at him under the wild mane of her Mohawk and carried on prying open pistachios one at a time.

"Thought you was going to sleep all day," she said.

"Could've used it."

"I hear that." She came to a pistachio that wouldn't open and held it up, looking for a seam. "Don't you hate that shit? Moving along, got a rhythm going on, and then, bam, a nut won't crack. Look at this stubborn little bitch here. What to do, right? Do I work this mother over until it gives it up?" Deja held open her jacket to show Gibson the gun holstered under her arm. "I know I smash it with Roscoe here, it'll sure enough open right quick, but for what? Everything inside be smashed too. Seems foolish. Got me thinking—Deja, there got to be a better option."

"You could let it go. You have a whole bag there. Why get hung up on one?"

"The pragmatic choice. One way to go." Deja contemplated the pistachio. "'Americans don't want to think. They want to know.' My man John Dewey said that. Me? I think Americans don't want to know. They want to believe. Want to feel. That's why I can't be throwing away no stubborn pistachio. 'Cause then I gotta be thinking about it. Wondering what's inside that make it be that way. Afraid if I don't find out, when I pull the next one out of the bag that I make the same mistake again. My people gotta *believe* that won't happen. You understand what I'm saying?"

A nurse stuck her head in the door to say that visiting hours were ending in fifteen minutes. They acknowledged her without breaking eye contact with each other. Judge Hammond Birk snored softly between them.

"I think you made that point loud and clear already," Gibson said.

"Weren't nobody home. Ain't nobody got dead. Can't say the same for my crew in West Virginia, you feel me?"

"So what now?"

"Your house . . . that what the government call a proportional response."

"Is that what that was?" Gibson said.

"That's what it is. And that's the way it can stay."

"If . . . ?"

"If I think we understand each other. See here, the danger of a proportional response is it embolden the ahistorical motherfucker. You ahistorical, Gibson Vaughn? You think you an innocent who been wronged? Thinking on revenge? Or you know your history? Admit hostilities began with you and recognize the proportionality herein?"

"If I do, then I get to walk out of here?"

"Your boy Swonger alive, ain't he?"

"Yeah, but you needed the farm. He works for you."

"Why? You want to come work for old Deja?" she said with a sly smile.

"I don't do that kind of work anymore."

Deja tossed the keys to his Yukon over the bed. "Yeah, inspiring how you gone straight."

The keys bounced off his hand, and he bent to pick them up. When he sat back up, Deja was standing and sweeping a pile of pistachio shells into a trash can.

"So what's it to be, Gibson Vaughn?" Deja asked.

It was funny. While he'd been busy plotting revenge on Damon Ogden, Deja Noble had been doing the same to him. He supposed Duke would make the case for retaliation. But Gibson didn't see what good it would do. It wasn't as if taking Ogden had fixed anything.

But he was avoiding the issue at hand. He'd made a promise to Gavin Swonger to leave Deja be. "Proportional," he said. "It was proportional."

"And I won't see you down VA Beach without an invitation."

"I don't even like the beach."

Deja nodded. "Yeah, it ain't healthy down there for pale white boys. All right, be cool now. Drive safe."

"Can I ask you a question?"

"You can ask one."

"Did it make you feel better?"

Deja considered it. "No. Felt worse. But feeling better ain't even the point."

"So what is?" Gibson asked.

"Moving forward. Only reason to do anything."

When Deja was gone, Gibson gathered up his empties but left the last bottle of RC Cola on the nightstand on the off chance that the judge remembered himself long enough to drink it. He squeezed the judge's shoulder and promised that he'd be back. At the front desk,

Gibson signed out of the logbook. Missing from the parking lot was the blue Yukon, but, two spots up, his silver Yukon had magically returned.

He slid behind the wheel. On the dashboard sat a threadbare Phillies baseball cap. Gibson turned it over in his hands and looked at the faded initials written into the red brim. "SDL"—Suzanne Davis Lombard. Bear's cap. He'd given it to Swonger for safekeeping before driving Merrick to the airfield that night in West Virginia. Had some part of him known then that he wouldn't be coming back? He didn't have much connecting him to his old life, and this old cap was an important reminder of where he'd come from. He tossed it in the backseat. That didn't mean he deserved to wear it anymore.

"Of course you do," Bear said. "That hat belongs to you. Put it on."

Gibson started the Yukon without answering.

"So you feel like taking Ogden 'moved you forward'?" Bear asked.

"What are you talking about?"

"I'm talking about what Deja Noble said."

"Were you eavesdropping?"

Bear ignored the question. "You don't feel better, do you? You're getting worse again."

"I'm just being tested."

"Tested?" Bear said, incredulous. "That's not how mental illness works."

"How would you know? You are mental illness."

"You're being mean."

"Everything will be better on Tuesday."

"Why? Because your dad says so? Where is he anyway? Notice how I'm the only one here these days? He abandoned you. That's what he does."

Gibson was instantly angry. "That's not fair."

Bear raised her hands, admitting she'd gone too far.

"Aren't you coming?" he asked.

"I'll see you at home."

"Bear, come on. Don't be like that."

"You still have the steering wheel," Bear said. "You're not spinning yet. There's still time."

She left him with that to chew over. Gibson took it slow on the way home, the memory of the spinout causing him to ease off the accelerator. He still arrived home in time for the second half of the Packers game. He'd never had any interest in football, but he rooted for Mrs. Nakamura's team to be a good guest. He fell asleep during the fourth quarter and woke around ten to the amused expression of his landlady. Hungry but too tired to do anything about it, Gibson excused himself and stumbled downstairs to sleep. He had another double at the diner in the morning. One more day until he knew if the plan had been for nothing.

CHAPTER SIXTEEN

On Tuesday morning, Gibson loaded the industrial dishwasher but kept one eye on the clock. 11:07. By now, Ogden's absence from work would have been noticed and logged. No panic at first. Even employees of the CIA had car trouble. But in the next hour they would begin making calls. When they couldn't reach him directly, Ogden's superiors would work their way down his emergency contact list. Someone would be dispatched to check his home. But it wouldn't be until Ogden's girlfriend revealed the texts from Friday night about being called back to the office that the Agency would hit the panic button. That's when Gibson would find how good the CIA really was.

Gibson had never held an especially high opinion of the CIA. During his time in the Marines, he'd always found Agency people insufferable and undeservedly arrogant. Much of that, he recognized, was sibling rivalry. The CIA wasn't held in the highest regard by the men and women of the Marine Corps Intelligence Support Activity. The CIA, hatched from the Office of Strategic Services after World War II, had for a time enjoyed being the only show in town. But in the modern era, the United States had an ever-expanding intelligence community with often overlapping responsibilities that required justifying their existence to Congress. It made for a competitive, jealous family.

The Activity had been founded precisely because the military viewed the CIA as selfish—a former only child that had never learned to play or share well with others.

None of that meant Gibson underestimated how seriously the CIA would treat the disappearance of one of their own. They had the resources to move heaven and earth to find Ogden. The only question was whether an abandoned power plant in Northern Virginia was in either one of those places.

Gibson threw on his coat and went out back to take his break. The fresh air felt good. He did not. Dreams of his revenge had sustained him during his ordeal, but it was time to admit the truth. He'd done what he and Duke had set out to do; it hadn't fixed him. If anything, he'd been getting worse all weekend, the symptoms of his madness returning with a vengeance. Like ants swarming over a discarded scrap of meat, the edge of his vision had been overrun and clouded. His thoughts were again becoming murky and indecipherable. The only time he felt decent was when the noise from the dishwasher drowned out his thoughts.

He'd been making excuses since throwing the dead bolts on Ogden's cell. Stalling. But if he'd beaten Damon Ogden, if he'd won like he kept telling himself he had, then why didn't it feel like a victory? He expected Bear to say she'd told him so, but, like Duke, she had disappeared. He called her name quietly, hoping she might hear him and come talk it over with him. But that had never been how it had worked; he was on his own. Gibson went back inside and got back to work. He still had a lot of dirty dishes to clean.

No longer concerned with establishing an alibi, Gibson shifted into the next phase of his operation: act natural, do nothing, and don't go anywhere near Ogden. Gibson performed his one-man show about a normal guy just trying to put his life back together, unsure if he had an audience but assuming he was playing to a packed house. He divested himself of anything that connected back to Ogden—burner phones and laptop were all scrubbed and discarded. He went to work. He went home. He applied for jobs that he'd never get. In the afternoons, he went to the movies—it would look odd if his routine changed immediately after Ogden vanished. Externally, his act looked compelling enough, but internally, doubts continued to fester and multiply. As did the feeling that his tenuous grasp on sanity was slipping once more.

The days dragged past.

He got it in his head that his food was being drugged and stopped eating. He took to sleeping on the floor of his bathroom with the door locked. The white walls reminded him of the cell, and it humiliated him to admit how safe it made him feel. He was desperate to know what was happening and how Ogden's disappearance was being investigated, but he resisted the urge to type his name into a search engine. By now, the NSA's computers would have added "Damon Ogden" to their index of keywords and would be scanning Internet traffic worldwide. If Ogden's name started popping up in searches originating from a coffee shop in Northern Virginia, that would change the focus of the investigation immediately. All of Gibson's misdirection would be for naught. So in the evenings, he was reduced to watching the local news and reading the papers, hoping for any mention of Ogden's disappearance.

On Thursday, almost a week after taking Ogden, Gibson found a brief article in the *Washington Post* Metro section about a missing Vienna, Virginia, man named Damon Ogden. It was short on specifics and more interesting for what it left out than for what it included. No mention of Ogden's employer. No suspicions of foul play. Only that his car had been found at an airport near Dulles. The low-key story was a long way from the breathless coverage a missing CIA officer would get splashed across cable news networks. Obviously, the CIA was playing the disappearance close to the vest and weren't ready to involve the media in any meaningful way. Gibson couldn't decide if that was a good sign or not. He just had to wait and wonder if he'd pulled it off. Wait for them to come at him . . . then he would know.

As it turned out, he had to wait only one more day. Friday afternoon after the lunch rush, Toby whistled sharply over the throb of the dishwasher. He did not look happy.

"That policeman is back."

Gibson snapped to attention. "What does he want?"

"He ordered pie, but that's not what he came for."

"Great."

Gibson frowned, hoping it concealed his delight. The appearance of Detective Bachmann represented the best-case scenario. The CIA would handle the bulk of the investigation internally, but they would need help sorting through secondary leads. For those, Langley would tap the FBI for assistance. Then there were the mutts. The leads that no one expected to pan out but that needed to be chased down anyway. Those would be tasked to local PDs. Gibson had expected that he'd wind up in one of those three baskets. It was inevitable, given his history with Ogden. The only question had been which basket. And now he had his answer.

Gibson found the detective sitting in a booth, enjoying a slice of apple pie. He took a seat opposite. Bachmann ignored him and continued savoring his pie. Gibson waited patiently for the games to begin and thought over what he thought he knew.

If he were a serious suspect, the CIA wouldn't have farmed him out to local police. They'd have either come at him a lot harder or, more than likely, not at all. They'd have sat back, set up surveillance, and waited and watched. They wouldn't have sent a cop to tip their hand for nothing. At this stage, the likeliest scenario was that the timing of Gibson's release and Ogden's disappearance had been noted. One of hundreds of leads, names, and angles to be sifted through, interviewed, and eliminated. Jim Bachmann had drawn that thankless task.

It made sense. Bachmann would have been tapped because he'd interviewed Gibson after his arrest. That gave the detective a pretext for this friendly chat over pie. He would lead with the house fire, starting in the past, but Bachmann was here for Ogden and would work the conversation around to the present. Gibson figured that his best bet was to play irritated and harassed but ultimately be helpful. And when Bachmann finally asked him about last weekend, Gibson would use it as a chance to lay out his alibi.

Bachmann made a satisfied noise and tapped the pie meaningfully. "I never order pie. Sometimes you don't know what you're missing."

"Don't you have any current cases?"

"I could have been enjoying pie all this time."

"Well, you have your whole life ahead of you."

"I do, don't I? That's a comforting thought," Bachmann said. "Gives me a reason to stop in regularly." He took another bite and pointed the fork in Gibson's direction. "You don't look so good."

"Been sick. Haven't been sleeping."

"Mhmm," Bachmann said noncommittally. "Any closer to telling me where you were the night your ex-wife's house went up?"

"I know where I wasn't."

"Be nice if it worked like that."

"Wouldn't it," Gibson agreed.

"How about lately?" asked Bachmann.

That didn't take long. "What about it?"

"A neighbor told your ex-wife that she saw a man matching your description on her front porch."

"What are you implying? That I zipped out to Seattle so I could lurk around my ex-wife's porch?"

"Did you?" Bachmann asked.

"This is pretty damned thin."

"Then you won't mind accounting for your whereabouts?" No mention of when, baiting Gibson to see if natural defensiveness would cause him to slip up and fill in that blank for Bachmann. A nice move.

Gibson spread his hands questioningly. "Where I was when?"

"Let's start with this past weekend. A show of good faith. Go a long way to keeping that resisting-arrest charge in my drawer."

Gibson sighed and cast his eyes down in defeat. "When?"

"Start with Friday."

Gibson took a breath, slowing himself. He didn't want to sound too eager. "I worked all day."

"Then what did you do?"

Gibson walked the detective through his entire alibi. Kept going right into Tuesday, but Bachmann cut him off. Gibson sat there while Bachmann finished scribbling notes. Bachmann took him through it again, asking questions, clarifying details. Gibson couldn't tell if the detective bought his story, which irritated him. That was all right. Being irritated fit the profile.

"What are you trying to pin on me now?" Gibson asked.

Bachmann studied him over the table. "You got something you want to tell me? Now would be the time. While I can still help you."

"I didn't burn the house down," Gibson said, intentionally misunderstanding the lifeline Bachmann was throwing him.

"All right. Have it your way."

"Have what my way?"

Bachmann stood and put his card on the table. "In case you think of anything." Then he pointed at the pie. "Get that for me."

On his way out, Bachmann stopped to ask Toby a few questions— no doubt verifying Gibson's shifts from the weekend. The detective shook Toby's hand and glanced back in Gibson's direction. Gibson waved. For the second time in a week, he'd won an important battle. And for the second time in a week, it felt like a loss. A Pyrrhic victory. Revenge hadn't fixed anything. Getting even with Damon Ogden was a sideshow, nothing more. He'd been crazy to think otherwise.

Maybe he'd had to take Ogden in order to know? It had felt better planning it than doing it, that much he knew. And having done it, and knowing that it hadn't fixed anything, he didn't know what to do about it. Even if he wanted to, he wasn't sure there was a way to walk it back. He'd made the bed he now lay in, and had lit it on fire too, for good measure.

On the way home, a squad car pulled in behind Gibson. He didn't think anything of it at first, but it stayed on his bumper even after he made a turn. A voice in his head urged him to floor it and make a run before the police had him completely boxed in. He resisted the temptation, even as the police stayed behind him for five more blocks.

He pulled off into a convenience store parking lot. The prowler followed. A second police car was already there. Was it waiting for him? How did they know that he'd pull over here, the voice asked. Gibson mimed a phone call, hand shaking, and lingered behind the wheel. The two officers chatted with each other, too smart to look Gibson's way. They strolled into the convenience store, talking animatedly between themselves. Neither looked Gibson's way as he backed slowly out of his spot. He kept an eye on the rearview mirror to make sure he wasn't being followed.

"You're being paranoid," Bear said from the passenger seat.

"Where have you been? I needed you."

"I'm here. I'm always here."

"I don't know what to do."

She looked at him pityingly. "Stop this," she said. "While there's time."

"I don't know how."

"He doesn't know who took him," she reminded him.

That was true. He couldn't undo the kidnapping, but that didn't mean Ogden had to stay kidnapped. If Gibson released him, what would Ogden really know for certain?

Could it be that simple?

CHAPTER SEVENTEEN

Under ideal circumstances, the evening rush hour around Washington, DC, was a snarled clusterfuck. It began as early as three in the afternoon and didn't taper until after seven. Toss in a steady "wintery mix"—weatherperson jargon for sleet, snow, and freezing rain—and traffic quickly went from bad to war crime. For reasons that defied easy explanation, DC drivers were notoriously awful at driving in the elements. Most reacted to snow as if seeing it for the very first time, either driving so cautiously as to be a danger or so fast that they became rudderless torpedoes the first time they tapped the brakes. Gibson had taken one look at the forecast and thanked his lucky stars. He was breaking his cardinal rule tonight, and he couldn't have asked for better weather.

Up ahead, a light went from green to yellow. Gibson watched a car fishtail miraculously to a stop without hitting anything. The driver looked around with a sheepish grin at his good luck. Judging by the GPS, not everyone was enjoying so blessed an evening commute. Gibson's traffic map showed most roads highlighted in red, yellow icons indicating accidents continuing to multiply. Fat snowflakes danced before his headlights. Good. Let it snow. Accidents and heavy snow gave him his best odds. He glanced in the rearview mirror; it had become a nervous tic since Bachmann's visit to the diner. Gibson doubted he could spot a tail if he had one, or lose one even if he did. But getting lost in the maelstrom of a winter's rush hour? That he could do.

He'd waited until after five p.m. to leave the diner. Traffic was already hopelessly knotted, and for the last hour he'd been in an endless cycle of stop-start, stop-start, one car length at a time, mile after mile. Visibility was down to about thirty feet, but after the sun went down, it dropped to a single car length. Gibson began switching lanes, getting on and off the beltway, doubling back again and again. If someone could follow him in this, they deserved to catch him. Around eight p.m., he pulled into a parking garage in downtown Bethesda and took a walk around the block. He bought a cup of coffee at a Dunkin' Donuts. He sat in the shop window, sipped his coffee, and waited.

Since Detective Bachmann's most recent visit, Gibson's thoughts had turned more and more to the past. To that brief, shining moment when he'd lived his best life. Near the end of his time in the Marines, when his work for the Activity had earned him praise and respect from the higher-ups, his marriage to Nicole had been rock solid, and Ellie had been the perfect, hyperactive cherry on top. With the clarity that only ever came too late, he saw the moment that he took his first meandering, careless step away from that life. He saw the subsequent fumbling steps that had been supposed to lead him home but only compounded his misery. The steps that had led him here. Steps that continued to lead him further and further away from anything that might reasonably be called a good life.

Wouldn't life be better if, like a video game, you could simply reload an earlier save and relive a decision until you made the right one? A foolish, Dickensian fantasy shared by all those who had reduced their failures to one decisive moment. Life wasn't a video game, and wishing wouldn't make it so. But he realized that, in a way, a video-game philosophy had crept into his thinking. All these unwinnable battles. He'd squandered the last few years struggling to reclaim his mythologized best life instead of working toward the best that life still had to offer him. He was still a young man; there should still be time. But there might not be opportunity.

At least not so long as Damon Ogden remained locked in that cell. Taking him had been a mistake. Gibson accepted that now. Ogden's imprisonment would never give him back what had been taken, would never heal him, would never even the score. Damon Ogden had to be freed. The question was how. Gibson's only advantage was that Ogden knew neither the identity of his abductor nor where he was being held. It needed to stay that way. Unfortunately, that eliminated the simplest approach: an anonymous tip that led to Ogden's cell. The cell would give investigators a crime scene to scour that would undoubtedly turn up a variety pack of Gibson Vaughn DNA. Ogden would have to be moved, which would violate the first commandment of his plan: stay away from Ogden for at least three months.

Unless he'd blundered badly, the name Gibson Vaughn should still be no more than a single data point in a sea of information that investigators were sifting through. Chances were remote that they'd initiated surveillance on him, but, in the end, that was nothing but supposition—he had no way to be sure. And if wrong, he'd lead investigators straight to Ogden, in which case his goose would be cooked and then shot twice for good measure. But that would simply be a chance he'd have to take. Couldn't go back, couldn't stand still, the only choice to move forward.

Through the front window, Gibson glanced up and down the block. Nothing suspicious jumped out at him; it was now or never.

––––––

The power plant rose ghostly against the night. Snow swirled around the plant's four smokestacks. It looked quite beautiful in a broken way. A medieval fortress standing vigil over some lost wilderness.

Gibson drove around back, took the keys from the ignition, and sat behind the wheel, listening to the wind. He half expected helicopters and a SWAT team to materialize out of the night sky. The snow continued to fall. He racked the slide of his gun, chambering the only round, and slipped it into his belt. One round would be all he'd need if he was indeed walking into a stakeout. No one else would suffer for his mistake.

In the Yukon's headlights, he saw Duke Vaughn waiting at the basement door. He'd changed into a charcoal suit and looked ready to go to battle with Senate foes across the aisle.

"Where have you been?" Gibson demanded. He couldn't believe his dad had the nerve to show up now after leaving him to twist in the wind.

"Don't do this, son. Don't lose faith now."

"Faith? You're not a priest. You're a figment of my imagination."

"These things take time," Duke said.

"Yeah, it's always another day. One more thing. Isn't it? It's bullshit."

"If you go in there, you're throwing away everything we've worked for."

"*We've* worked for?" Gibson said. "You abandoned me. I needed you. I've been all alone."

Duke didn't cede an inch. "You'll never feel normal again. Do you want that?"

"I don't want to be this man, Dad. I must have been crazy to listen to you."

"Well, now you're just throwing me softballs," Duke said with a grin.

"It was a mistake," Gibson said, peeling back the tape around the door. It was all intact and untouched. A reassuring sign. He turned on his lights and went down the steps. A thin coat of dust had settled undisturbed along the hall. Nothing seemed amiss. His feet echoed down the stairwell.

Duke waited at the first turn, shaking his head. "Please think this through. I raised you to be better than this."

"I'm not your son. You're not real. You're dead."

"As if you care."

Gibson took a wild swing at the thin air where he saw his father. He stumbled and almost fell.

"Strike one," Duke said. "Feel better?"

Gibson put a finger to his lips in a shushing gesture.

"Oh, knock it off," Duke said. "He can't hear me."

"You had your chance. Leave me alone."

"It's not that simple," his father said as Gibson brushed past him.

Outside the cell door, Gibson retrieved his gear from the cubbyhole and did an equipment check: stun gun, syringe, zip ties, hood. Through the peephole, Ogden stood motionless in the center of the room, staring intently at the door, Gibson's footfalls having announced his arrival. Apart from the beginnings of a beard, Ogden appeared unchanged by his brief imprisonment. One of the cases of food had been torn into, but the cell itself was well tended. Gibson read over the printed instructions on the white sheet of paper he carried:

You're going home today. Lie facedown on the ground, hands behind your head. If you move or speak, we'll try this again in a month.

Satisfied, Gibson knelt to slip the note under the door.

"Gibson Vaughn," Ogden said through the door, his voice full of authority and purpose. Gibson remembered that about him from West Virginia. Despite having been tortured and shot in the leg, Ogden had still talked as if he were in total control.

Gibson froze, staring stunned at the door.

"Vaughn. I know it's you out there."

Gibson stumbled away from the door and sat down hard with his back against the wall. How had he given himself away? He'd been so thorough.

"Took me a while to figure it out, but I have nothing but time, thanks to you. I asked myself, who would kidnap a CIA officer but ask no questions? It was a pretty short list. Plus, the cell is kind of a dead giveaway."

Gibson shut his eyes and cursed silently. There went plan A. If he released Ogden now, he would be in custody within hours.

"Got to say, I did not see you coming," Ogden continued. "Completely underestimated you. Should have given more credence to your military record. And you have to tell me how you found me; I'm dying to know. All the way around, an impressive operation. But what's your endgame? You're one man. You know how many people are looking for me right now? How long before they find you? What then? I don't know what point you're trying to make, but consider it made. What happened to you was regrettable, but I'd do it again. I won't apologize for doing my job. You were involved with the bin Laden operation. You more than most should understand that sometimes there's collateral damage in this world. I know it stings when it's our turn, but this? This isn't going to end well for you.

"Talk to me. We can work something out. You do know the sentencing guidelines for kidnapping a representative of the United States government, don't you? The Patriot Act is very specific about it. So talk to me. We come to some kind of accommodation, I'll put in a good word for you. Maybe save you from the worst of it. Unless, of course, you like needles."

Gibson reached for his gun and held it gingerly in both hands. There was always plan B. He wondered what the muzzle would feel like pressed to his temple.

He pushed the thought away and holstered the gun. He wasn't thinking clearly. What he needed was time to come up with an alternative. Ogden would be okay for another week. Gibson stood and went back up the stairs. Ogden heard him leaving and began barking his name, ordering him to come back. Then pleading. Then silence. Outside, the wintery mix had turned to regular old rain.

CHAPTER EIGHTEEN

After the debacle at the power plant, Gibson's grip on sanity continued to erode. More and more, his vigilance descended into paranoia. Every vehicle became a possible tail, anyone glancing in his direction a possible undercover. Unfamiliar faces at the Nighthawk looked suspicious. Gibson knew he was becoming irrational but couldn't control himself. It wore at his nerves, and he felt himself becoming twitchy. If Detective Bachmann came back for another friendly chat, Gibson didn't know if he could hold it together.

After his lengthy absence, Duke Vaughn seemed determined to make up for lost time. He hadn't left Gibson's side for a moment. A constant, glowering presence, Duke never gave his son a moment's peace. At work. At the movies. More and more talk, until Gibson couldn't even follow the story. He couldn't hold a conversation without Duke interrupting. At night, Duke stood over him, waiting to pick up where he'd left off when Gibson opened his eyes in the morning.

Nothing Gibson did brought him peace. He tried reasoning with Duke. When that had no effect, he pleaded with the ghost for mercy. Then he resorted to yelling back, which only succeeded in making him feel like the lunatic he was. Finally, Gibson lapsed into a monastic silence, trying and failing to ignore his father. How do you tune out a voice that started and ended in your own head? It was almost as if the old political hand were trying to filibuster Gibson's life.

It was working.

After days of trying to think of a solution, Gibson was still no closer to resolving the Ogden situation. So far he had four vague and unsatisfactory options—release Ogden, kill Ogden, kill himself. Or some combination of the above. One morning, after a restless night on the floor, a fifth option occurred to him. He could run, and tip off Ogden's people once he was off the grid. Not that there was such a place, not anymore. Bin Laden had proven that. If they wanted him badly enough, they would always be able to find him. And Gibson imagined they'd want him pretty bad. It would be a dangerous precedent for Langley to set, allowing someone who'd kidnapped one of their people to remain a free man.

Gibson made a circuit of his tiny apartment and checked to see if the strips of Scotch tape on the windows and front door were all undisturbed. All part of his paranoid morning ritual. Some people made coffee; Gibson made sure the CIA hadn't broken in while he slept. He really ought to write the adhesive-tape people a thank-you note. They probably hadn't considered do-it-yourself alarm system among its possible applications.

He peered out through the thin floral curtains that decorated the small window in his front door. Before he got in the shower, he liked to check the street. It helped calm him enough to get ready for work. A black SUV with tinted windows idled at the curb behind his Yukon.

"What are you doing now?" Duke asked.

"There's somebody out there."

"Oh, right, that would be the CIA."

"Why didn't you say anything?" Gibson heard the panic in his voice.

"What, are we on the same side now?"

"What do they want?"

"I told you not to go back to the power plant."

"No, actually, you didn't," Gibson said.

"Well, it was implied."

From this angle, Gibson couldn't see the plates, but the whole getup felt distinctly government issue. Although it didn't make any sense, them sitting there out in the open like that. Gibson figured they'd either surveil him or arrest him. Why tip their hand otherwise?

Duke leaned in to take a look for himself. "Flushing game."

"How's that?"

"They want you to break cover. They're trying to spook you."

"Well, it's working."

"Relax, kid, if they had something, they'd have driven a tank through your door already."

This was a true fact. "So what do I do?"

"I don't know . . . cowering here seems to be working pretty good so far."

Gibson felt suddenly vulnerable standing there in his socks and boxers. Ignoring Duke again, he went to find clothes, deciding the best course of action with the men outside was obliviousness. If they had him, they had him, and there wasn't anything he could do about that. Otherwise, he needed to stick to the plan. He reminded himself how he'd almost freaked out when the cop had followed him. *Don't over-react.* Maybe it was nothing but a parent waiting to pick up a carpool kid for school.

"Oh, I'm sure that's exactly what it is," Duke said.

Gibson locked his door and walked out to his car. Duke followed after taunting him with paranoid warnings of what would happen next. When the front doors of the black SUV popped opened, Duke chuckled. Two men in suits stepped out to meet him. Gibson scanned the street for their backup, resisting the urge to bolt. Instead, he planted his feet and let them come to him.

The driver, the older of the two, was white with bulldog eyes and a disappointed mouth. Broken blood vessels fanned up his nose like a map of the Amazon. He came around the car and joined his partner, a tall Sikh who wore a black turban that slanted down across his eyebrows and covered his ears. Unlike his partner, he glowed with good health. A lush black beard framed his imperial face, and his mustache came to manicured points. The bulldog held up a hand halfway between a greeting and a caution.

"Mr. Vaughn. A word?"

"I'm on my way to work." Gibson didn't know why he wasn't face-down and handcuffed already, but he would play along.

"How is the dishwashing business?" the bulldog asked.

His younger partner stared off into the middle distance, smiling as if remembering a funny line from the movie he'd watched only last night. It did little to endear him to Gibson.

"What do you want?"

"We'd like you to take a ride with us."

"Do you have a warrant?"

"We're not law enforcement, Mr. Vaughn."

Gibson didn't know whether to be relieved or not. The partner's smile broadened into a mirthless grin. He had the whitest teeth that Gibson had ever seen in real life.

"So who are you guys?" Gibson asked.

"My name is Cools," the bulldog said. "This is Mr. Sidhu."

"What kind of name is Cools?"

Cools blinked. "Belgian. So what do you say?"

"I say I'm going to be late for work," Gibson said.

"Take a ride," the older man said, as if reasoning with an uncooperative child. "We'll bring you right back after. Dishes will still be dirty."

"Where are we going?"

"Into the city to see an old friend."

"Who?" Gibson asked.

"Calista Dauplaise."

Served him right for wondering how his situation could get any worse. For the first time since the power plant, Duke Vaughn stopped talking. And for the first time since the power plant, Gibson's head cleared enough for him to think without it hurting.

"Oh, that old friend," Gibson said.

"What do you say? She just wants to catch up."

Gibson was pretty sure catching up was the last thing Calista wanted. But she wanted something, and that was reason enough to take a ride into the city. After Atlanta, they'd struck an uneasy truce. A truce that he regretted, even if he knew it had been the pragmatic decision. It had held for two and a half years, until just this minute. Article one—stay out of the other's way. If Calista was risking the status quo, Gibson needed to know why. She wouldn't go away, and he'd rather see her coming than waste time looking over his shoulder. He was doing enough of that as it was.

"Do I have a choice?" Gibson asked.

"A choice?" Cools asked. "Sure. You get to choose whether you get in the car under your power or ours."

"You really want to make a scene out here?"

"There won't be a scene," Mr. Sidhu said, speaking for the first time. He held open the back door of the SUV. Gibson saw no option but to play along.

Calista Dauplaise lived in a mansion built by her great-great-great-grandfather, Alexandre Dauplaise, in the aftermath of the War of 1812. His wife, Sophie, had christened the house Colline—Little Hill—upon her arrival from France. Seated at the top of Georgetown, it had been home to one of the oldest families in Washington going on three centuries now. Calista's ancestors had played a historic role in the nation's rise as statesmen, generals, and diplomats. A role that had waned in recent years, although Calista was singularly devoted to restoring her family to prominence. If only Duke Vaughn had intuited the ruthlessness of that devotion, how different life might be now. When Duke had threatened her plans, she had dispatched a monster to murder him, staging it as a suicide in the basement of the family home.

Gibson had been fifteen the day he tiptoed down the steps and saw his father's feet dangling in the air. Calista had sent the monster back for Gibson a decade later when he'd dug too deeply into Bear's disappearance. A strange little man with eyes at home in the dark and a voice that lacked several essentially human chromosomes. Gibson touched the scar across his throat, remembering the sound of the stool clattering across the floor and the way the rope bit into his neck. He'd be buried alongside his father had Jenn Charles and Dan Hendricks not come to his rescue.

Despite all that, when the time came, Gibson had made peace with Calista Dauplaise to protect Bear's daughter. It had been a hard deal to stomach, but he'd sided with the living over the dead, chosen to save an innocent girl before avenging his father. He wouldn't change that decision even if he could, but that didn't mean he'd ever felt entirely good about it. The guilt was a punishing weight. It fueled the twisted version of Duke that even now sat beside him in the backseat with murder in his eyes. Part of Gibson wished he hadn't stashed his gun out at the power plant; another part worried what might happen if he had it now.

"What should have happened three years ago," Duke said.

Gibson slumped back and wondered what could possibly tempt Calista to break the truce and invite him to her home. He was no closer to an answer when they crossed Arlington Memorial Bridge, the Lincoln Memorial rising up to greet them. They looped down onto Ohio Drive, which briefly became I-66 before they exited onto Pennsylvania Avenue at the south end of Georgetown. Crossing Rock Creek, they took a right and disappeared up the hill into the labyrinthine heart of old Georgetown.

Here we go, he thought.

"Here we go," Duke agreed.

A black, wrought-iron fence capped with golden spear points rose up on the right. Through the trees that edged the property, he glimpsed the house itself, an imposing, perfectly symmetrical Federal the length of a city block. That one woman called it home was almost enough to make Gibson consider communism.

A pair of uniformed guards stopped the SUV at the new gatehouse. It had been completely rebuilt since the last time he'd been here. Where before it had served a largely ornamental function, the new front gate looked capable of repelling an armored assault. Gibson counted a half dozen security cameras. All it lacked was a moat. Something or someone had put the fear of God into Calista. He didn't mind that at all.

At the top of the sloping drive, they circled the fountain that dominated the center of the driveway. Curving white quartz steps, thirty feet across at their widest point, led up to a towering front door. They stopped at the bottom, and Sidhu held the door for him again. The butler met them at the door. Gibson remembered him from the day that he'd come for Catherine, Bear's daughter. The butler remembered him as well.

"Hullo, sir. So good to see you again. Would you care for a beverage? Beer, isn't it?"

"Good memory, Davis, but a little early for me."

"If you insist, sir. May I take your coat?"

Davis ushered Gibson and his two chaperones down a high-ceilinged hallway. On one side, glass doors faced out onto the terrace that overlooked the gardens; on the other hung an art collection that would have stopped Toby Kalpar in his tracks—canvases by Winslow Homer, Henry Bacon, John Singer Sargent, among others. They passed through a door and into an antechamber where a fastidious, bespectacled man sat typing briskly at an antique desk. Jazz played soothingly in the background from speakers that Gibson couldn't see. Without looking up from his keyboard, the man instructed them to sit in an accent that Gibson's ear could narrow no further than West African. Cools and Sidhu did as they were told. Gibson followed suit.

"Who is he?" Gibson asked.

"Ms. Dauplaise's secretary," Sidhu explained.

The secretary glared at them over his glasses. "Quiet, please, gentlemen. There's no talking."

"Why don't you go fuck yourself with that?" Gibson suggested pleasantly.

The secretary froze with a satisfyingly prim, dismayed expression, then stood haughtily, five foot and maybe three hundred pounds. Gibson fixed him with a helpful smile. With a disappointed shake of his head, the secretary disappeared through a door behind his desk.

When he was gone, Sidhu spoke up. "That wasn't necessary."

"Felt necessary."

"Ms. Dauplaise only wants to talk. There's no call for profanity."

Gibson gave him a sidelong look. "Are you kidding me? Do you know who you work for? And cursing is where you draw the line? What kind of dipshittery is that?"

Sidhu began to rise, but Cools put a hand on his partner's shoulder. Reluctantly, Sidhu sat back down.

"Do not curse at me again," Sidhu said.

Gibson was weighing his options when the secretary returned and pointed to Cools and Sidhu. "She wishes to speak to you."

Gibson patted Sidhu on the knee. "Good talk."

His two chaperones followed the secretary into Calista's office, leaving Gibson alone. He wondered if this could be another of his hallucinations. Simply being back in Calista Dauplaise's home felt strange enough. But to be treated as a guest and not a prisoner . . . well, that was downright surreal. Gibson realized that Duke hadn't followed him into the house. Apparently it had taken Calista Dauplaise to drive his father away.

After a few minutes, the office door opened, and the three men returned.

"Ms. Dauplaise will see you now."

Calista's office might better have been described as a small library. Towering rosewood bookshelves encircled the room. The high ceiling necessitated a rolling ladder to access the upper shelves. The kind Gibson had only ever seen in black-and-white movies. All the books were leather-bound, and Gibson doubted he'd find one written in the last half century. At the far end of the room, an enormous printer's table dominated, completely bare apart from two brass desk lamps and a single stack of papers. Behind the desk, the curtains were drawn back on tall bay windows that let in the cool winter sunlight. In one of the window seats, Bear sat with a book open on her lap. The way she'd spent so many afternoons in Pamsrest when they were children. He didn't like her by the windows, which looked out over the gardens, at the bottom of which was a small family graveyard. Bear looked back at Gibson when he entered and smiled sadly. He shouldn't have brought her here; he just didn't know how not to do that.

In the center of the room, a pair of green leather chesterfield sofas flanked a crackling fireplace. Calista sat on one with her back to the door, a throw across her lap and her feet tucked up underneath her. On the low marble table between the chesterfields, a pot of tea steeped beside a stack of the day's newspapers and a black rotary telephone. Across the base, the phone had six square buttons, one red, the others clear for changing lines—straight out of the old spy movies that his dad loved. For a woman trying to drag her family into the new century, Calista lived a decidedly museum-quality life.

She didn't turn to greet Gibson but waited for him to circle into her line of sight. Calista did not adjust to the world; the world moved to suit her. She gave him an appraising nod, offered him a seat on the opposite sofa, and set to serving the tea. She poured two cups, to which she added milk and a single teaspoon of white sugar, all without asking if Gibson wanted tea, and if he did, how he took it. She pushed one of the cups a quarter inch in Gibson's direction and lifted the other to her lips and blew across it contemplatively. The normal timeframe to greet a guest had passed, and now they sat in awkward silence, neither inclined to be the first to speak.

It gave Gibson a moment to acclimate to being this close to Calista Dauplaise. Disappointingly, she appeared unchanged from their last encounter more than two years ago. If there were any justice in the world, recent history would have withered her. The naïve sentiment that the truly evil wore their sins on their skin. But like Dorian Gray, Calista Dauplaise must have had help to appear unblemished. One didn't look ageless at sixty-five without either medical or supernatural assistance. Gibson would have believed either.

Calista sipped her tea.

Gibson waited.

"You've lost weight," she said, breaking the deadlock. "You must tell me your secret."

As with everything Calista said, there were layers to the seeming compliment. Gibson wondered how much she knew, but, rather than take her bait, he forged ahead.

"We had a deal."

Calista set down her teacup. "And as far as I'm concerned, that arrangement stands."

"So what am I doing here?"

"Having tea."

"I hate tea," Gibson said.

"You were far more charming the first time we met."

"You want charm, maybe snatch people whose fathers you didn't kill."

Calista contemplated the wisdom of that.

"What am I doing here?" he asked a second time.

"I require your assistance," Calista replied.

Gibson put a fist to his lips but couldn't prevent the hiccup of laughter that escaped him. A full-throated laugh followed. It could have been mistaken for forced or fake, maybe it was, but he needed it to vent some of what he was feeling. It was either laugh or choke her to death. Calista's face dropped like a stone into a well. Not a woman accustomed to being laughed at, she struggled with how to respond, eventually choosing to conceal her displeasure behind her teacup. When Gibson's outburst subsided, he stood to go. That was all the catching up he had in him.

She didn't speak until he had his hand on the doorknob.

"Sit. Down."

He paused to look back at her; she still sat with her back stubbornly to the door like a parent refusing to acknowledge a child's tantrum. Gibson had used the same tactic on Ellie a time or two.

"You will want to hear this," she said.

"What?" Against his better judgment, Gibson took his hand from the doorknob.

"I am not speaking to you while you are standing behind me."

"Well, then turn your ass around."

Calista's back stiffened, but she didn't turn. He badly wanted to walk out on her, but it would be a meaningless victory, and he did want to know what was important enough for her to risk their cease-fire. He returned to the sofa where she could see him, but remained standing. Gratefully, he saw that Bear had gone from the room. He didn't want her here for this.

"All right," Gibson said. "What exactly do you need my help with?"

Calista took a sip of her tea before answering. "I need you to help me free George Abe."

CHAPTER NINETEEN

"He's alive?" Gibson asked.

Invoking the name of George Abe felt like a lure. Something Calista knew that he cared about enough to hear her out. She wasn't wrong. He'd more or less written off George after Jenn Charles had disappeared, but the mere mention of George's name sparked hope.

"More than that," Calista said, "I know who has him."

"Where is he?"

"That, I do not know," she replied.

"I knew it—" Gibson began.

Calista cut him off. "But, I do know where he will be in eight days."

Gibson sat down on the couch. She had his attention now, but he reminded himself to trust nothing that this woman said. Some of it would be true; she always built her deceptions on an honest foundation, but mixed in, often in plain sight, would be the lies and half-truths that masked her agenda. Whatever story she told him, it wouldn't be the whole picture. If he found himself believing her, he had only to remind himself that it had been Calista Dauplaise who had sent him after Bear despite knowing, from the very beginning, exactly where to find her.

"If you know where he'll be, what do you need me for? It's not as if you're short of goons, and we don't exactly trust each other."

"We certainly do not."

"So you can see where I might find that suspicious?"

Calista smiled. "Uncouth though you may be, you are a clever boy."

"And how did that work out for you the last time?"

"Poorly," Calista admitted.

"So what am I really doing here?"

"Any effort to free George Abe cannot be seen as coming from me."

Gibson understood Calista's angle now. He represented the perfect cover. Given their history, no one in their right mind would suspect they'd ever work together, and his personal relationship with George would both offer an explanation of his motives and also deflect attention away from her. Textbook Calista Dauplaise. He might be a clever boy, but she operated on an entirely different level.

"I saw all your new security. What are you afraid of, Calista?"

She pursed her lips as if tasting something that had spoiled. "Colonel Titus Stonewall Eskridge Jr."

"That cannot be a real person."

"Ordinarily, I would be inclined to agree with you."

"So who is he?"

"He is the CEO of Cold Harbor. A PMC—a private military contractor—"

"I know what a PMC is."

"Of course. Well, Cold Harbor is an especially unscrupulous one. No mean feat. Are you familiar with the organization?"

Only by reputation. And it was an ugly one. Cold Harbor was known as a small but ruthless outfit that took jobs other PMCs wouldn't touch. Took on clients that the United Nations would've preferred to see on trial in the Hague. In fact, if he remembered correctly, a couple of incidents in Africa had put Cold Harbor on the Hague's radar.

But none of what Gibson knew about Cold Harbor was current. Back when he'd served in the Marines, the Joint Chiefs had leaned on PMCs to an unprecedented degree. At least until Blackwater drove into Nisour Square in 2007. Since then, the Pentagon had retrenched its thinking on the wisdom of unleashing mercenaries over whom they exerted little operational control.

"If I am," Gibson said, "I don't remember."

"Oh, no, I will wager that you do. Colonel Eskridge was a close friend of the former vice president. Do you recall the men who attempted to seize you at the lake house in Pennsylvania?"

Gibson remembered only too well. Holed up with Jenn and Dan Hendricks in a house on Lake Erie, trying to piece together their next move. In Washington, George Abe had been arrested. Then men claiming to be FBI had rolled up to the lake house. All hell had broken loose, Jenn and Hendricks holding them off despite being hopelessly outgunned. Billy Casper had caught a bullet. It still amazed Gibson that any of them had survived the firefight.

Calista said, "They were Cold Harbor, working at the behest of Vice President Lombard."

"So Cold Harbor also took George?"

"And have held him ever since."

"Why would they keep him alive after Lombard *committed suicide* in Atlanta?" Gibson hung air quotes around "committed suicide." "Seems like an unnecessary risk."

"Ah, well, therein lies the rub. You see, dear Jennifer Charles shot and killed the leader of the Cold Harbor team."

"They all died one way or another."

"True, but that particular man's name was Titus Stonewall Eskridge the Third."

"Oh," Gibson said, fitting that into the puzzle. It was funny how one missing fact could change an entire narrative. "So Eskridge is taking it out on George?"

"Oh, heavens no. George is merely bait."

"For Jenn."

"Eskridge wants her quite badly. However, from what I gather, Jennifer Charles is a rather gifted operative, and despite his best efforts, he has yet to corner her. So they persist in this game of cat and mouse. She has made several audacious, if failed, attempts to liberate George while inflicting not inconsiderable damage to his organization over the last two years."

"How has this not made the news?"

"For the same reason that the catastrophe at the lake house went uninvestigated—Eskridge has gone to elaborate lengths to clean up after Jenn Charles. He has no interest in involving the authorities. Should he catch her, justice will be meted out in extremely personal terms. I shouldn't like to think about it. His thirst for revenge has quite unbalanced him." Calista paused just long enough for Gibson to wonder who she meant. "If you ask me, the entire affair has unflattering undertones of *Moby Dick*."

If true, Eskridge was messing with the wrong woman. Gibson smiled inwardly at the thought of Jenn Charles waging a one-woman war to free George Abe. It at least explained why she had been off the grid all this time. Still, he couldn't see how this served Calista's self-interests, and self-interests were the only interests that mattered to this woman.

"So what's Eskridge got on you?"

Calista smiled. "Prescient as ever. Colonel Eskridge has Benjamin Lombard over me. Several rather damning recordings, in point of fact. He and I differed considerably in our vision of the vice president's future, and Eskridge blames me for spoiling his plans. In a fit of pique, he threatened to release them after Benjamin took his own life—expose everything to ruin me."

"Why didn't he?"

"Because Colonel Eskridge is a pragmatic animal, or at least he was at the time. I helped him reconsider and see how valuable my connections in Washington could be to his business interests now that his patron was deceased."

"You cut a deal with Eskridge."

"Yes. A deal most unfavorable to myself, but the best I could hope for, given my tenuous bargaining position. It is an arrangement that I have tolerated for two years, however . . ." Calista paused to arrange her words. "Circumstances have changed, and my arrangement with Colonel Eskridge is no longer tenable."

"How have circumstances changed?" Gibson asked.

"That is not your concern apart from the opportunity it presents vis-à-vis George."

"Poor, dear George."

"Precisely," Calista agreed. "Colonel Eskridge has realized that the United States is no longer hospitable to his brand of PMC. He is in the process of relocating his operation to more permissive climes. Every two weeks, a Cold Harbor transport delivers personnel and equipment to Cold Harbor's new base of operations in North Africa."

"So? What does this have to do with George?"

"In eight days, George will be on that flight. Eskridge feels it will be easier to see Jenn Charles coming from Africa. Frankly, I think that girl has his number, but he's not short of confidence despite all evidence to the contrary." Calista added a thought: "In any case, this move to Africa will almost surely mean the end of poor, dear George."

"And how does this advance your cause? It's sure not poor, dear George's well-being."

"Well, no, that is your cause," Calista allowed. "But so long as George can be convinced to keep the peace, then I am willing to let bygones be bygones. Suzanne Lombard's affairs have been resolved in the best interests of all involved, and I have moved on from it." Calista paused to sip her tea. "My stake is Colonel Eskridge. You get George and simultaneously end the need for Jenn Charles to carry out a suicide mission in Africa. I get the plane. Or rather, what is on the plane."

"And what is on the plane?"

"That I do not know. But judging by the secrecy around it, Colonel Eskridge is swimming in very murky waters once more. I intend to see he drowns in them."

"What do you want from me?"

"I need you to assist my operative—"

"Operative?" Gibson interrupted sharply. If she thought he would work with the man who had killed his father and tried to hang Gibson, she was out of her damned mind.

She anticipated his concern. "No, it is not him. He has not worked for me since Atlanta. I simply need someone with your skill set to consult on this operation."

"What exactly is the objective of this operation?"

"I need the plane and its contents taken before it leaves US airspace." She said it as though it would be no harder than lifting the key to a gas-station restroom. And in eight days, no less.

"Is that all?" Gibson said incredulously.

"My confidence is commensurate to your abilities. Now, I think it best that you meet with my operative, who is waiting and will elaborate." Calista pressed a call button, and the door opened, her secretary filling it amply.

"Hold on," Gibson said. "Even if any of this is true, what makes you think I'd work for you again?"

"Self-preservation, Mr. Vaughn."

"We have a deal."

"This is a separate deal."

"How so?"

"Because the CIA is offering a substantial reward for information concerning the whereabouts of their missing man, and I have this."

Calista opened a manila folder and showed Gibson a photograph of him dragging Damon Ogden toward the power plant.

Whatever else might be true, Gibson admired Calista's discipline. Most people wouldn't have known to hold their trump card until the end. She'd allowed him to believe he controlled his fate. Believe that their conversation had been a negotiation rather than what it proved to be—a capitulation.

In a daze, he trailed Cools and Sidhu back down the long hall of Colline. His chaperones bundled him back into the SUV, and twenty minutes later, Gibson still felt like a boxer describing a knockout punch he hadn't seen coming. He couldn't even call it a sucker punch. After all, he'd prepped himself to be on his toes with Calista, and she'd still blind-sided him with ease. What the hell was he going to do now? Besides exactly what he was told.

"Never fails," Cools said. "They go in her office all tough and come out like spring lambs."

"He wasn't that tough to begin with," Sidhu said.

Cools's bulldog eyes considered Gibson in the rearview mirror. "That true, sweetheart? Were you ever tough?"

When Gibson didn't answer, Sidhu turned around in his seat. "What? Don't feel like cursing at me now?"

He really didn't.

"Where are we going?" Gibson asked.

"Reston. You have a meeting," Cools said.

Right, with Calista's operative—Gibson remembered now. He'd been a little distracted by Calista blowing up his fantasy that he'd gotten away with taking Ogden. When in fact, he'd signed over the deed to his freedom to the most dangerous person he'd ever met. Even if Gibson delivered his end, chances were that Calista would still feed him to the CIA. She'd said she needed to tidy up her affairs. Gibson certainly qualified as a mess. But he didn't see any choice but to play along for now. Hopefully something would come to him. How those chickens did love to roost.

Reston, Virginia, was an edge city founded in 1964, but hadn't boomed until 1984, when the Dulles Toll Road was finished. When

Gibson had been a kid, this had still been mostly farmland. Those days were over. Reston Town Center was about thirty minutes west of Washington, near Dulles International Airport. The thirty minutes depended on the roads being absolutely clear, which they almost never were. At rush hour, it could easily take an hour and a half.

Cools turned off into a newish development with underdeveloped trees that made the cookie-cutter houses appear even larger than they already were. There was a sameness to the landscape, and the street signs were still on back order. It made navigation tricky. Twice they stopped at the wrong house. Third time was the charm, and Cools pulled to the curb and threw the SUV confidently into park.

"Ring the bell," Sidhu advised.

"Aren't you coming in?"

"Oh, no, I don't think so," Cools said with a cold laugh. "We're not welcome."

Gibson looked up at the house uncertainly. It felt like a setup.

"Off you go. There's a good boy."

Gibson went up the walk to the house. He felt like a virgin who'd been led to the lip of a volcano. The front door sat under a small covered overhang; he rang the doorbell and stepped back into the sunshine. Seconds ticked by. He glanced back at the SUV, where his chaperones still watched. His bad feeling became a dreadful certainty that he was one of Calista's affairs about to be tidied up. He tensed at the sound of approaching footfalls, preparing to flee.

Then the damnedest thing happened.

Jenn Charles opened the door.

She looked different. They both did, of course, but Jenn looked deliberately different. Her eyes were a different color, and her black hair had been dyed blonde and cut short. Like a wolf in a lean winter, she'd shed pounds, and it showed in her face. She stood there in the doorway, letting him grapple with his surprise. Which he did by saying the dumbest thing that came to mind—simply to have something to say.

"Jenn?"

"Hi, Gibson."

"Jenn?"

"Surprise."

That was putting it mildly. "I've been looking all over for you."

"I know you have," she said with a weary smile.

"And you're in Reston?"

"You should come inside," she suggested. "Where it's warm."

It seemed a good idea, so he did.

CHAPTER TWENTY

Jenn led Gibson back to a kitchen that flowed into a great room. Everything was king-size, from the wall-mounted television to the over-stuffed couches and plush armchairs. The artwork looked as if it had been stolen from the lobby of an Indianapolis Hilton, and there were enough small pillows strewn about to build a scale replica of Stonehenge. Animal prints had made a comeback while he'd been locked away. The entire house smelled like a commercial for air fresheners—some man-made approximation of a glacial spring. A fire crackled cozily in a broad stone fireplace. This was all wrong. Jenn didn't belong here, in some subdivision in Reston, Virginia. It felt like stumbling across Amelia Earhart collecting tolls on the New Jersey Turnpike.

"Whose house is this?" Gibson asked.

"Airbnb."

"Oh, this is so weird."

"Coffee?" she asked and then turned away without waiting for an answer.

The first thing Gibson had ever noticed about Jenn Charles was her grace. She was calmer with a gun pointed at her than most people were tucked safely in bed. So the tremor in her hand when she poured the coffee caught him by surprise and made him a little sad. A reminder that change ran far deeper than the cosmetic.

"How long have you been here?"

"Couple of days."

"And before that?"

Jenn thought about it and shrugged. "Somewhere else."

"Yeah, me too."

They sipped their coffee uneasily, aware of wandering into a minefield that neither felt eager to explore.

"I should have gone with you," he said. "In Atlanta. I shouldn't have let you go after George by yourself."

"Let me?" She arched an eyebrow.

"I mean, we should have stuck together."

"Well, we didn't," she replied without it being an accusation. A simple statement of fact. She ran her fingers through her hair and rubbed the back of her neck. "Honestly, I didn't think it would be this hard."

"Still . . ." He appreciated her exonerating him, but it fell on guilt's deaf ears.

Jenn saw it in his face and came around the counter. She hugged him. His hands went around her, and he clung to her gratefully, ignoring the gun tucked against the small of her back.

"Why didn't you ask for my help?" he asked.

"Because you were doing well. Dan said that you had a good job lined up and that things were turning around for you. I didn't want to jeopardize that."

"Wait." Gibson stepped back. "When were you in touch with Hendricks?"

It was Jenn's turn to look guilty. "From the beginning."

"From the *beginning* beginning? Since Atlanta?"

Jenn nodded.

"Son of a bitch," Gibson said. "Son of a bitch." He kept saying it, hoping he'd start to feel less of a fool. It didn't help. All those phone calls had been nothing but a smoke screen. Hendricks had known all along that Jenn was alive and had left Gibson in the dark. "I'm going to kill him."

"Gibson," Jenn said. "Gibson. No, it's not Dan's fault. I told him to stand down. It was my call."

He picked up his mug and slammed it back down on the counter, slopping coffee everywhere. "Why? I thought you were dead, or worse. Do you really trust me that little?"

"That's not it," Jenn said. "That's not it at all."

"Do you know how much time I spent looking for you?"

"Yeah, I do."

"Then what the hell?"

Jenn sighed. "Because I knew you'd try to help, and I didn't want it."

Gibson would have thought that he'd graduated from hurt feelings at this point in his life, but he'd have been wrong.

"Why the hell not? Do you think I—"

"You'd done enough." She reached out and touched the scar at his throat. "We both thought you'd let it go." Jenn smiled at him. "But you're so damned stubborn. God, how Dan used to bitch at me about how he could set his watch by your calls."

"Great. I'm glad I was good for something," Gibson said bitterly.

"It meant a lot to me."

"Well, you're welcome." Gibson poured himself more coffee and took it over to the fireplace. He stood gazing into the flames. Jenn came and stood next to him. She nudged him with her shoulder.

"I should have told you," she said.

Admitting mistakes was not in Jenn Charles's blood; it surprised Gibson, but he wasn't inclined to be so easily placated. "You're damned right you should've."

"But I didn't, so quit pouting."

"Pouting?" Gibson said, not believing his ears.

"Yeah, you're pouting. Knock it off, already. I haven't seen you in two years, you big baby."

He looked at her, bracing for a fight, but she was grinning at him.

"Look, I said I was sorry."

"No, actually, you didn't."

Jenn thought about it. "Well, I meant to."

Gibson waited, but that was as close to an apology as Jenn got. And she was right, they hadn't seen each other in two years, and he didn't want to start with a fight.

"It's good to see you," Jenn said.

"Yeah, you too."

"So what happened to you?"

"What do you mean?" he asked, knowing exactly what she meant.

"I mean, you vanished. One second Dan can't get rid of you, and the next your ex-wife's house burns down and you're nowhere to be found. We thought you might be dead."

"I could say the same for you."

Jenn began to press the issue, but then her phone buzzed in her pocket. She frowned at the number and went into the next room to take the call. When she didn't return, Gibson wandered back to the kitchen to refill his coffee. Exploring, he stuck his head through a nearby door and found the dining room. Jenn had converted it into an office. A large white architectural map of Dulles International Airport had been taped to the dining room table. Arrows, circles, lists, and notes had been scrawled across the map in a variety of inks. A stack of legal pads sat beside a laptop. Gibson would have needed a laser to line up the row of multicolored Sharpies that precisely.

Casually, he reached out and jostled one of the Sharpies a quarter of an inch with his fingernail. That he knew someone well enough to mess with them like this made him happy. It felt more human than anything he'd done since his release. He cast around for another prank to play, but Jenn came back from her call.

"See you found my war room." Something in her voice told Gibson she would have rather he'd stayed in the living room.

"Tell me this airplane isn't flying out of Dulles."

"Is that a problem?"

"Dulles International Airport? Little bit, yeah."

"I thought you liked a challenge," Jenn said with false bravado. "Come on, let me show you the rest of the house."

She seemed eager to get him out of there, so he let her lead him on a tour of the upstairs. Of the four bedrooms, she'd taken the smallest for herself.

"You can take any of the others, but I had them put your stuff in here," she said, opening the last door.

"My stuff?"

Two black garbage bags and Toby's cardboard box had been set against the far wall. Gibson opened each one—it looked to be everything from his basement room.

"When?" he asked.

"An hour before you got here."

That meant they'd cleaned out his room while he'd been meeting with Calista. Further evidence of her calculating confidence. To beat him here, her people would have had to start packing him up as soon as he'd gotten into the SUV this morning. Calista had known she'd won before he even walked into her office.

"So I'm moving in?"

"That's Calista's intention. Until this is over."

"And my car?"

"It's in the garage," Jenn said.

"She's unbelievable."

"Doesn't miss a trick, does she?"

Something in Jenn's tone bothered him. He stopped rummaging through the garbage bags and looked up at her framed in the doorway. He wasn't sure how to say it.

"So I got to ask you something . . ."

"Just ask," Jenn said, a hardness creeping into her voice.

"How long have you been in bed with Calista Dauplaise?"

Jenn's eyes narrowed. "You mean, was I with her in Pennsylvania?"

"Just answer the question, Jenn. How long?"

Jenn ran her tongue over her front teeth. "About two months *after* Atlanta. She approached me, offering to bankroll my operation. She's got her reason, which is Eskridge, and I've got mine, which is George. And no, I don't trust her. But one thing they taught me at Langley is that the world is too complicated to do business only with your friends."

"Yeah, but Calista Dauplaise . . ."

"Yeah? That's pretty rich, coming from you. After everything she did to your family. Yet time came, you struck a bargain with her. Didn't you? Not that I'm not blaming you. Believe me, I understand. Sometimes all we can do is make the best deal that's on the table, and sometimes the enemy of my enemy is my friend. But don't hold me to a different standard."

"I had to ask."

"Did you?"

Jenn stalked out of the room and downstairs to the kitchen. Gibson heard the refrigerator open and slam shut. So much for not starting off with a fight.

"Yeah," Gibson said under his breath. "I've missed you too."

CHAPTER TWENTY-ONE

Reunion off to a roaring, dysfunctional start, the two took a break from each other. Jenn disappeared into the dining room, burying herself in work. Gibson left Toby a message, apologizing for missing his shift and explaining that he wouldn't be in for a couple of weeks. He left it vague, knowing this was probably his last strike with the Kalpars.

"Are you sure this is a good idea?" Bear asked after he hung up the phone.

"This is Jenn we're talking about."

"I know she's important to you," Bear said. "But you haven't dealt with the existing mess, and you're thinking about starting a whole new one. And what about Nicole's e-mail? You still need to explain. Fix things."

That had been on his mind since he'd first opened Nicole's e-mail. But he didn't know where to begin, and every time he reread what she'd written, he felt less certain. Calista's reappearance had only served to back up Nicole's argument.

"I don't see where I have a choice, Bear. If I don't play ball, Calista puts in a call to the CIA."

Unconvinced, Bear took her book and went looking for a quiet place to read. Gibson waited for Jenn to finish working, but she wasn't done being angry. He sorted through his belongings, unpacked only as much as needed, and put aside the few things that he actually cared enough about to take if he had to leave in a hurry.

Eventually, he got ready for bed. He was tired, but even with all the lights on, sleep wouldn't come for him. He crept past Jenn's door and went downstairs. Turning on the television, he surfed around until settling on a Paul Newman movie he'd never seen. Newman was driving a pickup down the sidewalk at Philip Seymour Hoffman. Unable to get comfortable on the wide, plush sofa, he curled up on the floor and watched the movie until he drifted off. He liked the background noise. A reminder that there was a world beyond these walls, and that was enough to help him sleep.

"Gibson. Gibson. Wake up."

His eyes flicked open. Jenn knelt beside him, shaking his shoulder.

"What is it?" he asked, only partially awake.

"You were screaming."

Wide awake now, he said, "I was what?"

"Screaming. Are you okay?"

He fought gravity to a sitting position and rubbed his face with both hands. "I'm sorry. Did I wake you up? I'm sorry."

"It's all right. Do you do that a lot?"

"I don't know."

He expected her to be irritated. They hadn't settled their argument before he'd gone to bed, but he saw only concern in her eyes.

Jenn said, "When you disappeared . . . Where did you really go?"

"You want the long version or the short?"

"Make it the long. I haven't had a normal conversation in ages."

"Won't be anything normal about it."

Jenn chuckled, and Gibson smiled at the implausibility of the situation. Two old friends reuniting on Calista Dauplaise's nickel. It was a tender goddamn moment. In many ways, they barely knew each other, but in other ways, ways that mattered more than Gibson could hope to articulate, this woman was the only person who might understand him.

Jenn sat on the floor beside him and waited for him to begin. At first, he was hesitant, but once he got rolling, he couldn't stop. He found he wanted to tell her the story. Needed to tell her. And as he talked, Gibson felt lighter and lighter. A wonderful, weightless relief. He couldn't think of anyone else he trusted to believe him. Jenn never interrupted but instead listened intently, letting it all tumble out. She never once looked away. He didn't think it would last, but he felt as close to right as he could remember.

The only part of the story he left out was kidnapping Damon Ogden. Jenn Charles had spent eight years in the CIA, and he doubted that even she would have much sympathy or understanding for what he'd done. After all, if he didn't, why should she?

"And then Jenn Charles opened the door. The end."

"Not if I can help it." She reached over and squeezed his hand and didn't let go. After that, they sat in silence. Side by side. She didn't ask questions. He didn't think he could say anything more. She didn't offer words of comfort, tell him she was sorry for his suffering, or promise him that things would get better. He didn't want to hear that anyway.

"Do you see them as people?" Jenn asked, referring to Bear and Duke.

He nodded. "As real as you or me."

"But you know they're not. Right? You can tell the difference."

"I do. Intellectually, I know. But . . ."

"They feel real."

"Something like that, yeah."

An old Robert De Niro movie played on the television. De Niro was in first class beside Charles Grodin, who was afraid to fly. But he wasn't really . . . it was all an act. Gibson had seen this one before; one of Duke's favorites. Gibson looked around for his father, expecting him to appear, but it was only Jenn and him. Of course, Jenn hadn't seen the movie—she was the only person he knew who made him feel hip—so they watched for a while until the tension had left the room.

"Come here," she said. "Get up on the couch."

"Why?"

"Just do it. Lie down."

"I can't sleep like that."

She stared small burn holes in his forehead until he did as she said.

"Happy?" he asked.

She climbed over him and lay behind him on the couch, fitting herself against his back. She put an arm around him and held him close to her.

"Sleep," she said. "I've got you."

He didn't remember anything after.

In the morning, Gibson woke up alone. He yawned contentedly. He felt oddly good. The best night's sleep he'd had since he couldn't say when. Since the cell. And now he no longer felt the urge to retreat back into sleep. Instead, he wanted to get up and help Jenn. Whatever she needed. He still had no idea what to do about Damon Ogden, but he believed that if he could help Jenn, it would make it easier to face the consequences of what he'd done.

"Aren't you going to fight me on this?" he asked Bear, who was watching him from across the room.

She closed her book carefully. "No, I think you're right."

"Really?" he said, failing to keep the surprise out of his voice. "You do?"

"I do."

"I think it might fix things."

"It's not going to fix anything," Bear said. "But you should help her anyway. She's your people."

Bear had a point. Jenn was his people. If only Calista had come for him before he'd taken Ogden. He laughed at the thought. Wishing that Calista Dauplaise had saved him from himself—it was pathetic. *Look forward, not back. Help Jenn. Figure out Ogden. One thing at a time.*

First up, he owed Jenn an apology.

Mind made up, he followed the smell of fresh-brewed coffee to the kitchen. He poured himself a cup and found Jenn working in the dining room. She didn't look up but carried on typing. Gibson sat down and drank his coffee. She came to the end of her thought and sat back.

"Morning," she said.

"I'm sorry," Gibson replied, not making eye contact, "about what I said yesterday about Calista. Just a lot to wrap my mind around."

"I'd want to know too."

Gibson had expected a longer discussion, but that seemed to settle the matter in her mind.

"So you want to tell me what you need me to do?" he asked.

The corners of Jenn's mouth inched downward.

"What?" he asked.

She turned to face him. "I think maybe you should sit this one out."

"What? No, I'm here to help."

"Gibson. Eskridge doesn't own kid gloves. If this goes bad, and it could, rotting in a cell would be a best-case scenario. Even if this goes good, we're going to be on the run afterward."

"Why?" Gibson asked.

"Because chances are airport security is going to know we were there. And shortly thereafter, so will the FBI and Homeland. There are simply too many cameras. Too many sets of eyes. We may not get caught in the act, but they are going to figure out what we did. And when they do, there will be serious consequences."

"So what are you going to do?"

"Take George out of the country. Lie low. Let the dust settle and see what we see."

"That's it?" Gibson was expecting something a little more elaborate.

"I've got seven days. That's it. There isn't time to plan this right. That's why I'm saying you don't have to do this. George doesn't mean to you what he means to me. I get that. You need time, Gibson. Eighteen months in solitary . . . It would cook anybody. From what you described to me, you've got serious PTSD."

"Oh, is that all?" Gibson tried to make a joke out of it. As if having a sense of humor about being crazy meant he had it under control.

"For starters."

"Look, maybe I got left in the microwave a little too long, but I'm all right. It's getting better."

"That's not good enough."

"Please. Let me help you."

"Listen to me, Gibson," she began. "I've been looking for George for over two years. In all that time, I've been close three, maybe four, times. Otherwise, I've been running from Cold Harbor. And they've gotten close seven or eight times. Damn close," Jenn said, and Gibson could see hard memories clouding her eyes. "I'm tired, Gibson. Real tired. I've been out here alone a long time. I have seven days left before my best, maybe my last, shot at getting George away from that son of a bitch. I don't have time for 'getting better.'"

"I get it, but I'm telling you: I know I can do this."

"How? At some point, we may have to be outside. How do you know you won't freak out? Or start arguing with your dead father?"

Because I kidnapped a CIA officer from his home and took him clean, Gibson thought to himself. *Or almost clean.* Instead, he said, "If I'm busy, I'm good. You just have to keep me busy."

She shook her head. "I'm trying to be a friend. Last night. The way you screamed? I thought you were dying. You're not up to this."

"Can I ask a practical question?" He went on after she grudgingly agreed. "You need a hacker, right? Who is your backup? Do you have time to replace me with someone you trust?"

Jenn frowned, clearly unhappy with the box he'd put her in. "No," she admitted.

"So let me do that much. Think of it as an audition. If I do good, you keep me on board. If not, sayonara, Gibson."

Jenn ran her tongue across her teeth, mulling it over. She didn't have a choice, and they both knew it.

He said, "Come on, quit making me beg, already. Let's get the band back together."

Jenn cracked her neck. "First off, we're not getting the band back together."

"Jenn!" Gibson said. "What do you need me to do? Give."

She sighed. "I need you to hack MWAA."

"Which would be what?"

"Metropolitan Washington Airports Authority. It leases Reagan and Dulles from the Department of Transportation. I need you to insert bogus credentials."

"For what reason?"

"To get an access badge to airport facilities at Dulles. Can you do it?"

"Sure."

Jenn smirked. "'Sure'? Just like that? You don't want to maybe do a little research first? Is that how you boys did things in the Activity?"

Gibson rolled his eyes. "I'll need a laptop. Unless interagency trash-talking is all you brought to the party."

Jenn went out to the garage and brought back a factory-sealed laptop. Nice one too. Very shiny. She cleared him a workspace on the dining room table, and then they spent the day working together side by side. Gibson thought it felt pretty good.

He started by browsing the front-facing MWAA website. It had always amazed him how helpful organizations were in contributing to their own security breaches. MWAA didn't disappoint him. He found a treasure trove of useful documents including one titled "Ronald Reagan Washington National Airport Badge Requirements" that listed credentialing requirements and procedures at both Reagan National and Dulles. He also gleaned that badges were handled by the Dulles Pass & ID Office and not airport police as he would have expected. He jotted notes on a legal pad and then settled in to work.

It had been dark for several hours when Gibson finally shut his laptop. He knew exactly how he would hack MWAA. Saw it in his mind's eye. Once again, work had cleared his head; he'd used the clarity to think through his situation generally and reached some stark decisions. He knew what had to be done about Ogden. It would hurt, but it was his only way forward. Like Deja had said, moving forward was all that mattered. He'd also decided what he needed to tell Nicole. That would be the hardest letter he'd ever written. Bear wasn't going to like it, but it needed to be done.

He nudged one of Jenn's pens out of place and went to find her.

"Well?" she asked.

"We're totally getting the band back together."

"Can you do it?"

"No problem, boss. I'll just need two things."

"Name them," Jenn said.

"A fingerprint scanner." He handed her a printout of the one he had spec'd out. "Found one on Amazon for seventy bucks."

"And second?"

"For you to admit we're getting the band back together."

"Gibson . . ."

"Fine. But I do need a round-trip ticket to Seattle."

Jenn blanched. "Why do you have to go to Seattle?"

"Who said anything about going to Seattle? I just need the ticket. Oh, and a suitcase, I guess."

The look of confusion on Jenn's face made Gibson inordinately happy.

CHAPTER TWENTY-TWO

At six in the morning, only a handful of bleary-eyed business travelers dotted the lonely concourse of Reagan National Airport. The only signs of life were the TSA checkpoints at either end of the main hall. Despite the soaring ceilings and panoramic windows, passengers rarely lingered to enjoy the view. The reason for the ticket to Seattle: Gibson expected to be here most of the day, and, if he camped out on the concourse, someone would eventually wonder what he was doing there. Better to blend in down at one of the gates. He'd parked in the long-term lot, even though he had no intention of catching his flight. His story needed to be consistent. If he drew attention from security, he was just on his way to Seattle to visit his daughter.

Gibson rolled his suitcase down to Terminal B and joined the bottleneck of business travelers catching early flights to cities like Chicago and New York. A TSA agent checked his boarding pass and ID and waved him through. Gibson grabbed a couple gray plastic bins for the conveyor belt and shuffled through the body scanner in his socks. Down at the main gate hub, he bought a coffee and found a seat far from his departure gate. A woman trying to wrangle two children glanced at him apologetically, and he smiled to let her know he wasn't bothered.

She smiled gratefully at her fellow traveler and went back to getting her kids situated.

The girl looked around Ellie's age; at least Ellie's age the last time Gibson had seen her. That had been a good day. He'd taken her to a movie and then for a banana split at the Nighthawk. The memory of her laughter made him grin. He held on to it, knowing he'd be making no new memories of his daughter in the foreseeable future. Maybe someday if he got lucky and she grew up forgiving. He thought about ditching the hack and catching the flight to Seattle after all. It was a pleasant fantasy as far as it went, but he couldn't keep the reality of his situation at bay long enough to take it seriously. With a sigh, Gibson opened his laptop and got to work.

He'd built a virtual machine on the laptop, nesting it on a Windows platform. A tool for maximizing resources on servers, multiple "virtual" machines could be run on one physical computer while keeping the data and functions completely isolated from one another. Each virtual computer had its own resources and existed completely independent of the others. There weren't many reasons to run a virtual computer on a laptop, but hacking an airport qualified. Although it took time to build, Gibson could erase all evidence of its existence in about forty seconds. If he drew unwanted attention, he could delete his virtual machine, and even if airport police seized his laptop, they would still not have the computer that had hacked them.

There were any number of programs for hacking Wi-Fi passwords, and all had plusses and minuses. Gibson preferred Aircrack-ng. The program tracked traffic to and from a router, gradually building the password from packet data. While it worked, he toggled over to the parent operating system and opened his résumé on the off chance anyone glanced over his shoulder. He sipped his coffee and waited; this was the easy part. Thirty minutes later, he logged into the Metropolitan Washington Airports Authority Wi-Fi. He was now inside their network.

To a point.

A network was a bit like a gated community, and the password only let him in the main gate. Inside were the servers, laptops, cell phones, and miscellaneous devices, each one a private residence—or network segment—that required the correct credentials. Gibson's virtual computer was uncredentialed, so he found an airport employee's computer connected to the airport Wi-Fi, attacked it, and borrowed its credentials to traverse the firewalls between network segments.

So far, so good.

Each network segment had a unique address, and his network mapper showed thousands of IP addresses connected to the MWAA network. Only the servers interested him, though, so he narrowed his search parameters. That left him with a couple hundred IP addresses to check. Still too many, but it was a start.

Security credentials would be stored in a database. SQL and Oracle were the industry standards. A quick search of the MWAA website careers page revealed that MWAA was currently hiring for a SQL database engineer. That narrowed it down. He used a port scanner called Nmap to hunt for servers that responded on 1433 and 1434, known SQL ports. This part took time because if he scanned hundreds of servers and their ports simultaneously, it would trigger alarms. Instead, he had to probe one server at a time, pausing between each. It took a few hours, but he narrowed the list to forty-six servers that responded on SQL ports.

After he missed his flight, he packed up and went to his gate. He told a tragic sob story about getting stuck in traffic on the way to the airport. Alaska Airlines ran only two daily flights to Seattle, and the second didn't depart until almost seven p.m. The gate attendant regretfully informed him it was already full but dutifully added his name to the standby list. Gibson feigned dismay at the news, but it gave him a legitimate pretext to linger at the gate for the rest of the day. All the time he would need. Gibson found a seat near the counter that let him keep his back, and more importantly his laptop, to the window. Then he got back to the business of hacking the airport.

Thousands of IP addresses were now forty-six: time to sing for his supper. From the MWAA website, he knew that Access Control was a unified system supporting security cameras, credentials, and badge readers. Those were both mission-critical systems, so MWAA would operate them as a cluster, ensuring redundancy should any one server fail.

A program called Wireshark sniffed packet traffic to the forty-six servers, hunting for data from the badge readers. Gibson waited patiently, at home in a familiar world in which he felt comfortable and capable. He'd never fit the antisocial hacker stereotype, but for the first time he felt the relief that the binary world offered to someone overwhelmed by people.

By noon, he'd identified the Access Control cluster. He took a break for lunch and then began a SQL injection attack to compromise the database so that he could add records. This step took a full five hours. Access granted, he spent time getting a feel for the server's database architecture. He looked at several preexisting employee records and credentials before creating his own. Entering his bogus information, he inserted the employee photograph that Jenn had taken, along with his scanned fingerprints.

Satisfied with his work, Gibson deleted the virtual machine as if it had never existed. Tomorrow, posing as an employee of Tyner Aviation, he would pay a visit to the Dulles Pass & ID Office, located in the main terminal across from baggage claim seven. There he could pick up a replacement green badge with escort authority and nonmovement area endorsements. That would give him the run of the place. He didn't know what good that would do him—Jenn had been less than forthcoming with details. He'd leave that up to her.

Gibson checked a nearby clock—still plenty of time to catch the seven o'clock to Seattle. He packed up and rolled his suitcase back to the parking garage. If anyone questioned him later why he'd been at the airport but never boarded a flight, he'd say he'd been on the way to confront his ex-wife in Seattle but thought better of it. Not far from the truth.

Jenn expected him to return directly to Reston, but he needed to make a couple of stops on the way. She wouldn't be happy, but the way he looked at it, he'd be doing her a favor. She needed new things to be grumpy about to take her mind off all the things that were already irritating her—an area in which Gibson excelled. He started the SUV, telling himself he was being unfair. While they still had a few trust issues to work out, it felt good to be around someone who knew him.

Still, she was going to be mightily pissed.

Gibson saw the top of the power plant above the trees. Duke leaned forward from the backseat like he'd been planning an ambush.

"These aren't your people," Duke said. "Jenn. George. They are not your responsibility. I care about my family. Your family. The people that you have failed again and again. The way you failed me."

"I'm doing the best I can," Gibson whispered.

"This is your best? That woman had me murdered, and what do you do? You cut deals. Another confessed to burning down my grand-daughter's house, and what do you do? You cut deals. Christ, boy. What does someone have to do to actually deserve your retribution?"

"I locked Ogden away like you wanted."

"And now, at the first setback, you're going to let him go again."

"It's not solving anything. I can't live like this."

"If that's true, then floor this thing. Drive us into the side of the power plant before you fail someone else. Die with that much dignity. You'd be doing us all a favor."

"Shut up," Gibson said as defiantly as he could, but his eyes went where Duke pointed. The SUV leapt forward, his knuckles white and taut on the steering wheel. The thought of letting go of all his pain was a tempting one. The chance to rest. To be free. It had seduced him before when he'd believed that the door would never open. He remembered the faded bloodstain on the floor of his cell and eased his foot off the accelerator.

"This isn't over," Duke warned.

Gibson didn't doubt him for a second. He drove around back and parked, waiting for his heart to slow. Everything looked status quo. He took the shopping bag from the passenger seat and went into the plant. At the bottom of the stairs, he took off his boots and padded down the service corridor in his socks. At the cell, he retrieved his gun from its hiding place and loaded a full clip. Just in case.

Through the peephole, he saw that Ogden lay motionless on his cot, back to the room. His efforts at housekeeping had deteriorated since Gibson's last visit. Food packaging littered the floor. Gibson sorted through his key ring.

"Think about what you're doing," Duke said. "Ogden is just guessing. You open that door, you're going to have to kill him."

"I don't *have* to do anything you say."

Gibson unlocked the cell and took a short wooden stool inside. Ogden didn't move. Gibson shut the door and sat with his back against the door. He rested the gun on his thigh and waited. Ogden rolled over, and the two men regarded each other.

"It's harder than you think it's going to be, isn't it?" Gibson said.

"Are you here to gloat?"

"I thought I would be, but no."

"Then what was the point?" Ogden asked.

"I needed you to know."

"Know what?" Ogden asked, lifting his head from the cot.

"That it mattered."

"So now what?"

"I haven't gotten that far. But I thought we should talk."

"Will you tell me one thing? How long have I been in here?"

Gibson nodded at the familiarity of the question. "I know, right? It's weird how time gets away from you."

"How long?"

"Three months," Gibson said with a straight face.

"Bullshit," Ogden said, but Gibson could hear the doubt in the man's voice.

"A week? A year? A lifetime."

"You're one crazy son of a bitch."

"Yeah, I am. Thank you for that."

Ogden swung himself into a sitting position. "What I did was justified."

"Doesn't make it right," Gibson said.

"The needs of the many exceed the needs of the few."

"Is that how you CIA boys justify the rendition of an American citizen on US soil? Was Poisonfeather really that valuable?"

"Do you know what China is?" Ogden asked. "It's the Soviet Union on steroids. It's Russia with a world-class economy and ten times the population. We literally spent the old USSR to death. That won't happen with China. They are strong, rich, ambitious, and spend close to two hundred billion a year on their military. So yes, Poisonfeather was that valuable. He was the best human intelligence resource that we've ever had inside their politburo. Poisonfeather was worth a thousand of you. I wasn't going to jeopardize my asset for some burnout Marine hacker."

"I wouldn't have said anything."

"Your history suggested otherwise. And if we're being candid, this little stunt hasn't done anything to change my mind."

"What happens if I let you go?"

"Death penalty," Ogden said without hesitation. "The Patriot Act is unambiguous on that point."

"And if I run?"

"We hunt you down. Death penalty."

"Shouldn't you be telling me what I want to hear?" Gibson said. "How if I let you go that you'll forget who it was who took you?"

"I would if I thought you were dumb enough to fall for it."

"I was dumb enough to take you."

"You got me there," Ogden agreed. "You ever kill anyone?"

Gibson shook his head. "No. And don't especially want to start now, but I'm not fond of needles."

"There might be one other move we could try."

"What's that?"

"How long have I been here? Really."

"Two weeks," Gibson said.

"It seems so much longer than that."

"You should try it for eighteen months."

Ogden stared at him without a response.

"You were saying."

Ogden lifted his chin. "Langley won't be anxious to admit that one of their people got snatched from under their nose. It's a bad precedent. Have I been on the news yet?"

Gibson shook his head.

"Good," Ogden said. "That's good. Chances are they'll want to keep it that way. Especially if they get me back in one piece."

"So what do I do?"

"You go in."

"To Langley?"

Ogden nodded. "Ask for a man named René Ambrose. He's my boss. Tell him you've got me. Offer to trade me for a plea deal."

"I'll have to do time?"

"Releasing me doesn't make this a wash, Vaughn. You'll still owe."

"How much time will I have to do?"

"Depends, but I'd guess ten to twenty. But I'll push your deal through. I give you my word."

Gibson whistled at the number. If he served twenty years, he would be in his fifties when he got out. Ellie would be almost thirty. Not comforting math.

"You have to kill him," Duke said.

"No, I'm not doing that."

"It's your only option," Ogden said.

"Shut up. I'm not talking to you."

"You want to do twenty years for this son of a bitch?" Duke said.

"If that's what it takes."

"Who the hell are you talking to?" Ogden asked.

"Oh, where are my manners? I should have introduced you two. This is my dead father. He thinks I should kill you."

"You're damn right I do," Duke agreed.

Ogden stared at the empty space where Duke stood. "You're actually insane."

"What the fuck else would I be?" Gibson yelled. "You've been here two weeks. That's nothing. Try eighteen months and see which of your ancestors shows up for a chat."

He didn't remember pointing the gun at Ogden or wrapping his finger around the trigger. Ogden's hands were up. He was talking, but Gibson couldn't hear him over the ringing in his ears. He drew a deep breath and eased his finger from the trigger.

"Nice try," Gibson said to Duke, who shrugged.

"That was all you, kid."

"All right," Gibson told Ogden. "You sit tight. I have a couple of things to take care of, and then I'll see how bad your boss wants you back."

"How do I know you'll come back?" Ogden's voice suddenly held a note of panic that Gibson knew all too well.

"I give you my word."

"Your word? What's that worth?"

"About the same as yours. No, wait, I saved your life in West Virginia. And I delivered you Charles Merrick. So a little more."

"You kidnapped me," Ogden said.

"Yeah, you weren't there at the time, but I promised you that too."

Ogden had no response to that, which Gibson appreciated. Ogden looked at the floor for a long time before finally asking the question on his mind.

"How long are you going to be gone?"

"A week or so."

"And how long is that?"

Gibson opened his shopping bag and took out an alarm clock. He set the time and slid it across the floor to Ogden.

"What's this?" Ogden asked.

"Your new best friend."

Ogden looked at the clock. "Is it morning or night?"

"Night."

Out in the service corridor, Gibson secured the cell door and leaned against the wall. He admired how Ogden had played it. He'd been both good and bad cop—hard and unforgiving, then bearing a ray of hope. Not an easy line to walk, but Ogden had made turning himself in sound like the smart play. Gibson agreed in principle. But he knew that if he walked into Langley he'd never see the light of day again. He'd have to figure something out.

After they got George.

CHAPTER TWENTY-THREE

Gibson sat in the back of the Nighthawk Diner and stared blankly at the laminated pages of the menu. After leaving the power plant, he should have driven straight back to Reston, but he needed time to think. He also needed to ask Toby Kalpar one last favor. The box of keepsakes that Toby had salvaged from his old apartment sat on the banquette beside Gibson. He opened it and took an inventory. Satisfied everything was there except for the pictures of Ellie that he'd kept for himself, he closed the box's flaps and went back to the menu.

His summit with Damon Ogden had left him somber and reflective. He hadn't expected a miracle, and Ogden hadn't told him anything that he didn't already suspect, but somehow hearing it aloud had crystalized his awareness that he had no outs left. Like a gambler down to his last dollar, he looked back on the chain of bad bets on long odds that had led him to this precipice and knew there was no way to get back what he'd lost. What he ought to do was take that last dollar back off the table before he lost it too. Not chase bad money with good.

Speaking of which, his hack today had violated a raft of statutes. Moreover, he hadn't even broken the laws because he thought it might get him home to Nicole and Ellie. The truth was, there hadn't been a way home for a long time. There might never have been one, but that hadn't stopped him from hoping. Hendricks had once warned him about the danger of hope. Hope was a cancer, Hendricks had said. A cancer that gnawed a person down to the bone. At the time, Gibson had dismissed the advice as self-serving cynicism. But he realized now that Hendricks hadn't meant *all* hope. Some hope was essential. Hendricks had meant the kind of hope that kept a person from accepting a hard truth. Hope that kept people from finding closure and moving on with their lives. The hope that a missing child might turn up alive and well after a decade. That your ex-wife might have an uncharacteristic change of heart. Or that the ones you loved would not suffer for your sins.

At this point, there was no way back to Ellie. He accepted that now. And given what he'd done and the consequences yet to be faced, he knew it to be for the best. He wiped at his eyes. It was a painful, heartbreaking thing to know that you were not in your own child's best interests. A bitter thing to accept about yourself when your biology screamed that she needed you to survive. But it was the other way around, wasn't it? He'd forfeited the right to argue differently.

So he'd helped Jenn because he could and because she needed him. Jenn was *also* family, not the kind that you were born into but the kind you built for yourself.

Duke snorted. "They're always special, aren't they? Suzanne. Birk. Jenn Charles."

"And you," Gibson said. "You were the first. Don't forget that you started all this."

His father had a point, though. Didn't Gibson always find a rationalization for how his wrongs added up to a right? Some justification to make things worse for himself. He'd been doing it since he was a boy, when he hacked Senator Benjamin Lombard. And again costing his family dearly when he'd joined the hunt for Suzanne Lombard, and later to help Judge Hammond Birk. Damon Ogden was only the icing on the cake. Yet here he went again, making things worse for himself.

Strange thing was, even knowing he was doing it, he saw no way to stop himself. He would help Jenn no matter the cost.

After all, they couldn't give him the death penalty twice.

So he had come to the Nighthawk to draw up his last will and testament. Such as it was.

When the waitress took his order, Gibson asked if Toby could stop by his table. Even if the Nighthawk was slammed, Toby always had a nod for Gibson when he came through the door. Toby had barely acknowledged him today. It had left him anxious, and when the food came, he picked over it, appetite gone. Toby slid into the booth while Gibson was paying the check. They stared at each other across their burned bridges. Toby's eyes held the weary gloss of a parent who'd changed the locks on his own child. Gibson started to speak, but Toby cut him off, his face hard and remote.

"The police came to my house. Asked to see the room where you slept. We were given a number to call if you came in." Toby turned a business card over in his fingers before handing it to Gibson. It belonged to Detective Jim Bachmann. On the back was written a cell phone number.

"What about?" Gibson asked.

"As if I would know. I am just some trusting fool. Why would I know anything?"

"I'm sorry."

"He stops by almost every day now, your detective," Toby said.

"Has he been by today?"

"No, not today."

"Did you? Call him?" Gibson asked.

"No. Should I have?"

"Yes, probably."

"What have you done, Gibson?"

In the past, Gibson had confided in Toby only with a sanitized, network-television version of events. Whether that was to protect Toby or Toby's perception of him, Gibson couldn't say. Toby had always had a hopeful indulgence for Gibson's impulsiveness. As if Toby saw something in him that Gibson himself did not. That faith, from someone so fundamentally good, had always made Gibson optimistic about the future. It was hard not to want to live up to Toby Kalpar's expectations. Gibson could see in Toby's expression that he had not, and more than that, he had finally exhausted his friend's considerable patience. This time there was no sanitized version. He'd crossed a divide, and not even Toby Kalpar would be able to find a silver lining.

"Why did you come?" Toby asked when it became clear Gibson would not answer his question. "Clearly it is not for more useless advice."

"Toby, I—"

"Please do not. What is it you want from me?"

"Would you keep this for me?" Gibson indicated the box. "If Ellie ever comes looking for me, will you give it to her? I want her to have it." He searched Toby's face. "Would you do that for me?"

Toby looked at the box a long time before meeting Gibson's eyes. "No. I will not involve myself with this any longer. I cannot."

Gibson nodded and couldn't stop. He let out a whistling sigh. "I understand. Sure. Probably for the best."

He counted out money to pay the check and gathered up his things. Toby looked away into the middle distance. Gibson stood and rested the box on the corner of the table. Toby had not moved.

"Thank you," Gibson said. "For everything. I'm sorry I let you down."

"He is here," Toby said.

In the reflection of the window, Gibson saw Detective Bachmann speaking to Sana. She stood so that Bachmann's back was to them, although the detective glanced around as they talked.

Gibson and Toby looked at each other. Toby's face was a mask to him. Gibson held his breath.

Toby said, "Go out through the kitchen. The back will be unlocked. He won't see you. Go quickly."

"Thank you."

Toby nodded once to acknowledge Gibson. "Do not come back."

———————

Gibson walked aimlessly for blocks, lugging his cardboard box. His Yukon, tucked into a back corner of the Nighthawk parking lot, was trapped until Bachmann left. It was the second time someone he cared about had told him to go away and stay away. First Nicole, now Toby. His ex-wife and his ex-champion. A smart man would take the hint.

He paused outside a FedEx office. Inside, the lights were still on, and a sleepy employee leaned against the counter. Gibson went inside and asked Greg—according to his name tag—how much to ship the box to Seattle. Greg weighed it and quoted him a price. Gibson agreed. While Greg filled out shipping information, Gibson borrowed a pen and wrote a long, rambling letter to Nicole. He read it over, crumpled it up, and started again, this time keeping it short and to the point.

Nicole, I got your e-mail and agree. I wish I didn't, but as usual you are right. This box is for Ellie. Someday. If you think she would want it. If you think she should have it. I'll leave that up to you. You were the best part of my life. I can only say that I am sorry that I've become the worst part of yours. I hope you find your best part out there. Take care of our girl. Yours, Gibson

He read it over again and still didn't like how it sounded, but Greg said he needed to close. Gibson handed over the letter and watched him tape up the box.

"You okay, bro?"

"What?" Gibson said.

Greg pointed to his own eyes and made an awkward expression. Gibson put a hand to his own face. It came away wet. He hadn't known he was crying.

"Allergies," he said lamely.

Greg nodded sagely. "Zyrtec. That shit's the bomb."

Gibson thanked him for the advice and dried his face on his sleeve. An electronic chime announced a customer's arrival.

Greg said. "Sorry, dudes. We're closed."

"It's all right. We're here for him."

Cools and Sidhu stood in the door. They wore matching winter overcoats with the collars flipped up, looking like a couple of cinema gangsters from an old black and white. Gibson thanked Greg for his help and went out the door. Calista's men parted to let him pass and then fanned out on his shoulders. Gibson turned in the direction of the Nighthawk and his car, but Cools blocked his way. Gibson squared up to him, filled with joyous anger to have someone tangible to vent his frustrations upon.

"You know, I appreciate the escort, but it's been a long day. Why don't you fuck off?"

There were two of them. He should have kept that in mind.

From behind, Sidhu drilled him in the kidney. It was a precise, expert blow, and only his puffy winter jacket saved Gibson from pissing blood for a week. As it was, it felt like a bottle of hot sauce had shattered inside him. His knees gave out, but Cools caught him before he could fall, spinning him around and pinning his arms to his sides. Sidhu stepped in close and delivered several shots to his midsection like a boxer working the heavy bag.

"Enough," Cools said.

Sidhu stepped back as Gibson slipped to the sidewalk and rested his face on the cold concrete. It felt heavenly. Sidhu grasped Gibson by the chin, forcing his head up.

"What did I tell you about cursing at me?"

Gibson couldn't muster enough breath to reply.

Duke said, "You know, one of these days I'd like to see you win a fight."

Cools and Sidhu hefted Gibson by the armpits and dragged him to an idling limousine. They opened the rear door and dumped Gibson onto the floor. Sidhu got in behind him and shut the door. Gibson rolled onto his back, tried and failed to catch his breath. Calista Dauplaise gazed down at him. She wore a floor-length gown that pooled at her feet, and a chandelier of a necklace. She held a program from the Washington National Opera.

"I have been anticipating Lisette Christou's debut for a year," Calista said. "Her Violetta Valéry is said to be peerless. But rather than enjoying the pageantry of *La Traviata*, I find myself in the back of my automobile to witness an entirely different tragedy unfold. Which is perplexing, because I feel certain that I made myself clear to you. Should I go ahead and make that call to Langley now?"

Gibson moved to sit up, but Sidhu put one of his size fourteens on Gibson's chest and pushed him down. From his back, Gibson said, "I just had to take care of a few things."

"Yes, I am quite aware of all your unscheduled stops today. Between the two of us, you really must learn how to spot a tail."

"Yeah," Gibson agreed. "It's been on my list."

"Why were you at the power plant this evening?"

"I talked to him."

"Did you, now? About what, precisely?"

"I told him I was going to let him go. Next week. After we get George back."

"Do you take me for a fool?" Calista asked and nodded at Sidhu, who drove his foot into Gibson's rib cage. "A detective spoke to the proprietor of the diner not two minutes after you departed. Did you pass the proprietor information from your hostage to give to the police? Are you actively attempting to sabotage me?"

"No. No, no, no," Gibson said, seeing where Calista was heading with this. Calista expected to be betrayed so she saw betrayal. "Toby has nothing to do with this. He knows nothing. That detective investigated the arson at my old house. He thinks I'm a suspect and won't leave me alone. That's it. I swear. Toby is not involved."

"So why were you at the diner tonight?" she asked.

"I had a box of . . ." Gibson didn't know how to describe it.

"Personal effects?"

"Sure. Stuff I wanted my daughter to have. I asked Toby to keep it for her. He refused."

"Why would you need him to do that?"

"Because I'll have to go to jail," Gibson said. Calista paled so he hurried on. "But not until after the plane. That's what I told Ogden. I promised to let him go. But only after Jenn and I take the plane."

Calista contemplated the premise of what he'd told her. He could see her testing the idea, looking for the lie. He shifted topics, trying to move the conversation further away from Toby Kalpar.

"The airport went totally smooth. We're all set there."

"Is that the truth?" she asked.

"I'll have the credentials when I get back from Dulles tomorrow."

"Well, you had better have, hadn't you?"

Calista gestured to Sidhu, who helped Gibson up into the seat opposite Calista. The two old enemies faced each other. Only a few feet apart, it felt as though Calista were studying him through opera glasses from the safe confines of a private box. Her finery made him feel more acutely like a guy who'd just had his ass kicked on a sidewalk. Calista uncrossed and recrossed her legs, which seemed to indicate that she'd reached some kind of conclusion.

"When was the last time you saw your daughter?" she asked. "What is her name? Eleanor, if I am not mistaken?"

Gibson bristled. "Don't. Don't bring my kid into this. I'm doing everything you asked me to do."

Sidhu leaned forward and put up a cautioning hand that said, *Calm down or finish this conversation back on the floor.*

Calista shook her head, trying to slow him down. "No, I apologize for the misunderstanding. That is not what I meant. I am not threatening Eleanor. Your daughter has nothing to fear from me."

Calista opened a small bar and, using silver tongs, dropped a single ice cube into two cut-crystal tumblers. She filled the glasses with scotch and passed one to Gibson as a peace offering.

"Did you know that I have a son?" she asked conversationally.

The change in subject and tone threw Gibson. "The one in Florida?"

"Yes, the same. I suppose I must have been rather unkind about him."

That was putting it mildly. Calista had talked about her son the way someone else might describe a mass murderer. His great offense had been shacking up with a woman and playing a lot of golf. And for living in Florida—Calista held a dim view of the entire state.

"What does your son have to do with anything?" Gibson said.

Calista puffed up ever so slightly. "I mentioned earlier that my circumstances had changed. Well, my son has been elected to Congress."

"He is a Dauplaise. More of your handiwork?"

"No, I had less than nothing to do with it." There was a note in Calista's voice that Gibson had never heard before. It took him a moment to put a name to it: regret. "There was a vacant seat. Party leaders approached him with promises to back him should he run."

"I thought all he did was golf."

"Yes, well. Recharging his batteries, I think he called it. Before that, he had been with a law firm in New York. He had been a partner for less than six months when he resigned unceremoniously, sold his apartment, and moved to Fort Lauderdale. It was a scandalous decision. One that, in retrospect, I did not take with the grace with which I might."

"Congratulations," Gibson said, feeling proud that he'd kept the derision out of his voice. A Dauplaise back in Congress would mean everything to Calista.

"Thank you. He has received a rather plum appointment to Ways and Means. His party holds him in high regard and is grooming him."

"Does your son's new position have something to do with Eskridge?"

"Nothing," Calista snapped. "And he never will. Of that, I assure you. My son has no part in my affairs. He now spends a good deal of time here in Washington. I have offered him the use of Colline, of course. It is the family home, and it is his. However, he prefers to rent a row house on Capitol Hill. To be closer to the action, he says. As if Georgetown were a suburb of Baltimore. His mother raised him to be diplomatic, you see. But he has not so much as set foot on the property. Nor have I been invited to meet my grandson."

"That must be hard."

"My influence is not what it once was, but I could have furnished him with introductions. Life is not easy for a freshman congressman, and I would have improved his lot dramatically. He is, however, intent on forging his own path and made it abundantly clear that neither I nor my counsel are welcome."

"Does he know what you've done?"

A pained expression crossed her face. "Sidhu, please wait up front. Have Mr. Cools raise the divider."

She waited until they were alone before she continued.

"I prefer that we not speak of these things in front of the help. No, my son is a sweet boy. An honorable man. If he knew, he would call the authorities himself. That said, he has his suspicions. He knows that I have not always been the most"—she paused, searching for the right word—"principled of actors."

"That's one way of putting it."

"Even though he is ashamed of me, there is nothing that I would not do for my son. We do not share a great deal, you and I, but I think in that we are much alike."

"Ellie's not ashamed of me."

"No, she's not old enough yet for that."

"Fuck you, lady," Gibson spat.

Color rose on Calista's neck and cheeks, but she made no move to respond. She sipped her drink and composed herself.

"My point, Mr. Vaughn, is that, hard as that is for me to admit or to accept, my son is correct to turn his back on me. And if he is to have an opportunity to make an authentic contribution to his country, then the miscalculations of my past must never become public knowledge."

"'Miscalculations'? You should have been in advertising."

Calista pushed through Gibson's interruption. "I will not permit my son to be tarred with my brush. As you have said, my word means nothing to you. I would not think as highly of you as I do if it did. You might be a vulgar, limited man, but you are a good one too. Far better than most recognize, and I know more than most what that has cost you. I tell you all this so you and I might understand each other. Once Mr. Eskridge has been neutralized, I intend to withdraw from public life. After this one last unprincipled action, I am through. I have no intention of moving against you, your family, or your friends. Not now, not ever. If for no other reason than it would place my son's career in jeopardy after I moved heaven and earth to protect him. Have I, at long last, made myself clear?"

"Yes."

"And do you believe me?"

"No," Gibson said. "Not now, not ever. But we can coexist. I am helping Jenn Charles and George Abe. Not you. As long as their interests continue to align with yours, then we have no problems. Anything happens to them, we will have a serious conversation. And like you said, you better than most know that I have a lot less to lose than you."

"Good," Calista said. "I think we understand each other at last."

CHAPTER TWENTY-FOUR

The Reston house smelled cozy and homey when Gibson came in from the garage. He had only picked at his meal at the diner, and the aroma of garlic and olive oil kicked his appetite in the ribs. His ex-wife was a natural, intuitive chef, the catering business she'd started after the divorce a testament to her culinary talent. Dinnertime in the Vaughn household had always been an event.

He slipped off his coat gingerly, wishing Nicole would appear around the corner in her socks and leggings to drag him into the kitchen and taste her work, indulging a tricky memory that he relived far too often. Like any drug, it brought a smaller and smaller high each time, chased by an emotional pit from which he had to climb. Made all the harder tonight, given what he'd put in the mail. It occurred to him that the fire had surely cost Nicole her business. She would have had to abandon it to take Ellie to safety. That killed him. She'd been so proud of what she'd built. One more thing that he'd taken away from her.

"In here," Jenn called.

Gibson followed her voice back to the kitchen, wincing with each step. He didn't think any ribs were broken, but Sidhu's handiwork made breathing a chore. Jenn sat at the counter, typing on her laptop, exactly where he'd left her this morning. No indication that she'd moved, apart from the stack of dirty dishes and pans soaking in the sink. An empty bottle of wine sat beside an empty glass.

"You cook?"

"I'm an adult," Jenn said. "Of course I cook."

"So what's for dinner?"

"Don't know, what are you making? Besides, the way I heard it, you already ate dinner."

"You talked to Calista," he said, using the refrigerator as an excuse not to make eye contact, but the anger in her voice was unmistakable. How much had Calista told Jenn about his day? He really didn't want to get into it with her about Ogden. They carried on the conversation while he foraged for fixings to make a sandwich.

"Of course I talked to her," Jenn said without pausing from her typing. "We're partners. That means we keep each other in the loop."

"You don't actually think you can trust her?" Gibson said.

"I don't trust anyone."

"Then why—"

"I trust motives," Jenn said.

He rolled his eyes. "Did she give you the same bullshit assurances she gave me? About going straight because of her congressman son? Saint Dauplaise?"

"Her son is the real deal."

"Oh, come on. He's a Dauplaise."

"You know what David Dauplaise has to gain by accepting her help? What he sacrificed by turning his back on her? She offered him the keys to the kingdom, and the only string attached was his mother. He still said no. Don't know how he did it, but somehow he grew up without Calista beating the integrity out of him. And he represents everything that she's fought for her entire life—he has the pedigree, the ambition, the talent, all wrapped up with a handsome chin dimple."

"Chin dimple?"

"Like the Grand Canyon. He's everything Calista thought she had in Benjamin Lombard, only he's a Dauplaise. So, yeah, I do believe her when she says she needs to tidy up her act and that Eskridge is the end of the line for her."

"Okay. I just want to be sure you didn't have a blind spot for her. She may have played straight with you so far, but this is the endgame. Keep in mind how that went for us the last time. Let's not make the same mistake that George did."

"Is this going to be a repeat of Pennsylvania?" She meant the operation to find Suzanne Lombard's kidnapper. At a key moment, Gibson had disobeyed Jenn's instructions to return to Washington and had gone rogue. It had been a bone of contention between them at the time, and he didn't like her throwing it in his face after so long.

"And how did that work out, Jenn? Which of us found him first?"

Her typing ceased with a satisfying, staccato clack. Gibson knew better than to push that particular button, but he'd already had his daily lecture from Calista. Instead of apologizing, he finished making his sandwich and cracked open a beer. Jenn held out her hand and snapped her fingers. He passed her the beer and opened another.

"No," he said, breaking the silence. "It's nothing like Pennsylvania. I just had to tie up a few things before we step off."

"'Step off'?" Jenn rolled her eyes. "Today was your audition. Remember? And you put everything in jeopardy with that stunt tonight. How close did the detective come to seeing you? In what universe but yours would this qualify as a passing grade?"

"The one where I hacked an airport for you. How about that one, huh?"

"It worked?" Jenn asked, somewhat appeased.

"Well, I won't know for sure until I don't get arrested tomorrow. But, yeah, it worked." He gave her the highlights of his incursion while he ate. "Tomorrow I drive out to Dulles and report that I lost my credentials. I'll have to fill out a lost-pass form, but that's a formality. Fifty bucks and my winning personality, and we're in business. So what do you say you put the pin back in the grenade?"

Jenn stared at him long enough that he began to brace himself for a fight. Finally, she took a long sip of her beer, shut her laptop, and stood up.

"Know how to play cribbage?"

Not what he'd expected. "Do I know what, now?"

"I'll be in the living room after you do the dishes."

"What?" he asked, although he knew the answer. "All of them?"

———————————————

"How do you know how to play cribbage?" Gibson asked when Jenn had finished showing him how pegging worked. It seemed like a game from another kind of lifetime.

"My grandmother played every card game ever invented."

Jenn's father had died in the Marine-barracks bombing in Beirut in 1983. She'd been two. His death had unraveled Beth Charles, who had deliberately and conscientiously taken refuge in a bottle of vodka before wrapping her pickup around a tree. Jenn's grandmother had taken her in, put a roof over her head.

"That sounds kind of nice," Gibson said.

Jenn nodded. "She wouldn't have a television in the house, but she'd gin rummy you to death if you let her."

Gibson had never gotten the sense that Jenn had been close to her grandmother, so marathon card games surprised him. Jenn read his mind.

"Cards was the only time she took a break from criticizing. And not always then."

They played a couple of practice hands until Gibson got the hang of the game. Jenn shuffled the deck and dealt for real.

"Did you like her?"

"She taught me to shoot," Jenn replied.

Gibson waited, but that was all the answer Jenn seemed inclined to give. "So I'm in trouble here is what you're saying?"

"Aren't you always?" she asked, turning over the four of spades from the deck. He played a six, and she laid the five of hearts. "Fifteen for two." She moved her peg two places forward on the board.

"It's part of my charm," Gibson said with a wry smile and played the eight of diamonds. "Twenty-three. So are you going to tell me your plan? I'm still hazy on why you didn't have me create credentials for both of us. Why just me? It doesn't make sense."

"Thirty-one for two," she announced triumphantly as she played an eight. Gibson stared forlornly at the board while Jenn used his remaining cards to score even more points.

He *was* in trouble here.

"Do you know what Category X means?" Jenn asked, shuffling and dealing the cards.

Gibson did. Cat X was the Homeland Security designation for US airports deemed high-value terrorist targets due to the volume of commercial passengers. Billions of dollars had been spent hardening Cat X facilities post 9/11, and only twenty-five airports had such a rating: Logan, O'Hare, JFK, LAX, SeaTac . . . Dulles.

"Actually, it works in our favor," Jenn said as she arranged her new hand. She picked two of her cards and put them in the crib. Gibson added two of his own. The game continued.

"How do you figure?"

Jenn paused and ran her tongue over her teeth the way she did when she was thinking.

"Cold Harbor operates a C-130 out of Dulles," Jenn said. "It resupplies Cold Harbor's base of operations in North Africa and supports its contracts there and in the Middle East. Cold Harbor is dirty as hell, but they keep a low profile at Dulles—everything by the book. My guess is that's why Eskridge is using it to fly George out of the country. In five years, they've never once been cited for a violation by customs inspectors, and no one will be looking at them too closely. Plus, Eskridge thinks that flying out of Dulles offers him a measure of protection. Who would be stupid enough to take down one of his shipments at a Cat X?"

"But we are? That stupid?"

Jenn ignored him. "Cold Harbor flights are guarded only by a skeleton detail plus flight crew plus whatever personnel are being transported to Africa. And because it's Category X, their materiel has to be sealed in shipping containers. They won't be armed."

"Yeah, but neither will we," Gibson reminded her. "Armed or not, how are we supposed to take George off a plane guarded by Cold Harbor mercs? Rock-paper-scissors them for him?"

"Who said we'd be unarmed?" Jenn said with a crafty smile.

"Jenn. I'll have a green badge, and that will give me the run of the airport, but I'll still have to pass through security to get on premises. There's no way I'm getting guns through. So unless you've been tunneling under security at night . . ."

"Are you familiar with the term 'security theater'?"

Gibson nodded. It was the criticism that the billions of dollars spent since 9/11 to upgrade security at American airports had had little impact on overall security. That all that the pantomime at TSA checkpoints accomplished was to create the illusion of increased safety.

Gibson said, "Doesn't mean they won't catch me carrying a gun into the terminals."

"That would be true if we were infiltrating *that* Dulles International Airport."

"There's another Dulles I haven't heard about?"

Jenn nodded and explained that there were, for all intents and purposes, two Dulles International Airports: commercial and general aviation, each one operating on two entirely different sets of security principles. "Cat X really only refers to the commercial side of the airport. The airline terminals. Where TSA puts the general public through their little shoeless, beltless parade—metal detectors, pat downs, all of that. Then there's GA—general aviation. That's the side of the airport that accommodates private aircraft—anything from a one-seat prop to Gulfstream jets. And private cargo planes for businesses like FedEx and UPS."

"And Cold Harbor."

"And Cold Harbor," she confirmed. "That's why you now work for Tyner Aviation. It's one of the FBOs—fixed-base operators—that provide services, such as fuel and maintenance, to private aircraft at Dulles."

"So no security theater in general aviation?"

"Why bother?" Jenn asked. "There's no one there to see it. I mean, they still have employees pass through security checks, but it's pretty nominal compared to the commercial terminals."

"Metal detectors?"

"Yes," Jenn said.

"So how do we get weapons in?"

"Simple. Fly them in."

That seemed like an even worse idea to Gibson. "Oh, come on. They don't search aircraft?"

"Not domestic. Have you ever been searched *after* landing?" Jenn asked. "For reasons known only to the FAA, inbound domestic aircraft to Cat X airports are trusted entities. And so are the pilots. Even if their point of origin is some Podunk airstrip with no security whatsoever."

Even to Gibson, who was accustomed to the vagaries of security, that sounded insane. She had to be overlooking something. "Are there at least separate runways? Fences?"

"Nope. There are only four runways at Dulles, and commercial and general aviation share them. General aviation flights simply taxi to separate hangars after landing."

"You're telling me that terrorists could land a plane, taxi to the commercial terminals, and launch an attack from the Jetway. And no one would know until bullets started flying?"

"As long as an aircraft has a legitimate tail number, it's free to land at any airport in the United States. Cat X included."

"That can't possibly be a thing," he said without much conviction.

"Afraid so. Good for us, though, huh?"

"So who's the pilot?"

"You're looking at her."

"You're a pilot?"

Jenn nodded. "Fixed wing and rotary. Just like my mom was."

"Man, you think you know a person."

"But that doesn't mean they let pilots wander around the tarmac. I'll need an escort once I exit the aircraft."

Suddenly his newly acquired credentials made sense. Jenn would fly weapons in, and Gibson's green badge would enable him to chaperone her anywhere she wanted to go. It shifted the terms of the engagement ever so slightly in their favor. Enough that, for the first time, Gibson could see how, if everything broke their way, they might just pull this off. A thought occurred to him.

"But, how do we—" Gibson began.

"Gibson," she interrupted. "There are about a millions buts, and I want to cover every damn one of them. But can we get into it tomorrow when you get back from Dulles? It's been a long day, and I just want to play cards."

"So does that mean I passed the audition?"

"Only if we're grading on a massive curve."

She went to the refrigerator for two more beers to sweeten the deal. Gibson chuckled and leaned back in his chair and put his hands over his head in a big stretch. The only thing Jenn Charles loved more than a tightly run operation was planning a tightly run operation. Instead, she was plying him with beer to entice him to shut up and play cards.

A more religious man might interpret this as a sign of the impending apocalypse. But a wise man took his beer, shut up, and shuffled.

They played until almost two in the morning. He lost far more than he won, but that made no difference to him. Kicking his butt seemed to unwind Jenn, and as she relaxed, she began talking. They both enjoyed the comforting camaraderie that comes of not having to pretend not to be broken. The high-tension wires that hummed constantly through his head these days subsided, and Gibson put everything else aside and focused on the simple task of making his friend smile. They swapped stories—Dan Hendricks a recurring theme—and Jenn even laughed a couple of times. She had a good laugh, and hearing it felt special, like catching a glimpse of a desert flower that bloomed only under extraordinary conditions.

Gibson's curiosity got the better of him, so he asked how Jenn had come to work for George. He regretted it immediately as the sparkle went out of Jenn's eyes, and she turned serious.

"You want to know why I'm doing this?"

"Something like that," Gibson admitted.

"George saved my life. More or less."

Gibson definitely hadn't heard this story and waited for her to go on. She ran her tongue across her teeth.

"My last assignment with the Agency, I was attached to Camp Chapman," she said. "Forward operating base in Afghanistan. Not far from the Pakistani border. I'd been on some remote bases before, but you needed a damn chopper just to get *back* to remote. You ever see *Apocalypse Now*? The scene where the Playboy Bunnies do a USO show and the troops literally riot at the sight of women? That's what it was like. Every day."

"I don't like where this is going."

Jenn smiled and tapped her front teeth. "These look pretty real, don't you think? The doctors in Germany . . ." She trailed off. "After I left the CIA, I was in not good shape. Let's leave it at that. Physically or spiritually. I wanted to press charges. The Agency made it clear they wouldn't back me up. Advised me to drop it. The assault and attempted rape of CIA personnel on an Army base by two sergeants was bad for business. *A severe hindrance to CIA operations in the region* was how it was put to me. Plus the Army threatened to charge me over the death of the other sergeant."

"You killed one?"

"Lost consciousness before I could kill the other one." Jenn sounded disappointed.

"And Langley tried to sweep it all under the rug?"

"Let's just say I found out that my loyalty was not reciprocal. I was a true believer—young, naïve. I did not take it at all well. At all. Sounds stupid to say about a job, but it felt like I'd had my heart broken. I felt that I'd been betrayed. Anyway. I holed up in an apartment in Nashville. Just hiding from the world. Not working. Burned through my savings in about eight months. Drinking pretty hard too. Vodka, like my mom. Thought for a while there that I'd wind up at the bottom of the Cumberland River."

"So what happened?"

"George Abe knocked on my door and offered me a job is what happened. I opened the door looking like something that would clog a garbage disposal, and there stood George in his perfectly pressed shirt and his perfectly pressed jeans. I mean, who presses their jeans?"

"That's exactly what I thought!" said Gibson. "Did you know him from somewhere?"

"Never seen him before in my life. I thought he was there to give me the good word of the Lord. Still don't know how he found me. Said I came highly recommended. But I still don't know by whom. So after I say no in about a dozen unpleasant ways, he spends three days talking sense to me until I finally give in. Drove back to DC with him. Got my fresh start. George Abe saved my life. That's why I'm doing it."

"That's a hell of a story," Gibson said.

"I know there's bad blood between you and him, but if we pull this off, I really suggest giving him a chance. He's good people."

"I might just do that."

"And on that note, I'm going to bed," Jenn said.

"Yeah, long day tomorrow."

"They're all long days from here on out."

"Good night," Gibson said, carrying their empties to the recycling bin.

"Gibson," Jenn said, stopping him. "I didn't mean what I said."

"About what?"

"About not trusting anybody. I trust George Abe with my life."

"I know you do."

"And you. I trust you. Even if you're an asshole sometimes."

Gibson nodded. "Maybe some more cribbage tomorrow night? Now that I'm actually ahead for once."

"In your dreams, Vaughn."

CHAPTER TWENTY-FIVE

They never did get back to the game. By morning, Jenn's smile was nothing but a distant memory, along with the deck of cards and her cribbage board. When she shook him awake a little before dawn, the bags under her eyes spoke of a restless night. As if she'd been berating herself for taking even a few hours for herself. From that moment on, she was all business. They had a lot of work to do and not a lot of time to do it.

"What?" Gibson asked and tried to roll away. "I'm not going out to Dulles until later when they get busy. Let me sleep."

"We're going for a run," Jenn said. "You've got six minutes."

"Sir, yes, sir," Gibson grumbled. He hadn't slept much either. He'd resolved to start sleeping in a bed, with no more than a night-light for company. It had been rough, but he was done coddling his demons. He might be a long way from being well, but he would fake it until he made it. That was his current thinking anyway.

"Five minutes fifty seconds," Jenn updated him and closed his door.

Gibson bounced from foot to foot, trying to get loose. Cold enough to see his own breath, the weather made his joints feel as if they'd been soldered in place. Jenn started what seemed for her an easy jog. Gibson labored to keep up. When she picked up the pace a mile out, he realized how far he had to go before regaining his old strength and wind.

"I thought we should talk before we get any deeper into the planning," Jenn said.

"As opposed to last night?"

"Calista has the house bugged."

The only part that surprised Gibson was that he hadn't anticipated it. "How do you know?"

"I swept the house the day I arrived. Dan might be the expert, but he taught me a thing or two."

"Wait," Gibson said, thinking back on everything that had been spoken over the past two days. "Why are you only telling me now?"

"Because I needed you to be convincing. We had to have those conversations, and Calista needed to hear us having them. I knew you would question my working with her, and I wanted her to hear me backing her up."

"So what? I was the patsy?"

"You were the convincer. It played better if you were sincere."

Gibson thought back to his confessional and telling Jenn about his eighteen months in solitary. The intimate, painful details that he'd shared. The thought of Calista Dauplaise listening made him sick to his stomach. He pulled up and stood with his hands on his hips, breathing hard.

"Your little speech about trusting me—quite a performance," he said. "Do you think Calista made popcorn?"

Jenn circled back to him, jogging in place. "We need to keep running. I don't know if they're watching."

"Was everything just a performance?"

"Yes," Jenn said. "And no. I meant what I said last night."

"And yet . . ."

"I trust you, Gibson, but I didn't know if you were up to it. You know you're not all there. I couldn't be sure you'd be able to pull it off."

"So why tell me now?"

"Because last night I realized that I needed to put my money where my mouth was. You've done everything I've asked. You're taking the same risks I am. And they are significant. You deserve to see the whole board." Jenn smiled ruefully. "And because, as you've pointed out, we've been on an operation before where I held out on you. Didn't work out too well for me."

"We should keep moving," Gibson said, breaking back into a jog. "In case they're watching."

They ran in silence. Jenn had a gift for offending him and then making it sound like the only sensible course of action. It drove him crazy, but once again, he couldn't argue with her reasoning. Forget admitting it, though; he wasn't feeling that magnanimous.

"So what do you think is on the plane?" Gibson asked.

"You mean Calista's prize? I wish I had some idea. My guess is that it's something on the export-control list. Technology, maybe? Eskridge is moving his operations to Africa. He's going to need a patron. He'll try and trade his cargo for protection and work."

"And we're going to turn that over to Calista Dauplaise?"

"Over my dead body," Jenn said.

"So what's the plan?"

"We don't have one yet."

"We should probably get on that."

"As soon as you get back from not getting arrested at Dulles." Jenn picked up the pace and left Gibson in her dust.

"Oh, right, that."

Gibson did not get arrested at Dulles.

After his little detour to the power plant and diner, Calista revoked his driving privileges for the duration. So he went to the airport under the watchful eye of Cools and Sidhu. They weren't the friendliest chauffeurs, but neither had taken another swing at him.

In the end, it was all rather anticlimactic. Gibson's falsified credentials in the database held up to the scrutiny of the clerk, who issued him a replacement badge. Next, Gibson tested his new green pass, which theoretically gave him the run of the airport. He was a little nervous at his first checkpoint, but he sailed through without a hitch.

Cools and Sidhu drove him back to Reston, where Jenn and he spent long hours poring over the map of the airport and planning the next steps of their operation, after which Gibson would make an incursion to test their assumptions. There was a risk to being too visible a presence around the airport, but there was also a risk to being a completely new face on the day of the operation. By showing up in the days preceding the operation, Gibson could learn his way around, get to know the security staff, and in turn, the staff could get to know Gibson Vaughn, a newly hired mechanic with Tyner Aviation.

Tyner Aviation was one of four fixed-base operators at Dulles that provided support services for general aviation aircraft. Jenn had chosen Tyner because it was the largest FBO and would give Gibson the best chance of going unnoticed. And also because its offices were on the far side of the airport from the Dulles Air Center, a series of private hangars in the northeast corner of the airport, including the one that Cold Harbor staged its flights out of: Hangar Six.

His cover as a mechanic at Tyner held up from day one, allowing Gibson to poke around and ask questions without drawing attention to himself. The new mechanic was a genial sort of fellow but not all that quick on the uptake. As a result, he asked a lot of rudimentary questions about the airport. No one held it against him, though, because he was very sweet about it, and they'd all been new once too.

Gibson returned with the results of his reconnaissance, and then he and Jenn began all over. Both taking turns playing devil's advocate, looking for holes in their thinking. Tearing it to shreds and stitching it back together again. During their morning runs, they used the same tactic to propose ways to keep Eskridge's classified materials from falling into Calista's hands. Then back to the airport went Gibson with fresh questions. Soon, the gaps in their plan narrowed. They did their best to anticipate the ways that things could go sideways on them and write contingencies into their script. Jenn projected an air of confidence that Gibson played into, but they both knew that the airport represented a complex and chaotic target. There were simply too many moving pieces to see everything coming. The risks were high, and the chance of taking George Abe cleanly was low.

Gibson's crash course on Titus Stonewall Eskridge Jr. had been sobering. Eskridge was smart, ruthless, and adaptive. A survivor. Going up against a man like Eskridge under ideal circumstances would be risky, and these circumstances were far from ideal. They didn't know what they'd be walking into in Hangar Six. And if by some miracle Eskridge didn't kill them, they still had Calista Dauplaise to contend with. Jenn, George, and Gibson represented dangerous loose ends to Calista, just as Eskridge did.

Jenn compensated by working longer and harder. She lived for exactly this. She probably had precise, printed mission specs for brushing her teeth. She went over everything in meticulous detail while Gibson took notes. Any element that they couldn't account for went on a master list to be worked out later. She'd drill him until he could recite the mission details backward and forward. If the past was any indication, there would be a quiz later.

"So why don't we get Hendricks in on this?" Gibson suggested one afternoon during a marathon planning session. "I know he'd come. Another set of reliable hands would up our odds on this a lot."

"Can't. Cold Harbor has eyes on him. If he suddenly decamped for the East Coast, Eskridge would know we were making a play for his aircraft. Besides, he's already doing an important job. We know from Calista that Eskridge is surveilling Dan. He and I've spent the last month establishing a false narrative that I am in hiding somewhere on the West Coast. Dan has been openly begging me for a meet. So far I've resisted, but the day before Dulles, I will agree to a meet in the Castro. Ideally, that will give Eskridge a false sense of security and give us the freedom to operate here."

Gibson nodded. "If you're in San Francisco, you can't very well be at Dulles."

"Something like that," she said. "Eskridge had eyes on you too. Another reason I had to stay away from you. But Cold Harbor lost track of you when you disappeared. That's the only reason we thought it safe to reach out."

"Well, it's a shame. We could use Dan here."

"That we could," she said and went back to work.

With a day to spare, Gibson thought they had things nailed down as well as they could on this timetable. But, true to form, Jenn got one of her bad feelings, and they spent the morning reviewing every phase of the operation. Gibson groaned inwardly but resisted the urge to intentionally forget details. He was almost punchy enough to find it funny but not punchy enough to think Jenn would too. In the end, they agreed on the necessity of Gibson making one more trip out to Dulles.

When he returned to the house, he found Jenn in the midst of an equipment and weapons check, a ritual that had evolved into her cleaning every weapon and re-handloading every magazine.

"If it jams on me, I want it to be my fault."

"Happy to be off the hook for that one," he said.

"How did it go at the airport?"

"We may have a small problem."

"Tell me," she said.

The plan called for Jenn to fly into Dulles in a small aircraft rented out of Ohio. After she landed, Gibson would need to pick her up in a Tyner Aviation vehicle. Most of the vehicles inside the airport's security perimeter were parked with keys in the ignition. However, Tyner personnel kept a watchful eye on them. Tyner also had a parking lot outside security. It wasn't nearly as carefully monitored, but no keys were left in vehicles there. If he managed to commandeer a vehicle from that parking lot, Gibson would also need to cross through security to get into the airport. Neither option was ideal, and he'd gone back to the airport to determine the lesser of two evils.

"So I could probably take a vehicle from inside the fence, but after that we're rolling the dice on how long before someone raises the alarm. Might be two hours, might be ten minutes. There's just no way to know."

"So it's got to be a vehicle from outside the lot."

"That would be my vote."

"You don't happen to know how to hot-wire a car?"

"No," Gibson said. He'd been giving this issue a lot of thought, and he had a solution. Jenn wasn't going to like it. Without ever meeting him, she wasn't going to like it one little bit. "But I know a guy."

"You know a guy? Why do I suddenly feel like I'm about to get an STD?"

Gibson described Gavin Swonger to her.

"And there it is," Jenn said in disbelief. "You want to recruit a white-trash, convicted car thief? Are you out of your goddamn mind? There's no time to vet him. I leave in less than eight hours. Calista's going to brick."

"Then let her brick. Look, I'm all for scouring LinkedIn for a Harvard-educated car thief, but I don't know how many of those we're going to find."

"Gibson . . ."

"We're twenty-four hours out. You have a better idea?"

215

"You've worked with this guy?"

"In West Virginia. I'll vouch for him."

Jenn looked as if she'd been given the choice between having her fingers smashed with a hammer or smashed with a rock. "Fine, give your guy a call. I'll smooth things over with Calista. God help me."

Swonger didn't take any convincing at all. He agreed before Gibson even finished laying out what he needed. Gibson brought up payment, and Swonger shut him down.

"Dog, how many times I got to tell you? Your paper's no good here."

"Thanks, Swonger."

"Not a thing. See you mañana." Swonger hung up.

Calista took significantly more persuasion, and Jenn didn't come back downstairs for an hour. When she finally reappeared, they squared away the house ahead of their departure tomorrow. A cleaning crew would follow after them and scour the house from top to bottom, but they wanted to be sure they hadn't left anything incriminating behind.

They cooked dinner together—steaks, grilled brussels sprouts, and pureed cauliflower that, despite Gibson's skepticism, actually tasted exactly like mashed potatoes. It was intended as a morale booster, but it felt too much like a last meal. They ate in silence, then Gibson did the dishes while Jenn burned their plans in the fireplace.

Afterward, Gibson found Jenn watching the Super Bowl with the volume off. He wasn't much of a football fan but found it disconcerting that he hadn't even known the game was on. Another facet of American life from which he felt disconnected. He got the last two beers and dropped onto the couch beside Jenn. They clinked bottle necks to George. Two orphans off to rescue a surrogate father. Gibson couldn't decide whether it was noble or pathetic.

"When did you move in with your grandmother?"

"Eight or nine?" Jenn said. "I'm not actually sure."

"It's weird the way it gets foggy beyond a certain point."

"You too?"

"Only the things I want to remember. The things I don't care about are what I remember best."

Jenn chuckled and raised her beer in agreement.

"Do you remember your mom?" Gibson asked.

"Not real well. Some days, I can only remember the bad things, like you said, but I know there was more to her than that. What about you? Do you remember your dad?"

"I thought I did. Now I think I just make him up as I go along."

"That's the beautiful thing about memories—they're whatever you don't need them to be." She finished her beer, slapped Gibson on the knee, and pried herself up off the couch. "I'm for bed."

Gibson slept a few hours but woke up after two, heart hammering in his chest, afraid he'd been screaming again. He was grateful not to see Jenn staring down at him, bleary-eyed. Only Bear kept vigil tonight, watching from a nearby armchair. She brought her book over and held it out for him to read to her.

"I can't, Bear," Gibson said. "I can't read to you anymore."

Her brow furrowed. "Why not?"

"Because it's not good for me."

Bear stood there looking hurt. It unnerved Gibson, who rolled over and put his back to the ghost. He checked his e-mail again to see if maybe Nicole had written him back. He'd been checking it obsessively for the past few days. His box should have arrived by now, and he kept thinking that he might hear from her. He hadn't. He put the phone aside and lay staring at the back of the couch. Eventually he slept.

Jenn left shortly after dawn. She had a long drive to an airfield in Ohio, where she'd rented a small two-seat Cessna. Gibson rose before her and made breakfast, the only meal he'd ever mastered. Jenn looked it over appreciatively but wolfed down only a slice of bacon. She said she was too amped up to eat. At the door, she hugged him tightly. It reminded him of when they'd said good-bye at the motel in Atlanta.

Even though he'd be seeing her in a matter of hours, it still felt forbidding and final.

She said, "I'll see you tonight."

"11:34 p.m."

"Don't keep me waiting."

"Sir, yes, sir," Gibson said with a grin, trying to force himself into a better mood.

"Smart-ass."

Cools waited for Jenn in the driveway. The first time Gibson had seen him without his partner. Cools helped Jenn load her gear into the trunk. She paused before getting into the passenger seat and gave Gibson an almost imperceptible nod. He returned it and watched them back out of the driveway. When they were out of sight, Gibson shut the door and finished his own preparations.

CHAPTER TWENTY-SIX

It was a beautiful, clear winter night at Dulles, and Gibson hated it. The light of the waning moon was enough to pick out details in the tree line on the far side of the airport. The forecast had called for flurries, but the temperature hovered stubbornly just above freezing, and Doppler weather radar showed all precipitation missing the airport to the north. Snow didn't seem too much to ask. A little fog. A swarm of locusts. Anything to provide a little camouflage, but no, the airport was lit up like a ballpark before a night game.

Swonger knelt to tie his boots for the second time in one hundred yards. Gibson shot him a glance.

"And yet you can hot-wire a car."

"One of my laces broke, dog." Swonger held up the ends for Gibson to see. "They uneven as shit now."

Gibson looked away and sighed. No battle plan survived contact with the enemy—he didn't know who had said that, but they probably hadn't had Swonger's shoelaces in mind. Ahead, the iconic main terminal rose up like a cresting wave. If tonight it finally broke, he and Swonger would be washed away.

"You're a goddamn poet," Duke said.

Since Jenn left this morning, Duke had been his constant companion, lurking silently in the periphery of Gibson's vision. He reminded himself that Duke wasn't real and that he could choose to control it. Easier said than done. The problem with insanity was how incredibly sane it felt. He bit his tongue and said nothing to the smirking ghost of his father.

When commercial passengers approached Dulles, they paid attention only to the main terminal. But to either side stood cargo hangars and the fixed-base operators that supported general aviation. Tyner Aviation was on the left. Jenn would arrive at an FBO on the right side, as far from Tyner as possible. The plan required Gibson to drive around the airport, between the commercial terminals, and pick Jenn up. That was where Swonger came in.

Swonger finished his shoelace surgery, and they strolled across the Tyner Aviation parking lot. Gibson had a spare Tyner Aviation uniform, and from a distance it almost looked like it fit Swonger. They talked loudly and about nothing. Swonger's first rule of boosting cars: act like you owned it.

"Ain't nobody gonna stop you stealing your own car," Swonger said.

They stopped at a panel van with a Tyner Aviation logo along the side. Swonger went to work on the lock, chatting away the entire time. Gibson waited on the passenger side and kept a lookout. When the lock didn't pop right open, Gibson slapped the window to get Swonger's attention.

"I'm freezing out here," he said.

"Fresh air. Good for you."

"That's jet fumes, Swonger."

The lock popped open at last.

"Losing your touch?" Gibson asked.

"I missed you, dog. You my blue sky on a cloudy day."

"Any time now."

"These boys need to service their shit," Swonger groused. "That lock stiffer than my daddy's knees."

Inside the van, Swonger set about hot-wiring the ignition by the light of his cell phone. Gibson checked the time: a few minutes before eleven. The last of the overnight international flights to Europe would be taxiing out to the runways. Assuming she was on schedule, Jenn's Cessna would land in thirty-five minutes. According to Cold Harbor's flight plan, their C-130 had a two a.m. scheduled departure. That would leave two hours and change to secure Cold Harbor's enormous cargo aircraft, rescue George, and get the hell out of Dodge.

Gibson had spent a restless last day in the house, waiting for his ride. Pacing the halls to avoid his father. To his surprise, it had been Cools who had collected him. He'd just completed a nonstop round-trip drive to Jenn's Ohio airfield and was working on a nasty cold. The bags under his eyes were swollen and dark. Sidhu had been nowhere to be seen.

"Where's your partner?" Gibson had asked.

"Busy, but I'll let him know you missed him."

"Just thought you two were a package deal."

"Jesus, Vaughn."

"Are you not allowed to curse in front of him either?"

"Was one beating not enough for you?"

They'd driven to the parking lot of a P. F. Chang's off I-66. Maybe the beer in Swonger's hand had soured things, but it had not been love at first sight for Cools. Swonger had been, well, Swonger about it. Cools had looked like he'd just found blood in his stool.

"This is your guy?" Cools had demanded. "What trailer park did you find this prize in?"

Swonger had thrown his half-full beer at Cools's feet and provided graphic instructions on how to impregnate himself. It had almost come to blows, but Gibson had separated the two men.

"He better come through," Cools had said, letting the implied threat hang between them.

As much as it would have surprised Gibson eighteen months ago, the one part of the plan about which he had zero doubts was Gavin Swonger. Gibson didn't have many friends, but Swonger had mysteriously become one of them. In the pale light of Swonger's cell phone, Gibson watched him hot-wire the van. How many people had a friend who would commit a felony for them, no questions asked?

Too late, Gibson spotted movement out of the corner of his eye. A roaming airport police officer appeared from between two parked vehicles. The steam of his breath swirled above the officer like smoke after a hard-fought battle. Gibson watched him veer in their direction.

"We've been made," Gibson whispered. "Someone's coming."

Swonger glanced over the dashboard at the approaching officer, but his hands didn't stop working. "I need another minute."

Gibson sized up the situation and didn't like how it looked— two guys sitting in a dark van in the middle of the night. Swonger wore a Tyner uniform but no credentials; he wouldn't stand up to a semi-careful inspection. The fact that they didn't have keys to the van wouldn't help matters either.

"Pop the hood," Gibson said and unzipped his coat far enough that his credentials were visible. He got out, ignored the security guard, and propped up the hood. Scanning the engine, he loosened a connection at the base of the fuse block.

"Try the lights," he told Swonger.

Nothing happened, which was predictable since he'd disconnected the battery. Gibson cursed for the benefit of the officer, who had appeared at his side.

"Having some car trouble?" the officer asked in a friendly tone, but his eyes were narrow and alert. He had a round white face that the cold had mottled pink like uncooked bacon.

"Yeah, engine won't turn over," Gibson confirmed. He faced the officer so his credentials were in plain sight.

"Battery?" the officer asked, stepping around Gibson to get a look at Swonger. Swonger gave the officer an incongruous thumbs-up.

"That was my thought, but the clamps are all good," Gibson said. "Cheap bastards need to service these vehicles regularly. It's getting ridiculous."

"Sounds like your boss knows my boss," the officer said. "Have you checked the fuses?"

"I would if I could see what I was doing."

The officer flicked on a long-barreled Maglite and shone it on the engine. "Let's take a look."

"You are a lifesaver."

"To protect and illuminate," the officer replied.

Gibson forced a chuckle. "I like that."

Together they leaned over the engine block. Gibson hesitated, granting him a head start. He hoped the officer would spot the problem on his own. Playing the hero felt good, and generally people would avoid undermining that narrative. In this case by not asking questions that might reveal that he'd helped to steal a car. The officer's hand went out and felt around the sparkplug caps.

"Anything?" Swonger asked, sticking his head out the window. "I'm ready to get goin', already."

"I think we're going to have to call in for a jump," Gibson said.

"Hold on," the officer said. He held up the loose connector. "Think I found your problem."

Gibson grinned at him. "Son of a gun."

The officer reattached it, and Gibson told Swonger to give it another try. The van started right up. Gibson clapped the officer on the shoulder.

"By the power invested in me, I make you an honorary mechanic."

"You're a mechanic?" the officer asked.

"Don't tell anyone about this. My review's coming up."

The officer looked amused at this tidbit, and Gibson could see him arranging the story in his mind to tell his buddies later. Gibson had a feeling he wouldn't come out well in the officer's version—some numbnuts aircraft mechanic too dumb to check his own fuse block. *That's all right*, Gibson thought. The officer had earned it.

Gibson let the hood drop, and the two men shook hands. Swonger leaned out the window to offer his thanks, and the officer strolled off on his rounds.

"That was close," Gibson whispered.

"You breaking into an airport, dog. What were you expecting? One of them little mints on your pillow?"

Gibson didn't have a rebuttal to that. Instead, he had Swonger show him the toggle switch that he'd jury-rigged under the dashboard, bypassing the ignition switch. Swonger started the van and shut it off several times.

"Simple as that," Swonger said. "Oh, you might need this." He held up half of a car key—just the bow and shoulder. Swonger fitted it in the ignition switch. "In case some mook sticks his nose in."

"Damn, that's perfect. Thank you." Gibson put out a hand.

"Ain't nothing. Sure you don't want me to stick around? Somebody need to watch your back."

"No, if this thing goes sideways, grand theft will be the tip of the iceberg," Gibson said.

"So who you helping this time?"

"What do you mean?"

Swonger tilted his head and arched his eyebrows. "Come on. We both know you ain't the type to break into no airport. So stands to reason somebody laid a sob story on you. Hope it's at least a girl this time and not some wrinkly-ass judge."

"Actually, it is a she."

"There it is!" Swonger whooped.

"But I wouldn't go calling her a girl to her face."

"Now we talking. Now we talking!" Swonger grinned mischievously. "Is she fine? She's fine, isn't she? Tell me she's fine."

Gibson put up a hand begging for Swonger to stop, but he was smiling. "It's not like that."

Swonger groaned and threw his arms up to the heavens. "Aw, you killing me. Why you got to be so damn selfless? Makes me want to pop you one. Answer me this: What's in it for Gibson? You got to hit that, dog."

"What's in it for you, helping Lea?" Gibson retorted.

At the mention of Lea's name, Swonger stopped and turned somber. "You right. You right. My bad." He stared out the window at the runways. "But maybe, after this is over, you find something for you?"

Gibson didn't know how to explain that there wasn't going to be an afterward for him. He realized he'd been saying good-bye to the people and places that made up his life. Casting them off before whatever came next. Swonger was another piece of that old life. The last piece, as fate would have it. This time tomorrow, he'd either be dead or in custody. He smiled at his friend.

Swonger narrowed his eyes. "Dog . . . you about to burst into song or some shit? Why you giving me the Disney-princess eyes?"

Gibson chuckled. "Something like that," he said and handed Swonger an envelope with five thousand dollars inside.

Swonger tried to give it back. "What I tell you? Don't want your money."

"It isn't my money. And believe me, she can spare it. Take it."

Swonger relented and ran his thumb through the stack of bills approvingly. "Was going to hit the casino up in DC anyway. Now it be like playing with house money. Gonna play me some blackjack tonight, boy."

"There's a casino in DC?"

"MGM National Harbor. Dog, you really went away."

And would again once this was over. One way or another.

CHAPTER TWENTY-SEVEN

The van idled at the checkpoint, waiting to be cleared through from land-side to air-side. Gibson knew one of the officers on duty. They said hello, and Gibson handed him his badge. The officer disappeared into the security booth to run the plates and Gibson's credentials. Gibson counted at least four security cameras. It made him jittery knowing this was the point of no return, but he chatted amiably with the officer. He was pulling it off fine until Duke piped up.

"Tell him how the airport looks like a wave. I bet he's a poetry lover too."

Gibson's head snapped around before he could stop himself. He glared at his father and mouthed, "Shut up." When he turned back, the officer had a troubled look on his face.

"You all right, pal?"

Gibson did his best to play it off, improvising a story about headaches and neck pain. The officer didn't seem overly sympathetic. Gibson tried to change the subject, get the conversation rolling again, but the officer stepped back and cut him off.

"Sir, step out of the vehicle."

Gibson asked what the problem was, but the officer only repeated his command, so he did as he was told. Duke looked pleased with himself. The officer kept a watchful eye on him until the other officer came back from the booth with Gibson's badge. He gave his partner a questioning look.

"What's going on?"

The officers conferred in whispers while Gibson wondered how far he'd get if he ran. He kicked himself for falling for Duke's provocation. He'd made progress learning to block out Duke and Bear, but when it counted, he'd failed. Jenn had been right. It was over before it even began, and it was all his fault. He'd blown it.

"All right, Gibson. You're good to go," the first officer said, handing him back his badge.

Gibson looked at it in surprise. "Everything okay?"

"Yeah, he's new like you. Good guy. Little gung ho is all."

Gibson got back in the van and watched the gate open. The officer told him to take care of his neck and slapped the side of the van. Not exactly how he'd drawn it up, but he was through to the air-side. He wouldn't get that lucky twice. "Keep it together," he repeated aloud over and over like a mantra.

The commercial wing of Dulles was composed of three parallel terminals. When Gibson had been a kid, mobile lounges—lumbering, seventy-ton, buslike vehicles—had shuttled passengers back and forth between the main concourse and the outer terminals. It was a slow, inefficient system, and in 2010, Dulles had finally replaced the mobile lounges with an underground rail system, but Gibson still felt nostalgic for the old buses. It had been exhilarating to be out on the tarmac among the behemoths as they started, then stopped, showing deference for the gleaming 747s. Almost like being on safari among dinosaurs—at least to a little boy.

Gibson felt a trace of that now as he steered the van along Alpha Road, a utility corridor that fronted the main concourse. Everything was scaled to enormous proportions; his van was dwarfed by the aircraft and larger service vehicles. Jenn had reviewed the protocols and procedures for driving on this part of the airport, but Gibson worried he'd make a mistake and a late-arriving Airbus would bulldoze him into the tarmac. He took it slow and made nervous full stops like a kid taking his first driver's test.

"You remember when we flew out of here?" he asked Duke.

"If you remember, I remember."

"You knew every aircraft."

"I made all of that up," Duke said.

"No, you didn't."

"Call it eighty-twenty, then." Duke winked at him, and for a moment Gibson saw his father. His real father, not the angry ghoul that his subconscious had birthed. Duke Vaughn wouldn't have wanted any of this for his son. He hadn't been a vengeful or spiteful man. It would sadden him to know Gibson had fallen so far. Gibson thought that was an important idea and one worth holding on to.

"You're not the man I thought you'd be," Duke said.

"I know. Me neither."

His father looked taken aback at how easily Gibson had acquiesced. "What's wrong with you?"

"I don't want to fight with you anymore," Gibson said.

"That's too bad, because I'm not done fighting with you."

"I know," Gibson said and turned off Alpha Road. The van disappeared between the satellite buildings that provided support services for the terminals and airlines. He followed the signs for NW Service Road. To his right, the van passed a series of freight hangars, and even at this late hour they were a beehive of activity. Commercial flights stopped before midnight, but cargo flights came and went around the clock. Overnight shipping meant exactly that. Out the driver's side window, the runways stretched out of sight. He checked the time. Jenn should be on the ground by now. He accelerated as much as he dared.

Near the end of NW Service Road, Gibson saw Russert Aviation, a fixed-base operator and competitor of Tyner Aviation. All manner of private aircraft were parked around the Russert offices and hangars—from single-engine Cessnas and small Learjets all the way up to corporate Gulfstreams that ran into the tens of millions of dollars.

He parked the van at the curb by the main doors. Jenn would be inside, and he waited two minutes for her to make herself scarce. He took the old Phillies cap from the pocket of his jacket and rubbed the brim between his thumb and forefinger. When it was time, he put the cap back in his pocket and got out of the van. Duke was there waiting for him.

"Good luck," his father said.

"Really?"

"Just trying it out. Don't get used to it."

Gibson pushed through the revolving doors into Russert Aviation. Indistinct jazz filled the wide, tastefully furnished lobby, which reminded Gibson of a hotel. Russert offered a gourmet bistro, conference room, fitness center, and showers. Everything needed for a budding jet-set lifestyle. At this late hour, the lights, tastefully dimmed, accentuated the views out the floor-to-ceiling windows. Not that there was anyone there to appreciate the effect apart from the counter agent, who greeted Gibson with a cheerful wave.

"Greetings, friend!" the counter agent said as if Gibson's unexpected appearance had just made life worth living again. The man's perky, energetic persona belied the fact that it was almost midnight. A night owl for the night shift, and a little ray of sunshine on a cold, dark night. Although Russert was technically a competitor of Gibson's putative employer, he hadn't seen any trace of rivalry among the employees, who largely saw themselves as brothers-in-arms against the barely controlled chaos of airport life. Gibson was depending on exactly that now.

They exchanged pleasantries while the agent continued typing busily at his terminal. Behind him sat Jenn's brand-new luggage—four expensive, hard-sided suitcases decorated in brash floral patterns that proved money didn't buy taste. Overkill, perhaps, but their weapons and gear weighed significantly more than clothes, so they'd chosen to spread them out to avoid raising suspicion. The counter agent finished typing and looked up at Gibson.

"So what brings you to our humble corner of the world?"

Gibson leaned on the counter and adopted a weary posture. This part of the plan demanded finesse, because to work it required his new friend here to break protocol. If the counter agent picked up the phone and called over to Tyner Aviation, then they were cooked. It would be the sensible thing to do, so Gibson would have to give the man a good reason not to do it.

Gibson looked around the empty lobby. "Well, I was hoping you could help me out, but it doesn't look like it."

"Sorry to hear that. What's the problem?"

"Well, I've sort of lost a plane," Gibson confessed.

"You lost a what, now? How is that . . ."

The counter agent trailed off as a woman burst out of the bathroom at the far end of the lobby. Gibson turned and joined him in staring. Intellectually, he knew it was Jenn, but that didn't mean he recognized her.

She had warned him that she intended to go bold and loud, but he hadn't known exactly what that meant until now. She wore a cap-sleeve black cocktail napkin of a dress with a plunging V-neck that ended not far from where Gibson imagined her belly button to be. That was about all it did leave to the imagination. Add to that four-inch heels and enough gold jewelry to start a new currency, and the garishness of her luggage suddenly made much more sense. The oversized black sunglasses were an especially nice touch, given the hour.

Jenn crossed the lobby toward them much the way German panzers had crossed into Poland—rampant and undeniable. She had not been subtle applying makeup—her cheekbones stood out like defiant cliffs, and the cruel red of her lips accentuated a contemptuous sneer. She slapped a burgundy Chanel handbag down on the counter like she'd just planted a flag on a newly conquered continent.

"Well," Jenn demanded in a hard Russian accent. "Have you found my fucking flight yet?"

Gibson bit down on his tongue to stifle a laugh at her audacity. It worked perfectly.

"No, but I am still looking," the counter agent said.

"I cannot be late," she said. "If you make me late, I will . . ." She finished her threat in Russian before returning to English. "How is it you cannot find an airplane? Are there so many that you do not know where one is? Are you an idiot?"

"Ma'am, I am looking, but I have nothing scheduled for this morning. Are you certain you have the right day?"

Jenn's expression turned to molten rage. Through clenched teeth, a stream of hot Russian poured out. Gibson didn't speak a word himself, but he knew tone of voice well enough to know that the counter agent's family had just been cursed for generations to come. The counter agent looked miserable but stood politely by while Jenn belittled him. Somehow his helpful smile never wavered. Gibson waited for an opening and threw him a lifeline.

"Excuse me. Did you say you were meeting a plane?" Gibson asked, but the counter agent wasn't getting off that easy. It took Gibson three more attempts before Jenn deigned to acknowledge his existence. Her performance was so convincing that, for a moment, Gibson felt irritated by her grandstanding. He knew she was good, but he had no idea she was this good. He hadn't known Jenn in her CIA days, but the Agency had been fools to let her get away.

"What?" she demanded, turning on Gibson as if taken aback that there was anyone else in the building. "What is it you want?"

"You're supposed to meet a plane?"

"Yes, this is what I am saying. Are you also an idiot?"

Gibson glanced over at the counter agent. They were nearing the sales pitch, and Gibson wanted to take his temperature. The counter agent gave him a helpless, sympathetic nod, which Gibson took as a positive indicator. To help push the needle a little further in their favor, Jenn went back to assaulting him in Russian. Gibson let her go a few more rounds before stepping in again.

"Are you a guest of Rupert Delgado?" Gibson asked.

"*Da.* This is what I am trying to tell this fool."

"All right, there's been a bit of a mix-up," Gibson said.

"She's your missing plane?" the counter agent asked with relief in his voice.

"What mix-up?" Jenn asked suspiciously.

"You're at the wrong FBO. When you landed, you should have been directed to Tyner Aviation. This is Russert."

"Tyner! Russert! I do not care. Why did you do this?" Jenn demanded, summoning her inner Romanov.

"Ma'am, that was aircraft control, not us. The important thing now is that Mr. Delgado is ready to go," Gibson said.

"And I am not?" Jenn pronounced, emphatically gesturing to her own figure. If she'd had a mic in her hand, she'd have dropped it.

"All right, then," Gibson said, clapping his hands together. "Let's get you to that plane."

"What about her aircraft?" The counter agent was pointing out to the ramp. "It can't stay here."

Gibson played crestfallen. For obvious reasons, protocol required an aircraft be in its designated location. Proper procedure called for Jenn's plane to be relocated immediately.

Gibson nodded emphatically. "Yeah, of course. Where's her pilot? Are they still air-side? Can they move it?"

"She's the pilot," the counter agent said.

"She's a pilot?" Gibson feigned disbelief.

He didn't know how Jenn made herself flush on command, but she went the color of red-wine vinegar. She snatched a cell phone from her purse and walked away from the counter and launched into a fresh tirade to an imaginary girlfriend.

"Wow," Gibson mouthed despairingly at the counter agent, who exhaled in relief at the momentary reprieve.

"Who is Rupert Delgado?" the counter agent asked.

"Real estate. Worth a couple billion. Not the world's nicest guy, if you know what I mean."

"Yeah, I know the type. When does Delgado's jet leave?"

Gibson checked the time. "Twenty minutes."

"Want me to call over to your desk? Tell them to hold his flight while we take care of this?"

Gibson took his time pretending to weigh the pros and cons in his mind. They'd reached the moment of truth, wherein the mark was convinced to break the rules to help a total stranger. But for it to work, Gibson couldn't ask for the favor. It needed to be offered. So far, though, despite being sympathetic, the counter agent had played it by the book. Which meant it was time for the calculated gamble that lay at the center of their deception. Gibson had hoped it wouldn't come to this.

"Yeah, may as well," Gibson said. "Delgado's going to peel my face off."

The counter agent picked up the phone.

Jenn hung up her imaginary call with a snarl and pivoted on Gibson. "*Nyet. Nyet.* You do not call. Rupert will not be happy. Not with me, with you. You understand me? We go now to the plane, or you will need new employment."

Jenn kept up her threats in an escalating spiral as Gibson begged her to be reasonable. Out of the corner of his eye, he watched the phone hover in the counter agent's hand. *Have a heart.* Slowly, slowly, it lowered back into its cradle.

"How soon can you get back here?" the counter agent asked.

Jenn and Gibson went silent in unison.

"Give me an hour?" Gibson said.

"How about two?"

Gibson could have kissed him.

CHAPTER TWENTY-EIGHT

"You speak Russian?" Gibson asked when they were safely in the van.

"Don't you?" She held his gaze stonily for a long moment. The corner of her mouth flickered up in the memory of a smile.

"I thought his head was going to explode."

"Let's go before he changes his mind."

That sounded like a real good idea. Gibson threw the van in reverse and backed out. The Dulles Air Center and Titus Eskridge's Hangar Six were all the way around on the far side of the airport, past Tyner Aviation. While Gibson drove them back the way he had come, Jenn disappeared into the back and opened one of the suitcases. She peeled off her dress, all the jewelry, and changed into black BDUs.

"Now I see why you're helping her," Duke said with a smile.

"Eyes front, Dad."

"And another angel gets his wings."

Jenn climbed back into the front seat to pull on her boots. With her Russian party-girl hair and makeup, it made for an interesting dichotomy.

"What?" she asked suspiciously.

"You got a little something on your face."

"Oh, shut the hell up. You know how long it would take to get all this off? I used so much hair spray it's like a fiberglass beehive."

"No . . . you looked—"

"Make peace with God before you finish that sentence."

The adrenaline relief of coming within a hair's breadth of disaster made them both a little giddy. For a few minutes, they bantered back and forth like a couple of kids who had snuck out of the house past curfew. Quickly, though, the gravity of the situation reimposed itself, and they fell silent as the van passed between the main terminals. The operation had already had three close calls—the cop when Swonger hot-wired the van, the security guard at the checkpoint, and then the counter agent. Not being cats, they were fast running out of lives.

The Cold Harbor flight wouldn't depart for ninety minutes, which allowed Gibson to make a wide detour around the Tyner Aviation offices. The last thing they needed was for someone to glance up and wonder where one of their trucks was going at this hour. It gave Jenn time to review the next phase of the plan. Both knew it front to back, but Gibson let her talk. It focused her and settled him down. And if they were being absolutely honest, this was the point when their meticulous planning became little more than a series of branching contingencies. What the Marines called a fragmentary order—a set of standard operating procedures when plans needed to be drawn up in the field—if this, then that; if that, then this.

The difference was, Marine units spent countless hours drilling those standard operating procedures. Jenn and Gibson had worked through theirs only in theory. They were a unit in name only. And to make matters worse, they were going up against professional mercenaries who had trained together for years. They had the element of surprise going for them and not much else.

Sometimes that was enough.

Calista had a source inside the company who had given them a detailed snapshot of a typical Cold Harbor supply run. But this flight was anything but typical. Eskridge was smuggling a kidnapped US citizen out of the country along with his mysterious cargo. Secrecy surrounding tonight had been draconian. Already deeply paranoid, Eskridge had managed all aspects of the flight personally. No one outside his immediate circle had been included, and Calista hadn't dared push too hard for fear of raising suspicion.

So Jenn and Gibson had planned for multiple contingencies, aware that Hangar Six would remain an unknown until they had eyes on it. Hence the four large suitcases—Jenn was prepared to fight several different battles depending on what they walked into in Hangar Six. Would Eskridge stick to his script and maintain Cold Harbor's low profile? Or would he ramp up security and risk drawing unwanted attention from customs agents? They were about to find out.

Jenn slung a lightweight nylon tactical rig over her shoulders as the Dulles Air Center rose into view. A white, V-shaped series of six interconnected hangars, the Air Center had its offices and customer center at the pivot, with three hangars on each side. Hangar Six was the last hangar on the northern wing and large enough to park a 747.

From the outside, the customer center looked much the same as Russert Aviation, except that Gibson saw no one at the front desk. He tried the doors, but they were locked. He rang the overnight buzzer and hopped from foot to foot in the cold. A minute passed. He rang again. Jenn nodded tensely from the dark of the van when he glanced back. Finally, a woman in her forties appeared. She wore the expression of a pretty nineties sitcom wife whose plus-size husband had gotten up to his predictable shenanigans. Through the glass door, she asked what Gibson wanted. The keys in her hand jangled, but she made no move to unlock the door.

"Yeah, hi," Gibson said. "Did Mindy talk to you? I'm here to borrow a jack stand."

"I haven't talked to a Mindy."

"Mindy didn't call? No, of course she didn't. Unbelievable," he said, making it sound like the most believable thing he'd heard all year. Typical Mindy.

"How long do you need it?"

"An hour, maybe two. Tops."

She considered the request for a moment before kneeling to unlatch the door's floor lock. After he was inside, she almost went to relock it behind him, but laziness won out. This was Dulles . . . what could happen?

Gibson followed her through the lobby and into a back office. The same featureless jazz as Tyner Aviation's played overhead. It gave Gibson the surreal feeling that he wasn't making any progress at all. Duke sat in one of the armchairs in the lobby. He whistled tunelessly as his son passed.

One half of the large back office was divided by a series of cubicles. A photocopier. Community table. A bank of security monitors occupied another corner. If the three men in the office hadn't looked up at Gibson, they might have seen Jenn slip in the front door. Gibson raised a hand in greeting. Two looked to be mechanics, the third a customer service rep. Gibson didn't spot any aspiring heroes among them, but one of the mechanics was a powerfully built man with camshaft arms. Gibson would keep an eye on him.

"Any of you talk to a Mindy?" the sitcom wife asked.

The three men shook their heads.

"Unbelievable," Gibson said again.

"Don't worry about it. We all know a Mindy," she said.

Without knowing the details or Mindy, the room chuckled in agreement. More than love or family, incompetent management crossed all culture and language.

Gibson grinned at them appreciatively. "Lot of you fellas here tonight," he said. "How many of you do they have working this late?"

That provoked some grumbling.

"Six," said one mechanic.

"You believe that?" the other mechanic said.

"We have a late flight going out," the sitcom wife explained. "After that, most of us are out of here."

"Except me," the customer service agent said. "I'm here forever."

"I hear that," Gibson commiserated and took out his phone. He called Jenn, who picked up on the first ring.

"Mindy," Gibson said, rolling his eyes for the benefit of the crowd. "I'm over at DAC. Who did you talk to here?" He shook his head at her explanation. "Fine. Fine. Whatever. They're going to help us out anyway, but it makes me look stupid is what it does." He feigned listening again and made noises as though she were asking him a question. "Yeah, well, we have four total. I've ordered spares because two are missing. No, I'm not sure where they are. Yeah, six total."

Jenn confirmed the numbers and gave him a thirty-second count. Gibson hung up and threw his hands up at the ceiling dramatically.

"Fucking Mindy," one of the mechanics said on his behalf.

"I appreciate the assist, guys." Gibson walked toward them under the pretense of shaking their hands, starting with the big mechanic. He wanted to be in the way in case any of them took their bravery pills this morning.

Jenn kicked in the office door.

She was a specter clad in black from head to foot. A balaclava concealed her face. But Gibson bet the only detail they'd remember was the barrel of the Remington shotgun. Shotguns had a funny way of erasing all other memories. It was loaded with nonlethal beanbag rounds, but the only way to know would be to take one to the chest. It was a steep learning curve, and it would take a hardy soul to sit for that exam.

Jenn racked the slide and yelled at them to get their hands up. Barking instructions—hard, decisive commands. Controlling the room. Allowing no time for anyone to even think about fighting back. Gibson raised his hands and backed up into the group.

Jenn herded them out of the office, back through the lobby, and into the conference room. She shifted into a soothing, calm voice. "Stay quiet. Do as you're told. No one will be hurt." She repeated it over and over. A lullaby for a child woken by a terrible nightmare. She ordered them facedown on the ground, fingers laced behind their heads. When everyone was down, she prodded Gibson in the side with her boot. "You. Up."

"You just told me to get down," Gibson complained, climbing to his feet. "Make up your mind."

The sitcom wife hissed at him to shut up and do it. She seemed to press herself even deeper into the carpet as if her own obedience could compensate for Gibson's mouthiness.

Jenn dropped a bag of zip ties at Gibson's feet and ordered him to hog-tie the other four. Gibson moved down the line as quickly as he could while still playing the unwilling accomplice. The shotgun leveled at his chest made for a convincing prop. His four new friends peered up fearfully, but no one struggled and no one fought back. When all four were secured, gagged, and hooded, Jenn ordered Gibson back down on the ground. They waited a minute and went back to the Air Center office and got to work.

First things first: Gibson hacked into the Dulles Air Center computers and disabled the server that recorded security footage. He deleted the last thirty minutes. They'd been recorded by enough cameras across Dulles to put them away for a long, long time, but the last thirty minutes had been especially damning. The next thirty might be even worse.

He left the cameras functional, however, so Jenn could confirm no stray personnel wandering about where they shouldn't. Satisfied, Jenn had Gibson switch all of the monitors to the various camera angles inside Hangar Six. They huddled before the monitors and studied the lay of the land, eager to finally know what they were up against.

In the center of the hangar sat a slate-gray Lockheed C-130 Hercules. A wide, slow-moving beast with the top speed of an aerodynamic brick, it wasn't fast, comfortable, or pretty. But it was durable and got you there in one piece. Gibson had flown in one like it more times than he could count in the Marines. A military workhorse since the 1950s, the C-130 had been designed as a troop and cargo transport. But it had also been adapted to myriad other roles in its sixty-plus-year lifespan. Its wings stretched 133 feet, tip to tip, but the hangar was large enough that a pair of medium-size jets were parked comfortably against the north wall.

The C-130's four turboprop engines couldn't be safely started inside the hangar. That explained the two missing mechanics, who were attaching a ramp vehicle to tow the aircraft outside. Jenn sketched out the interior of the enormous hangar. Besides the mechanics, they counted two Cold Harbor mercenaries guarding the hangar's interior doors and another pair guarding the exterior access door. Five more huddled at the bottom of the C-130's ramp. All wore desert camos, but none was visibly armed.

As far as they could tell, Eskridge had indeed played it low-key, relying on the safety provided by Dulles. Still, nine unarmed mercenaries spread out across a hangar this size would be a lot more difficult to control than a roomful of airport staff. And that accounted only for the ones they could see. They had no view of the aircraft's interior. Calista had insisted that the bulk of Cold Harbor's personnel had already decamped for North Africa, but Gibson knew from experience how many men a C-130 could hold. If it had more than a skeleton flight crew tonight, they would have some hard decisions to make. Gibson feared that Jenn had already made them. She viewed everyone associated with Cold Harbor as complicit. If they encountered heavy resistance taking the plane, she wouldn't hesitate to kill them all.

Kill them all or die trying.

Jenn pointed to a man holding a clipboard. "That one is the loadmaster. He'll have the manifest. We're going to want to talk to him. The rest look like mercs."

"That's a lot of men."

"Agreed."

"We need to thin the herd," Gibson said. "Bring some of them to us."

"What do you have in mind?"

They both studied the flickering images, looking for an answer. Gibson wanted to avoid a bloodbath if possible. He had an idea.

"The hangar door is closed," Gibson said.

"And?"

"The master override is computer controlled. I saw it when I was in their system. If we kill the hangar door, someone's going to have to come check on it."

Jenn liked that idea. Together they sketched out a plan and went out to the van for her suitcases. She unpacked the gear they would need while Gibson used the office's computer to lock down the hangar door. Then they waited and watched.

The clock ticked closer to one a.m.

The mechanics finished hooking up the ramp vehicle. One walked over to a control box mounted on the wall between the exterior access door and the enormous retractable hangar door. On the silent monitors, Jenn and Gibson watched the mechanic turn a key and punch a green button. Nothing happened. The mechanic tried it several more times. The two Cold Harbor mercs guarding the exterior access door gathered around and gave it a try. Still nothing. The other mechanic wandered over, and the four of them diligently troubleshot the problem before eventually reaching the consensus opinion that it didn't work.

One of the men standing at the rear of the C-130 strode across the hangar to find out what was happening. He had the bearing of a man whose schedule was being blown all to hell.

"I know him. Name is Norrgard. He's the leader and a mean son of a bitch," Jenn said and leaned in to study his flickering image. "Control him, and we control the room."

Down in the hangar, a decision had been reached. Accompanied by two Cold Harbor mercs, one of the mechanics hustled across the hangar. They went out a smaller door and into the service corridor that connected the hangars and the Dulles Air Center offices. The man that Jenn had identified as the leader updated the rest of his team on the situation. The second mechanic went back to the ramp vehicle and made himself comfortable behind the wheel.

Gibson reactivated the hangar-door controls.

Then they got ready for company.

CHAPTER TWENTY-NINE

The mechanic from the hangar was thicker than Gibson, but his shirt fit passably if Gibson tucked it in all the way.

"How do I look?" Gibson asked.

"Like you shrunk in the wash," Jenn said.

"That's not reassuring."

"Relax. You're a mechanic, not a male model."

"The mechanic in the hangar will know I'm wrong."

"He'll be a hundred feet away. Keep your head down and keep moving. You'll be fine."

"I think fine is optimistic," Gibson said. "Do you think he'll be on board?"

"No, Eskridge is too smart to be anywhere near this."

"I meant George."

"He has to be," Jenn said with a weariness that reinforced Gibson's belief that she had reached the end of her line.

They both had.

He thought about what that meant on the long, cold walk down the corridor to Hangar Six. He might die tonight, and he greeted the idea with indifference. If anything, it would be a relief. What little he had left to lose had already been lost. No matter what happened tonight, Damon Ogden and a prison cell waited for him. Knowing there was no way back and only one way forward, he felt weightless and, strangely, free.

Despite Jenn's reassurances, he was still worried that the mechanic would see him and sound the alarm. Gibson pulled his Phillies baseball cap from his jacket pocket. He ran his fingers across the brim as he did sometimes when he needed good luck.

"Put it on," Bear said. "Or do you still think you don't deserve to?"

"It's complicated."

They came to the hangar door. He considered the cap again. It would really help conceal his face, but still he hesitated.

"Put it on," she said again with the gentle lilt of someone coaxing a nervous puppy into the open.

He did as she asked and fitted it low over his eyes.

Bear looked him over with a kind smile. "It suits you."

"If you say so," Gibson replied and opened the door.

The cameras hadn't conveyed the enormity of the hangar. The ceilings soared overhead like a cathedral, and every sound was answered by a faraway echo. Even the enormous C-130, in the center of the hangar, looked insignificant by comparison. There would be nowhere to hide if things went wrong. And he'd be in enemy territory the entire way. As if to remind him of that fact, the two mercs guarding the door stepped into his path.

"Heard you boys broke my hangar," he said and shook his canvas tool bag for effect. Neither cracked a smile.

"Hurry up," one said. "We're running late."

"You stopped me."

That observation did little to endear him to them or to move them out of his way. He squeezed between them and walked toward the control panel, which was diagonally across the hangar. It looked like a day's hike between here and there. Unfortunately, the C-130 sat between here and there. His feet wanted to take the long way around to avoid the three mercs at the bottom of the C-130's ramp. But he was keenly aware that they were all watching him now, so he forced himself to walk straight toward them. At the aircraft, Gibson glanced up the ramp but didn't see a platoon of men lying in wait.

"Doesn't mean they're not in there," Duke said pleasantly.

Gibson ignored him.

The leader—the one Jenn had identified as Norrgard—was an imposing man with Scandinavian features and a dissatisfied scowl that had etched deep lines around his mouth and clearly made smiling more trouble than it was worth. He was Eskridge's right hand at Cold Harbor, and Jenn had sketched out his string of atrocities across Nigeria in 2014. Just on the off chance Gibson wasn't terrified before.

Norrgard paused as Gibson approached. With military precision, he snapped his arm crisply at the elbow and examined his wristwatch. "Take your time, sweetheart," he told Gibson with a voice that reminded Gibson of every drill instructor at Parris Island—one part disgust, one part *what is the world coming to?*, two parts *I ought to charge you for breathing my air.*

"I'm going, aren't I?" Gibson said.

Norrgard looked from Gibson to the interior door and back to Gibson. "Where are my men?" he asked, meaning the two mercs sent to check on the problem with the hangar door. Jenn had subdued them and tied them up with the others.

"The hell should I know?" Gibson said. "The pisser?"

"Together?"

"Maybe they like to hold hands. Look, you want me to fix the door or go chaperone your boys? Your call."

The big Scandinavian bristled but only cocked a thumb toward the control panel. "Get that door open or I'll polish my foot in your ass."

"Aye, aye, *capitaine*," Gibson said with a mock salute.

Crossing the hangar, Gibson adjusted his cap still lower and slung the tool bag over his shoulder so that his right arm concealed his face.

As he came around the C-130, the other mechanic called out a greeting from the driver's seat of the ramp vehicle. Gibson raised his free arm and gave an ironic thumbs-up. Hopefully, the mechanic wouldn't get ambitious and come offer to help.

"So, what seems to be the trouble, boys?" Gibson asked the final two Cold Harbor mercs who stood guard by the exterior hangar door.

"Door don't work," one said with the stupid accuracy of the mechanically disinclined. He pointed at the open access panel.

"Why don't I take a look-see," Gibson said and knelt to unzip his bag. Among the tools, he saw the Taser and a Glock. He reached for the flashlight instead and shone it into the access panel, nodding thoughtfully as if he had a clue what he was doing. Out of the corner of his eye, he saw the other mechanic moseying in his direction. That narrowed Gibson's timetable considerably. He estimated twenty seconds before the mechanic got a good look at him and raised the alarm. He didn't like how close the two Cold Harbor mercs stood to him, but there wasn't time to do anything about them now. Gibson only hoped that Jenn was in position.

He reached up into the access panel and mimed fiddling with the wiring. Then he stood, dusted off his dustless hands, and punched the oversized green button on the control panel. The enormous retractable door began to open. Given its size, Gibson had assumed it would be deafening, but the motors rumbled quietly overhead. He realized this was the same gambit he'd tried in Damon Ogden's garage. After everything that had happened, all he'd done was trade one garage for a much larger, much more dangerous one. As he reached for the Glock and not the Taser, the symmetry of his life struck him as darkly funny.

A hand slapped him on the back.

Behind him, the mechanic congratulated him on troubleshooting the problem. Simultaneously, from the far side of the aircraft, a shotgun discharged. Once. Twice. Rumbling through the hangar like distant thunder.

Everything slowed down.

Everyone turned to see.

Everyone but Gibson.

The two Cold Harbor mercs took several tentative steps toward the aircraft. It bought Gibson critical yards.

He pointed the Glock at the ceiling and fired twice.

The mechanic flinched as thousands of years of survival instinct drove him into a crouch. Gibson shoved him hard to the ground, barking at them to get down, facedown. The mechanic rolled into a ball and covered his head with his arms.

The two Cold Harbor men didn't flinch, decades of training sublimating their base drives. They pivoted smoothly, assessed the threat, and moved quickly apart to create two targets from one. It reminded Gibson of pack hunters circling prey. He yelled for them to get down, but instead, they showed their hands and kept moving laterally and forward.

The warning shots had been a mistake. The Corps had taught him better than this. You didn't shoot to warn. You didn't shoot to wound. If it came time to pull the trigger, you aimed center mass and put your man down. Now they knew he meant to take them alive—a weakness they aimed to exploit. Gibson repeated his command, drifting to his right, back against the wall, buying himself time—compounding his error.

He'd lost the initiative and control of the situation. Either he took it back or he'd have to kill them both.

Or they'd kill him.

He wasn't wild about either of those options.

Both men outweighed him substantially, so with no good option, Gibson went for the man to his left. Straight at him. Gun level with his eyes. When the man's stare shifted to Gibson's gun barrel, he knew he had a chance.

The Marines taught unarmed, close-quarters combat that someone with a sense of humor had once dubbed "Semper Fu." In it, rifles and sidearms became hand-to-hand weapons that could deliver devastating attacks. Of course, the Marines assumed the magazine would be empty by that point. Gibson figured it would work either way.

At the last moment, the man brought his arms up in a defensive posture, but not fast enough to stop the heel of the Glock from breaking his nose. Like a faucet, blood gushed down the man's face. Gibson hit him again squarely in the eye socket.

The man dropped and lay motionless.

Gibson spun, looking for the partner, who was closing like a linebacker, low and fast. Six feet . . . five feet . . . He didn't see another way.

Gibson shot him twice in the chest.

The man went down and clutched his chest. Labored breathing but no blood. Gibson said a silent prayer to the inventor of ballistic armor.

"Smart move," Gibson said, patting the merc's vest.

"Fuck you," the merc wheezed.

"Roll over."

Gibson had just finished restraining all three when gunfire erupted from inside the C-130.

CHAPTER THIRTY

Gibson sprinted across the hangar toward the desperate sounds of battle. When he got close, he slowed and crept alongside the fuselage toward the rear of the aircraft. As if on cue, the gunfire stopped, and the hangar fell ominously silent. Using the ramp as cover, Gibson surveyed the scene.

Jenn's handiwork lay all around. A trail of bodies led from the hangar door to the bottom of the C-130's ramp. Miraculously, none was dead. The guards at the hangar door had taken beanbag rounds to the head. They'd be out for a while yet, and Gibson didn't envy them their concussions when they regained consciousness. He saw where she'd discarded her shotgun on the run and switched to a compact MP7. The big Scandinavian and the loadmaster lay trussed up like Christmas trees on the way home from the lot. They peered up at Gibson with murderous eyes.

"Was that fast enough for you?" Gibson asked.

Norrgard sneered at him. "I'll remember you said that." Even restrained, the man made it a meaningful threat.

Movement from inside the aircraft snapped Gibson to attention. He crouched beside the ramp and aimed into the darkness. Waited breathlessly. He heard movement before he saw it. His finger slipped off the trigger guard of its own volition.

"It's me," Jenn called loudly. "I'm coming out."

She appeared at the top of the ramp. Her MP7 dangled loosely from its harness. Blood was splattered across her chest and dripped from her arms and from her hands. Gibson felt his heart climb his throat and try to punch its way out.

"It's not mine," Jenn said.

Gibson felt a wave of relief, but then he realized what that meant. He dropped his head and asked, "How many?"

"Two. Both of the pilots."

The big Scandinavian roared and struggled against his restraints. He vowed revenge in the blunt poetry of soldiers. Called her all the words men saved for women that they hated. "How many is that now?" he demanded. "How many have you killed?"

Jenn came down the ramp and knelt beside him. Her hand wrapped around the grip of her MP7, and for a moment Gibson thought she meant to add the Scandinavian to her résumé. The Scandinavian must have believed it too, because his jaw snapped shut.

"You stop holding hostages, Norrgard, and I'll stop filling body bags with your men. How's that?" She snatched up the loadmaster's clipboard and flipped through the cargo manifest. "George isn't on board," she said to Gibson.

"What?"

"He's not on board," she said again, the frustration ringing in her voice.

She held out the clipboard. Gibson took it and ran up the ramp into the plane. They didn't have a lot of time.

The cargo bay of a C-130 was nine feet high, forty feet in length, and ten feet across at its widest point. Down the center of the hold sat pallets of equipment wrapped in plastic and tethered in place by thick straps. The pallets were shoulder height, and narrow pathways had been left on either side. Gibson worked quickly, scanning the cargo manifest and comparing it against the pallet tags.

"Replacement parts for vehicles."

"Ammunition."

"Medical supplies."

"Computers."

Customs had signed off on the manifest. Everything looked official. There was no sign of George.

At the bulkhead behind the last pallet, Gibson found where the two pilots had made their stand. They lay, one on top of the other, like two brothers wrestling on the living room floor. Brass casings lay all around in the grease and blood. One had died instantly, but the second had clung to life until he'd bled out. Gibson saw where Jenn had tried to administer first aid.

Gibson stepped over the bodies and went up the cockpit ladder with the absurd hope that George Abe would be there waiting to be discovered. Nothing. He went down the other side of the aircraft, praying for a miracle, but finished his lap around the hold without spotting anything that Jenn had missed. He hated to think that they'd done this for nothing. Killed two men. Jenn had kept it bottled up tight, but he knew her well enough to see that she'd gotten her hopes up. How would she respond if she'd missed again? And how had they? Had Calista been wrong or had Eskridge smelled a rat?

Was this a trap?

"Anything?" Jenn asked, looking up the ramp at him. She still knelt beside Norrgard. Her hand still rested on the pistol grip of the MP7.

"Nothing. What about him?" Gibson pointed to the big Scandinavian. "What does he have to say?"

"Says he doesn't know."

"Do you believe him?"

"I think I need to ask him another way."

Gibson didn't like the sound of that. Jenn had experience as an interrogator from her time in the CIA. At a time when the country's definition of torture had been far more flexible than it was now. Given her state of mind, Norrgard would be lucky if it stopped at enhanced interrogation.

Gibson said, "We don't have that kind of time."

Jenn checked her watch and grimaced. "Maybe they're bringing him in at the last minute?"

"And maybe the pilots called for reinforcements. Maybe this is a trap."

"You don't know that," Jenn said.

"We don't know anything. That's my point. We're into wishful-thinking territory here," he said, even as he felt himself losing her attention. "Jenn. It's time to leave. We have to stick to the plan."

Jenn looked despairingly from the aircraft to the hangar doors and back. Her eyes settled on Norrgard.

"Where the fuck is he?"

"Where you'll never find him. The colonel is on to you, bitch."

"Bullshit," Jenn said and pressed the muzzle of the MP7 to his head. She asked her question again. Over and over. With each repetition, a little more of the humanity drained out of her voice. Gibson recognized it—his father's ghost's voice in the days leading up to taking Damon Ogden.

Duke scoffed. "Don't try and pin this on me."

"I'm only going to ask you one more time," Jenn said, her face an unreadable mask.

"Jenn!" Gibson said.

"What?" she screamed back.

"We have to go. Now."

He put a hand on her shoulder. Jenn pulled away. She looked pale and shell-shocked. Staring at nothing. If hope was a cancer, as Dan Hendricks insisted, then Gibson thought Jenn might be a terminal case.

He feared that she would curl up and surrender. He said her name again but got no response. It was like standing outside a dark house, ringing the bell, unsure if anyone was even home. He tried again, and this time he saw the lights flicker on in her eyes.

"Jenn?"

She drew a deep breath and finally met his eyes. "All right. We'll go."

The C-130 lumbered down the runway and rose reluctantly into the night sky. It should have been a great feeling. Against all odds, they'd come through an impossible gauntlet unscathed. They'd broken dozens of laws, killed two men, and pulled off an epic heist, stealing an airplane right off a runway at a Cat X airport. It was the stuff of legend.

Except it wasn't. It had all been for nothing, and now Jenn had no choice but to flee the country. That had been the plan all along, but she was doing so without George. They'd failed, and as the ramifications of that failure sunk in, Jenn retreated further and further into a shell.

Gibson watched her carefully. Military C-130s flew with a flight crew of four. Cold Harbor had gotten by with three, combining the flight engineer and navigator into one position. It was definitely not an aircraft designed to be flown solo. It could be done, but a pilot would need to be focused. That was not how Gibson would describe Jenn at present.

He needn't have worried. Whatever disappointment she felt, she didn't allow it to affect her professionalism. She took the plane to ten thousand feet and leveled off. According to the flight plan that Cold Harbor had filed, the first leg took them to Caracas, Venezuela. The two-thousand-mile flight was right at the edge of the C-130's operational range, but Caracas was exactly Titus Eskridge's kind of lawless.

He could refuel away from prying eyes before making the next leg to Fortaleza, Brazil.

Their arrangement with Calista called for them to divert to a small airfield in Virginia. There they would turn over the C-130 and its cargo to Calista. A second aircraft would fly Jenn and George out of the country.

No chance that would happen.

Calista had been an ally, but it was an arrangement that had run its course and would not outlive the night. She was every bit as ruthless as Eskridge. Gibson still hadn't discarded the idea that Calista had used George as bait to get them to do her dirty work. This was Calista—anything was possible.

Jenn's true intention, which they had devised during their morning jogs, was to keep to Cold Harbor's original flight plan for three hours before filing a new flight plan that took them to an airfield in southern Florida. There they would scuttle the C-130 so that neither Eskridge nor Calista could claim its cargo. Jenn had arranged their own transportation out of the country from Florida. Gibson intended to wait until the last minute to tell her that he wouldn't be coming with her. Although now that they were missing George, he didn't know what she would do.

He tried several times to start the conversation about their next move, but she rebuffed him.

She engaged the autopilot and stood up.

"What are you doing?" Gibson asked.

"We're over the Atlantic," Jenn said, her voice flat and affectless over the headsets. The engines made it hard to be heard without them.

"So?" he asked, finding that somewhat ominous. "Jenn? So?"

"So I'll be right back."

"Jenn. We should decide what we're going to do."

"I know that."

"So where are you going?" Gibson asked.

"To clean up my mess."

"Let me help you."

"No. One of us has to be in the cockpit at all times. Stay here and don't touch anything."

"I'm not a child," he said, realizing how petulant it made him sound. But he was tired and disappointed too.

"Everyone's a child in a cockpit."

Gibson followed her down the ladder to the cockpit door. Concerned about her mental state, he wanted to keep an eye on her. The absurdity of it wasn't lost on him. A crazy man looking out for her mental health. Although, now that he thought about it, he felt more lucid than he had in a long time. His sanity had faded in and out since his release. During his preparations to take Damon Ogden, he'd mistakenly thought he'd been improving. But he'd crashed and crashed hard immediately after. He'd felt the same improvement working with Jenn but didn't trust it to last. He didn't feel that way now. Even though the job was over, he still felt in focus and almost like himself again. Hijacking an airplane might have been a bad idea, but it didn't feel like a crazy one.

Now if he could just get rid of his dad.

"Dream on, son," Duke said from the copilot's seat. He didn't have a headset, but Gibson could hear him just fine.

One at a time, Jenn dragged the bodies the length of the cargo bay. Rigor hadn't set in, but the narrow pathway made it a difficult obstacle course. She lowered the ramp. Wind whipped through the plane, and the temperature dropped thirty degrees in an instant. It hadn't been all that warm to start.

She hauled up the first body and sent it tumbling into the night. At ten thousand feet, hitting the water would pulverize the body. Mother Nature would take care of the rest. An undignified kind of funeral.

Gibson wondered what his name had been. If he'd been married or had any children.

"Go after him. Ask him," Duke suggested.

"Go to hell."

"No, I'm serious. You're going to turn yourself in anyway, right? They're going to execute you for what you've done. So what's the difference? Why don't you die with a little dignity instead of tied to a table, turning blue while Ogden watches from the audience. His smug fucking face will be the last thing you'll see. And when it's over, he'll take his girlfriend's kids out for ice cream and never think about you again."

"No, he's willing to make a deal."

"A deal . . . what is that? Take a leap. Fly. It will be beautiful. At least that way, Ogden suffers too."

"No, I'm not going to be that man."

"You're not a man at all."

It wasn't the first time the ghost of Duke Vaughn had voiced such a sentiment, and each time it had knocked the wind out of Gibson. Not so now. Now his words meant nothing to Gibson. Duke sensed it, faltered, fell silent.

A buzzer sounded in Gibson's ear. An incoming call on Cold Harbor's sat phone, which had been wired into the aircraft's control panel. It could be only one person. Gibson punched a button on the console and connected the call. No one spoke. Gibson wasn't in the mood for games, so he hung up. The phone rang again a minute later.

"Hello, Titus," Gibson said. "Fancy hearing from you."

"Dan Hendricks. I should have killed you two years ago." Eskridge's voice was smooth and untroubled.

Hendricks didn't sound anything like Gibson, but over the roar of the engines, it would be hard to identify voices. It made sense that Eskridge would assume Gibson was Hendricks.

"Dan is in California," Gibson said.

"No, you're not," Eskridge said confidently. "Where is Jennifer Charles?"

"She's feeding the fish. What do you want?"

"I want my aircraft."

"Yeah, we kind of like it, though."

"You can't stay in the air forever," Eskridge replied.

"Who's to say?"

"As if you have the fifty thousand to refuel it. And even if you did, it's my aircraft. I can track your location anywhere in the world. There's nowhere you can land that I won't find it. And you."

"Yeah, but it'll be a smoking wreck when you do. Or maybe we'll start rolling cargo into the ocean. There's got to be something irreplaceable on board."

That provoked a long pause. Gibson could almost hear Eskridge trying to compose himself before replying.

"What do you want?"

"Maybe we could work out a trade," Gibson said, floating the idea. Perhaps there would still be a way to get George back safely. If Calista was at least right about Eskridge smuggling classified materials, then it might be valuable enough to exchange for George.

"And what exactly is it you want?" Eskridge asked.

Gibson started to say "George Abe," but he caught himself. The din made it hard to read tone of voice, but something about Eskridge's question rubbed Gibson the wrong way. It should have been ironic and knowing, but Eskridge had almost sounded sincere. As if he didn't know the answer. Gibson decided to bluff.

"Well, we've got George, but we could really use a relocation fund to help him get settled. I'm thinking something in the mid-seven figures."

Jenn appeared in the cockpit door with a questioning look on her face. Gibson put a finger to his lips. This was the moment of truth.

"That's high, but I think we can come to an accommodation. I can go as high as two million."

"Three."

"Can you guarantee Charles will agree?"

Gibson pretended to think about it. "I'll convince her. Let me call you back."

Gibson hung up and grinned at Jenn.

"What?" she said.

"Eskridge just offered me three million for the plane."

"So?"

"So, I think George is on board."

CHAPTER THIRTY-ONE

"Convince me," Jenn said with the skepticism of someone who'd opened her front door to a pushy salesman.

Gibson described his impromptu negotiation with Eskridge. The strangeness of Eskridge asking what they wanted for his aircraft. "He didn't miss a beat when I said we had George."

"Maybe he was bluffing too."

"Why? It's a dumb bluff. What does he gain?"

Jenn thought about it, wary of getting her hopes up again so soon. Gibson pressed her.

"Let's divert to Florida now. Get on the ground as soon as possible and go through all the cargo containers. He's got to be in one of them."

"No. That we're not doing," she said.

Jenn took Eskridge's threat seriously. Without a doubt, Cold Harbor had a GPS tracking device on board in addition to the aircraft's transponder, but finding it, much less deactivating it, would be impossible in flight. It was a key reason they'd always planned to ditch the plane. The moment the C-130 set down, Eskridge would scramble whatever Cold Harbor assets remained on the Eastern Seaboard. The clock would be ticking, and she didn't want to get caught on the ground searching for George.

Cold Harbor

"So what's the alternative?" he asked.

"We search them in flight."

He didn't like the answer and told her so, then he told her again, but in the end, they did it her way. It was an incredibly bad idea and a recipe for getting themselves killed. The pallets and their cargo were lashed to the deck and secured with heavy tarps for good reason. A patch of heavy chop could turn an unsecured container into a sledgehammer, its contents into shrapnel. Jenn wanted to be the one to conduct the search, but she needed to stay in the cockpit and guide them around any rough stuff. That was how Gibson came to find himself unstrapping and uncovering pallets while the C-130 was still midflight.

Gibson started at the aft end of the hold and worked his way forward. The first few pallets held a mixture of aluminum ULD (unit load device) containers of various sizes. He had only two hours before they were scheduled to divert to Florida, so he did his best to streamline the process—eliminating any containers too small to hold a man. It was still slow going, as, once he'd gone through a pallet's containers, they had to be resecured before he could move on.

It didn't help that Jenn demanded constant updates. It made him tense, and as he worked his way methodically up the hold with nothing to show for it, he began to second-guess himself, replaying Eskridge's words in his head. Had he read something into them that he'd only wanted to hear?

The heaviest pallet on any flight would always be positioned between the wings. In this case, it was ordnance. Through the clear plastic tarp, Gibson saw ammunition cans and crates of claymores. The only way George would fit in there was in pieces. A morbid thought, but he gave the ammunition cans a second look. From what he knew of Eskridge, it wasn't outside the realm of possibility. Gibson skipped checking further. For now.

The power of positive thought in action.

261

Something about the fifth pallet struck him as odd. Unlike the others, it held only one large ULD container. Externally, it looked no different from the others, but when Gibson rapped the butt of his knife against the side, it felt different. Denser. He wished he could hear the sound over the engines, but even so, he felt a familiar and fearful hopefulness.

"What is it?" Jenn said in his ear. He'd been talking steadily, narrating his progress, and she'd heard him fall silent.

"Nothing yet. Hold one."

"Gibson!"

"Give me a minute."

He worked his way around the container, loosening the ratchet straps, and threw back the tarp. The ULD was even bigger than he'd assumed. The size of a prefab shed that you might find at the end of a garden. With fingers crossed, Gibson opened the double doors. A wall of computer-monitor boxes greeted him. He double-checked the manifest—sure enough, pallet five should be nothing but computers. But better safe than sorry.

First he unpacked the monitors. Threw them aside, only to reach another wall of equipment. This time boxes of tower computers.

Frustrated, he almost quit. He had to cut corners where possible to save time, considering how much more he had to do. But on a hunch, he pried out one box and reached through the gap it left in the wall of boxes. He touched something smooth and metallic . . . with rounded edges. The cargo bay was dimly lit, and the interior of the ULD was virtually pitch-black. He shone his flashlight through the opening—whatever it was, it wasn't more computer boxes.

Gibson worked faster, clearing away the remaining boxes to reveal what looked like an old-fashioned refrigerator door, only wider and held shut with dead bolts and latches. He unlocked it but needed both hands to pry the door open. He rested his flashlight on the ground, but it rolled away, casting shadows against the wall of the container. Inch by inch, the door gave way.

In the gloom, he saw movement. A water bottle rolled out and bumped against his foot. He groped around for his flashlight and held it up. A layer of thick white foam padding covered the interior. He ran the flashlight's beam across the interior of the strange container. There, in a corner, crouched George Abe.

They'd found him. They'd actually found him. Gibson felt an unfamiliar flutter in his chest. He realized it was the feeling of hope fulfilled. He kind of liked it.

Gibson called George by name, but the roar of the engines drowned him out. Pressed against the back wall, George held up a hand to shield his eyes. He looked terrified. A beaten dog. Gibson realized George couldn't see a thing, so he squatted down on his heels and turned the flashlight on himself.

"You're safe now," Gibson said, even though he knew he couldn't be heard.

George squinted, head tilted to one side. Recognition flickered across his face, and he darted forward and threw his arms around Gibson. It knocked Gibson on his back. He felt George sobbing and simply held on to him. Gibson knew how it felt when a door that would never open finally did.

"What's happening?" Jenn asked.

"He's here. I've got him," Gibson told her and then said to George, "I've got you." It seemed important to say.

In the dark of the container, he held George and listened to Jenn whoop with joy. He smiled. It felt good. He would need this memory for what came next. How he would miss these people when it came time to say good-bye.

CHAPTER THIRTY-TWO

Jenn and George's reunion was emotionally wrenching to watch. She tried to hold it together, but when George put his arms around her, she broke down. Seeing Jenn Charles cry was like catching a glimpse of that stoic uncle, the one who never showed any emotion, wiping away an unguarded tear. It should have been obvious, but he hadn't realized until that moment how much of a father figure George Abe was to her. Gibson backed out of the cockpit. He went down to the cargo bay, repacked the container, and lashed it to the bulkhead.

When he returned to the cockpit, Jenn had composed herself. She'd found a blanket and wrapped it around George, who sat in the navigator's chair. She was on one knee beside him, holding his hand. By the light of the control panel, Gibson saw clearly the ruin of George Abe. It was hard to believe the man sitting swaddled in the navigator's seat was the same man. The man who had approached him at the Nighthawk to find Suzanne Lombard had been an ageless, perfectly manicured composition. But two years of beatings had rearranged the smooth, flawless planes of George's face. The cockpit headset covered ears that had been turned to cauliflower. His left eye drooped, and a knot on the bridge of his nose marked where it folded over to one side. Teeth were missing, and his jaw looked swollen and misshapen. And Gibson knew the damage wasn't restricted to his face. George had needed Gibson's help getting to the cockpit, and Gibson had felt the profound limp. George looked like a coffee mug that had been shattered and glued back together.

Now, with his eyes glazed over, George had the disoriented look of athletes who had pushed themselves beyond the point of failure. Gibson wondered if he'd worn the same expression the day the CIA had dumped him back at Dule Tree Airfield. He remembered the unbearable flood of thoughts and emotions. How overwhelming freedom had felt. They hadn't had identical experiences by any stretch of the imagination, but Gibson knew it would be a while before George came to grips with his new reality.

Now that they had George, Jenn needed to call Calista. Calista had no way of making contact, and they were already overdue. By now, she would be getting . . . well, there was no telling what Calista would be getting, but it wouldn't be pleasant. She would need reassurance that everything was on track. Sooner or later, Calista would smell a rat, and it was impossible to predict how she would react. They needed to buy themselves as much time as possible once they altered course for Florida. Gibson would wait until they were on the ground to tell Jenn that he couldn't go with them. She wouldn't have time to argue it with him then. George needed medical attention, and that would be her first priority.

"Jenn. You need to make the call to Calista."

At the mention of the name, George's eyes cleared. He shook his hand free from Jenn's grip. "Why would you need to call *her*?"

Jenn began to explain their fragile alliance with Calista Dauplaise, but George cut her short. With a snarl, he threw himself at Jenn. He was breathtakingly fast, knocking her back and pinning her to the floor. George's hands went for Jenn's throat, and she didn't defend herself but instead tried to explain.

For his part, George didn't seem in an explanation frame of mind.

Gibson put George in a full nelson and dragged him off her. George was stronger than he looked and tried to wrestle free. Their feet got tangled up, and Gibson went over on his back. George landed hard on him, knocking the wind out of him. George drilled him in the ribs with an elbow and used the recoil to spring to his feet.

George had clearly oversold how weak he was. Maybe he'd been doing it for years, playing possum, waiting for a window of opportunity to make an escape. Jenn's MP7 was slung over the back of the chair, and by the time Gibson clambered to his feet, it was in George's hands and pointed at Jenn's head.

"Sir, please," Jenn said. "What are you doing?"

"You're working for Calista?"

"Put the gun down, and I'll explain. If you hit something in here, we all die."

"Then we all die." George's hands shook, but his voice was steady. "Now answer my question. Are you working for Calista Dauplaise?"

"It's complicated."

"It's not complicated. Yes or no?"

"No, sir," Jenn said. "Not exactly."

"What have you done? Calista *gave* me to Cold Harbor. She had Michael killed. She watched them put a bullet in the back of his head. I knelt beside him while his blood soaked into the dirt. I was next."

George meant Michael Rilling, the missing former IT director at Abe Consulting Group. There had been an internal leak, and Jenn and Gibson had long suspected Rilling of selling them out. He'd been missing since Cold Harbor had kidnapped George, and they'd assumed Michael was in hiding. Now they knew better. Jenn blanched at the news.

"I didn't know that, sir," Jenn said.

"So how can you be working for her?"

For George, the world had stopped turning more than two years ago. He knew only what Titus Eskridge wanted him to know. And for two years, he'd felt only what Titus Eskridge wanted him to feel. In a way, George still knelt in the dirt beside Mike Rilling. Calista's betrayal would be as fresh and raw to George as the day it happened. In his world, Calista and Eskridge were still partners. Gibson understood. He'd been there himself.

It didn't mean he wasn't losing patience, though. After what Jenn had done to rescue him, the risks she'd taken, to have George point a gun in her face? It pissed Gibson off. His ribs hurt. He was tired. The benefit of the doubt didn't seem like too much to ask.

"You're being an asshole," Gibson told George.

George and Jenn both looked at him, incredulous.

"Gibson!" Jenn said.

"No, I'm serious," Gibson said, then to George, "Do you know what she's been through to find you? What she's sacrificed? She hasn't stopped looking for you since the day you disappeared. So how about a little benefit of the doubt? We both know what Calista is. What she's done. Better than you, probably. Like how she had my father murdered. For instance. But she was the only way to get you back, so we did what we had to do."

George faltered, eyes widening. He had known Duke Vaughn well. They'd both worked for Senator Benjamin Lombard—Duke his chief of staff, George his head of security. Duke had been a beloved figure, and his suicide had affected everyone who knew him.

"Duke was murdered?"

"Yeah, by Calista's psycho. Same guy who tried to hang me from the same spot." Gibson pulled his collar down to reveal the scar around his throat. "And weren't you partners with Calista before either of us? Yet here I am. It's an imperfect world. So why don't you stop pointing a gun at the woman who just saved your life?"

George looked down at the gun in his hands as if he didn't know how it had gotten there. Ashamed, he held it out to Jenn, who unloaded it and stowed the magazine.

Even if it had achieved the desired effect, Gibson still felt disgusted with himself for losing his temper. No one had treated him that way after his release. But maybe he wouldn't be in the mess he found himself in if someone had. Then again, who was he kidding? No one had ever talked him out of a bad idea in his life.

George sat down, rubbed his face thoughtfully. "I apologize. My social graces don't appear to be what they once were. Would one of you be so kind as to catch me up on what I've missed?"

Where even to begin? Jenn sketched out their current situation. There would be time later to tell the whole story, but for now she gave him a severely streamlined version of the last couple of years. George took it all in and, to his credit, kept his questions to a minimum.

"I owe you both an apology," George said. "It is my fault this woman is in our lives. You're right about that, Gibson. And you've both paid a heavy price for my negligence. I hope you can forgive me." He looked at each of them in turn, searching their faces.

"There's nothing to forgive, George," Jenn said. "We all paid."

"Amen," Gibson said.

George nodded gratefully. Jenn adjusted the blanket around his shoulders and squeezed his arm. It was a damned touching scene. One they didn't have time for at the moment. Gibson looked at Jenn and tapped the back of his wrist. She nodded in agreement and slid into the pilot's seat. Gibson saw her steel herself before dialing Calista Dauplaise. Gibson patched in George's headset so he could listen along. The phone barely rang before Calista picked up. As if she'd been holding the phone anticipating the call.

"Hello, Jennifer. I had expected to hear from you earlier."

At the sound of her voice, George stiffened in his seat. His hands went white around the armrests.

"We ran into complications," Jenn explained.

"I see. And what is the prognosis?"

"We have the plane. We're in the air now."

"Tremendous news. And George?"

"We have him."

Calista waited expectantly, but Jenn didn't elaborate beyond that. George looked like he had walked into a foreign movie halfway through and was trying to guess the plot.

"When should I expect you?" Calista asked as if planning a late supper.

"I'd estimate a little over three hours. On our way to you now." In three hours, they'd be on the ground in Florida. By the time Calista figured out she'd been double-crossed, Jenn and George would already have switched aircraft and be on their way to Europe.

"I see," Calista said.

"Is everything set on your end? I'd like to—"

"Jennifer. Please spare me," Calista said, the temperature of her voice dropping precipitously. "I am not, when last I checked, in Venezuela."

Jenn and Gibson traded a look, knowing what it meant. Somehow Calista had gotten access to the plane's GPS and was tracking their course, the same as Eskridge. They should have anticipated that.

Calista said, "I apologize. Have I interrupted your performance? Would you care to finish?"

"No, I'm good."

"I suppose it was to be expected, but I will admit to some small disappointment. I held out some hope that, after so long, we understood one another."

"Oh, I think I understand you," Jenn said. "Don't you worry."

"Yes. As I understand *you*, Jennifer."

Something in the tone of Calista's voice made Gibson alert. She didn't sound defeated. Or even angry. She practically purred with haughty self-satisfaction. Readying the other shoe for its long drop. Jenn heard it too.

"All right," Jenn said. "I don't see any point in belaboring this. Good-bye, Calista."

"A moment more, if I may?" Calista said.

Jenn's hand hovered over the button on the console, caught between the desire to hang up and wanting to know why Calista sounded so damned assured. They'd lost a little of their head start, but they should still be all right. Still, her hand hovered.

"What do you want?" Jenn asked.

"Someone would like a word."

For a moment, Gibson conjured an elaborate conspiracy in which Calista and Eskridge were still partners. It was all a trap designed to get them all together in one place. The plane would explode any moment. It was absurd for any number of reasons, but it felt undeniably true in his head.

Duke whistled. "That's paranoid even by my standards."

"Jenn, I'm sorry. I didn't see them coming."

It was Dan Hendricks. Calista had him.

Gibson flashed back to his conversation with Eskridge. He hadn't given it much credence at the time, but Eskridge had been sure that Dan Hendricks wasn't in California. Looked like he had known better.

"It's okay," Jenn said. "What happened? Where are you?"

"I'm in Virginia. They took me yesterday at dawn."

Jenn looked furious. "Are you okay? Have you been hurt?"

"No, I'm fine. Embarrassed but fine. How's George?"

"He's okay. He's here."

"Well, that's something."

Calista came back on the line. "That's enough. You will have plenty of time to reminisce later."

"So you were always planning on betraying me?"

"No, you silly girl. I was always planning on you betraying me. And I mean that as a compliment, Jennifer. You're far too smart to trust me. This was all foreseeable. We are, in the end, coerced by the choices we have made, repeating them time and time again. Isn't that right,

Gibson? I trust you're listening in. Perhaps George is as well. Hello, my old friend."

"You think kidnapping Dan is going to convince me to trust you?" Jenn said.

"I merely flew Daniel out from California to remind you of the importance of honoring your agreements."

"So what do you want?" Jenn said.

"Only what we agreed. Bring me my aircraft."

"And what happens then?"

"You take what is yours. I take what is mine. We part ways and never see each other again."

Jenn covered the headset's microphone and looked at Gibson for confirmation. He nodded. It wasn't even a question. Dan and he might never have gotten on like a house on fire, but Hendricks was one of them. They couldn't leave him behind. Not with Calista. The real question was George. He'd been free for less than an hour, and now they were contemplating taking him back to the woman who had put him there. It was asking a lot. They turned around in their seats to face George.

Gibson didn't think he'd ever forget it. Even beaten and broken in places, George radiated a noble fury. In another time, he would have been right at home astride a horse addressing his troops. The way he looked each of them in the eyes gave Gibson goose bumps.

"Let's go get our man," he said.

And that was that.

"We're on our way," Jenn told Calista.

"Three hours, Jennifer. Turn the aircraft around and under no circumstances deviate from my heading. Do not appeal again to my baser instincts."

"Three hours," Jenn confirmed and disconnected the call.

CHAPTER THIRTY-THREE

"Anything?" Jenn asked over the headset.

"Not a damn thing," Gibson said without bothering to hide his frustration.

For the last two hours, as they returned north to meet Calista in Virginia, he'd torn the hold apart, looking for whatever she had gone to all this trouble to obtain. He knew it was a fool's errand. Like looking for a needle in a haystack. Worse. At least Gibson knew a needle when he saw one. Calista's prize could be anything. Any size. It could be a microchip or a large piece of hardware. For all Gibson knew, he'd already held it in his hands.

They felt beaten. To work this hard to free George only for Dan Hendricks to take his place felt like a cruel zero-sum game. They'd planned it all so carefully, or thought they had, yet Calista had outmaneuvered them once again. Up in the cockpit, Jenn and George were busy strategizing. Over his headset, Gibson could hear them proposing and rejecting one plan after another. Another waste of energy since they had no clear picture of what Calista had waiting for them. That was why Gibson remained down in the hold, hunting blindly. If he got lucky, supremely lucky, they'd have a much stronger bargaining position when they landed. So he kept looking despite the odds. Like every failed gambler before him, he had this ridiculous idea that he was "due," somehow.

"Gibson," Jenn said. "Wrap it up and get back up here."

He felt the plane begin to descend. They were out of time, and they were out of options. Gibson took one last look down the length of the cargo bay, hoping maybe he'd missed the flashing neon "Classified Material Inside" sign. If only they had something, anything, Calista needed. The irony of course was that they did, they just didn't know what it was they had. He sighed and made his way forward. Calista Dauplaise held all the cards, and for the life of him, Gibson couldn't figure out if they'd even been dealt into the game.

Gibson strapped himself into the copilot's chair beside Jenn. Out the cockpit window, he could see the lights of the Northern Virginia suburbs. To the east, the sun was cresting the horizon one more time. Once again, he was on board a plane at dawn, landing with no control over what came next. At least this time, he wasn't shackled with a hood over his eyes. Whatever it was, he would see it coming. And he was among friends. That was no small thing. Of course, knowing Calista, they might all wish for a blindfold sooner rather than later.

If only they had found it . . . But wait . . . He thought for a moment. Calista didn't know that, did she? What if they bluffed? Threatened to destroy it? No. It was a stupid play. You couldn't trade what you didn't have. Especially when you didn't know what you didn't have. All they had was the plane itself.

Suddenly, Gibson sat up straight. *We have the plane.*

"Jenn," he said. "I might have an idea."

The C-130 landed hard, bouncing on one wheel. A strong gust lifted the plane off the runway and tried to turn it sideways. Jenn compensated as best she could, but the big aircraft fought her all the way back to the ground, as if the C-130 were even more reluctant than they to land there. Once she wrestled the wheels down, Jenn powered down, and the aircraft settled into the earth. They decelerated down the runway.

It was a small airfield with two runways side by side. At the far end stood three small hangars, all of which would fit easily inside one of the Dulles Air Center hangars. The center hangar was open, and lights were on. They taxied toward it. Jenn made a tight turn so that the tail of the aircraft faced the hangar. As the aircraft turned, he saw Calista's limousine inside the hangar. Behind it, her henchmen's SUV idled. He didn't see Cools, Sidhu, or anyone else, but they would be there, out of sight. Waiting.

"Go," Jenn said as soon as it was safe.

Gibson and George hustled back to the hold to prepare. Jenn had wanted George to stay in the cockpit out of harm's way, but he wasn't having it. Not while Calista had Hendricks. Gibson admired him for that. They worked quickly, no time to set up anything elaborate. When Jenn joined them, she looked at what they'd jury-rigged and whistled.

"I don't know if that will work," she said.

Gibson didn't disagree but said, "You have a better idea?"

She did not. It would have to do. He handed her one of the three controllers.

No one knew what to expect when they lowered the ramp. They readied themselves as best they knew how. Jenn swapped a full clip into her MP7. George stood a little ways off and tucked the gun that Jenn had handed him out of sight. Gibson popped the clip from his Glock and checked it. It hadn't been fired, but he did it anyway to steady his hands.

They looked one to the other.

"This reminds me of a story," George said.

They waited for him to go on, but he didn't appear inclined to share it.

"What do you think?" Gibson asked Jenn.

"Let's not get killed."

"Solid plan."

George said, "If it's me she wants, we make the trade."

Jenn looked aghast. "She wants Eskridge's cargo as a bargaining chip."

"And if there is no bargaining chip?"

Neither Jenn nor Gibson had considered the possibility that it was another of Calista's inventions. That George had been the target all along.

"Why would she want you?" Gibson asked.

"Who can say? But I think that if I've proven anything, it's that I'm not the best at anticipating Calista's motives." He gestured to his scarred face.

Gibson laughed despite himself. George joined him. Jenn stifled a smile. It was a morbid joke, but gallows humor was the only kind left to them. Gibson would have happily stayed in this moment. This was where he was meant to be. The people he was meant to be with. He wanted to remember this feeling so he could hold on to it afterward. He would need it.

"Why are you so happy?" Jenn asked.

"I'll tell you later."

"You are certifiable," she said.

He didn't argue.

Jenn activated the ramp, and the hydraulics whined into life. The ramp descended. Gibson would have wagered that Calista would be nowhere in sight. That she would be safely tucked away while her men secured the aircraft. He would have lost that bet.

Calista Dauplaise stood at the foot of the ramp. She wore a sable coat that fell to her ankles, and an oversized fur hat. A tsarina come to view the war. Her limousine now idled behind her, broadside to the aircraft. Cools stood behind it. The cold had worsened in only a few hours. His nose was an angry red, and the bags under his eyes had turned a sickly pork-chop gray. He rested a shotgun on the roof of the limo, pointed at no one.

Each side stared at the other for a long moment. As if they had all somehow expected to end up here, but now that the moment had arrived were uncertain what came next. Calista watched Jenn intently. Chances were she'd never had a gun pointed at her before, and you never forgot your first time. Especially when the person holding it was someone like Jenn Charles. Cools eased the stock of the shotgun to his shoulder and trained it on Jenn. Calista put out a gloved hand, fingers spread wide, and when she spoke, her voice did not carry its usual authority.

"Jennifer. I assure you that is not necessary."

Jenn looked unmoved by her appeal and held up the green controller.

"And what would that be?" Calista asked.

Cools knew. "A claymore detonator."

"That's right," Jenn said. "We each have one."

"So you have a couple antipersonnel devices," said Cools. "What's that going to do?"

"They're attached to the wing root. Aimed at the external fuel tanks on the wings," Jenn said.

Calista glanced back at Cools, who no longer looked sure of the situation.

"Your point?" Calista asked.

"I figure there's still enough fuel left to turn this plane to slag. That and whatever it is you want so badly."

Calista regarded Jenn coolly. "If I am not mistaken, you are standing inside said aircraft."

"I'm aware. Are you ready to die?"

"Not quite yet," Calista replied.

"So let's all keep our heads. I want Dan."

"George," Calista said. "A word, if I may?"

"No, you'll talk to—" Jenn began.

George started down the ramp toward Calista, Jenn barking at him to stop. When he didn't, she followed him halfway down the ramp and stopped, unwilling to surrender the cover of the aircraft. Gibson dropped to one knee at the top of the ramp. He scanned the nearby hangars. He didn't see Sidhu. Or anyone else, for that matter. Not exactly the overwhelming display of force that he'd anticipated. In some ways, he would have preferred it. At least then he would have known Calista's intentions.

George stopped outside arm's reach. The two old friends, business partners, and enemies looked each other over.

"Hello, George," Calista said.

"Calista," George answered.

George's face was serene, and from his voice, Gibson wouldn't have known that this woman's betrayal had resulted in two years of brutal imprisonment. Getting her first good look at George, even Calista's practiced detachment couldn't quite mask her shock. Despite her many atrocities, she'd rarely had to look one in the eye.

"It's different up close, isn't it?" George said.

"Yes. It is. I am, however, pleased to see you."

"I've no doubt," George said. "You have one of our people."

"He is unharmed. I assure you."

George chuckled. "I have always appreciated your sense of humor."

"Let us not resort to unpleasantness. I am here in good faith. No one is threatening you, and your Mr. Hendricks is hale and hearty. I had an arrangement with Jennifer. I wish for it to be honored and to be permitted to board my aircraft."

"Not until we see him," George said.

"We do not have a lot of time for all of this. Eskridge is tracking his aircraft. Cold Harbor is already en route. It would be wise to be elsewhere when he arrives."

"Then you had better hurry."

With a put-upon sigh, she turned to Cools, who spoke into a microphone clipped to his sleeve. "Bring him up."

In the hangar, the headlights of the SUV came on. It drove toward them slowly.

Cools sneezed violently.

Jenn's weapon jerked up at him, reacting faster than her mind could interpret what it had heard. Cools swung up the shotgun in self-defense.

The SUV rolled to a stop fifty feet away.

"Mr. Cools, lower your weapon," Calista said.

"Not until she does."

The only sounds Gibson heard were the wind and his heart.

"Mr. Cools. Do as you are told."

"Hell no," Cools said. "Tell her to put it down."

Still on one knee, Gibson tightened his grip on the Glock but didn't draw it. For a moment, the tentative truce seemed poised to unravel over a sneeze. As good a reason as any to kill each other, Gibson reckoned. The danger of brinksmanship was that no one could afford to be the first to back down. It set a bad precedent.

Then something wholly unexpected happened.

Calista Dauplaise stepped between Cools and Jenn. She held her hands out to them, poised like a conductor before a symphony. Slowly, she brought her hands down. "Both of you. Lower your weapons."

Stunned, Cools and Jenn both complied.

Calista produced a handkerchief and thrust it across the limousine. "Blow your nose, Mr. Cools."

He took the handkerchief sheepishly.

"And for God's sake, bring up the car."

Chastened, Cools called back and then blew his nose while the SUV made a wide, lazy arc and came to a stop behind the limousine. Sidhu got out and circled around to the passenger door on its hangar side. He opened it but looked to Calista for confirmation before reaching into the limousine and pulling Hendricks out of the car. Hendricks's arms were bound behind his back. He looked irritated, but then again, that was his natural state. In the two years since Gibson had last seen him, the white vitiligo spots had expanded across Hendricks's face. It made him appear older than Gibson's memory of him.

Dan looked across the two car roofs at George. "Hey, boss," he said as though they'd seen each other only the day before.

"I'm sorry for this," George said.

"My own fault."

"You all right, Dan?" Jenn asked.

"I could use a cigarette."

Sidhu put a hand on top of Hendricks's head, forced him back into the limousine, and slammed the door.

"What happens now?" George said to Calista.

"How many ways do I have to say it?"

"Maybe just once more."

"I have an arrangement with Jennifer. I have honored my commitments. It is time for her to honor hers. The aircraft is mine. You are all free to leave. There is your transportation as agreed upon, fueled and ready to depart," Calista said, extending a hand toward a Gulfstream IV parked a hundred yards away. "Take it and go in good health."

"And you think we would let you have whatever is on board?" Jenn said.

"You have won a great victory today, Jennifer. This is the price to secure it. Or you can wait for Eskridge to arrive and lose everything," Calista said, then called out, "How far away are they?"

"Twenty-two minutes," Cools answered.

"How do we even know that plane is safe?" Gibson asked of the Gulfstream.

Calista turned to George. "The boy has a point. We find ourselves in a predicament, you and I. I require your trust, and you would be fools to give it."

"That is a fair assessment," George said. "So what now?"

"You already know the answer."

"Do I?"

"If you stay, you will all die in approximately twenty-one minutes. That is a certainty. Whereas if you go, there is a chance that I have tampered with your aircraft and that you will die while airborne. So which do you prefer? The chance or the certainty?"

"You should've been in politics," George said.

"I have always been in politics." Calista gave her men a signal. Sidhu brought Hendricks back out and this time uncuffed his wrists. "Good-bye, George." She took off a glove and put out her hand, palm up.

After a moment, George placed his detonator in it. "Be careful with that," he said and started to limp toward the Gulfstream.

Jenn looked uncertain but followed George's lead and came the rest of the way down the ramp and handed her detonator to Calista too. Calista held them both daintily until Cools came and relieved her of them. Gibson was last. He handed his detonator directly to Cools. Calista gave him a meaningful look but said nothing. They backed away from the C-130, and Hendricks circled around to join them. He put George's arm around his neck as they broke into a hobbled jog. Hendricks grunted at them in greeting. A more fitting reunion would have to wait. They had a plane to catch.

Most of them anyway.

Gibson wanted badly to have second thoughts. To forget the name Damon Ogden and get on board with Jenn and George and Hendricks. He dreaded the thought of giving this up, this sense of belonging. He could flee with them and give the CIA Ogden's location from a safe distance. But it would be selfish. Ogden wasn't the bygones-be-bygones type. Eventually, the CIA would come for Gibson, and he couldn't be anywhere near Jenn or George or Hendricks when they did. He wouldn't subject his new family to that risk.

They were at the gangway now. Hendricks helped George up the airstairs and into the Gulfstream. Gibson slowed to a stop and called out to Jenn.

She stopped and came back to him. "You're not coming, are you?"

"I want to. You have no idea."

"Whatever it is, we can handle it."

He held out the Glock. "I know, but you shouldn't have to."

"What is it?" she asked but took the gun.

"Thank you," he said. "For letting me help."

"Couldn't have done it without you. Even if you are certifiable."

"I'm aware of that."

"You waited until I couldn't talk you out of it, didn't you?"

He nodded.

"Dick move, Vaughn," she said and handed him a claim check printed in German. "If you change your mind—"

"I won't."

"If you change your mind, fly to Frankfurt, Germany. Go to luggage storage in Terminal One, Concourse B. You got all that?"

"Yeah. What's there?"

"I have a go bag. It'll be there for the next three months. There's some travel money inside. A phone with one preprogrammed number. Call it. When it answers, say any three words, but only three words. No matter what the voice on the other end says or asks. They will put you in touch with me no matter where I am."

"Should I be wearing a pink carnation?" Where he was going, he knew it would be far longer than three months, but he pretended in the moment. It was a pleasant self-deception.

"Couldn't hurt," she said.

She put an arm around his neck, kissed him on the cheek, and hugged him. They stood there in the cold dawn until Gibson broke away.

"You have to go," he said.

They were out of time.

"I hate this. We made it," Jenn said. "Come with us."

"I wish I could, but I can't. You have to leave me."

Grudgingly, Jenn went up the airstairs. At the top, she looked back at him. It took everything in him to keep his feet planted. After she closed the hatch, George appeared at one of the windows. He put a palm to the glass. Gibson raised a hand in farewell, then stood and watched the Gulfstream taxi out to the runway.

They'd pulled it off. How about that? The stuff of legends.

Bear stood beside him. "You did it. Amazing."

"They're going to be okay."

"Because of you. You should be proud."

"I guess I should be."

"Are you okay?" Bear asked, watching him carefully.

"I'm scared."

"I know. Are you ready?"

He thought he might be.

He put on the Phillies cap, shielding his eyes from the sun at the horizon.

"It really does suit you," Bear said with a smile.

This time he didn't argue with her. He liked the way it fit him. It meant something to him, even if it was a strange thing for your life to be summed up by a beat-up old cap.

Together they turned and walked back toward Calista. What were the chances she might give him a ride out of here?

CHAPTER THIRTY-FOUR

"I thought perhaps you had suffered a change of heart," Calista said. She stood by the open door of her limousine, warming herself. Cools had been banished to a safe distance, where he coughed into the back of his wrist.

"Just seeing them off," Gibson said.

"That must have been difficult, I am sure."

Sidhu emerged from the aircraft with a three-ring binder that looked like the flight manual from the cockpit. Calista took it and snapped through the pages impatiently. When she found what she was looking for, she popped the hinges and removed a laminated sleeve. The discarded binder fell to the ground, and a gust sent paper dancing across the tarmac.

"That's where it was?" Gibson asked.

"Sometimes plain sight is the best hiding place."

"And you knew what it was all along."

Calista gave him a pitying look for having ever thought otherwise. "May I ask what your intentions are now?"

"I'm going to turn myself in to him. Work out a deal if I can."

"I see." She paused as Cools whispered something to her. "And how do you foresee that conversation will turn out?"

Gibson didn't have any idea and didn't care to discuss it with her. "I'm hoping for the best."

"Yes," Calista said. "Wouldn't that be novel?"

Gibson grimaced but said nothing.

Calista said, "Before you go, would you do me the courtesy of lending me a few minutes of your time?"

"Shouldn't we all be getting out of here? Isn't Eskridge due any minute now?"

It was Calista's turn to make a face.

"He is coming?" Gibson said.

"Oh, most assuredly, he is on his way. However, I perhaps exaggerated the imminence of his arrival. You and I have a little time yet. There is a matter I wish to discuss."

Calista got into the limousine and waited. When Gibson hesitated, she held up a thermos enticingly. He reminded himself that this was exactly how Hansel and Gretel had wound up in an oven. He got in anyway. Cools shut the door behind him. At least it was warm in an oven.

Calista poured coffee into china cups and handed him one. Beside her sat an enormous willow picnic basket, from which she served him a croissant on a small plate. His stomach growled as he tore off a hunk. It had been more than twelve hours since he'd last eaten. Flakes of pastry tumbled onto his lap, which he swept to the floor. When he glanced up, Calista was staring at him. She let her eyes drift slowly to the carpet, gravely disappointed. Chastened, Gibson took his next bite over the plate. Crumbs exploded everywhere anyway, and he gave up. Who served croissants in a car?

Throughout, he kept one eye on the laminated sleeve balanced on Calista's knees. Inside he could see a plain brown interdepartmental envelope tied shut with string looped between two red buttons. Calista opened the envelope. Out slid a thick sheaf of papers. She leafed through them carefully while she sipped her coffee. The faintest of smiles played across her lips. She caught Gibson watching her.

"Our Mr. Eskridge has been an exceedingly naughty boy," Calista said, returning the papers to the envelope and the envelope to the laminate sleeve.

"What was it we stole for you?" Gibson asked.

"It is in your best interests not to know."

"Always good to have you looking out for me," Gibson said.

"As you wish," Calista said, holding out the envelope. "See for yourself."

Gibson didn't take it.

"Wise boy," she said. "Mr. Eskridge has gained possession of the identities of certain key contacts inside Israel. Unique resources that our intelligence community has developed over the course of many years. Along with methodology and vulnerabilities—everything an ambitious intelligence service would need to turn the source for itself."

Gibson felt himself physically shrink away from the envelope. As if the envelope itself were radioactive. If it was actually what Calista said, then it was beyond dangerous. The value of intelligence depended entirely on being the only one in its possession. If it became common knowledge, then it conferred little advantage. There was nothing the CIA prized more or protected more ruthlessly. The last eighteen months had been proof of exactly that.

"You're kidding, right?" Gibson asked.

"Indeed not. Mr. Eskridge has a buyer in the Middle East who will, in exchange, sponsor Cold Harbor as it transitions its operations entirely to that region of the world. Not the sort of thing one would be wise to transmit electronically, so Mr. Eskridge meant to fly these documents overseas. Paper is still the best firewall in the world."

Gibson nodded. It's what he would have done in Eskridge's place. Hand-couriering documents might be slow and expensive, but it was immune to a hack.

"So what's your angle?" Gibson asked. "Hold it for ransom to him to get him off you?"

"No, that would offer but a short-term solution. I wish to resolve this troubling relationship once and for all."

"So what, then?"

"I wish to entrust it to your care," Calista said and held out the laminated sleeve. This time Gibson did take it, as much out of surprise as anything. He turned it over in his hands suspiciously, trying to see the hook inside Calista's bait. Calista said, "Someone in the CIA must be made aware that they have been compromised, and by whom."

"Me? You want me to deliver it?"

"Well, you do know such an individual. I think perhaps it would be worth something to him," Calista said, pausing for effect. "Don't you?"

It would. Gibson could scarcely wrap his mind around it. Damon Ogden was first and foremost a patriot. He wouldn't like it, but he would make any deal to keep such information off the open market. This potentially changed everything, and Gibson saw possibilities for his life that he thought had been lost. But coming from Calista Dauplaise, he dared not get his hopes up. It had to be a trick. He had to be standing over a trapdoor where she had maneuvered him.

"Why would you do this for me? I don't understand."

Calista smiled. "Ah, I understand your confusion. Why would I do you this kindness?"

"Something like that."

"The answer is that I am certainly not doing it for you. I am clearing the way for my son. Tidying up my affairs, which certainly encompasses Mr. Eskridge. However, the scope of my affairs also encompasses

George and Jennifer and Daniel. And it encompasses you too. As such, it suits my interests that your present dilemma resolve favorably. I have asked myself what you know that might be traded to the CIA for a more lenient sentence. The fates of Suzanne and Benjamin Lombard come to mind. But the resulting scandal would scuttle my son's career in politics before it truly begins. However, I think we can agree that the documents now in your hands make a far more compelling bargaining chip than my family's good name."

A knock came on the limousine's window. Calista lowered it fractionally.

Cools said, "It's time, Ms. Dauplaise."

She acknowledged him and closed the window. They sat there for a moment in the still of the limousine.

"As much as I do enjoy our time together, I am afraid that duty calls." Calista leaned forward. "Do we have an understanding? Will you do this one last service for me?"

"Yeah, I'll do it. But not for you."

"Excellent," Calista said as if they'd agreed on a restaurant. She knocked on the window, and Cools held open the door. Gibson followed her out. Cools and Sidhu looked uneasy. Both anxious to be gone before Cold Harbor arrived.

"Gentlemen, your services are no longer required," Calista said, turning to her men. She handed each an envelope. Confused, the two men opened them and thumbed through a thick stack of bills. "Consider this your severance," she said.

"Ma'am?" Cools said. "Are you sure about this?"

"I do hope your cold improves," Calista said. "You may keep the SUV. The title has been transferred to your name, Mr. Cools. My limousine will remain here. As will Mr. Vaughn."

Cools and Sidhu glanced at Gibson and then at each other. They came to a silent conclusion. Without another word, they hustled to the SUV and drove away. When they were out of sight, Calista handed Gibson a key.

"What's this?" he asked.

"The key to your automobile. I had it delivered in the expectation that we would reach an accord. You will find it in a small lot beyond the fence behind these hangars. Eskridge will not look there so long as you wait until he departs."

"What will you do?"

"I must see that Mr. Eskridge is greeted properly. He and I have much to discuss."

"He'll kill you."

"I am touched by your concern," Calista said, pulling her fur coat tight around her. "But I have the situation under control."

"If you say so," he said, meaning it to sound dismissive, but he had no doubt that she did. She'd orchestrated everything exactly to her liking. He'd have admired her if she wasn't so damned contemptible.

"I do say so," she said and held out a hand. He shook it. The first time that he had ever touched her. She was shivering, or trembling. It was impossible to say which.

"One last thing," Calista said. "There is a laptop in the passenger seat of your vehicle. Show the recording on it to your prisoner along with the documents in the sleeve. I believe it will paint a rather damning picture of dear Mr. Eskridge."

"A recording of what?"

"You will see. But now it's time for you to go."

Gibson lingered a moment longer. It seemed there should be more to say to this woman who had loomed so large over his life. Who had brought so much suffering to so many. The thought that she might pull this off, and that he'd helped her to do it . . . Tidy her affairs, as she called it, and simply retire from the world so that her son might be king—it sickened him. But what could he say to her that would make a difference, to her or to him? He'd wasted too much of his life on dreams of revenge that, in the end, always proved hollow. Allowed those dreams to consume him.

That ended now.

Calista was right.

It was time to go.

CHAPTER THIRTY-FIVE

Duke leaned against the SUV, waiting on Gibson. Gone was the charcoal suit, replaced by chinos and a polo shirt as if it were a summer's day at Pamsrest. Gibson braced for whatever would come next. Another diatribe about how ashamed Duke was to call him son.

But to his surprise, his father looked up and smiled. A gentle and kind smile. One Gibson knew well. A smile straight from his childhood. The one that said, *It's just you and me, kid, against all comers.* The one that promised a late-night milkshake at the nearest diner. Gibson couldn't remember the last time he'd seen it, but he knew how much he'd missed it.

"Don't know that we have time for a milkshake," his father said with a wink.

"Probably not. Rain check, then?"

"You betcha. Now let's get you in where it's warm."

Gibson unlocked his car and got behind the steering wheel. His breath immediately fogged the windshield, and he started the engine so he could run the heater. In the backseat was the duffel bag of clothes that Gibson had left at the Reston house to be destroyed. On top of it was his passport and an envelope with a credit card in his name. "In case of emergencies," read a yellow sticky.

In the passenger seat sat Calista's laptop, connected to a large external battery. He peeled off another yellow sticky from the touchpad: "Click record." Suspicious, he tapped the spacebar, and the screen blinked to life. He saw a video feed from the runway. A split screen showing two different angles of the rear of the C-130 and the limousine. Calista had had the area wired for video and sound. What was she up to?

Gibson started recording the scene and put on the headphones connected to the laptop. At first, all he could hear was the wind. Then the back door of the limousine opened, and Calista stepped out. She stood defiantly in the cold, holding her china cup and saucer. Gibson heard the rumble of approaching vehicles. Calista turned to greet the two panel vans that roared into frame and slammed to a halt.

Cold Harbor mercenaries leapt from the backs of both vans. Unlike their brethren at Dulles, these men were armed for war. A pair disappeared up the ramp and into the aircraft. Two more cleared the limousine, checking the front and back. The remaining men fanned out to secure the nearby hangar. None paid Calista any attention as she stood stoically sipping her coffee.

Titus Stonewall Eskridge Jr. clambered out of the passenger seat like a man buried beneath the bodies of his enemies. His photographs did not do him justice. Well into his fifties, he carried himself with the arrogant bravado of a twenty-two-year-old athlete. The scar that ran down his jawline pulled the corner of his mouth into a permanent scowl. Gibson doubted he'd ever been a handsome man, but he could see the blunt-hewn charisma that would inspire awe in a certain kind of man. The gun Eskridge held in his right hand looked anxious for a target.

"You are too late for coffee, I am afraid," Calista said.

In answer, Eskridge cracked her across the face with the butt of his gun. She went down hard. Her china coffee cup shattered, but Calista Dauplaise didn't make a sound. She worked herself back to a sitting position, found her hat, and repositioned it atop her head. It wasn't the reaction Titus had expected. He stood over her, unsure of himself. Clearly not a familiar or comfortable feeling.

"You always did lack imagination, Titus," she said and glanced toward the flight manual, which still lay on the tarmac, bleeding pages. "It's one of your more charming qualities."

Eskridge followed her eyes and let out an inchoate roar. He snatched up the binder and paged through it furiously, flinging it away when he'd confirmed what he already feared.

"Get up."

"I do wish you'd make up your mind," Calista said, rising shakily to her feet. She was hurt worse than she let on, and Gibson could hear the pain in her voice.

"Do you have it?" Eskridge demanded.

Calista gave him a disappointed look that Gibson knew well. "Of course not. It is far, far from here now."

"You've been working with that bitch Charles."

"I always was. How has it taken you so long to catch up?"

"And?" he said. "What do you think you've accomplished? You don't think I have another copy?"

"In fact, I am counting on it."

"Bullshit," Eskridge snarled. "If that's true, why are you still here?"

"So that you would know it was me, and so that I might see firsthand."

"See what?"

Calista drew herself up to her full height. "You run."

Gibson didn't doubt that Calista thought she had the situation under control. She had a plan. She always had a plan, but for the life of him he couldn't see it. This wasn't like her. Sticking around to gloat. Eskridge wasn't the kind of man you goaded. If she kept on this way, she really would get herself killed.

And, like that, Gibson understood her plan.

"And why would I do that?"

"Because the CIA takes a rather dim view of treason, Titus."

"To hell with Israel," Eskridge said. "Those sons of bitches have it coming."

"Be sure to mention that in your interrogation. Everything you stole is on its way to Langley, along with your particulars. I expect you will be a most popular fellow in a few short hours. The belle of the ball, as it were. If I were you, I would—"

She never finished that sentence. Eskridge's right arm flashed up, and Calista crumpled to the tarmac alongside the flight manual. Her hat rolled away again, but this time she didn't sit up and she didn't reach for it. The gunshot echoed across the airfield. For a moment, Eskridge stood rooted to the spot, as did his men. Then he holstered his gun and began shouting orders to refuel the C-130.

"What are you looking at?" he bellowed. "I want to be wheels up in thirty!"

One of his men moved toward Calista, and Eskridge snapped at him to leave her where she lay. Then he stood there and admired his handiwork with the sneer of a man whose temper had gotten the better of him. Slowly, his chin dropped to his chest, and he ran a calloused hand down his face as if someone had spat on it.

Gibson took off the headphones and turned off the SUV's engine, suddenly paranoid that it might be heard from the runway. He sat in silence, watching Cold Harbor bring up a fuel truck, unsure how he felt about what he'd witnessed. How *should* he feel? Calista didn't deserve better, but she deserved something else. He didn't know what that might be, though, so this would have to do.

Calista had never struck him as the suicidal type, but this clearly had been her plan all along. She had fallen prey to the same ruthless calculus behind all her decisions. Everything she did, she did for her family's legacy. Anyone who threatened it or stood in its way paid a terrible price: Duke Vaughn, Suzanne Lombard, Michael Rilling, George Abe, Benjamin Lombard. She'd had her own sister murdered. And those were just the ones Gibson knew of. Nothing and no one was immune. Not even Calista Dauplaise herself.

How long had it taken her to reach the conclusion that she herself had become a threat? To admit that she would always be a scandal away from toppling her son? That if she died, at least, the threat died with her? It would have made perfect sense in her mind. He doubted that she had questioned it for even a moment.

And he'd be damned if it hadn't worked. Her affairs were now in order. She had settled up with those who would settle, mortally wounded those who would not. Eskridge would soon be branded a traitor and a murderer. And somehow, Calista had managed to die a martyr and a patriot. That was quite some trick.

Gibson didn't dare restart the engine until he saw the C-130 rise above the trees. While he waited, he changed out of his Tyner Aviation uniform and into something less conspicuous. Then he powered up his cell phone, which had been off since before Dulles. He hadn't had any calls or texts, but his phone vibrated to let him know he had an e-mail. It was from Nicole and had arrived last night. There was no message, but attached was a photograph of Ellie.

His daughter stood on a grassy field in a dirty soccer uniform. In her hands, she held a trophy of a girl kicking a ball. She smiled, but something had caught her eye, and she looked past the camera. Perhaps a group of girls calling her to join them? Gibson wiped away a tear. He couldn't believe how she'd shot up in the last eighteen months. She was all legs and would be tall like her mother. His daughter.

His eye flicked up at the image of Calista lying on the runway, alone beside her limousine. One of her legs was twisted under her at a cartoonish angle. Gibson shut the phone rather than look back at Ellie. He didn't want to associate the two images in his mind. Besides, he still had one errand left to run for Calista.

And hopefully for him as well.

CHAPTER THIRTY-SIX

The radio that morning was dominated by stories of a brazen midnight attack at Dulles International Airport by armed assailants. As he drove, Gibson skipped around the dial listening to the various accounts. No one could agree on a motive. There were conflicting reports coming out of Hangar Six as to whether anyone had been killed. He listened to two commentators argue about whether it qualified as a terrorist attack. The number, race, and gender of the attackers varied from station to station. Although whether that was genuine confusion or intentional misdirection by the FBI, Gibson didn't know. But it was only a matter of time before they put it together if they hadn't already.

A lap around the power plant turned up nothing out of the ordinary. Gibson parked and went inside with the laptop and headphones, the laminated sleeve, and a bag of drive-through burgers. The burgers were meant as a peace offering; he'd inhaled his on the way there. At the end of the service corridor, he started to collect the hood and restraints from their hiding place but stopped. It made no difference whether Ogden knew where he'd been held. They were past all that now. Gibson took the gun, though; they weren't past that quite yet.

Ogden sat on the floor in the corner of his cell. He licked his lips at the sight of Gibson but made no move to rise. The cell and its resident had both taken a turn for the worse. The alarm clock lay smashed against a wall, and trash littered the floor. The cell stank like old, moldy shoes in the back of a forgotten gym locker. Ogden was filthy, and his jumpsuit was stained and torn. His beard was matted and thick except for one bare patch where he had obsessively yanked out the hairs. Ogden kept on licking his lips and staring at him.

Gibson put down the stool and sat down. Neither man spoke. He slid the bag of burgers across the floor, scattering protein bar wrappers in its wake. It glided to a halt against Ogden's foot. For a minute, he ignored it but then caught the scent of real food. He snatched up the bag, tore open the wrapper, and ate the first burger ravenously.

"I'd slow down," Gibson said. "Or it will make you sick."

Ogden didn't acknowledge the advice and took a bite of the second burger, chewing methodically.

"I made the same mistake. I had burgers for my first meal too. At a truck stop in West Virginia where you guys dumped me. Unless you count a banana as a meal, but really that was more of a snack."

"I didn't think you were coming back," Ogden said, speaking for the first time. He'd finished both burgers and seemed more aware of his surroundings.

"That why you broke the alarm clock?"

Ogden cut to the chase. "Did you talk to my people? Am I getting out of here? Do we have a deal?"

"No, I haven't talked to them," Gibson said. "I don't think there's time for that now."

"Why not?"

"There's something you need to read," Gibson said. He crossed the room and placed the laminated sleeve on the cot.

"What is it?" Ogden asked, climbing to his feet.

"I don't know," Gibson said and waited by the door.

Ogden sat on the edge of the cot and slid the papers out of the envelope. As he read, his eyes narrowed, and his body language changed. He sat forward intently, leaning over the pages as he read. Halfway through, he glanced up at Gibson disbelievingly before returning to his reading.

"Where did you get this?" he demanded when he was finished. "Do you know what this means?"

"It means you've been breached."

"This is treason, Vaughn."

"That's kind of the point." Gibson handed him the laptop and headphones before Ogden could reach any more premature conclusions.

Ogden watched in mute fascination. Gibson saw him flinch at Calista's death. When it was over, Ogden put the laptop aside and thought long and hard about what he'd seen.

"When was this taken?" Ogden asked.

"A few hours ago."

"Who is the man?"

"Titus Stonewall Eskridge Jr. That's actually his real name, by the way. He fronts a PMC called Cold Harbor."

"I know of them."

"Good, because he already has a buyer lined up in the Middle East."

"How did you get this?" Ogden asked. "Scratch that, I don't care. I suppose you think this buys you immunity for kidnapping me?"

"Nope."

"No?" Ogden asked, surprised.

"No, because it never happened."

"Brother, you live in a fantasy world."

"It didn't happen, Damon. You've been running me this whole time. Ever since I got out. This was your operation from the start. A damned impressive piece of work too."

"You actually think I'm going to go along with that?"

"Why not? This way you get to be the hero again. I don't know about you, but that sounds a whole lot better than admitting you got taken like a bitch and locked in a bathroom for a month. Does Langley give promotions for being a victim?"

"Easy on that talk," Ogden said angrily, but Gibson could see him considering the proposition.

"Take all the time you need," Gibson said. "But keep in mind that C-130 is in the air and on its way to North Africa."

That got Ogden's attention. "Let's say I agree to go along with this. What happens now?"

Gibson slid a garbage bag across to him.

"What's this?" Ogden asked.

"Your suit. Unless you'd rather go to work dressed like that."

CHAPTER THIRTY-SEVEN

An unassuming green sign announced the exit for the George Bush Center for Intelligence. Beneath it, attached to one of the legs as if an afterthought, a small white sign read: "Authorized Vehicles Only." Gibson's Yukon definitely didn't qualify. The New Headquarters Building wasn't visible from Dolley Madison Boulevard, but it was back there beyond the trees. Gibson could almost feel it. He turned off at the exit and pulled to the side of the road. The security gate was up around the bend about a hundred yards, but this was as close as he intended to get. Ogden would have to walk the rest of the way.

"Sure you don't want to come in for a minute? Say hello," Ogden said. "I'm sure everyone is dying to meet you."

"That sounds like a real bad first date."

"You understand that if they want you, they'll just come get you."

"Then come get me. But I have faith that you can sell it to them."

"It's a pretty big sell. They're going to have questions."

"And you've got answers," Gibson said, pointing to the laptop and laminated sleeve resting on Ogden's knees. "Do we have a deal?"

"Yeah, we have a deal. But don't think this clears the slate between you and me."

"No," Gibson said. "But I figure it's a good start."

"I'm not entirely comfortable with having to constantly check my rearview mirror for you. Wondering if you've had a change of heart."

"Believe me, I feel the same about you. So I'll be leaving the country tonight. Put a little distance between us."

"You understand it had better be one-way. You go, you stay gone," Ogden said.

"I know, and I will. But I'm going to need you to call off the dogs first."

"What are you talking about?"

"Yeah, so there was kind of a . . . thing last night."

"What . . . thing?" Ogden said.

Gibson described the events at Dulles. It already felt like a lifetime ago. He made no mention of Jenn or George, but otherwise it was 80 percent true. He fudged only a little around the edges, but by the time he finished, Ogden's jaw was hanging open.

"Do you know how many laws you broke?" Ogden said.

"None. I was working for you. It was a matter of national security."

"Are you kidding me? We don't have jurisdiction over something like that. You know the shit storm that will come down if I claim the CIA was running an operation on US soil? Homeland and the FBI are going to bend us over."

"Well, gosh, Damon, I'm real sorry that saving the CIA's ass, again, is so damned inconvenient. Next time, I'll be sure to let the bad guys fly away."

"All right, all right, I'll figure something out. But I'm not going to be able to hold them off forever."

"Just until tonight. If I get detained, I'm going to have quite a story to tell," Gibson said.

"If you get detained, you're not going to get a chance to."

"I guess we'll see."

"I guess we will."

Ogden stepped out of the vehicle and shut the door gently. He buttoned his jacket against the cold. His suit didn't fit him properly anymore and hung loosely off his shoulders. He turned back as if he wanted to say something. Gibson lowered the window, but by then Ogden had changed his mind and turned away.

In the backseat, Duke Vaughn and Bear sat side by side. Duke had an RC Cola in his hand. Bear was kicking the back of the seat with her feet.

"You're gonna miss your flight at this rate," Duke said.

"Yeah, let's go already," Bear said agreeably.

Gibson had never seen his ghosts together before. It meant something, but he didn't know what. Duke handed the RC Cola to Bear, who took a tentative sip. She grinned at the sweetness. Duke produced a second bottle, and they clinked necks, a silent toast. Gibson watched them in the rearview mirror. It made him happy to see them together. He liked that they were finally getting along, which, crazy as it sounded, felt important. It gave him hope for the future. His father caught his eye and tapped his watch.

Agreed.

Gibson shifted back into gear and made a U-turn. In the rearview mirror, he saw Ogden running up the road in the direction of the guardhouse. When you added it all up, they'd spent perhaps two hours of their lives together. It was peculiar hating a man one barely knew. You ended up hating the idea of the man more than the man himself, filling in the blanks, making up the parts you couldn't know. Damon Ogden didn't actually seem like all that bad a guy. Still, he hoped it would be the last time he ever saw him.

He made the drive to Dulles International Airport braced for the police to box him in and force him onto the shoulder. In the back, Duke and Bear whispered to each other. He'd always been able to hear them clearly, no matter the noise, but now he found himself straining to catch what they were saying. At first it unnerved him, but after a few miles it felt strangely soothing, and he forgot that they were there at all. The main terminal of the airport rose up at the end of the road. In the daylight, its distinctive swoop glistened like the wing of an aircraft in flight. He parked in its shadow and left the doors unlocked. The keys went on the dashboard, the gun in the glove compartment. The bullets disappeared down a storm drain.

Duke and Bear followed him into the terminal. Bear had trouble keeping up in the crowd, and Duke had to take her hand. It was strange being back here again so soon. In the aftermath of last night's incident, security was on an emergency footing. In addition to airport police, Gibson saw FBI and Homeland Security. A pair of armed soldiers in urban camos eyed him as he passed by. He prayed Ogden had held up his end of the bargain and that he wasn't walking into an ambush. He rubbed the brim of his Phillies cap; he needed its good luck right about now.

The heightened security had snarled progress at the check-in counters. A line fifty passengers deep snaked in front of the Lufthansa desk. He took his place and, while he waited, took out his phone so he could look at the photograph of Ellie. For one wonderful moment, he contemplated getting out of line and finding a flight to Seattle. A tap on his shoulder ended his reverie and reminded him why it was an impossibility. He spun around, expecting the barrel of a gun, but found only an apologetic German tourist with a question. Gibson answered as best he could.

When Gibson finally made it to the counter, he handed over his passport and asked for a one-way ticket to Frankfurt. The fare was almost three thousand dollars. Next time, try and book in advance, the schoolmarmish counter agent advised. He paid with Calista's credit card and asked for a window seat. An eternity passed while she entered his information. She scanned his passport, and he could feel himself sweating. She kept glancing up at him until he felt certain she was stalling while security got into position.

"You're all set." She handed him back his passport and circled his departure gate on his boarding pass.

It felt too easy. Far too easy. An airport police officer with a service dog passed him without a second glance. Maybe they were waiting to take him at the TSA checkpoint.

He made his way through the crowd and found Duke and Bear waiting for him.

"This is where we say good-bye, kiddo," Duke said.

"You're not coming?" Gibson asked.

"We don't have tickets," Bear said.

"We're going to stay here," Duke said. "Keep an eye on things while you're gone. Now get going."

"Yeah, get going," Bear said with a grin.

Gibson knew it was for the best, but the thought of losing them hurt all the same. He didn't care if that made him crazy. He picked up his bag and turned to get into line for security.

"Is that your Phillies cap?" Duke asked Bear.

"Yes, but I gave it to him."

"Suits him."

"That's what I keep saying," she said.

After that, Gibson couldn't hear them anymore.

The TSA checkpoint was swamped, but his flight didn't leave for ninety minutes, so he would still make it. He shuffled ahead, stop-start, pushing his duffel bag forward with his foot. It took an agonizingly long time to get to the head of the line. With each step, he expecting to be dragged out of line and handcuffed.

He glanced back over his shoulder but saw only Duke and Bear, who stood on the concourse waiting for him to pass through security. Bear was giggling. Duke must have been telling tall tales about something or other. His father had always had the golden touch with kids. Bear glanced up at Gibson and waved. He waved back. His father smiled and winked his trademark wink.

The line moved again, and Gibson shouldered his bag. A TSA worker beckoned him forward to her podium. She scanned his boarding pass, frowning as she read her display. Gibson's throat tightened, and he forced a smile, holding it despite feeling like a grinning idiot. She scribbled her initials on his boarding pass and handed it back along with his passport.

"Have a good flight," she said.

"You too," he said automatically, but before he could correct his mistake, she waved the next passenger forward.

And like that, he was through.

He picked up a plastic tub and looked back one last time. Duke held Bear by the hand, and together they turned away and walked down the concourse. Gibson watched them until they disappeared from sight.

The line was backing up behind him. Gibson took off his shoes and belt, put what little he owned on the conveyor belt, and stepped into the machine to be scanned. He raised his hands above his head and stood still while the rotating arm circled him. A bored TSA agent looked at a small monitor, nodded, and waved Gibson through to the other side.

ACKNOWLEDGMENTS

I wrote the first chapter of *Cold Harbor* halfway through the first draft of *Poisonfeather*. I had a midnight epiphany, clambered back out of bed, and wrote a first draft. Then I locked it in a metaphorical drawer, went back to work on *Poisonfeather*, and tried not to think about what I had in store for Gibson. I always knew that *Poisonfeather* would be hard on him, but it wasn't until then that I realized exactly how hard. But, if *Poisonfeather* is about hubris, then *Cold Harbor* is about what comes after the fall. When the limitless expectations of youth dim and the realization sinks in that some bells can't be unrung. It was a book and a subject that required a lot of unpacking and thought before I could write it. For me, that meant talking it out, for which I am indebted to my friends and family who served as readers and ears. For this, I offer a heartfelt thank-you to Allie Heiman, Steve Konkoly, Daisy Weill, Michelle Mutert, Drew Anderson, Vanessa Brimner, Steve Feldhaus, Kit Manougian, Melanie Danilko, and Eric Schwerin.

Thanks to Gracie Doyle and everyone at Thomas & Mercer. You are a marvelous team. I'm grateful for everything you've done to bring Gibson Vaughn into the world. But mostly the Oreos.

Thanks to Ed "The Editor" Stackler who, for six weeks every year, does a masterful job of making me sound far more polished than I actually am. Working with you gives me a reason to look forward to February. I "just" couldn't do it without you.

Thanks to David Hale Smith, a great agent and a better friend. You make it look easy. I know it's not, but it makes writing books a lot less stressful knowing you're out there taking her easy for all us sinners.

Thanks to Deirdre M. Lofft for sitting down and answering my questions about Virginia PD. Any liberties taken are mine and not hers.

Thanks to Nathan and Patrick Hughes for all things Marine Corps. More than anything, I would hate to get this wrong, so I appreciate your keeping me on the straight and narrow.

And finally, thanks to Michael Tyner for taking every crazy idea that pops into my head and finding a plausible real-world solution. You are an amazing coconspirator, and I pity anyone foolish enough to cross you. I have your bail money should it ever come to that.

ABOUT THE AUTHOR

Matthew FitzSimmons is the author of the bestselling Gibson Vaughn series, which includes *The Short Drop* and *Poisonfeather*. Born in Illinois and raised in London, England, he now lives in Washington, DC, where he taught English literature and theater at a private high school for more than a decade.